HIGH SEASON

www.penguin.co.uk

ALSO BY KATIE BISHOP

The Girls of Summer

HIGH SEASON

Katie Bishop

bantam

TRANSWORLD PUBLISHERS
Penguin Random House, One Embassy Gardens,
8 Viaduct Gardens, London SW11 7BW
www.penguin.co.uk

Transworld is part of the Penguin Random House group of companies
whose addresses can be found at global.penguinrandomhouse.com

First published in Great Britain in 2025 by Bantam
an imprint of Transworld Publishers

Copyright © Katie Bishop 2025

Katie Bishop has asserted her right under the Copyright,
Designs and Patents Act 1988 to be identified as the author of this work.

This book is a work of fiction and, except in the case of historical fact,
any resemblance to actual persons, living or dead, is purely coincidental.

Every effort has been made to obtain the necessary permissions with
reference to copyright material, both illustrative and quoted. We apologize
for any omissions in this respect and will be pleased to make the
appropriate acknowledgements in any future edition.

A CIP catalogue record for this book
is available from the British Library.

ISBNs
9781787636026 hb
9781787636033 tpb

Designed by Gabriel Guma
All emojis designed by OpenMoji –the open-source emoji and icon project. License:
CC BY-SA 4.0

Printed and bound in Great Britain by Clays Ltd, Elcograf S.p.A.

The authorized representative in the EEA is Penguin Random House Ireland,
Morrison Chambers, 32 Nassau Street, Dublin D02 YH68.

Penguin Random House values and supports copyright. Copyright fuels creativity, encourages diverse voices, promotes freedom of expression and supports a vibrant culture. Thank you for purchasing an authorized edition of this book and for respecting intellectual property laws by not reproducing, scanning or distributing any part of it by any means without permission. You are supporting authors and enabling Penguin Random House to continue to publish books for everyone. No part of this book may be used or reproduced in any manner for the purpose of training artificial intelligence technologies or systems. In accordance with Article 4(3) of the DSM Directive 2019/790, Penguin Random House expressly reserves this work from the text and data mining exception.

Penguin Random House is committed to a sustainable future
for our business, our readers and our planet. This book is made
from Forest Stewardship Council® certified paper.

For Joe

THE BIRTHDAY PARTY

There is a soft, sleepy light on the water.

Later, Nina will think of it as the color of rust. Sunlight through a bottle of sweet, dark rum. The very last embers of an almost-extinguished fire.

Later, Nina will remember that the heat was heavy, like swimming through warm honey. That the grass was stiff and sharp from lack of moisture. That the tiles, cracked with heat and age, were warmed through. How they felt against her feet. How, in the distance, she could hear the adults talking and laughing. The clink of a cocktail glass; the unmistakable sound of her mother's voice, wavy with drink.

Later, Nina will remember how, earlier in the day, she sat out too long in the sun and her shoulders turned pink. How she had eaten a sandwich for lunch, cheese and tomato wilted in the humidity, the bread curling at the edges. How her mother had been exasperated with her.

Go and bother someone else, why can't you?

How Nina had trailed down the steps that led from the house to the beach, all tangled up with anger at the unfairness of it all. How her sandal had caught on an uneven step, the white leather strap tearing, forcing her to limp back up the hill. Onto the path that would take her past the pool, flat and still and glowing.

But now, Nina does not think about the color of the water. She doesn't think about the heat, or the grass, or the tiles. She doesn't think about the fact that her stepfather will be irritated with them all tomorrow, that her mother will be small and apologetic. She does not think about any of these things.

All Nina thinks is that there is a dead girl in the water. There is a dead girl in the water, and only Nina knows what happened to her.

PART ONE

ONE

TWENTY YEARS LATER

2024

The dinner party had been Ryan's idea.

He had suggested it a week ago, when he and Nina were having drinks at his members' club in Soho—an anniversary date that had morphed into an impromptu celebration of the job offer that had landed in her inbox that morning.

"Your first proper, grown-up job," he had said. "That's worth cracking a bottle of good wine for, surely."

Nina had tried to rebuff the idea at first. She was twenty-five, after all, and it had taken her much longer than most to arrive at the promised land of full-time employment. The fact that she had only just secured her first salaried wage—something that almost all her friends had enjoyed for years—felt like an embarrassing admission rather than something to celebrate. But Ryan was adamant. He would plan it all. Nina wouldn't have to worry about a thing.

Now they've had several bottles of good wine, more than Nina has kept count of. She's tipsy; a starry haze has settled over the evening, the sun melting just below the rooftop beyond their flat. The table is strewn with empty plates, still slicked with salad dressing and seafood shells, everyone too drunk to suggest clearing up. Nina sits on the windowsill, her glass half-empty, her white wine warmed through with the early summer heat, as Ryan tops up everyone's drinks.

"Cheers." Her brother Blake leans over from his seat on the sofa to clink his glass against hers. "You worked hard for this, you know. You deserve it."

Nina can tell that he's drunk by the way the rims of their glasses tap together slightly too hard, a tiny tsunami of wine sloshing over the edge. She *has* worked hard for this. A postgraduate degree and years of clinical training, not to mention the endless job applications, the slog of rejections before, finally the offer that came through last week. An assistant clinical psychologist role at a small London clinic.

"*Child* psychology, though," Blake says now, shaking his head. "Bit close to the bone, don't you think?"

"So you've said," says Nina. "About twenty times, actually."

She gives him a gentle nudge.

"Come on, Blake," she says, smiling. "You understand why."

He sits back heavily in the chair. "I just think it's a bit . . . morbid, isn't it? You know that Mum's still hoping you'll change your mind."

Nina takes another sip of her wine. Châteauneuf-du-Pape Blanc. Their mother's favorite.

"That's not all she's hoping you'll change your mind about," Blake says.

He reaches out for Nina's hand.

"Come back this summer," he says, his voice wheedling. "Please. It would mean a lot to Mum. It would mean a lot to *me*."

"You know I can't," Nina says.

She starts to stand. Extracts her hand from Blake's.

"I'll go and sort pudding."

"Nina, don't be like that. I didn't mean to—"

"It's fine, Blake. Just not tonight, OK? Not when Ryan's put so much effort in. We'll talk about it another time."

Later, Nina fills the sink full of scalding hot water. The flat has two dishwashers, but she likes to wash up by hand. She likes to look out over the city through the kitchen window as she scrubs, a small, mindless task as voices drift from the living room. Blake and Ryan are discussing her brother's flight to the South of France tomorrow, his plans to spend summer with their mother at the family home on the Côte d'Azur. Her best friend Claire is fussing with the antique record player that once belonged to Nina's grandfather.

Nina piles pans into the sink to soak. Outside the enormous sash window, the sky has that strange cerebral quality that only comes at the cusp of summer. Pink clouds blossoming against a purple twilight. Heat crawling upward as if trying to escape the city.

Nina always forgets how suffocating London gets at this time of year. How the air tastes of car fumes, the roads tangled up with people escaping for cooler patches of the country. Smoke from balcony barbecues. Sweat rising from bodies packed into tube carriages. The warm tarmac, the rubbish starting to stew and bake in unemptied bins. Not for the first time, she has the overwhelming urge to take Blake up on his offer. To go back to the place that somehow, in spite of everything, still feels like home.

"God, I would *kill* for this kitchen."

Claire marches through the industrial glass doors that lead from the lounge, a pile of plates stacked up in her hands—three scraped, only Nina's almost untouched. She deposits them on the countertop and runs her fingers down her linen skirt as if checking that she hasn't dropped the dregs of four sticky toffee puddings down herself. She hasn't, of course. Nina's best friend always looks astonishingly put together, with her rotating selection of pastel-colored headbands and the same signature lipstick that she's worn every day since Nina met her when they were both eighteen, on their first day of university. Nina had stayed close to home, in London, her mother insisting that she wouldn't be able to cope with a big move. Still, she had been terrified on her first day, embarrassed that her mum had insisted on their private driver dropping her off at her halls of residence. She had clutched a bottle of gin that she had planned on using as a peace offering for her new flatmates as the porter informed her, one eyebrow raised, that John Lewis furniture deliveries had been arriving for her small single room all week (*Well, you can't sleep in a bed that* someone else *has already slept in*, her mother announced when Nina had called her, mortified, as the porter looked on).

Claire had bowled into the shared kitchen just as Nina, red-faced, oversaw a Fortnum & Mason order that the delivery driver had insisted on transporting straight to her refrigerator.

"Gin!" she had announced, spotting the forgotten bottle abandoned on the countertop. "It always makes me a bit loopy, but I never learn. I've got tonic in my groceries somewhere, if you want to do a trade?"

It was one of the things that had drawn Nina to her. Claire seemed like someone who was completely unfazeable.

"Ryan's flat is *incredible*," Claire continues. "How much did he pay for this place again?"

Nina doesn't remind her that it isn't Ryan's flat. Not anymore. It's *their* flat now. Has been since Nina moved in eight months ago. But Claire's mistake is understandable. There's so little of Nina in the swathes of marble, the engineered-wood floors, the way the entire flat is rigged up with gadgets—speakers and smart systems running through the walls like veins. Nina makes a mental note to put up some pictures before Claire comes round again. She should ask Blake what happened to all of the art that their mother had in storage. Perhaps she could find something a little more like Nina.

"It needed work. He got a good deal," Nina says, even though it's not exactly true. She hates talking money. Wants to avoid getting into a discussion about how Ryan is technically letting her live here for free, an agreement that started when Nina was job hunting and which has yet to lapse. She's offered to pay rent, of course, but Ryan said that it wouldn't be fair when only his name was on the mortgage.

"Hey, your brother is looking *good* tonight," Claire says, lowering her voice. "Did you say that he broke up with . . . what's her name?"

"Jazmin?"

"That was it. Jazmin. Because I kind of got a vibe from him over dinner. Did you notice?"

Nina turns away to hide her smile. She's used to people being this way around her brother. She had barely even got a chance to know Jazmin before Blake mentioned, in passing, that he had a date with a girl he'd met at an art gallery opening.

"What about Jazmin?" she had asked.

"Oh, *Jazmin*," Blake had said, as if Nina was bringing up a long-lost acquaintance rather than the girl they'd all been out to dinner with the week prior. "Well, we wanted different things."

As usual, Nina had wanted to say. Blake is in his late thirties, but he seems so far from settling down that Nina sometimes feels embarrassed by how early she herself has fallen into long-term coupledom. She has become used to meeting a new girlfriend of Blake's every few months, some sweet and beautiful woman who seems completely besotted with her brother.

"You know Blake," Nina says. "He can turn on the charm when he wants to. Don't read too much into it."

"Right," says Claire. "Oh well. My turn eventually."

She bumps her hip against Nina's to show that she's joking.

"Hey, your phone was going off, by the way. Want me to grab it for you?"

"It can wait," says Nina. She pulls the plug from the sink so the water can drain, disappearing in a swirl. She is here. She is with all of the people that she cares about the most. "Whoever it is, I'm sure they can wait."

Claire sways slightly on her feet, wraps her arm around Nina and pulls her close.

"I'm so proud of you, babe," she says. "You're killing it."

And somehow, Nina can't quite bring herself to point out Claire's poor choice of words.

TWO

2024

Nina had told Ryan what happened to her sister on their second date. He had been sitting across from her, pouring her a glass of red wine.

"So," he had said. "Do you have any siblings?"

The restaurant hummed around them, as if Ryan hadn't asked Nina the question that she had spent most of her life dreading.

"It's a bit complicated," she had said.

And it had all begun there.

Nina had met Ryan two weeks earlier at a recruitment fair in a drafty university hall. Ryan ran a technology start-up that had a stand, and even though Nina didn't have the slightest interest in data programming she lingered, picking up a leaflet and pretending to read. He had asked her if she was considering a career in the tech sector, and when she admitted that she was already signed up to do a psychology master's next year and had only come along to keep her best friend Claire company, he had grinned.

"A master's in psychology?" he said. "Well, clearly you're too smart to work for us."

She had liked him immediately.

"Why psychology?" he had asked her on their first date, at a cocktail bar with views over the Thames.

Nina had taken a sip of the too-sweet mojito she already regretted ordering and considered her answer.

"I want to be able to understand people," she had said.

"Do you think that you need psychology to understand people?"

"I think that you need psychology to understand *yourself*, never mind other people," she had said, and then been faintly embarrassed by how easily the answer came. What it might say about her. She did not want this smart, older guy who seemed so self-assured to think she was the sort of person who didn't really know or understand herself, in spite of her psychology degree.

But he had just nodded, and pushed his square-framed glasses up the bridge of his nose in a way that Nina found sweet, and slightly nerdy. Attractive in a way she couldn't quite quantify.

"Good answer," he had said, as if it were a test and Nina had passed.

It was Ryan who had suggested dinner for their second date. The idea had felt strangely adult, a performance of romance that Nina wasn't used to. Dinner dates were the things that her mother used to go on, and the words evoked memories of perfume and silken dresses, her mother patting her hair in front of a long mirror and telling Nina and Blake that there was food on a plate in the refrigerator if they got hungry. Nina was more accustomed to university romances. Sleeping with a guy long enough during her first year to eventually be called his girlfriend. A friend with benefits she had fallen for two terms before who got a place on a graduate scheme in America, and had looked at Nina with genuine disbelief when she suggested there might be something more between them.

But she liked how confident Ryan was. How intelligent, and interesting. She liked that he seemed completely oblivious to celebrity gossip, furrowing his brows and saying *Who?* when Nina referenced Kris Jenner.

She liked the way he looked at her with approval in his eyes. The way it made her feel.

And now, she was sitting across the table from him, knowing that what she was about to say could change everything.

"I've got a brother," she said. "Blake. He's twelve years older than me."

From the table next to them came the rise and fall of laughter. A murmur of conversation.

Nina took a deep breath.

"And I had a sister," she said. "She and Blake were twins. But she died when she was seventeen."

She had Ryan's full attention now.

"Oh my god," he said. "I'm so sorry."

"It was a long time ago."

"But still. That must have been terrible."

"I don't really remember much about it," said Nina. "I was only five."

She lifted her drink and took a long, slow sip. The heat of the alcohol slid straight through her. She set down her glass harder than she had intended.

"It was actually a pretty big thing, at the time," Nina allowed. "She was killed by somebody."

Ryan didn't speak. Didn't move.

"There was a trial," Nina said. "A girl whose mother worked for us, the housekeeper's daughter. She used to spend all her time around our house. Babysitting me, or helping out with the housework. She was sixteen. I had to give evidence."

For the first time in Nina's life, the words came easily. It was something she'd talked about so rarely, even though it was often the first thing that people knew about her. She hadn't even told Claire until they'd been friends for over a year, one night after drinking cheap merlot out of coffee mugs, sprawled on Nina's bed.

"I already knew," Claire had confessed, her mouth stained red. For the first time in all the months Nina had known her, she was bashful rather than brash. Embarrassed for Nina, for thinking that she had a secret, when all the world knew.

Ryan's eyes widened.

"You gave evidence when you were five?"

"I had to," Nina said. "I was the only one who saw."

"You saw?"

His voice was quiet now.

"Yes," said Nina. "I saw."

"God," he said. "That's . . . well. It must be awful. To have seen that. How could you . . ."

He shook his head, the words seeming to fail him.

"It must be terrible for you. To be able to remember seeing that."

Nina swallowed.

"Memory's strange," she said. "It's hard for me to . . . the details. You know?"

Ryan didn't say anything, and Nina staggered to fill the space.

"I mostly remember the trial," she said. "And the aftermath—being taken into a room and asked to draw what happened. I remember exactly what I drew. The pool. My sister—Tamara. Her name was Tamara. And her. Bending down. Pushing her under the water. Josie Jackson. She denied everything, of course. Said that I must have made the whole thing up."

She paused to take a sip of water, her mouth suddenly too dry after too much wine. How could she explain it? The gray rooms and long corridors. The year of Nina's life that seemed lost to that drawing, entire days and weeks stretching out between the felt-tip lines. The blue of the pool. The black squiggle of Tamara's hair. The fluorescent pink of Josie Jackson's arms.

And all the years since. How she had had to move schools because the other girls seemed afraid of her, as if death was catching. How, even though the police and the social workers spoke gently to her—telling her she'd done the right thing, that Josie Jackson was a bad person and needed to be punished—Nina had felt a bolt of guilt so intense that she had become obsessive about strange things. Handwashing. Counting. Flicking light switches on and off. Believing that if she didn't track her steps in units of one hundred then some omnipotent force would take another member of her family away. Chewing each mouthful exactly twenty times until her jaw ached and she had no appetite left. Developing an intense anxiety around food, hiding it in napkins and flushing it down the toilet.

Of course, she had had years of therapy. Stuffed animals, and concerned-looking doctors. The nerve-ending fizzle of pain if anyone ever asked Nina if she had a sister. The way Nina still had to change the channel or leave the room if a courtroom drama ever came up on the television in her university common room.

Nina couldn't explain these things, and so she didn't. Instead, she looked Ryan straight in the eye.

"The funny thing is that when I think of it now, that's what I see. That picture. It's a trauma response, I suppose. It's easier to remember the picture than the real thing."

She was speaking too quickly, running out of air. She took a deep breath.

"That's why I want to be a psychologist, really," she said. "I want to help other people—children especially—who've experienced trauma at a very young age. I want to be able to show people that you can survive it."

Ryan's brow furrowed. He was looking just beyond her. As if he hadn't heard what she'd said.

"But if you don't remember it," he said, "how do you know you *weren't* making it up? Kids make things up all the time, right? They make believe. How do you know that you were telling the truth?"

Just then, the waiter turned up with their mains. He topped up their waters, asked if they'd like any sauces, delivered a steak knife to the side of Ryan's plate with an aplomb that suggested he was delivering a ceremonial sword rather than a simple item of cutlery. By the time he left, the question seemed forgotten. Ryan had moved on. He was already asking about the verdict. How high the cost of a life really was for the woman who killed Tamara, his curiosity shifting into sympathy.

Later, Nina would learn that Ryan was the kind of person who threw out big questions without thinking about the consequences. That his mind was always whirring, searching. It was the kind of *blue-sky thinking* that his investors were always saying he had, the *looking outside the box* that had made him a start-up CEO at twenty-two. Always inquisitive, always moving quickly on to the next curiosity.

So Ryan had forgotten the question.

Ryan had forgotten the question, but Nina had not. She could not.

Nina would never forget Ryan asking her that question, because it was the first time that anyone had ever said the thing she had always wondered. The hum of fear and guilt that had lodged itself in the back of her brain and refused to budge. The thing that she had always ignored, pushed down, starved out.

And now Ryan, with his straightforwardness, his lack of complication, had simply said it out loud. And now, Nina could only think about that question.

She thought about it all through dinner. When they agreed to order a second bottle of wine, instead of pudding. When Ryan insisted on paying the whole bill, and Nina was briefly struck with the surprise of how differently people could treat her when they didn't know who her family were.

She thought about it in the taxi on the way back to her flat. When she unlocked the door, and Ryan whistled and said that he'd expected student digs, not a mansion flat in Chelsea with paneled walls and a four-poster bed so large that Nina's mother often joked it would never fit through the doorway when she moved out.

She thought about it as she explained that the flat had belonged to her grandfather. That she had been living here since their second year of university, after her mother made a fuss about the small, damp student house that Nina had planned to move into with Claire and some of her coursemates, asking, *Why on earth would you live there when there's a perfectly nice flat you could live in for free?* That, like everything in Nina's life, the flat was inherited, another thing passed down through the family that Nina felt she had no right to, but somehow ended up accepting anyway. That she hated the stiff-backed mid-century furnishings, the paintings that were worth more than most people earned in a year, the bar cart heaving with sticky bottles of Cointreau and Pernod that Nina always cringed at when she brought back her beer-drinking friends from the student union.

She thought about it when Ryan kissed her as she was midway through explaining all of this, his hands cupping her face beneath the chin, his mouth hot and firm against hers. As he led her to the bedroom. When he had taken off her dress, his mouth moving all the way down her body, her neck, the soft outward rise of her hip bones.

Even as he entered her, all Nina could think about was what he had said back in the restaurant.

How do you know that you were telling the truth?

The morning after the dinner party, Nina wakes to a pulse in the back of her head, an ache behind her eyes, the sour-mouthed dryness that accompanies a hangover. The room is dark, a benefit of the hideously expensive blackout blinds that Ryan had imported from Germany, but Nina can tell from the panicked feeling in her chest and the fact that Ryan's side of the bed is empty that she has overslept.

She rolls over and fumbles on the bedside table for her phone. Instead, her hand knocks against a wineglass. Her memories from the night are blurred. Ryan getting annoyed when she failed to put a coaster down on the bedside table. Claire insisting that they do their go-to karaoke routine from their university days—"Don't Go Breaking My Heart" by Elton John and Kiki Dee, with Claire usually ending up taking over both parts. Blake asking Nina again if she'd fly out with him tomorrow, *One last chance, sis.* And did Blake and Claire *leave* together? Nina manages to drag herself up to sit, wincing as she does.

Ryan is already in the kitchen dressed in a shirt and chinos, standing, even though there's a barstool beside him. He's religious with tracking everything from his screentime to his steps, and his latest endeavor is to spend at least eight hours per day on his feet. He doesn't look up from his screen as Nina enters, his fingers tapping against the keypad.

"Morning, sleeping beauty," he says cheerfully. "Or should I say afternoon?"

"What time is it?"

"Quarter past nine. There's coffee in the pot if you want it."

"Let me just brush my teeth first. I'm disgusting."

"You left your phone out here, by the way," he calls after her as she crosses into the hallway. "I put it on charge in the living room for you."

"Thanks."

Nina swipes her phone off the coffee table as she passes and locks the bathroom door behind her. She sits on the lowered toilet lid as she ignores the pile of notifications at the bottom of her screen to tap into her conversation with Claire.

I feel like shit this morning. Make me feel better and tell me you didn't go home with my brother last night?

She stands to switch the shower on and leans against the sink, thumbing through messages that she missed last night while the water heats. A notification from Instagram; a newsletter from a psychology magazine she's long subscribed to but almost never reads; an email sent at half eight this morning from her soon-to-be employer reminding her to read through her contract and let them know if she has any questions. Then, farther down, a subject line that makes her breath catch in her chest.

Tamara Drayton case: twentieth-anniversary documentary (interview request)

The room is hot, filling with steam. Nina has to wipe a film of moisture from her phone screen to make out the text. She has a sick, heavy feeling in her stomach as she scans the message, her eyes skimming too quickly to take much in.

Notorious murder case. Youngest-ever witness. Access to case files.

Before she knows what she's doing, Nina is crouching on the bathroom floor, the tiles damp beneath her skin.

Renewed attention on case. Unreliable witness. Tragic death. Josie Jackson.

She's lightheaded, her heart falling into beat with the hard drum of water against the ceramic shower stall. She has to close her eyes for a moment. Slow her breath. She tries to remember her exercises from therapy. A long, deep inhale through her nose. A slow exhale through her mouth. When she opens her eyes, the screen seems too bright. The words of the message stark. She scrolls back to the top of the email and reads the whole thing from start to finish, lingering over each word.

She reads the email through twice. Turns off the shower, and then reads it a third time. She only realizes that she's clenching her jaw when it begins to throb, a sharp pain that cuts through the dull ache of her hangover.

Give me some credit, Claire has responded. Solo taxi home for me. I actually feel OK. Maybe I'm still drunk?

Nina ignores the message. Finds her brother's number.

What time's your flight? she types. And is it too late for me to get a seat?

She presses send and then waits, her thumbs hovering above the keypad. Then, before her brother has a chance to open the message, she types out a second text.

We need to talk about Josie Jackson.

THREE

2004

SIX WEEKS BEFORE THE BIRTHDAY PARTY

On the day before high season began, Josie Jackson and Hannah Bailey broke into the Draytons' swimming pool.

They slipped down the steps, away from the house and onto the broad, flat terrace that stretched out toward the sea. They peeled back the cover to reveal the water, newly cleaned and chemical. They snorted with laughter and hushed each other, even as they both squealed, dive-bombing into the deep end, scattering the quiet of the late-spring air.

They swam lengths as the sun set over the endless flat of the sea. They splashed each other, and saw who could hold their breath the longest. They did handstands, their feet sticking out of the water like flowers breaking through earth. Like they used to when they were children.

Afterward, they stretched out on the ground, their skin wet and stinking of chlorine. The early evening sky was golden, and the water on their bare legs and stomachs glittered.

"Maybe their flight will get delayed," said Josie.

"Maybe they'll decide to stay in London this summer."

"Maybe they'll decide they're sick of this house and give it to us."

Josie nudged Hannah, her elbow sharp in her best friend's ribs.

"You would hate if they didn't come," she said. "You'd be heartbroken. You've been counting down the days 'til Blake turns up."

Hannah wriggled away from her.

"He might not even be coming this year," she said.

Josie stretched her hands above her head, as if reaching for the last gasps of the day's heat.

"He'll be here," she said. "He will."

Just then came the distinctive sound of Josie's mother's voice, its wiry, perpetually anxious edge drifting down the hill.

"Josie May Jackson, what are you doing with that pool cover?"

They scrambled to their feet before Patricia Jackson could make it down the steps, pulling clothes over their damp bodies, laughing, scurrying to haul the pool cover back on, dashing out the side gate. Leaving only wet footprints behind.

Josie and Hannah first met when Josie was ten, Hannah eleven. Josie was new to the town, her family having moved to the Côte d'Azur two weeks earlier. The total upending of Josie's life back in the UK had come out of the blue. Her taxi-driver dad had met a bloke at the pub who told him that he could make good money working as a private driver for rich expats in the South of France, and within a month they were packing their bags.

Like many of the transitions in Josie's life (their relocation from London to Kent after her dad remortgaged their house to invest in a timeshare company that never got off the ground; the time she and her brother had to leave the school her mum said she'd *moved heaven and earth* to get them into when her dad got into a physical fight with the head teacher at parents' evening; the summer he'd taken them all to Disneyland and then they'd had to do a midnight flit because he'd borrowed the money from a dodgy moneylender to pay for it), the move was characterized by a flurry of hope and optimism followed by a shift to quiet fury and disappointment. They arrived in autumn to find the beaches empty, the village quiet, the flurry of high season stilled. Most of the people who owned the sprawling holiday homes had already gone home for winter, and the work that Josie's dad had been promised failed to materialize. Instead, he would spend all day at home, smoking at the kitchen table, cracking open bottles of beer at increasingly early hours of the afternoon. Josie found herself leaving the house more and more often to escape the simmer of tension. She ventured along coastal paths, climbed the trees that lined the winding road to their house. She could stay out for hours, if she had to. Often, she felt like she did.

The first day that Josie met Hannah was a Saturday, the temperature cool, the streets silent. Josie had been able to feel the threat of an argument settling between her parents in the same way that you can feel moisture in the air before a storm. The heaviness had sent her scurrying out of the house and—in an effort to fill time—down toward the beach.

She was remembering how her dad had taken the whole family there on their first morning in France, loud and grinning, buying her and her brother ice cream even though it wasn't quite warm enough, treating her mum to a brand-new swimming costume from one of the boutiques that lined the seafront still making the most of end-season stragglers. They had been happy. Excited. Her dad had said how great it would be for Josie and her brother, Calvin, to grow up so close to the sea. Josie had dripped ice cream down her T-shirt, and her mum hadn't even gotten cross about it. In fact, she had been beaming, pink-faced, looking at Josie's dad in a way that she rarely did anymore.

Josie wanted the peace and hope of that day to return. She felt, somehow, that if she could make it to the beach, things might feel all right again.

She found her way to the town easily, navigating the rows of shuttered-up restaurants and shops. She located the road that ran parallel to the sea, but somehow couldn't find the path that led onto the beach. She walked up and down and only found rows of pastel-painted buildings, doors with FERMÉ POUR L'HIVER scrawled on hand-painted signs. Her shoes were beginning to rub, and there was a tightness in her chest. She thought again of her parents arguing. The black mood that had descended on their new home. She *had* to find the beach.

That was when she saw a girl sitting on the front terrace of a shop, her head bent over an exercise book. Long, bare legs and strawberry-blond hair. Snorkels and wetsuits strung up above her, swinging in the breeze.

"'Scuse me," Josie called out. "Do you know the way to the sea?"

The girl's head jerked up. She frowned. She had light gray eyes, sun-bronzed skin.

"Yeah," the girl said slowly. "You just need to take the footpath, at the end of the street."

She lifted her biro to point toward a row of shops.

"It looks like an alley at first. Down the side of that blue house on the left?"

Josie nodded.

"Oh yeah," she said, trying to sound like she'd simply forgotten. "Thanks."

She knew that she looked out of place here, with her scruffy ponytail and bitten-down fingernails. Skin that was scorched with freckles, a dead giveaway that she hadn't spent much time in the sun. Not knowing her way to the sea was surely unforgivable, a sign that she was an outsider.

"Wait."

Josie turned around. The girl was putting her exercise book down beside her.

"Are you . . ." she said. "Where are your parents?"

Josie shrugged. Scuffed her shoe against the pavement.

"Back at the house," she says. "We just moved in."

"Which house?"

"Up over the hill."

"You walked all the way down here by yourself?" The girl tilted her head to one side. "Do they mind? You must only be—"

"I'm ten."

Josie couldn't stop a note of defiance creeping into her voice. She was small for her age, the smallest in her school year back in Kent. People often thought she was younger than she was.

"They don't mind you coming down here on your own?" the girl repeated.

Josie shrugged again, slowly this time, reluctant.

"They're fighting," she said. "Anyway. Thanks very much."

She stepped back again, toward the footpath.

"Wait."

The girl was standing now.

"I was actually thinking of going for a swim," she said. "I'll come with you."

She brushed sand from her thighs. Sand seemed to get everywhere, out here.

"I'm Hannah, by the way."

"Josie."

Hannah smiled.

"Let's go," she said. "The waves are perfect at this time of day."

※

Now, Josie and Hannah left the Draytons' pool and walked to the beach, back to the exact place where they swam that first day. They'd been like sisters since then, inseparable for the last six years. Josie, who turned up here without being able to speak a word of French. Hannah, who was bilingual by dint of having a British father but had never quite made friends with the other kids at the international school over the hill, on account of always having to spend her weekends helping out at her parents' dive shop. Who, Josie now knew, had only gone down to the beach with her that first day because she had seen a small, lost girl and been afraid of what might happen to her. What could come of a child who didn't yet understand the sea. Its depth and currents. The way a wave could seize hold of you and fill your lungs.

To Josie, they fit together like salt and sand, even though they made a strange pairing: Hannah, who at seventeen was almost six feet tall, with long, thin limbs and a sea of strawberry-blond hair; Josie, who was barely five feet, with a squat, compact frame and short, dark hair that she only ever wore tied up. Hannah, who had developed a way of making herself smaller, hunching her spine and folding her arms across her newly blossomed chest. Josie, who was loud and outspoken. Who had a habit of saying the wrong thing at the wrong time. Who never really cared when she did.

"I'm going in," said Josie. "Want to come?"

Hannah shook her head.

"It'll take forever to dry out now the sun's gone down," she said. "I'll wait here."

Josie stripped off her shorts and T-shirt and waded out until the waves lapped against her waist. Then she held her breath and plunged beneath the surface.

The water was dark, the twilight sky pale and high above her. She closed her eyes. She started to swim. When the beach was a distant sliver, the hill a black shadow against a hollow sky, she flipped onto her back and spread her arms and legs out wide. She floated, starfished, her ears beneath the surface so that she could hear the beat of her own heart.

This was where she felt happiest. Most peaceful. On the edge of something bigger than herself.

When Josie had been submerged for so long that she could feel her skin begin to soften and salinate, she swam back to shore. Short, sharp strokes that made her arms ache. Hannah was waiting exactly where she'd left her, tracing shapes in the sand with a stick. A star. A sun. A spiral. *J + H* in large, twirling letters. Josie collapsed down next to her, scattering sand across the sun.

"Good swim?"

"Beautiful."

Josie leaned back, her elbows in the damp sand.

"I hate this bit," she said. "Waiting for them all. Feeling like we're on hold until they get here."

Josie always felt restless as summer approached. To her, the divide between the end of spring and the start of summer was clear and defined. Before summer, this place seemed to belong to her and Hannah. The beach was desolate. The villas that dotted the hill were quiet, dust sheets thrown over furniture, vast bellies of emptiness. They would roam the rooms of the Draytons' house, where Josie's mum had gotten a job working as a housekeeper after Josie's dad walked out just a year after they arrived in France. They would sneak onto the terrace to watch the sunset. They would do their homework at great wooden dining tables made to seat fifteen people.

Then, high season would begin. Cars pulled up in driveways, families filled the grand estates, and beaches heaved with day-trippers. Hannah's parents would work late. Josie's mother would be perpetually exhausted and irritable, run ragged by the Draytons. Josie would often have to help out, babysitting the youngest Drayton kid or doing errands down in the town.

At night, there would be bonfires on the sand, the teenage children of their employers carrying down crates of beer, leaving bottles scattered like seashells. The bay that belonged to Hannah and Josie for most of the year would belong to them instead, and the two girls could only slip in through back doors, handing out drinks at parties or accepting twenty-euro notes in exchange for babysitting work, or the occasional tutoring job for parents who wanted to improve their children's French.

Hannah tossed the stick that she had been drawing with.

"I don't know," she said. "I'm kind of looking forward to it this year."

Josie snorted.

"Looking forward to having to work every weekend and be at some posh person's beck and call twenty-four hours a day?"

"Oh, come on. You hardly have to work. Looking after a few kids for a couple of hours a week. And we could use the extra money. *You* could use the extra money. Aren't you saving?"

Josie had been saving for as long as she could remember. She had showed Hannah her piggy bank the first time her new friend had visited the dilapidated house up on the hill that her dad had insisted was a *fixer-upper* but then refused to so much as replace a lightbulb.

"I'm going traveling, soon as I turn eighteen," she said. "I'm going to see the world."

Now sixteen, she stuck pictures of far-flung places up on her bedroom wall, dreamed about different cities the way that her classmates talked about their dream universities. Hanoi. Buenos Aires. Sydney.

"Don't you think it can be fun?" persisted Hannah. "Everything comes to life in summer, you know? It's how this place is supposed to be."

A quiet fell between them. The soft roar of stones rolling beneath the waves.

"I like it better when it's just us," said Josie at last.

Hannah stretched out so that her face was turned toward the sky.

"I have a good feeling about this year," she said. "I think this is going to be the best summer yet."

FOUR

2024

The flight is short, but there's something about airplanes that drains Nina. She always emerges exhausted, her body tightly wound and her muscles sore, even though Ryan insisted on paying for business-class seats.

"Remind me," says Ryan, as they queue at passport control. "What's your mum's new boyfriend called again?"

"Jonas," says Nina. "You met him at Christmas, remember?"

Ryan frowns.

"Small guy?" he says. "Going bald?"

"No, you're thinking of Hamish. Hamish was at least two boyfriends ago. Keep up."

Ryan shakes his head.

"I don't know how you keep track of them all," he says. "Your mum's boyfriends just seem to blend together, after a certain point."

Nina shifts her carry-on bag from one shoulder to another.

"As long as they're boyfriends, not husbands," she says. "Lucky for you, you missed her husband phase."

Ryan ducks down to plant a kiss on top of her head.

"Hope you're not going to take after your mum," he says. "I don't fancy being the starter husband."

Nina feels a dim pulse of pleasure. They've been together for almost four years, but the ease with which Ryan talks about them getting married still surprises her. He's been like that from the start, telling her on their fourth date that he could see himself being with her *forever*. They've been to three weddings already this year, all friends of his, and only two weeks ago Nina caught him lingering over her jewelry box, fingering an opal ring that Nina recently had resized. She pretended not to notice.

Now, she thinks of how lucky she is. How, when she realized that Blake's flight was fully booked, Ryan had been the one to find them seats for the next day. How he had calmly read through the email and offered to call his lawyer, talked about the whole thing as if it was something small and insignificant. An annoyance, rather than something that felt like it had the potential to upend her entire life.

"Thanks for doing this," Nina says. "Coming out here with me. I know work's busy for you right now, and—"

Ryan is already waving one hand, unlocking his phone with the other as he scans for new messages.

"It's fine," he says. "I was planning on working from home anyway. Working from your mum's place won't make much difference if it's only for a few days."

His eyes flit up from the screen.

"It *is* only for a few days, right?"

Nina nods.

"Yeah, yeah. Of course. I just want to talk to Mum and Blake about this in person. And anyway, my job starts next week. We have an excuse to leave if Mum tries to guilt-trip us into staying."

Ryan doesn't ask what she means by this. He knows that Nina hates coming back to France, hates that she is expected to return to the Côte d'Azur every year for her mother's birthday party. She even missed her graduation for it, flying out when her coursemates were enjoying their last few weeks of university. While they were donning robes, Nina had been counseling her mother through a particularly dramatic breakdown about a dress that hadn't fit her properly.

But then, three years ago, as Nina was complaining yet again about her mum, Ryan had simply said: *But what if you* didn't *go back this summer?*, and Nina had instantly felt a weight that she hadn't known was there lift. In spite of the furious voicemails, the lengthy messages, Nina had not been back to the Côte d'Azur since.

She likes it better this way, and she knows that Ryan does, too. He is someone who believes that perfection is possible, who talks about optimization as though he truly believes that it is a thing that can be applied not just to his work projects but to his personal life. Nina's family—her demanding mother, her dead sister—are things that he cannot fix, cannot optimize. He cannot make them neat, and good, and shiny in the way their London life is, and she knows that this bothers him. They *both* prefer to stay away from the Côte d'Azur, if they can help it.

The passport line begins to move forward, a shuffle of restless bodies, everyone anxious to get out of the artificial cool of the airport toward the promise of the summer air.

"It's the right thing to do, to come back," Nina says, even though she knows that Ryan is engrossed in his phone, no longer listening. "It's something I *have* to do."

※

The house used to be beautiful.

It's a landmark. Has been ever since Nina's grandfather built it back in the 1950s. A gem on the Côte d'Azur. A villa of terracotta stone sprawling against the rough jut of the hill. A broad terrace that reaches out toward the ocean, as if the entire house is preparing to dive in.

Back when Nina's grandfather had bought the land, this corner of the South of France was a secret. A strange place, almost untouched. A famous American writer had built a house down in the bay back in the 1920s and published a bestselling memoir about summers when the Jazz Age elite would descend on his home. Gatsby-esque parties and afternoons drinking Sidecars by the pool. Torrid affairs and drunken fallouts, intense friendships formed over pre-dinner cocktails.

By the time Nina's grandfather broke ground, the famous writer was dead from liver disease and a new elite had begun to move in. Hollywood actors seduced by the romanticism of European summers and British socialites tired of war-torn cities. This land offered the promise of glamor and escape, a not-so-long-ago past that now felt very far away. A golden age to be recaptured.

Nina's grandfather was the legendary Conrad Drayton, a film producer who had made his money in the golden age of cinema. The birth of Nina's mother, Evelyn—his only known child—was the result of a fling with a young, aspiring actress who had happily signed away her parental rights, worried that a baby would get in the way of her fledgling career. Within a few years, she would be a washed-up starlet with a drug addiction, and Conrad Drayton would be reveling in his latest—and in his mind, greatest—role as a doting father. Evelyn Drayton had grown up between London and the Côte d'Azur, passed around at parties before she could walk, drinking martinis with dinner by the time she was thirteen. Even now, she has a habit of namedropping the people that she holidayed with back then. Sixties supermodels. Retired Hollywood stars. She talks about secret parties, skinny-dipping at midnight, margaritas out on the balcony with people so impossibly famous that Nina has to double-check her mother has got their names right. Sometimes, Nina can feel the ghosts of them sipping aperitifs on the terrace, watching sunsets over the broad expanse of sea.

Evelyn inherited the house when she was nineteen, after a catastrophic heart attack had seized her father's right ventricle as he sipped on a strong cocktail out on the terrace. The housekeeper, who had been away visiting her son, had found him three days later, still stretched out on a sun lounger as if he had only laid down for an afternoon nap. *The heat had sped up decomposition*, Evelyn would sometimes tell them after a few drinks. They had wanted an open casket, but couldn't.

"Imagine the flies," Ryan said to Nina, after Evelyn had regaled them with the story the first and only time, before now, that Nina had brought him out there. He looked thoughtful. "Still. It's the best place to go, your favorite place in the world. That view? Better than a shitty nursing home, at any rate."

Nina wasn't sure about that. Sometimes she wondered why Evelyn had wanted to keep this house, which seemed steeped in bad luck. A place where death lurked beneath beauty.

There has always been a rawness to it. Something stark in the way that it protrudes from the cliff face. How great stretches of it sprawl out from the hillside, as though defying gravity. The unusual geometry—Nina's grandfather insisted on designing it himself, and windows and artfully placed decks open onto vistas of sky, giving the impression that the world has fallen away, or that one wrong turn could send you toppling over the edge, cascading down toward the sea.

The house used to be beautiful, and in a way, it still is. But now, it also has an air of neglect, a feeling that it belongs to a different time. Salt has sped up the structure's decay, vines crawling up the walls and knotting into window frames, plaster cracking where the house has performed a ragged breath, an expanding exhale in the midday heat and a retraction in the cooler months.

Over time, the sun has bleached the terra-cotta stone, the sea air ravaging the walls. The orange-red has faded to a shade of salmon, and now the locals call it the pink house. *La maison rose.*

Nina knows that Evelyn can no longer afford the upkeep, has never really been able to afford the upkeep. It seems, somehow, as if the house was always supposed to crumble into the mountainside. As if nothing so big, so sumptuous, so overblown is supposed to last forever.

It always struck Nina as a tremendous hubris, to build a house so close to the water. As though you were tempting nature to tear it to shreds.

"They're out on the terrace," Sandra, the Draytons' housekeeper, says when she opens the front door.

She doesn't comment on the fact that she hasn't seen Nina for three years, or the panicked phone call that she answered yesterday. She just steps neatly back into the large, cool entrance hall, almost untouched since Nina's grandfather first carved the huge stone staircase.

Nina thanks her and leaves Ryan behind, unloading their bags from the taxi. She knows which terrace Sandra means. They only use one terrace now, the smaller of the two, located at the back of the house. They avoid the larger terrace, jutting out toward the sea at the side of the property. Evelyn was never quite able to match up the tiles when the pool was filled in, and so the shadow of it remains, sketched out in lighter stone. A pale, rectangular ghost that none of them can stand to look at.

Nina can see her mother and Blake before she reaches them, the patio doors that lead from the kitchen closed tight against the heat. They sit in the shade of bougainvillea, a knot of vines as old as the house, an open bottle of wine on the table between them. As if nothing has changed.

Nina takes a deep breath and pushes against the door.

"Darling."

As usual, Evelyn looks beautiful and undone. Nina is used to her mother turning heads. She was an it-girl in the seventies and eighties, a newly minted heiress who had walked runways and been the muse of artists that she still liked to mention after a couple of glasses of wine. Nina has seen the pictures of her, too skinny, too much thick black eyeliner, her hair always looking artfully messy.

Now in her sixties, her look has barely evolved. Her long auburn hair is half-knotted on top of her head in an elaborate arrangement. She wears a silk dress as if she's heading for cocktails at the Ritz rather than waiting for the arrival of her daughter. A cigarette hangs from her hand, even though the last time Nina saw her mother back in London she had sworn that she was giving it up. Her most recent boyfriend, Jonas, is a health freak at least twenty years her junior. Evelyn has been considering taking up running.

"You decided to grace us with your presence then." Evelyn's voice is artificially bright as Nina swoops to plant a careful kiss on her cheek. "Honestly. Most people would *die* for a holiday home in the South of France, and here's my daughter having to be practically dragged here!"

She lets out a high, girlish laugh.

"Well, sit down, darling, sit down," she says. "Sandra will fetch you a glass. Blake picked up this gorgeous bottle of white."

"You'll love this, Nina." Blake is lounging back in his chair, tapping the bottle with one finger. "It's really good stuff."

"I'm OK, thanks." Nina slides into the seat opposite her mother. She can already hear that her voice is tight. This place still sets something off inside her, makes her feel like the world is slightly too narrow, like everything has come a little too close, in spite of the wide vistas of space around them. "We need to talk."

"Oh, yes?" Evelyn says mildly. "What about?"

Nina's head twitches between Blake and her mother.

"I called you about this yesterday," she says. "It's the whole reason I came—"

"Oh, *that*." Evelyn waves one hand, dispersing a cloud of cigarette smoke. "Well, surely you haven't come back just to talk about *that*, darling? And anyway, you've only just arrived. I'm so thrilled to have you here. Can't we just enjoy this evening? Can't we just have a lovely time, the four of us?"

Sandra emerges from the kitchen, delivering two wineglasses without being asked. She places them down on the table and slips wordlessly away.

"I've been so looking forward to this, darling," Evelyn is saying. Her voice is light. Hopeful. "Both of my children. Back in my favorite place in the world. Well, it's just like old times, isn't it? I don't get enough of the two of you. That's the sad thing about your children growing up, you know? You think that you have them forever, and then they grow up and go, and it feels like the time has just disappeared from you—"

"We'll have plenty of time to talk about the email, Nina," Blake says, quietly. He lifts the bottle to fill Nina's glass. "But you must be knackered. Will Ryan want a glass, d'you think?"

"Maybe. I don't know. He's just putting the bags upstairs . . ."

Nina trails off, her gaze twitches between her brother and mother, dazed. She's not been able to think of anything else since she received the email. For the last thirty-two hours, the words have been wedged somewhere between her throat and her heart, rising up every now and again like bile.

Social media sleuths. Flawed testimony. Josie Jackson.

"They emailed you, too, didn't they?" she says.

"Oh, darling," says Evelyn. She taps her cigarette against a glass ashtray. "You know I don't read emails. Blake's filled me in a bit, of course, but really. It just seems like a load of old nonsense, don't you think?"

"They're making a documentary," says Nina. "They're coming back here to film. They're going to interview Josie Jackson. And they think I lied about what happened to Tamara."

Her voice tremors. They never say Tamara's name out loud, not in front of Evelyn. Her mother's face doesn't move, but Nina sees a muscle twitch in her neck. Sees her drag more deeply on her cigarette.

"Come on, Nina," Blake says, level. "They're not saying you *lied*. It's just a theory. Just a silly theory, made up by people with too much time on their hands. People have said all sorts over the years about what happened."

"We just have to do what we always do," Evelyn says, cutting loudly across Blake. "We don't engage. We ignore them. And we threaten them with legal, if needed."

She takes a long drag on her cigarette and continues with a smoky exhale, her voice louder, an octave too high.

"I remember in the early eighties when the papers said that Blake's father was having an affair with a European princess—an actual European princess! Well! It was everywhere, as you can imagine. Paparazzi outside of hotel rooms. The works. We ignored the whole thing. Didn't say a word. It blew over, of course. Yesterday's news is tomorrow's fish-and-chips paper."

"He probably *was* having an affair with a European princess, knowing Dad," Blake says dryly. "And anyway. Nobody reads actual newspapers these days. And fish and chips don't get wrapped up in newspapers anymore, either."

"But people read stuff online," says Nina. "And people watch true crime documentaries, and listen to podcasts, and that stuff stays on the internet forever. Nobody forgets about it."

Evelyn taps her cigarette against the ashtray impatiently.

"Well, I don't know about that, darling," she says.

"And don't you think we should *want* to hear what they have to say?" says Nina. "If they think that this documentary could reveal something new about what happened to Tamara, shouldn't we help with that? Maybe we should *want* to be a part of it?"

Evelyn flings her hands upward.

"Not this again," she says. Her loud brightness has cracked, and her voice sounds strained. "First the bloody child psychology and now—"

"Nina." Blake's voice is firm now, speaking over their mother. "We know what Josie Jackson did. No amount of documentaries or amateur sleuths is going to change that. We say nothing. And we stick together. Like we always do. Like we always have done, all this time."

Nina catches a look in his eye then. A promise. *Later*, it says. *We'll talk about this later.*

"There's no use spoiling our holiday," Evelyn says. Her voice wavers on the last word. Her eyes are very wide, and she has a strangely childlike look to her, the threat of tears. "I've been looking forward to having you both here. Don't ruin it, Nina."

Nina's mouth slides shut. She has the distinct impression that she somehow manages to spoil things. But what else can you expect when at five years old you were given information that had the power to wreck someone's life?

"Come on," Evelyn continues. "Drink up. We're celebrating, aren't we? The whole family here. Everyone back together."

Nina picks up her glass. She is gripping the stem so tightly that she is surprised it doesn't shatter.

"To summer!" Evelyn says.

"To summer," echoes Blake, lifting his own drink.

When Nina raises her glass to her lips, Blake doesn't break her gaze.

FIVE

2004

SIX WEEKS BEFORE THE BIRTHDAY PARTY

When she was a child, Hannah Bailey used to collect stories about Evelyn Drayton.

This town, this stretch of coastline, was all that Hannah had ever known. Her parents had met while backpacking in Thailand in the early eighties. Her dad, an East Londoner, said he had found her mum impossibly glamorous, with her thick French accent and her harem pants. Her mum said she had found him too brash, too boyish, and yet somehow, they had clicked. They had traveled the world together until Hannah's mum realized she was pregnant—an accident, as the story went. That was when they had decided to move to this stretch of coast, far from the metropolises where they had each grown up. A former holiday haunt of artists and bohemians that teetered with the promise of becoming the next hippie paradise.

But dominated by villas that belonged to old-money families who drifted in and out with the good weather, the offbeat Eden Hannah's parents had hoped for never quite materialized. The dive shop that they plugged all of their savings into survived off the occasional family who would placate bored teenagers with the promise of scuba lessons, or children with the inflatable rafts they stocked to the ceiling. Somehow, each summer trudged in and out, and Hannah and her parents were still here.

Hannah knew everything about this town. She was a watcher. That was what her mother used to say about her. She would often report that even when Hannah was a toddler, she was happiest sitting quietly and observing. She would perch behind the counter of the dive shop, her eyes following customers, solemn and still. Absorbing details until she understood the intricate dynamics between families and friendships. Hannah knew everything about everyone, her mum once said. Hannah was good with secrets.

As far back as Hannah could remember, she understood that Evelyn Drayton was special. She heard how people talked about her. The reverence in the way they said her name. Even though Hannah didn't really understand what fame was, couldn't comprehend Evelyn's past as a celebrated socialite, she understood glamor. She understood that this woman was different. That there was something fascinating about her. Something that made Hannah long to be a Drayton.

Throughout her childhood, she collected stories about the family like a magpie hunting for bright, shiny things. She learned that Evelyn's name had once been synonymous with celebrity wild childs; that after she inherited her father's vast fortune at nineteen, she had regularly been spotted falling out of nightclubs, memorialized in paparazzi shots of her holding hands with bad-boy actors and aristocrats that sold to the tabloids for hundreds of thousands of pounds. She learned Evelyn had been married four times, twice to the same person. That her first husband was rock star Rocco Mae. That they'd had an infamously torrid and intense romance in the eighties. That they'd married when she was pregnant with twins, the pictures of Evelyn's rounded belly at their Vegas wedding splashed across gossip pages. That they were often branded as the new Richard Burton and Liz Taylor, the new Sid and Nancy—couples whose self-destructiveness outstripped their romance.

Hannah learned that Rocco and Evelyn divorced when the twins were just babies, after rumors of infidelity on both sides, but had been unable to stay away from each other. They had remarried in the nineties and divorced again three years later, when Rocco left for a supermodel ten years younger than Evelyn.

Then there was Evelyn's second husband—technically also her third husband—who had been arrested for trashing a hotel room at the Ritz. Evelyn's youngest child, Nina, was born not long after their marriage, and not long before their quickie divorce. She was the result of an affair—the papers speculating that the father was anyone from an heir to an ancient European fortune to the pink house's pool boy. Evelyn never confirmed either way. She bulldozed through the rumors by getting engaged to her fourth husband, a much younger American named Harrison Andreas, after just two weeks of a whirlwind romance.

"The Draytons are basically royalty around here," Hannah had said when Josie's mother landed the job of housekeeper at the pink house. "Everyone knows who they are."

Josie had shrugged. It was the summer her dad left, and she had been quieter than usual. Spending more time at the dive shop, or down on the beach.

"So?" she had said. "That doesn't make them better than us."

And Hannah hadn't answered, because Josie was younger, and she hadn't lived here as long, and she didn't understand yet. She didn't know what it meant, to be the Draytons. What it meant to be talked about, recognized. To know that you could enter a room and people would jump to make sure you were comfortable. To not have to worry about what next year would bring, or the year after that. The certainty of being part of a world where the rules were made to benefit you, where the parties were never-ending. Where the schools you would attend, the jobs you would hold, and the people you would be friends with were all decided before you could even walk.

To Hannah, it sounded like perfection.

✺

There was always a cocktail party the first night the Draytons arrived in the South of France. To Hannah, it signaled the start of high season. As darkness fell, the pink house would glow against the hillside, tiki lamps on the terrace, the glimmer of fairy lights. Every room lit up after a winter of darkness. A clear announcement that the Draytons were back in town.

Hannah had promised to arrive early this year. There was a virus going around, and some of the local girls who had been hired to help were sick. Patricia needed an extra pair of hands, and Josie would be tied up with her usual job of looking after Nina, keeping her out of the way of the adults. But there had been a problem at the dive shop, a missing cash box, and by the time Hannah turned up, guests were already scattered throughout the hall, hired waitstaff offering up trays of cocktails. Their eyes glazed over Hannah as she weaved through to the kitchen, sweat-damp from jogging to the pink house in an attempt to make up time. It was a lifelong discipline, the art of spotting money a mile off. The ease that it carried. The confidence that Hannah lacked. To Evelyn Drayton's guests, Hannah was almost invisible.

At the kitchen island, Patricia was lining up canapés on a ceramic platter, morsels of goat cheese smeared on top of figs and neat, square croustades, each crowned with a delicate fold of salmon.

"I'm so sorry, Pat—" Hannah started.

"Josie's outside," Patricia said, not looking up from her work, her hands moving rapidly. "By the pool. Here, you can take these out."

She wiped her hands on a tea towel before opening the fridge, pulling out a plate of sandwiches.

"Nina won't eat anything except cheese sandwiches at the minute," she said, an exhaustion in her voice. "I've tried to put some cucumbers in so she's getting at least a bit of something green. Josie might be able to persuade her. Nina listens to her, though god knows why."

Hannah took the plate without saying a word.

※

Josie was not by the pool, where Hannah had expected her to be. Hannah circled the terrace twice, weaving through clusters of women in long dresses and men in open-necked shirts, a waiter cleaning up a smashed martini glass. She traced the familiar route through the inside of the house, across the broad entrance hall, the living room with views over the sea, the library that Evelyn's latest husband, Harrison, had insisted they convert into an office, even though he had no discernible job. She paused at the foot of the stairs, knowing that she wasn't supposed to go up. When the Draytons were back, the house that Josie and Hannah roamed through all the rest of the year became off-limits. But then, Hannah had been told to take sandwiches for Nina.

She walked up the stairs quickly, two at a time, afraid she might be caught and questioned. She paused at the top, listening for the sound of a child playing, the high-pitched murmur of Nina's voice. She could only hear the hum of music from the ground floor, the clinking of glasses, the buzz of conversation. And then, a sound from the end of the corridor. She quickened her pace, expecting to recognize Nina and Josie's distinctive chatter. Her footsteps slowed. The voices were unmistakably adult. Urgent. She drew closer. The open door of Evelyn's bedroom.

"I saw it. I *saw* you looking at her."

"Bullshit."

"I saw it, Harrison. Do you think I'm blind?"

A short, sharp laugh.

"I think that you're crazy, Evelyn. That's what I think. I think that you make shit up when you want attention."

"How *dare* you? How dare you call me crazy?"

"Don't fucking touch me."

"I hate you. I hate you."

"I said don't *fucking*—"

There was a hard, quick sound, the brute noise of skin on skin. Hannah instinctively took a step back, as if she herself had been hit. Back into the doorway of the closest room, out of sight. There was a silence. It was worse than the sound of them fighting. It was terrible and vast. It felt like it would last forever.

"Evelyn."

Harrison's voice was weak this time. Appalled.

"No."

"I didn't—"

"Get *away* from me."

Then, an arm reaching around Hannah, the heat of a body, the feel of someone's breath against the back of her neck as the door was pushed shut.

"You know," a voice said. "You really shouldn't be sneaking around like this. You might hear things you don't want to know."

※

Blake's room was dark, the air tight and sweet-smelling. The scent of teenage boy: body spray and the earthy stench of weed. A deep blue lamp cast the room in an unearthly glow, the reflection of the molten wax patterning the ceiling. It would have been something that Blake's father, Rocco Mae, bought for him, Hannah could tell. After spending six years in and out of the Draytons' house, she could recognize something that a man who didn't really know his son would buy. A thing that he might think a teenager would like.

Blake moved from behind Hannah toward the bed where another boy lay, a spliff glowing orange in one hand. As her eyes adjusted to the half gloom, Hannah recognized him as Blake's best friend, Barnaby. She knew him, of course. She knew all the intricate networks that webbed the summer residents together. Families and step-families and friends, people who belonged to the same members' clubs back in London, or had drank together at university. She had grown up with these kids, knew where their families wintered, the names of the boarding schools they went to back in England. Barnaby's parents were property developers, well-known for building garish mega mansions. Their own house was an ugly monstrosity on the other side of the bay.

"I was just looking for Josie," Hannah said. She held up the plate, as if it was evidence. "Patricia asked me to bring up some sandwiches, for the kids."

"You don't have to explain yourself to us, H," Blake said, with an ease that made her flush. "I would just hate for Evelyn to catch you up here when she's on the warpath."

"Is she ..." Hannah paused. "Is she ... OK? Do you think you should check on her?"

"You don't want to get between her and Harrison when they're like this."

A voice from the other side of the room made Hannah jump. She hadn't seen her, sprawled in the window alcove, her legs propped up against the wall.

Tamara Drayton.

Blake and Tamara were of course not identical, and yet it still always struck Hannah with a kind of surprise how different they were. Blake had sandy blond hair, skin that turned tan easily. He had a way of fitting in, an easy confidence that filled whatever space he occupied.

Tamara, on the other hand, had short, dark hair cut into a pixie crop. Skin pale from deliberately staying out of the sun. A habit of wearing thick, black eyeliner. She was confident, too, but in a different way. A spiky way that seemed to draw a circle around herself, a warning not to enter. She said things that other people wouldn't, Blake often slipping in to soften her words.

The only way either twin appeared to have taken after their mother at all was Tamara's tendency to have a cigarette perpetually hanging from one hand. She smoked roll-ups, and Patricia was constantly sweeping up dropped scraps of tobacco at the pink house, muttering that anyone with Drayton money would smoke proper cigarettes, if they had half a brain.

Yet in spite of their physical differences, Blake and Tamara had myriad similarities, things that were more difficult to put your finger on. The way they tilted their heads when they were listening carefully. The way they laughed. The slant of their noses. The specific slang they used, the way they spoke a beat more slowly than seemed necessary.

Blake had once mentioned that when they were children, they had developed a secret twin-speak and that it would drive Evelyn mad. The two of them, communicating in a language their mother was unable to access.

Tamara tilted her head then, in that specific way Hannah recognized.

"It's like foreplay to them," Tamara said. "All this yelling at each other, accusing each other of fucking other people. It's their thing."

In the half-light, Hannah could see Barnaby pulling a face. Tamara drew on the thin roll-up, exhaling a stream of damp, musky smoke into the air. It was so muggy, like nobody had opened a window in days. Was Hannah imagining that she was getting light-headed?

"So, what's new round here?" Tamara drawled, as if they'd only been talking about the weather. "What have we missed while we've been rotting in London all winter?"

There was a taunt to her voice, and Hannah wondered if she was being mocked. She lifted her chin.

"Oh, you know," Hannah said. "It's been quiet. Always is, until summer."

Blake sat down heavily on the bed.

"Oh, come on," he said, kindly. "I bet you have loads of gossip. Stuff that goes on behind closed doors when we're not here."

"Upstairs, downstairs shit," said Barnaby.

Tamara snorted. Blake's leg jerked out to kick him, a movement subtle enough that Hannah almost didn't catch it.

"I just meant . . . you guys who live here must have the run of the place, right? And your dad runs that restaurant, doesn't he? Down by the beach."

"Actually—"

"Barnaby, you're such an idiot," said Blake. "H's parents run the dive shop, remember?"

"Oh, yeah," said Barnaby, in a way that suggested he didn't.

There was a pause that seemed to go on slightly too long.

"Anyway," said Hannah, breaking it. "I should probably go and find Josie."

"I'll come with you." Blake stood up. "Two pairs of eyes are better than one, right?"

"Bro," said Barnaby, the upper-class cut of his accent dragging against the word. "I thought we were gonna go get that vodka?"

"I'll get it on the way back," Blake said. "Chill."

He turned to Hannah.

"Come on then, H," he said. "Let's go and find your friend and my elusive sister."

Blake offered to carry the sandwiches. It left Hannah unsure what to do with her hands. They felt ungainly swinging next to her sides, hanging gorilla-like, drawing attention to her long limbs, the fact that she was half an inch taller than Blake. She folded them across her chest, but then remembered that she had read a magazine segment by a body language expert saying that doing so would make her look hostile and unapproachable. In the end, she settled for burying them in the pockets of her denim shorts as they circled the ground floor of the house.

"They were supposed to be by the pool," she said.

"Probably Nina, leading Josie astray," said Blake, and Hannah had to glance up to check that he was joking.

"Hey," he said. "Sorry about them. Tamara and Barnaby. They think they're being funny, but—"

"It's fine," said Hannah, too quickly. "I can take a joke."

"But they shouldn't take the piss out of you like that," he said.

The words, said so easily, confirmed Hannah's fears. That they were, in fact, mocking her. She tried not to let her face show the hurt scrabbling to the surface.

"Barnaby's always been kind of a dick," Blake continued, not noticing. "But I dunno what's going on with Tamara lately. Usually I know exactly what she's thinking, but she's different this summer."

They rounded out of the patio doors and onto the terrace. Even though Hannah had spent years going in and out of this house, the beauty of it never lessened. The deep blue glow of the swimming pool. The sea, pink with twilight, glinting with the last traces of sun. Guests had begun to dip their feet in the pool, their trouser legs rolled up, silk skirts spooling around thighs. The rattle of ice in a cocktail shaker. The distant pop of a champagne cork.

"Down here," said Blake.

His hand reached out and brushed the inward curve of Hannah's spine so lightly that it could have been a breeze, the shifting of clothes against her skin. She shivered, in spite of the warmth of the night. She was remembering last summer, a day when Blake had invited her and Josie down to the beach with him and his friends for the first time. How they had cracked open bottles of beer with their perfect, dentist-straightened teeth. Grilled hamburgers on disposable barbecues and eaten them on plain white buns with squirts of ketchup, sand peppering each mouthful.

How they had climbed up the cliffs and dive-bombed into the water. How she and Blake had jumped at the same time, their fingertips stretched out toward each other, as if trying to touch.

How, in that dark, tumbling moment after submersion—that second of panic when your body wants to fight for the surface but isn't sure which way is up—his hand caught hers. All of a sudden, the water had cleared, and she had seen him, his face close, the breath that escaped him tangling up with hers, pockets of water rising up toward the light together.

For a moment, it was just them. They were the only people in the world.

And then, he had let go of her hand. Kicked up toward the world above, his body rising toward the shattered light of the sun.

When Hannah had surfaced, Blake was laughing. Splashing. He flipped onto his back and swam quickly and easily over to where his friends were waiting for him. The moment was over so fast, but Hannah could still feel it. His hand. His thigh brushing up against hers.

She thought about that moment often. All through last summer, when she would see Blake occasionally, with his friends or at the pink house, and both of them would act as if nothing had happened. In September, when the Draytons went back to London, and she clung on to the memory of that moment while her parents worried about whether they could afford to keep the shop open for another year, what they would do if they had to sell. In spring, when the prospect of summer loomed back into view, and Hannah dared to let herself imagine what it might be like when Blake returned. To imagine other things—his hands against her skin. His body. Him, touching her in the way that she had only ever touched herself.

Somehow, Hannah never mentioned the moment she and Blake

had shared to Josie, even though they told each other everything. It felt private, somehow. Sacred. It was the warm hum in the pit of Hannah's stomach when Josie teased her about having a crush on Blake. A secret that only she and he shared.

"Knew it," he said, leaning over the balustrades at the edge of the terrace.

Peering up at them, crouched on a slope of grass below, Josie and Nina. Dolls strewn on the ground around them, resplendent in tulle party frocks.

"This is Nina's favorite place right now," Blake said.

"She didn't want to be around all the people," Josie shot back.

"I know that feeling," said Blake.

He stepped back so that Josie and Nina disappeared from view, and held out the plate of sandwiches toward Hannah.

"You have fun down there," he said.

She took the plate, aware of the brush of her hand against his.

"Hey," he said. "What are you doing tomorrow night?"

She shrugged. She was supposed to be tutoring; a family who were renting a property down by the beach for the summer had gone to great lengths to tell Hannah how important it was that their children were fully immersed in the culture.

"Nothing much," she said.

He tilted his head to one side so that his hair fell in his face.

"I think it's time we showed you girls what a real party is."

SIX

2024

When the sky is golden and Nina's head is hazy from heat, she crosses through the garden room at the side of the house. Outside, a set of stone steps leads down an entire story to the terrace where once a pool stretched out toward the sea. Below it, beneath the balustrade, a meandering garden that used to bloom with rose bushes and lavender, a second set of steps that lead all the way down to the beach. Now, the grass is scrubby, the bushes overgrown. Evelyn hasn't hired gardeners for a very long time.

It's the time of day when the air thickens, soupy and warm, so dense that you can almost taste it. Salt and honey. Charcoal left smoldering after grilling meat outdoors.

Nina leaves the house through the same door that she ran through all those years ago. Screaming. The eyes of a dozen adults turned toward her.

She remembers it. She does.

Or, at least, she thinks she does. She can see it now. A little girl, her sandal torn, a tear-streaked face. One hand pointing in the direction of the pool.

She can visualize the entire thing.

Whether or not that is the same as remembering it, she isn't exactly sure.

Nina has spent much of her life grappling with this fact. She has read books. Attended lectures. Earned degrees. Sat on a dozen therapy couches and been told over and over again that what she is experiencing is normal, for someone who has been through what she has. She has spent years trying to understand this strange confluence of memory and truth, grappling with the idea that these things are not exactly the same. She knows about false memory, and about how trauma can create great, gaping holes in your vision of the past. She knows that people's memories are the most accurate in the eleven months immediately after the event, and then become hazy afterward, complicated by retelling and rehashing a story. She knows that she should be reassured by the speed with which she was interviewed by the police. The clarity that she apparently possessed back then.

And yet, no matter how many books Nina reads or how many letters get added on to the end of her name, nothing quite delivers the certainty she longs for. She has never quite managed to quell the hum of uncertainty that loudens whenever she thinks of her sister.

Ryan is out on the terrace, pacing across the tiles, his phone held close to his face. When he sees her, he shoots a thumbs-up. He points toward the handset.

Work, he mouths.

He rolls his eyes, both a performance and a promise that he won't be long. He didn't know the Draytons, all those years ago. He doesn't realize that he is standing in the exact spot where they pulled Tamara out of the water, her skin glistening, her face an unnatural, terrible shade of gray.

Nina remembers that. She's sure she does.

"You won't make yourself feel any better, coming out here, you know."

Her brother, so close behind her that she can feel his breath tickling her cheek.

She turns and reaches her arms out, and he's there, ready to pull her into a hug.

"Why do you always sneak up on people like that?" she says, her voice muffled against his shoulder.

"Habit," he says. "Mum's just come down from her pre-dinner nap and is requesting martinis. You want one?"

He nods back toward the house. Toward the other terrace, with its quiet and its safety. A place where they can pretend that this terrace doesn't exist, and the events that took place here twenty years ago, didn't happen.

"Or," Blake says, seeming to catch Nina's hesitation. "I can get us an incredibly expensive bottle of wine and we can drink our troubles away very far from our mother."

Nina exhales. She didn't realize how tight her shoulders were until they release. How desperate she is to be away from everyone else.

"That sounds completely perfect."

❋

They go to the balcony that leads out from the master bedroom.

Even now, at the age of twenty-five, Nina feels that there is something delicious and rebellious about sitting there. They were never allowed when they were children. Evelyn always insisted that she needed something just for herself. Herself, and whichever boyfriend she had hauled along for the summer. Nina hadn't even known the balcony existed until she was sixteen and Blake had shown her where the key was hidden, the two of them sneaking up when their mother was out for the evening. Nina still remembers the strangeness of it, the discordance in something so new, so unfamiliar, having been here all along.

Blake places down a bottle of wine and two glasses, pouring them both generous measures.

"I thought she'd given up," Nina says, nodding to another overflowing ashtray abandoned on the low table between them.

"Ah, right," says Blake. "You haven't seen her since she was with Jonas."

"She broke up with Jonas?"

"Jonas broke up with *her*, to be totally accurate. Think her polo club membership was cramping his style."

"Good. His homemade kombucha was terrible."

"Vile. Who brews their own kombucha?"

"Unemployed men in their forties, I suppose."

"Jonas was in his forties?"

"Yep."

"He looked good for it."

"Maybe there actually was something in the whole paleo thing."

They both raise their glasses and take large slugs of wine. From below, Nina hears Evelyn's voice, Sandra's response.

"Do you really think we should ignore it?" Nina says. "This documentary? Or were you just saying that in front of Mum?"

Blake takes a moment to answer. His gaze is fixed out on the sea beyond them, burnished by the late afternoon light.

"I think Mum's probably right," Blake says at last, slowly, as if he's considering this even as he speaks. "People have always talked about the case. People have always said things. And these documentary makers? Unless they say they have any new information, what good can it do us? What's done is done, Nina. Nothing can change that."

"You didn't read the email, did you?"

"I skimmed it," Blake says, with a small shrug. "You know I'm always getting people emailing me about the case. Most of them are nutters, to be honest—"

"But this is different," Nina cuts him off. "Blake. I think you should read it."

For a moment her brother doesn't speak.

"Fine," he says. "Show me."

Nina pulls out her phone, even though she could recite every word at this point. That there's been a popular online miniseries about the Tamara Drayton case, from a well-known true crime influencer who has blown up on TikTok. A *slew of new tips and information* has emerged in its wake. The serendipitous timing—here, the producer almost seemed giddy—with the twentieth anniversary of Tamara Drayton's death.

> *We've asked the host of the TikTok series if they'd like to front the documentary and we're delighted to say that they've*

accepted. We've also been in touch with a number of sources close to the case, and many individuals wish to come forward to share their side of the story, in the wake of the renewed interest. But what we're still looking for is a member of the Drayton family who is willing to speak out about what happened that summer. And we believe that you—Nina Drayton—are the missing piece to the puzzle.

Twenty years ago, you became the youngest-ever witness in a French murder case. We believe that the trial was flawed, and that someone so young should never have been able to testify. Whether you agree with this premise or not, we feel that it's important for you to have the opportunity to share your truth. What do you remember about your sister's death, and the resulting trial? Do you, as someone with firsthand experience, think that a five-year-old is a reliable witness?

We know you've never spoken out about your role in this life-altering case. But we feel now could be the perfect time. If Josie Jackson is innocent, as a growing number of people believe, you could be the only one who knows the truth.

Nina watches as Blake scans the message. As he reaches the end, he shrugs.

"So?" he says. "Just like I said. No new evidence. Nothing of merit. Trying to pretend that they're on your side, that they've got your best interest at heart, when all they really want is to drag our family through the mud again. Just like the rest of them."

There's a stab of resentment in his voice. Nina has to remember to temper her response. To remind herself what her mother and Blake went through all those years ago. After all, she had been so young, and protected from the media firestorm. But her mother and Blake had been right at the heart of it. She knows that it still hurts them both, the things that were said about Tamara.

"But the video series that they're talking about," Nina says. "Blake, I watched it, and—"

Blake lifts his glass and drains it in one.

"See," he says, placing it down hard on the table. "This is the problem. You watch this rubbish online, and you fall into an internet rabbit hole, and next thing you know, everyone's a conspiracy theorist. Even you, the person who actually *knows* what happened. The person who was *actually* there."

Nina closes her mouth. She knows about how internet conspiracy theories work. She has a master's in psychology, for goodness' sake.

"Nina," Blake's voice is softer now, almost sad. "What you went through back then was traumatic. Incredibly, deeply traumatic. It's no surprise that you keep coming back to it. That you have this . . . this *obsession* with it. But this isn't healthy."

He reaches out, places one hand over hers.

"This is exactly why Mum didn't want you to get into all this child psychology stuff," he says. "All this worrying. All this trying to understand what you saw. What happened. Some stuff is beyond our ability to understand. Some stuff is cruel, and senseless, and terrible. Some stuff can't be explained away with . . . with bloody *therapy*, Nina."

He takes a deep breath. His eyes are wet. She hates that she cannot leave alone something that hurts him so much.

"What Josie Jackson did was terrible," he says. "It was evil, and brutal, and monstrous. *She's* monstrous. And what you did was the right thing. But you've spent your entire life feeling guilty about it. And I understand. I can't imagine what it must have been like, to have had all that weight on you. To have had to say something that sent someone to prison. And maybe all of that responsibility shouldn't have been put on a kid. Maybe this producer got that bit right. But the important thing is that *you* got it right, too, Nina. You put our sister's killer in jail. And you have nothing to feel guilty about. You have nothing, and nobody, to answer to."

On the horizon, the sun is close to setting. The sea is a bloody, violent shade of red.

"Do you ever think about her?" Nina asks, softly. "Tamara?"

Blake stiffens, his glass still to his lips.

"I hardly remember her," Nina continues. "I feel bad about it sometimes. This person—my sister—totally changed our lives. And I can only remember snatches of her, weird things. Like, I can remember how she smelled, but not how she looked. Don't you think that's strange?"

Blake lowers his glass.

"Memory is strange," he says quietly. "You of all people know that. You can't control the things you hold on to."

"But I wonder if we'd talked about her more, if I'd remember. If we had any pictures of her out—"

"Mum couldn't cope with it," Blake says. "You know she couldn't."

"But it's been so long . . ."

"Like you said, you don't remember, Nina. You don't know what it was like."

He sets down his glass and threads his hands together in front of him.

"I was older. I saw what it did to Mum. It almost killed her," he says. "People cope in their own ways, Nina. You have to let them."

For a second, there's quiet between them.

"Kitty used to think we were morbid, coming out here every year," Blake says at last.

"Kitty?"

Nina hasn't heard Blake mention his most long-term girlfriend for a while. Before they broke up last year, Kitty had been around for almost eighteen months, a marathon-length relationship for Blake. Nina had liked her. She was sad when they had broken up.

"Yeah," says Blake. "When you stopped coming out here, she said that she got it. She said most people would have sold this place, after what happened. I told her it was fine. That we've been coming back for so long we barely think about it anymore." He pauses, a note of dark mirth slipping between the edges of his words. "I guess I was wrong about that."

Just then, they hear Ryan's voice coming from the terrace below, the sound of a chair being pulled out.

"I should probably go back down," says Nina. "They'll be wondering where we've gone."

Blake lifts the wine bottle to refill his glass.

"I might stay here," he says. "Finish this off."

Nina stands.

"I'll make your excuses."

Their eyes catch, a glimmer of camaraderie between them. The thing about having a mother like Evelyn Drayton is that it bonds you. Nobody else will ever understand Nina quite like Blake does.

"Oh, and Nina?" Blake says. "I'm not going to tell you what to do about this documentary. But just . . . just think of Mum, OK? She can't go through it all again. She lost her daughter. *I* lost my twin sister. Is this really what our family needs? I don't know if we can relive losing Tamara again."

SEVEN

2004

SIX WEEKS BEFORE THE BIRTHDAY PARTY

"You can't seriously want to go, though?" said Josie.

She and Hannah were sitting on the very edge of the Draytons' pool. On the terrace, Nina was engaged in an intense imaginary game of mummies and daddies, pretending to smoke a cigarette fashioned out of a cocktail straw.

"Why not?" said Hannah.

Josie screwed up her nose.

"Because it'll be lame," she said. "All those posh twats showing off about where they're going on their gap years and which car their parents got them for their latest birthday. I'd be so bored I'd scream."

"Oh, come on, that's not what they're like. Not all of them, anyway."

"I hated it when we went to the beach with them last year. They all thought it was weird we were there. You could tell."

"But we were invited."

"*You* were invited."

"Blake said that you could come, too. He specifically mentioned you by name."

"Well, aren't I the lucky one?"

Josie put on a faux upper-class accent, sticking her chin up in the air.

"I am so *thrilled* that Master Blake deigned to invite me to his piss-up on the beach."

Hannah nudged her friend, elbow in her ribs.

"Come on. You know what I mean."

"You go by yourself. I'll stay here and hang out with Nina." Josie turned around to look at Nina. "Right, Nina? I'll just hang out with you. My little best buddy."

At the sound of her name, Nina bowled over and piled into Josie's lap, wrapping her plump arms around her neck.

"Ouch," Josie said, laughing. "You're getting heavy."

Although she always complained to her mum about Evelyn's babysitting demands, Josie adored the youngest Drayton. Nina was smart and happy, in spite of her dysfunctional family. Josie liked spending summer days with her, teaching her to swim in the Draytons' pool, or taking her down to the beach.

Josie would never say this out loud, but she really believed that Nina loved her, too. She saw how Nina would look at her with the complete trust and uncomplicated adulation that only very small children have. She liked how, unlike her mother and older siblings, Nina couldn't see the rigid walls that separated them. She didn't understand that Josie was different from her. She just saw the older girl who played with her, and made her snacks, and took her out of the house when Evelyn was on the warpath.

Josie always knew to do that; she remembered what it was like, being trapped with a parent whose rages sent the entire mood of the house swinging.

"Darling?"

A voice drifted from the other side of the patio. Evelyn, swanning across the terrace toward them. She wore a silk robe, even though it was early afternoon, and a large pair of sunglasses. Her feet were bare, her hair looking slept-in. A trail of violet smoke followed her, a cigarette clutched in one hand.

"Darling," she said, vaguely in the direction of her daughter. "Have you had a nice swim?"

She didn't seem to notice that Nina wasn't wet, or that she was still wearing the same summer dress that Patricia had wrestled her into that morning. She didn't wait for an answer.

"Have either of you seen Harrison?"

She directed the question toward Josie and Hannah.

"No," Hannah said. "Sorry. I thought he was upstairs."

"Hmm," said Evelyn. "No."

She sucked on her cigarette as if it was an oxygen tube.

"You've not seen Harrison, have you, Nina, sweetheart? You don't know where Harrison's gone?"

Nina's mouth was a firm line, shut hard. She shook her head vigorously, her eyes wide.

"Fucker," said Evelyn, beneath her breath.

For a second, she just stood there, swaying slightly. Her eyebrows furrowed as if she was trying to figure out the answer to a particularly complicated question.

"OK," she said at last. "Well. You girls send him upstairs if you see him, won't you?"

"Will do," said Josie.

"Wonderful. Great. Well, you enjoy your swim."

They watched as she walked unsteadily back toward the house.

"Jesus," Josie said, under her breath. "She's even worse than last year."

"What do you mean?"

"What do I mean? Hannah, look at her. She's a mess." She glanced around to check that Nina wasn't listening. "My mum reckons Harrison's leaving her."

"Seriously?"

Josie nodded.

"Apparently, people are saying that he's met someone else, and everyone knows it. Evelyn's in complete denial about it."

"Shit."

"Shit is right."

Josie leaned back, her palms flat against the tiles.

"I reckon this'll be the last summer that they're all together. It's kind of sad, actually, when you think about it. I think Evelyn genuinely thought that this was *it*, this time. And Nina hasn't really known any other dad."

A silence fell between them as they watched Nina play.

"Do you think Nina knows?"

"'Course not."

"What about Blake? Do you think he knows?"

Josie groaned, and the moment was broken.

"Do you ever think about anything else?"

Hannah reached down into the water, flipping her hand across the surface to splash her friend.

"Hey!"

"Come to the party with me. Please."

"You're not going to let this go, are you?"

"Absolutely not."

Josie reached down to splash Hannah back.

"Fine. But only for an hour. Two hours, tops."

"Deal."

"And Hannah?"

"Yeah?"

"Just . . . I don't want you getting your hopes up too much with Blake, OK?"

She had seen it. The way that her friend looked at Blake Drayton. The way that she talked about him. She'd gently teased Hannah about it for months, but now, with the Draytons back for the season, the issue felt urgent. Josie couldn't stand to see her friend getting hurt.

"People like him," Josie said. "They don't go for people like us."

Hannah shrugged.

"I'm not getting my hopes up," she said. "It's only a party. But I think it'll be fun."

EIGHT

2024

That night, Nina can't sleep.

She tries all of her usual tricks. White noise in her headphones. Lavender-scented oil smeared on her pressure points. The three-hundred-pound eye mask Ryan had bought her last Christmas that promised to engulf her in darkness like nothing she's ever experienced before.

None of it works. Nothing slows her heartbeat. Takes her into the relief of dreams.

She gives up sometime around four in the morning. She goes downstairs and pours herself an ice-cold glass of water, picks a waxy orange out of her mother's fruit bowl. Back home, Nina buys so much fruit that she keeps it in an oversized salad dish. Plump strawberries and green-skinned mangoes. She is compulsive about arranging them, the art of having something wholesome and fresh and beautiful on display promising an order and an aesthetic to her life that usually feels just out of reach. She rarely actually eats any of the fruit herself, buying more than she can conceivably get through. In summer, it often rots before she can throw it away, apples furring with mold, sugar-drunk fruit flies cavorting in her kitchen. Now, she peels the orange, and slides one plump segment into her mouth. Chews it until her jaw aches.

She sits at the kitchen counter and pulls out her phone. She types her own name into the search bar.

Googling herself is not new to Nina. She's always resisted having an online profile, maintaining only a private Instagram account with a small circle of friends as her followers. Still, her silence does not stop her name cropping up in dozens of search results. Most of the plentiful information about her online refers to her as *private* or *elusive*. Remarks that: *Now an adult, Nina Drayton has never spoken out about the case.* She is referenced in long reads about *former it-girl and famous heiress Evelyn Drayton* and *the many scandals of the Drayton family*. True crime blogs and Reddit threads about Tamara's death name-drop her. Archived articles from that summer and the months following relay the timeline of the investigation, and eventually, the trial.

Nina knows these results by heart. She's stayed up late, clicking on links that have already turned purple to show that she's visited them before, so many times that the web pages begin to resemble bruises. Violet sprawls of text, each an old wound to be pressed upon.

Now, when the results load, Nina is greeted by fresh links. They send a jolt of surprise through her, like new trees breaking through the earth overnight in a landscape that she has known for years.

Why are people suddenly talking about the Josie Jackson case again?

Newly commissioned documentary promises to "pull back the cover" on the noughties' most notorious murder trial

The true-crime TikTokker bringing attention back to long-ago crimes

Nina clicks on this last link. It brings her through to an article in an online pop-culture magazine with brightly colored graphics and thick, blocky text. A large picture of a young woman with veins of bright red running through her box-dye black hair, a nose ring, tattoos snaking her arms.

> Imogen Faye is better known by her online moniker, true-crimefangirl_2002. That's the name she's been going by since she first created a TikTok account in 2020. Back then, Faye,

who was eighteen at the time, was interested in sharing stories about her longtime fascination—the female victims of notorious murders, many of them that had taken place before Faye was even born. But little did she know how popular her videos would become.

Now just twenty-two, Faye is one of the world's most-followed true-crime influencers. She attracted thousands of fans with short series about notorious murders from the noughties. But it wasn't until her most recent story, the infamous case of society heiress Tamara Drayton, that television producers started sniffing around her channel.

There's a video linked below, a freeze-frame of Imogen Faye looking mid-speech, a faintly gleeful expression on her face. Nina clicks. Brings her face close to the screen.

The video quality is razor sharp, despite the informality of the background. A bedroom, the sprawl of unmade sheets. Throw pillows. Red-painted walls, with three framed mugshots in black-and-white. They could seem artsy, if Nina didn't recognize them from the true crime shows Ryan occasionally watches, even though she tells him that she hates them. A trio of notorious serial killers, their faces impassive, faintly brooding. If you didn't know, you might think that they were actors or rock stars, the kind of men that the young woman beaming at the camera might have impossible crushes on.

"Hi, true crime besties," truecrimefangirl_2002 gushes into the camera. "Boy, do I have a story for you today. Real, hot-off-the-press, juicy, *exclusive* gossip for my murder girlies."

Nina has already watched this video so many times, she could almost mouth along. She recognizes the American accent, each dramatic pause, each tattoo that snakes the length of this girl's arms.

"So, you probably remember the Tamara Drayton case."

A picture of Tamara flashes on the screen. Nina's chest still clenches. Her sister. Blake's twin. The traces of her brother, so familiar to Nina, echoed in the face of a girl that Nina barely knew. Barely remembers.

"So, this case *slaps*, it's literally one of my faves. It was *big* back in the noughties. Super rich family, pretty famous in the UK. The mom's a big deal, some kind of socialite like they have over there? Anyway, they have this crazy huge mansion in France, always throwing these big, glamorous parties. Like, you have got to be *seen* at these things, you know? But then at one of these bashes, Evelyn's oldest daughter, Tamara Drayton, gets found unconscious in the pool. At first, they think she's dead, but they pull her out and Bingo! She's got a pulse. Or at least she does for a few hours longer, before she dies at a local hospital. So, yeah. Like, some real Agatha Christie shit. Except for not really, because the whole thing actually ends up being pretty cut and dry. Turns out Tamara's sister, Nina Drayton, who was just five years old at the time, saw exactly what happened. And oh boy, was she quick to point the finger."

The picture of Tamara is replaced by a photograph that Nina has seen dozens of times before. Josie Jackson, back when she was sixteen. Frowning from beneath a blunt-cut fringe. Furious. Defiant.

"Nina says that she saw the babysitter, Josie Jackson, drown her sister. Turns out, these girls had a longstanding feud and a fight got out of hand. Little Nina Drayton even testifies in court. And this is a huge deal. She's one of the youngest people to ever give evidence in a murder trial, and basically the entire case rests on this. So, Josie Jackson gets convicted. Case closed, right?"

The girl grins broadly. A tongue piercing glints in her mouth.

"Besties, no. Wrong. Because we true-crime junkies are sleuthing hard, and lots of us think Josie Jackson is kinda fire, right? I mean, she seems low-key badass. And there is so much about this case that doesn't make sense. And at the heart of it is Nina Drayton, a little girl whose testimony changed everything. So drop a like if you are obsessed with this case, too, and you want to know the truth because I am—"

Nina exits the video. Without the whine of Imogen Faye's voice, the kitchen feels eerily quiet. Light is beginning to filter through the patio doors, the sun rising early at this time of year.

She can't sit here waiting for morning. She'll go insane.

All of a sudden, Nina has an urgent, desperate desire to run.

⁕

Outside the light is pale, the air cool. The sky is glazed yellow with the promise of a new day.

Nina deliberately chooses a difficult route. Up the winding roads to the top of the hill. A run that will make her legs ache, her lungs burn. That will generate enough pain to put her back into her body instead of keeping her trapped in her head. Her muscles are coiled tight. They only loosen when she begins to run.

Exercise has always been this to Nina. A punishment and a pleasure. Every time her feet hit the ground, a wave of elation pulses through her. Proof that she is pushing herself. A promise that she is making herself into a better, stronger, thinner person. A more likable person. All the things that Nina wants to be and fears she isn't.

Running is the one thing that stops her thinking too much. The one thing that quashes the anxiety that so often rages beneath the surface of her skin. When she weaned herself off her anxiety medication last year—with the help of a new therapist, an expert in obsessive-compulsive disorders who had a less laissez-faire attitude to pills than the psychiatrist she'd seen since childhood—running had filled the gap. She had spent countless mornings since then discovering Ryan's side of the city, pounding across London as the light turned from indigo, to a dusky gray, to the blanched brightness of an English spring.

The medication had been a feature of her life ever since Tamara died. It had been crucial, back then, to get Nina through nights where she would wake up screaming, torn from dreams of her sister's broken body. She still remembers those grasping, consuming visions, so terrifying that she would refuse to go to bed. She developed a trick of eating as little as possible in the evening, cutting her dinner into smaller and smaller mouthfuls, pushing food around her plate, so that she would be too hungry to fall asleep. The feeling of control it gave her was addictive, even back then. It was the first time Nina had understood how badly she needed that power.

As she navigated the difficult months of the trial, and then those strange, lost years when Tamara's death faded into the distance, Nina stopped being able to imagine existing without the pills she swallowed with her morning orange juice. They blunted the sharp edges of her mind, made the world manageable, even when the other kids whispered about her on the playground or dared one another to ask what it was like to see a dead body (the fact that Nina had not, as it turned out, actually seen a dead body didn't seem to bother them. It was as close as any of them had got to seeing a dead body, and that was good enough for them). She had a scaffolding around her life that held her up, and medication was the central beam.

It wasn't until she started her master's degree that she considered stopping. In a lecture on the dangers of prescribing to children, Nina realized that she didn't actually know what it was like to *not* be on the cocktail of pills that she had been taking since she was five years old.

How could she assess children—perhaps even refer them on to doctors who would dish out the same medications that Nina had been on for years—if she didn't even remember what she felt like without them?

By the time Nina summits the hill, her body is coated in a thin veil of sweat, and her chest is on fire. There is a tang of bile in her throat. She has to stop at the side of the road, bending over double, expecting herself to vomit. When she doesn't, she straightens up and keeps running. She runs until all she can focus on is the in, out of her breath, the ache of her knees and hips each time her feet strike the ground. Just as she has done on so many mornings since she first threw away the foil packets that had filled her bathroom cabinet for years, Nina runs until she can't feel anything anymore.

When she reaches the end of her planned route, she still can't stand to go home. Instead, she walks all the way down to the beach. She sits on the damp sand, not caring that her leggings are getting wet. The sound of the waves is colossal against the quiet of dawn.

It feels like she is sitting on the edge of the world.

※

It's almost seven by the time Nina gets back to the house. The endorphins have hit, that much-promised runner's high threading like a current beneath her skin.

The morning feels clean and fresh and full. A better day. She'll do what Blake says, she thinks. She'll delete the email. Maybe she'll block the sender. She'll go home tomorrow, back to her life in London. To her flat with Ryan, and her new job. All the good things that she has managed to wrestle out of the bad things that happened to her family. All the ways that she is not defined by the death of her sister.

Nina expects everyone to still be in bed. Evelyn and Blake are late sleepers, and even Ryan, who is up at the crack of dawn to work out and take his endless supplements back in London, often sleeps until midmorning whenever they leave the city, his body seeming to demand a break.

Nina unlocks the side door quietly, prepared to tiptoe upstairs. To shower, and then perhaps to coil back into bed beside her boyfriend, to wake him slowly with her touch.

She stops dead when she hears voices drifting in from the kitchen.

"She'll be in a good mood when she gets back. It's later that we'll have to keep an eye on her."

Nina doesn't move. It's Ryan, his back to her, his hands resting on the kitchen island. Seated on the chaise longue closest to the window, she can make out the top of her mother's head.

"I'm worried, you know," Evelyn says. "We tried so hard to protect her at the time. I knew this degree of hers could only lead to trouble. *Child* psychology, of all things! Such a ridiculous idea. Most people would want to move on. To forget about it. Not be confronting what happened to them, over and over again."

"She's good at what she does," Ryan says, and Nina feels a stir of gratitude toward him. "And she cares about her work. She genuinely wants to help people."

She should go in now. Evelyn would never know that she'd heard.

"But I've often wondered how much of it is *really* about helping people, and how much of it is a way of dealing with the guilt," Ryan says. "A way of figuring out what happened to her, I suppose. I think that's why she did her dissertation on child memory formation and trauma. Like, if she can figure out what she doesn't remember, and if she can figure out *why* she doesn't remember it, she might be able to convince herself that she told the truth."

Nina's skin turns to ice.

"But she *does* remember," Evelyn's voice is knife-sharp. "It's hardly the kind of thing that you forget."

"Not everything," Ryan says. "She doesn't remember everything."

There's a quiet then. A stillness. Nina has to force her breath to slow. She is almost scared that, if she doesn't, they might be able to hear the beating of her heart.

"I hate to ask you this," Ryan says, "but did you ever wonder if it was the truth? If Josie Jackson really did do it? Did you believe Nina, right from the start?"

A silence. Evelyn is taking much too long to answer.

"I had to," she says at last. "What other option was there?"

Nina's stomach drops. She takes a step back. There is an ache in her temples, her throat. The threat of tears.

She cannot listen to this. She cannot hear her own mother and boyfriend doubting her. Sounding just like the people online, so quick to tear her down.

She goes upstairs, treading slowly on the stone steps, careful not to make any sound. She goes to the farthest bathroom and switches on the shower, so hot that she has to stifle a squeal when the water hits her skin. She washes away the sweat and the sand, scrubs as if she could buffer away the terrible, awful feeling that nobody believes her.

When her skin is scarlet with heat, she emerges and stands naked, dripping on the bathroom floor. She lifts her phone up from the sink. She had left it there this morning, when she was changing for her run. Another lifetime now, it feels. When she presses the unlock button, the still image of truecrimefangirl_2002 flushes the screen. Smiling. Gleeful. Goading Nina on.

Nina clicks into her emails and pulls up the message that started this entire thing. She taps against the small reply icon. Begins to type.

Hi, she writes. I think I'm ready to talk.

PART TWO

@TRUECRIMEFANGIRL_2002
POSTED SIX WEEKS AGO

Oh hey, my little true crime freaks, thanks for coming back.

OK, so first of all, let me just say that this whole thing is *blowing up*. Like, for real, I have not been able to keep up with all of your comments and messages. But please keep them coming, I am loving the support and I am loving all of the tea you guys have been spilling. And trust me, you guys are going to want to keep watching, because the DMs are coming in *hot*.

So, guys, I thought today I'd talk a little bit about the facts of the case. Because, as ever with this kind of case, context is everything. So, let's get into it.

Tamara Drayton was discovered unconscious in the pool of the family home on the Côte d'Azur at approximately 10:25 P.M. on the twentieth of August, 2004—the night of her mother's forty-second birthday party. Up until then, it had been a pretty normal summer. People said that Tamara had been maybe a little withdrawn, a little moody, but also, like, that wouldn't be unusual for a seventeen-year-old who probably didn't want to spend all summer with her family? Believe me, I've been there.

Tamara was reportedly last seen at the party by her twin brother, Blake, at around ten o'clock. Blake reported that he saw Tamara talking to Josie Jackson in the entrance hall of the house, and several other sightings confirmed that Tamara was seen leaving the house through the back door, although police were not able to verify what time these sightings took place. Some witnesses said that she was alone, and others say that she may have been with a young woman, although because most of the guests did not know Josie Jackson, police also weren't able to positively confirm these sightings. And it's 2004, so it's not like everyone has CCTV or, like, Ring doorbells or whatever.

Now, guests at the party first knew something was up when Nina Drayton was heard screaming outside. She was found alone by the pool, having discovered her sister unconscious in the water. Tamara was pulled from the pool by partygoers, and was found to have a pulse, so an ambulance was called. Reports suggest that, although a large crowd had gathered outside, Josie Jackson did not arrive at the pool until five to ten minutes later—which was used as proof that she had had time to dispose of evidence.

The ambulance arrived, and Tamara died in the hospital around eight hours later. Police immediately thought her death seemed suspicious. But, it wasn't until a couple of days later—when little Nina Drayton started to spill—that things really started to get juicy. And that's when attention really started to shift onto Josie Jackson.

So there it is, the cold hard facts of the case. And I get it. So far, it's sounding like Josie Jackson is guilty, right? But over the next couple of videos, I'll be explaining more about the case, including some of the evidence that was, like, seriously sus. Like and follow to make sure you don't miss it.

Annamay897: Grrrl you are doing the lords work

JosieJacksonisinnocent: Yes to all the JJ fangirls! She was always my favorite murderer but now she might be my favorite NOT a murderer!? Lolllll

TamaraDrayton123: It's giving murder girl summer

Miribelle . . . : Always knew there was something shady AF about this case

Jadestargirl: Not here for all the Josie Jackson defenders. You're totally ignoring all of the crazy stuff that came out about JJ in the trial. That girl was twisted. Josie Jackson is the epitome of EVIL!

NINE

2024

It rains on the day that Josie Jackson returns to the Côte d'Azur.

"Madness," says Calvin. "It doesn't rain for weeks, and then *this*. On today of all days."

He dashes from the car to the house, swearing loudly, a suitcase flailing from each hand. The dirt drive, which Josie remembers being baked hard by sun, a trail of orange dust always marking her legs, has turned to mud. Calvin splashes through puddles that look, in the cooling evening light, the color of blood.

The air is thick. The rain is hot. Josie turns her face skyward. She closes her eyes and stretches her arms out, as if she cannot get enough of the feel of water against her skin. As if she has never been caught in a rainstorm before. As if she cannot bear to go inside.

※

"It looks like shit in here," Josie says, as the door shuts behind her.

Calvin drops a suitcase on the floor.

"Thanks," he says. "There's fresh towels upstairs. I thought you might want to take a shower."

"A shower?"

"I had one put in. A couple of years ago. After . . ."

He tilts his head, letting the words fall into the silence.

"After Mum died?" Josie fills in for him.

He ducks his head and Josie sees the dart of sadness still within him. She knows. She feels it, too, except her sadness is tinged with regret. Guilt.

"After I took over the house," he says instead.

He holds out one of the bags toward her. It feels light. Too light to contain almost everything Josie owns.

"Am I in . . ." She pauses. "Am I in my old bedroom?"

It's all so ancient and so new, all at the same time. So much time has passed. There are so many things that they don't know about each other.

"It's your bedroom," her brother says. "That hasn't changed."

※

The shower is slow and creaking, in spite of its relative newness. The water is a thin, lackluster stream, which takes forever to heat up, but is scalding when it does. Still, Josie stands beneath it for a long time. She washes her hair with a slim, damp sliver of soap. She lets her body grow pink, slightly singed. Her fingers crumple into a soft concertina of skin.

When Josie finally steps out, the room is full of steam. Her lungs ache with the heat of each inhale. She feels clean and warm in a way that she hasn't in a while, right down to her bones.

She pulls her damp hair back into a ponytail. She hasn't had it cut for months and her roots are growing out, brown bleeding into the yellow blond. She should really get it redone, and soon. Before too many people have time to notice her. She has already agonized over this for weeks, catching sight of herself in full-length mirrors and wondering if there is anything left of the old Josie. The short, freckled girl from twenty years ago. Anything that people might recognize.

She wipes condensation from the small mirror that she has looked in a hundred times before and lets this version of herself stare back, scrutinize. She is different now, she tells herself. She is an entirely new person.

She gets changed in the bathroom, the tiles slippery with moisture, a suitcase sprawled open on the floor. She can't stand to go to her bedroom. Not yet. Later, when she is tired enough to collapse into bed without thinking too much. When she can pretend that this is somewhere new, someplace she has never been before. A place that might eventually feel like home.

※

"I thought you might want a beer," Calvin says when Josie walks down the stairs that lead into the kitchen. A pan of tomato sauce is bubbling on the ancient stovetop, and her brother is ladling wet tendrils of pasta into bowls.

"Sit," he says. "Make yourself at home."

Josie traces the knots of the table, places where the wood has collected a thick scuzz of age, softened varnish and decades of spilled drinks, hot mugs scorching its surface. She touches a cigarette burn that her father made years ago, the orange butt smoldering against the thinning varnish. Thinks of her mother, sitting here with her head in her hands, on the day that he left them.

Calvin sets the plates down in front of them, the sauce a vivid and unnatural red, a heap of pale cheese wilting on top.

"Looks good," Josie lies.

Calvin sits opposite her and shovels a forkful into his mouth.

"So, what have you been doing for work lately?" Josie asks.

"This and that."

Calvin's fork continues to move rhythmically from his plate to his mouth, scooping up more pasta before he's even finished chewing.

"Up at the house?"

She doesn't need to say which house. His fork stills.

"Jo," he says. "I haven't been to the house in years."

"You didn't want to?"

He snorts.

"Not really a case of whether I wanted to or not. It's not like they'd let me anywhere near the place."

"They had Mum in their house, though," Josie says. "Mum worked for them right up until . . ." she trails off. The look on Calvin's face tells her all she needs to know.

"Didn't she?" she says, her voice wavering. "She worked there until she died, didn't she?"

"Is that what she told you?" Calvin asks.

Josie doesn't answer. He sighs. His chair scrapes back against the stone floor as he stands and gathers up his plate.

"'Course she did," he says. "She always wanted to protect you. Never wanted to give you anything else to worry about."

He drops his plate in the sink, letting it clatter against the cracked porcelain. For a moment he stays there, his hands resting against the countertop. Then he straightens.

"Look," he says. "It's been a long day. I might go to bed. But help yourself to whatever you want. Beer. Stuff out of the fridge. Whatever."

For a moment, Josie sees her brother as she used to know him. Limbs too long for his body, skin too pale for the summer heat. A perpetual streak of sunburn on the bridge of his nose.

"A lot happened," he says. "After you left."

The rain outside is heavy now, beating down on the roof, a wall of sound against the vast quiet of the house.

"It never went back to how it was," he says. "Don't expect things to be the same as they used to be. Everything's different now."

TEN

2004
SIX WEEKS BEFORE THE BIRTHDAY PARTY

Barnaby picked them up for the party in a bright red convertible that Hannah knew his parents had gifted him for passing his driving test, honking his horn, laughing as he pulled up outside the pink house. Tamara raised her eyebrows when she came outside and saw Hannah and Josie waiting there. She opened the car door and collapsed onto the front seat.

"You invited them," she said to her brother. "You can cram into the back with them."

Hannah felt Josie stiffen beside her. She expected her best friend to make a sharp comment, and was surprised when she simply clambered into the backseat, not looking at Tamara as she did.

Barnaby made a big performance of rolling down the roof before they set off. Hannah slipped into the middle seat, between Blake and Josie, painfully conscious of the warmth of his body beside hers. Keeping her leg still to preserve the half inch of space between them, until the muscles of her hip started to twitch.

In the muggy heat, Hannah's thighs stuck to the leather seat. She had chosen the kind of outfit that she saw the teenage girls who descended here every summer wear. Gladiator sandals, as if Hannah wasn't the kind of person who had to walk everywhere, trainers the only footwear that made any sense. Small, gold earrings that she had sneaked out of her mother's jewelry box.

Her parents had been fighting earlier. They often seemed to be fighting. The landlord wanted to increase the rent on the shop. They couldn't afford it.

This summer, money—or specifically the lack thereof—had seemed to loom larger than ever before. A few months ago, her dad, exhausted and irritable after a long shift, had looked horrified when he had found Hannah at the kitchen table, university prospectuses spread out in front of her.

Most of the kids at the international school where Hannah had a scholarship were planning on going to universities in the UK or America, and Hannah had long had her heart set on England. She had grown up reading Enid Blyton's boarding school stories, had begged her mum to drive her to an English-language bookshop so that she could buy the latest Harry Potter. She had spent a long time coming up with her shortlist, all for universities in the UK, a country she had never lived in but in some ways still considered her home. Bath. York. Edinburgh. Oxford, an idea that still felt so crazy, so dizzying, that she could barely dare to think about it. Her teacher said that she had a good chance, as long as she knuckled down a bit this year. Cut down on the tutoring. Dedicated a bit more time to her own studies.

Hannah felt as though she had been waiting all her life to go to university in England. To be shoulder to shoulder with people like Blake and Tamara and Barnaby, on a level with them for the first time in her life. A place where her intellect would permit her into the parts of society that had been out of bounds to her all her life.

"Want a beer?" Barnaby said, taking one hand off the steering wheel to grope in the footwell beside Tamara's bare legs.

They had been driving for almost an hour, far enough away for the roads to become unfamiliar, Barnaby navigating corners too quickly.

The car swerved as Tamara slapped Barnaby's hand away and bent down herself, retrieving two bottles. She passed them back without looking over her shoulder.

Hannah handed a bottle to Blake and then hesitated before pressing the second into Josie's hands. She could feel her friend growing tense beside her, fidgeting against the creaking seats. Hannah had promised that they could leave whenever she wanted to, but by now it was becoming clear that they'd have no way of getting back by themselves.

"How much farther?" Josie asked.

"Not far," Blake said. He cracked the bottle of beer open with his teeth and held it out to Hannah. "We're getting close."

Hannah took the bottle from him.

"Whose party is it anyway?"

"It's one of my friends," said Tamara, her eyes still fixed on the road ahead, arms folded across her chest. "From school. Her parents are away. It'll be cool."

Just then, Barnaby jerked the steering wheel, pulled away from the main road onto a thin, single-lane track.

"Pretty sure it's down here," he said.

"Wait until you guys see this place," said Tamara. For the first time the entire car ride there was a gleam of excitement in her voice. "You're gonna freak."

The house rose into view like the moon edging up into the night sky, pale and luminous. It was modern, built into a cliff face, with sharp, white edges, a spotlit façade. The kind of house that Hannah dreamed of living in, one day.

"It's beautiful," she said.

"It's just like all the other houses round here?" Josie said, causing Hannah to kick her beneath the seat.

Blake laughed.

"I forgot that it's completely impossible to impress Josie Jackson," he said.

Barnaby pulled on the handbrake.

"I think I'd be a bit more impressed if I lived in basically a shack," he said.

The air stiffened.

"What?" said Barnaby. "She can give it out, but she can't take it?"

Josie unclipped her seatbelt.

"Oh," she said. "I can take it. Believe me, I can take whatever you guys have to say about me."

※

They stayed much later than Hannah had intended. Late enough that people had begun to peel off, a drunken girl passed out on a sofa, kids clustered around a coffee table snorting coke through rolled-up bank notes, something that Hannah thought people only did in films. Outside, a group of boys cheered each other on as they took turns at climbing out of an upper-floor window and plummeting, meters below, into the glassy, illuminated stretch of the pool.

Somehow, between going down to the kitchen to get another drink and returning back to the upstairs window ledge where they had perched for the last hour, Hannah had lost Josie. Somehow, she didn't particularly mind. She drifted through the house, a vodka tonic clutched in one hand, feeling faintly as if she were watching herself from above. She had drunk enough that, for the first time in a while, she wasn't thinking about if anyone was looking at her, or whether she seemed out of place. She was imagining that she lived here. That this was her party. That all these people were here for her.

Blake must have seen her before she saw him. When she caught his eye across the room, he was already staring. Already watching her. He was in a group, a girl with long, highlighted hair, a boy whose body was angled hungrily in her direction. He left them, wordlessly, and they didn't seem to notice. He was walking straight to Hannah with such purpose that she was briefly unsure of herself, briefly certain that he would pass her by, on to somebody else. But, instead, he stopped right in front of her.

"I thought I'd lost you," he said, and the idea that he might have been looking for her sent a shiver straight through Hannah's core.

He took her hand.

"Come on," he said. "Let's get some air."

They were only just outside when Barnaby leaped on them, wrapping his arms around Blake's shoulders. His face was pink, an alcohol-induced flush. Hannah could tell he had taken something from his wide eyes and starry pupils, the way his body twitched. His hair was soaking wet, and in the aquatic glow of the pool his teeth looked sharp and bone-white as he grinned.

"Mate," he said, enunciating the vowel of the word, stretching it out long. "You've got to give it a go. Jumping off the roof. It's crazy."

Blake shook him off.

"Nah," he said. "I'm alright."

"Aw, come on," Barnaby said. "Don't be chicken."

"Seriously, mate," said Blake. "I'm good."

Barnaby looked around, his eyes settling on Hannah as if he was seeing her for the first time.

"You'll do it, Hannah, right?"

"I don't—"

"Aw, come on," he said again. "You went off the cliffs last year, right? You were the only one of the girls who'd do it. I remember."

He slid away from Blake, wrapped his arm around Hannah. She could smell something chemical and metallic on his breath.

"None of the other girls would *ever*," he said conspiratorially, and Hannah knew exactly what he meant. None of the other girls with money, with parents with good jobs, with the kind of status that Hannah could only dream of would ever. The kind of girls who didn't have to prove themselves.

She eased herself away from him.

"The cliffs are different," she said. "I've been jumping off those cliffs since I was a kid."

It was true. The things that Barnaby and Blake thought were daring, an escape from reality, the kind of adrenaline spike that their lives back in the UK denied them, were routine for her. The coastline had always been her playground.

"So?" said Barnaby, a slur encircling the edge of the word. "You should be able to show us how it's done then, right?"

She knew that he was baiting her. It was the oldest trick in the book, after all, that appeal to her ego. But still, her eyes drifted up to the second-story ledge. Not a huge drop. Twelve or fifteen feet.

"Come on," said Barnaby. "What are you scared of?"

"Give it a rest, mate," Blake said. "She said she doesn't want to."

"Actually, I will," said Hannah.

They both looked at her.

"You don't have to," said Blake.

"I want to," Hannah said. "It isn't that high."

Barnaby whooped.

"Yes, Hannah!" he said. He turned toward the cluster of teenage boys at the edge of the water. "Hey! You guys! Hannah's gonna jump."

There was a flurry of cheers.

"I don't have a swimming costume," she said.

Barnaby grinned.

"You could always do a skinny dip."

She ignored him. Turned to Blake. For once she felt bigger than everyone here. Stronger.

"You want to come, too?" she said, breezy, as if the thought had only just occurred to her.

She saw him swallow.

"You're not going to make the lady do it alone, are you, Blake?" said Barnaby, taunting.

"Yeah," said Blake. "Yeah. 'Course I'll come."

With more confidence than she felt, Hannah reached down and took his hand. There was another volley of whoops. A wolf whistle.

"Come on," she said. "Let's do this."

He knew the way upstairs, so he led. She could feel his pulse, fast and soft, like the beat of a butterfly's wings against the inside of her wrist.

"You can back out, if you want," he said, when they reached the first floor. "Barnaby's drunk. And he's an idiot. No one will care."

"Do you want to back out?" she asked.

He looked right at her then.

"Not if you don't," he said.

She gave his hand the tiniest squeeze.

"I don't," she said.

She was sure that she wouldn't back out either, until they reached the roof. It was a flat plain above the patio. You had to climb out of a window to reach it, one leg and then the other, until they were back in the muggy night air. That was the first time Hannah thought that maybe this was a bad idea. That she understood how far the pool was from the house. The stretch of ground that they would have to clear, the hard white stone below. A primal, gut twist of something that told her not to jump. An ancient survival instinct.

Below them, someone started to clap slowly. Just one person at first, and then more, until a sea of hands moved back and forth, a rhythmic wave, a beat that drew them closer to the edge.

"Ready?"

Blake said the word so softly, so close to her, that Hannah was certain she could feel it vibrate in the air between them. Beyond the pool, where earlier the sea had unfolded a dark and brilliant blue, there was now only darkness. A vast stretch of nothing. Only the sound of waves far below them. Only the feel of Hannah's heart beating hard in her chest.

"Ready," she said.

And then they jumped.

At first, it didn't feel like they were falling at all. There was a second, after Hannah's legs pushed away from the concrete beneath her feet, when she seemed to fly. Straight outward, toward the dark expanse of sea.

And then, that give of gravity, the catch of oxygen in her throat, the flail of her arms, her body's last-ditch effort to stop the inevitability of the fall. In less than the stretch of a heartbeat, the slam of her body against the surface of the pool. The roar of sound as she was submerged.

She opened her eyes, the water white around her, stirred by the impact. She held her breath as it cleared, and there he was. Blake, illuminated by the pool lights, reaching his hands out toward her. It reminded her of last year, when she saw him beneath the ocean after they jumped from the cliffs. That fragile moment when it felt like they were the only people in the world.

This time, with the surface of the water too broken for anyone to see, he took her hand. Their lips met, as if they were exchanging oxygen.

As if he was breathing life into her lungs.

22 August 2004, 13:21
Interview subject: Nina Drayton
Interview type: First interview

Present is the interview subject's mother, **Evelyn Drayton**, child support worker **Delphine Simon**, legal representative for the Drayton family, **Florent Portier**, and translator **Felicity Carmichael**.
Leading the interview is lead investigator **Martine Allard**.
We have confirmed that the interviewing officers have the appropriate level of training to conduct an interview with a minor, and will conduct the interview in English, where possible. For the purposes of this transcription, any translations have been omitted. For a full version in the original languages, please contact the appropriate records office.

M Allard: Can you tell me how old you are, Nina?
E Drayton: It's OK, Nina, you can tell the lady.
Nina: I'm five.
M Allard: Five! Goodness. So grown up. And when will you be six?
Nina: September.
M Allard: That's so soon. What are you going to get for your birthday?
Nina: New doll.
M Allard: A new doll. That's what my little girl got for her birthday, too. She's four.
That's a nice doll that you have there with you. Did Mummy get that for you?
Nina: Mmmhmm.
M Allard: Does she have a name?

Nina: Tamara.

M Allard: Tamara. That's your sister's name, too, isn't it? Do you know that we're here to talk about Tamara today, Nina? About your sister, Tamara?
Can you say it out loud, Nina? You're nodding your head now, and that means . . .

Nina: Yes.

M Allard: So you know we're here to talk about your sister, Tamara, today?

Nina: Yes.

M Allard: Do you know what happened to Tamara, Nina?

Nina: She went in the pool.

M Allard: Yes. She did go in the pool, didn't she? And your mummy's told us that you saw what happened to Tamara in the pool. Do you remember telling your mummy that?
Out loud again, please, Nina.

Nina: Yes.

M Allard: Can you tell me what you saw, Nina? Can you tell me what happened when you saw Tamara in the pool?

Nina: She was under the water.

M Allard: That's right. And how did she get under the water? Can you remember what happened to her before?

Nina: They were fighting.

M Allard: Who was fighting, Nina?

Nina: Tamara.

M Allard: Tamara and who else?

Nina: Josie.

M Allard: And what happened when they were fighting?

Nina: They were pushing, and she went under the water, and I was scared.

E Drayton: Nina, darling, you have to say *who* went under the water. You have to be specific. You have to say *Tamara* went under the water.

M Allard: Ms. Drayton, if we could just not interrupt Nina during this part of the interview, please.

Nina: Yes.

M Allard: What are you saying yes to, Nina?

Nina: That she went under the water.

M Allard: That they were pushing and Tamara went under the water?

Nina: Yes.

M Allard: And what happened then?

Nina: I was scared and I was trying not to cry 'cos I was scared.

M Allard: Yes, you've been very brave, Nina. And you're being very brave now telling us all these things. Now, we need you to be a bit more brave and tell us what happened next. What happened after Tamara went under the water?

Nina: I don't know.

M Allard: Was Josie trying to help Nina? Out loud again, please, Nina.

Nina: No.

M Allard: Do you think Josie was trying to hurt Tamara?

E Drayton: You can tell them, darling. Tell the lady what you told me.

Nina: I was scared and I was crying.

D Simon: Inspector Allard, the child is becoming visibly distressed, I think that it's time we took a break.

M Allard: We can take a break.

D Simon: Nina, you are doing such a good job. Shall we have a little rest now? We can get you some juice?

M Allard: Pausing this interview at thirteen thirty seven.

END OF TRANSCRIPT.

ELEVEN

2024

The rain lifts. The sky clears. Josie walks out of the door of her childhood home before the sun is fully up.

The air out here feels familiar to Josie, as much a part of her as her skin and bones. Muggy with nighttime warmth, the smell of jasmine and mimosa sweet on the breeze. Carpenter bees humming over a patch of lavender at the end of the driveway, their violet wings almost black in the hazy light of dawn. Josie walks straight past them, purposeful, stretching a broken night's sleep out of her body.

This is only the second time that Josie has been back in the last twenty years.

The first time was ten years ago, when she was first released from prison. She had to give an address, so she had named her childhood home, the only place that had rooted her to the outside world for all the years she was locked away. She stayed for just two nights, her mother hopeful, her hands knotted in front of her as she asked if Josie had slept alright, if she wanted anything. She had bought all the food Josie had loved most, back when she lived here last. Ritz crackers with orange globs of cheese, brightly colored cereal, plastic bottles of Capri-Sun. Things for another version of Josie, a person that she had long grown out of.

Josie had pretended not to notice when her mother's shoulders had drooped in disappointment when she thought her daughter wasn't looking, the piles of snacks left untouched.

Josie had left the next day. She had not returned.

Now, everything is exactly as she remembers it. The cluster of houses, all identical to the one she grew up in, crouched in a dip in the landscape, as if gathered for protection. The rolling upward tilt of the ground, the tree-lined road, wide enough for just one car. The baked earth. The walk that Josie used to do every day throughout the summer, as far back as she could remember, accompanying her mother to the house on the other side of the hill.

The route is longer than Josie remembers it, and soon her calves are aching, a seam of sweat where her clothes meet her skin. She had dressed quickly, in a pair of denim shorts and a T-shirt, the same heart-shaped necklace that she wears every day. Hauled a backpack onto her shoulders, which now weighs her down. She has to stop to catch her breath right before the hilt of the hill. Then, when the burning in her chest has faded, she walks the final few steps over the top. Over into what feels like another world.

The sky opens wide. Before her, a sharp decline straight down toward the sea, that brilliant azure that gives this place its name. Villas are nestled in the creases of the landscape, the artificial blue of swimming pools glinting against the red earth, like fat, shining beetles warming themselves in the sun. Farther down, the white strip of the beach, the pastel-painted town stuffed with designer boutiques and expensive restaurants that Josie's mother could never afford to take them to.

Josie has imagined this view so many times that seeing it sends a sharp, awful pain through the center of her chest. She used to dream about it—not when she was locked up, when her dreams were messy and jagged, nothing in them feeling quite real—but after she was released. In London, where she had gone with the vague idea that she might track down her dad. Where she had stayed in a hostel south of the river, asked for a copy of the Yellow Pages and then tried calling every D. Jackson in the city.

Finally, a girl in her dorm room, incredulous that Josie didn't have a smartphone, showed her how to use the free computers in the lobby. And there, over the sound of backpackers playing drinking games, travelers checking in for the night, Josie found the stories that her dad had sold to the papers after her arrest.

"I Always Knew She Was Evil," Says Teen Murderer's Dad

Dad Says Ex-Wife to Blame for Josie Jackson's Murderous Streak

Josie Jackson's Dad Speaks Out on His KILLER Daughter's Release

Josie hadn't wanted to find him so much, after that.

That was when the dreams started. There was also alcohol, and clubs. Sex, a thing that had felt so mystical and off-limits to her before, was suddenly readily available. There was an older boyfriend; a terrible breakup. A short prison stint, this time for theft, after a one-night stand reported Josie for slipping his wallet off the bedside table as she left. The kind of crime that might have warranted an eye roll from the police for anyone else. But the rules were different for Josie Jackson. The rules were different when everyone knew what you'd done.

She struggled to get jobs. Her name was too ubiquitous, and it was so easy to Google people now. She worked, briefly, in a nightclub that paid cash-in-hand. She started to lie, beginning to go by Josie Jones instead of Jackson. She considered making things official, changing her name legally, but she would have needed two witnesses to sign the documentation and she hadn't been able to face telling her new friends or colleagues who she really was, knowing that word would spread quickly. She paid for everything in cash. She didn't speak to anyone from her old life. It was easy to pretend. Shockingly easy to become someone else.

She fell hopelessly in love with a man who grew up in a small suburban town and worked as a joiner. They had moved to Devon together, and Josie got a job in a local tea room that didn't ask for references. For a year or two, she felt that her life was finally coming together. That was, until her boyfriend had found her passport and seen her real name. She would never forget the way that he had looked at her.

"You killed someone," he had said.

"You're not listening to me," Josie had protested. "You don't understand."

But she could see, on his face, that he was beyond listening. She knew that there was no return, once someone looked at you with that kind of undisguised disgust. There was no coming back from it.

England felt ruined for Josie after that. The streets were stained with her spoiled love, and she saw her ex on every corner, in the backs of strangers' heads in the supermarket or in the reflections of passing cars.

She tried Paris, and a series of cash-in-hand jobs. Cleaning. Delivering pizza. Working the coat check at an expensive restaurant. She used to listen to people from her small, dark enclosure as she collected and carefully tagged their jackets. She heard them talk about their nights; their real, tax-paying jobs; the bars that they would go to next. Sometimes, they mentioned the places that Josie had once dreamed she'd visit: Rome, New York, Vienna.

She lived in a small, damp flat with three other girls who seemed as lost as she was. On the nights when they had spare cash—which was rare—they would band together for drinks, a cheap bottle of wine consumed on the sunken living room sofa, a night out at a club that would leave smudged stamps on their arms. Josie would close her eyes and reach her arms up to the throbbing lights, dance so hard that the others would tease her about it. She would try and imagine that she was young, and carefree, just like thousands of other people who had come to the city before her. That her life was ahead of her. That her world hadn't, in many ways, ended almost two decades ago.

But then a French newspaper ran a double-page spread on JOSIE JACKSON: FRANCE'S MOST NOTORIOUS KILLER. WHERE IS SHE NOW? accompanied by grainy, unflattering photographs of Josie. Sitting on the doorstep of her flat after one of their nights out, her eyes looking sunken, her hair greasy. Emerging from a cleaning job, a mop and bucket in hand. Waiting for a bus, almost but not quite looking at the camera, her pupils glazed, her mouth downturned.

Of course, Josie knew that nobody looks good with a hangover, or on the way home from a long and exhausting shift. Josie knew that, with the right camera angle, her hair freshly washed, a slick of mascara, she looked fine. Pretty, even, if she put a bit of effort in. Yet in these photos, there was a darkness. In these photos she looked, Josie knew, like someone who could kill.

Josie had thumbed through the article on her phone, a terrible sickness in her stomach. When she finished, she had to find the nearest public restroom and hang her head over the toilet bowl until the feeling passed.

When she returned to her flat that night, she found the door double-locked from the inside, her belongings on the street outside.

That was when Josie called Calvin from a phone booth next to a busy intersection, the roar of traffic so loud in the background that she had to shout.

"I want to come home," she had said.

The line had fizzed and crackled. And then, her brother's voice, sounding like it came from another world.

"You took your time."

*

Josie takes a shortcut to the village. She avoids the road that zigzags down to the bay, instead following a route of faded footpaths that spiral through thickets of trees. Her trainers catch against stones, and branches skim the skin of her calves.

There are people who spend every summer here and never find this footpath, Josie thinks. Who wouldn't dream of walking in the early August heat. There are two completely separate versions of this small patch of coastline. One for people like her. And one for people like the Draytons.

It takes her longer than she remembers to reach sea level. The path skews sideways, and she wonders if she took a wrong turn. And then, just when she is about to pull out her phone and check, the trees thin. The path joins into pavement and the smell of the sea hits her. Salt and sulfur. A fragrance that takes her straight back to her childhood. She breathes in deeply. Fills her lungs.

The shape of the street is the same, but everything else is different. New restaurants. Shops transformed into wine bars. Bars turned into boutiques. Josie stops outside a dive store, the one place that seems to have stayed the same, seems to have weathered all the changes of this place, boogie boards and wetsuits still strung up outside.

Of all the places to survive. Of all the places that Josie never thought she would see again.

She hovers for a moment on the opposite side of the street, watching a disembodied wetsuit swing in the breeze. She remembers her first morning here. Seeing this street. That shop.

She lifts her eyes to the windows above the storefront and sees a flicker of movement. A shadow, behind a blank stretch of glass. Somebody is watching her. Josie steps back, looks down at the pavement. Walks away, as if there is nothing to see.

※

Josie finds the café easily. Calvin had written down the name for her on a slip of paper that she tucked into the back pocket of her shorts. She checks it now, as she pushes against the locked front door. She jiggles the handle. Presses her hands to the glass to shield her eyes from the light, and peers inside.

A woman emerges from the darkness, holding up a pair of fingers. *Two seconds.* She's younger than Josie, maybe in her mid-twenties, with a pile of dark curls on top of her head and an easy, trusting smile as she scrabbles to unlock the door. Josie can see what Calvin likes about her.

"We're not open yet," she says, her voice bright as the door swings open, a blast of cool air releasing from within.

"I know. I'm Josie? Calvin's sister?"

The woman blinks. A smile spreads across her face.

"Josie!" she says. "You're early. I don't think the producer is turning up until . . . what? Eight?"

"Yeah, I just . . ." Josie shrugs, spreading her palms out wide. "I didn't have much else on."

"Yeah, yeah, sure."

The woman steps back to let Josie pass. Inside, the air is mellow and inviting, the scent of fresh coffee, pastries baking.

"I'm Gabby, by the way."

"I know. Calvin told me. And I can't tell you how much I appreciate this, Gabby. Letting us use this place before opening time. I didn't want to invite anyone over to the house, and I didn't want to attract attention so—"

Gabby is already waving Josie's thanks away.

"A friend of Calvin's is a friend of mine," she says, and Josie is struck by how easy she makes it seem. "Can I get you anything? Coffee? Water?"

"Water would be great, thanks."

"Still? Sparkling?"

"Tap is fine. Thanks."

Gabby disappears into the back of the shop and there's a clatter of cupboards opening, taps being rattled. Josie sits at a seat closest to the window and then stands, chooses a table near to the back of the shop instead. She experiments with both of the seats. Her back to the wall, or her back to the café. Her hands drum against the bare skin of her calves. The smell of pastries makes her stomach ache, but she can't stand the thought of eating.

"Here you go." Gabby emerges with a glass of water. "I have some stuff to be getting on with round the back, but just give me a shout if you need anything, OK?"

Josie nods. Her hands close around the glass as if confirming its solidity.

"Oh and Josie?"

Gabby is hovering. An uncertainty crosses her face.

"I didn't believe it," Gabby says. "What they said about . . . you know."

Without meaning to, Josie's hands tighten around the glass. Gabby looks embarrassed, as if she's said too much.

"I just wanted you to know. So we get off on the right foot."

Josie is silent.

"Well," says Gabby, flustered now. Her hands flutter against a stack of napkins on one of the tables, starting to fold them and then unfold them unnecessarily, an invented task. "You let me know if I can help out with anything."

※

The producer is late.

Not unforgivably late. Not even to the point of being rude, really. But late enough for Josie, who was thirty-two minutes early, to become anxious. To begin to glance at her watch every thirty seconds. To think, with concern, about what they will do if the meeting runs over. If Gabby will have to open the café late. If Josie, on her first day here, will be an inconvenience, yet again, to the people around her.

Then, at exactly twelve minutes past eight, a woman dressed in a linen shirt and wide-legged trousers, the kind of effortless chic that always baffles and sparks longing in Josie in equal measure, glides up to the door. She has square-framed glasses, her hair pulled into a tortoiseshell claw. She looks exactly how Josie would imagine a documentary producer to look. Elegant and full of energy. When she sees Josie through the glass she smiles, raises up one hand in a wave.

"Josie Jackson," she says as soon as she piles through the door. "I really can't tell you how excited everyone is that you're here."

Josie doesn't answer. She's not used to people being pleased to see her. She half stands until the producer waves her down.

"No! No, don't get up for me. I'm late, I know. I'm so sorry. We had a planning meeting last night that ran over and I ended up staying up late to brainstorm some ideas and . . . well. It's so good to meet you, I suppose is what I'm trying to say. I'm Katherine."

She holds out one hand toward Josie. Josie takes it, tentatively.

"I'll get an espresso, please," the woman says, before Gabby has a chance to ask for her order. "Double."

She collapses into the chair opposite Josie.

"*Well*," she says. "Look at you, back here! It must be crazy for you!"

Josie nods. Opens her mouth.

"Did you want anything, by the way?" Katherine is already asking. "Coffee? Breakfast? All on us, of course."

Josie smiles tightly.

"I'm good with water, thanks."

"So well-behaved of you. I'm a total caffeine addict. You have to be in this line of work. Speaking of which, I am *so* excited to talk to you about the documentary. The team and I have been here for a week so far, conducting preliminary interviews and so on, and my god! This place! It's beautiful. And then this undercurrent of *darkness*. Such terrible things that have happened here, over the years, Tamara Drayton's death included, of course. It's completely delicious. Perfect for TV."

Josie can feel her face stiffening. The muscles of her cheeks starting to ache with the rictus smile that she's somehow managed to maintain throughout this monologue.

"And your story—my god. It's just *devastating*. I can't imagine how it must have been for you. To have all of those things said about you, everything out in a public forum. I'm so glad we managed to track you down. So glad we're able to tell your side of the story now."

Josie manages a nod. Swallows.

"Well, yeah," she says. "It's . . . well. It was pretty terrible."

"I have to ask you, of course." Katherine lowers her voice, conspiratorial. "*Did* you do it?"

The nerves inside Josie quiver. Stall. Something within her collapses. Katherine is laughing.

"I mean, of *course* you're not going to tell me," she says. "But you have to ask, you know? You can't *not* ask the question."

Josie bends down to unzip her backpack.

"OK, OK. We'll revisit that one later," Katherine is saying cheerily.

Josie straightens.

"Here," she says. She drops a cardboard file on the table. It's so thick, so stuffed with papers, that it falls with a satisfying thud that silences Katherine.

"The case file," Josie says. "That's what you wanted, right?"

"Josie." Katherine looks like the only thing stopping her from whisking the file up from the table immediately is Gabby approaching with her double espresso. "My god. You *star*. You're the only person who can request most of this stuff, but even then we weren't sure they'd grant access to all of it."

"It's all there," Josie said. "Everything they'd give me, at least. I looked through it. It's mostly boring legal stuff, but I'm sure there's something you can use."

"Of course, of course. I'm sure there'll be plenty we can sink our teeth into. We'll get it copied today and get this back to you."

Josie zips her backpack up with one decisive motion.

"It's fine," she says. "You can keep it. I don't want it."

"You don't—?"

"No."

Josie stands.

"Enjoy your coffee."

She almost delights in the panic that flashes in Katherine's eyes.

"But—I thought we could set up your first interview? Or at least have a chat through what information you might be able to offer us about—"

"I said I'd help," Josie says. "And I got you the case files. I didn't say that I'd be interviewed. Or talk about the case, for that matter."

"But Josie." Katherine has flushed an unflattering shade of pink. Her coffee remains untouched in front of her. She forces out a strained-sounding laugh. "You're our star interviewee! This documentary could be so good for you. It could change people's opinion of you. Convince them of your innocence."

"I think it might be difficult to do that," says Josie, "when the people making the documentary aren't convinced of my innocence themselves."

A look of horror dawns on Katherine's face.

"Is this because I asked if you did it?" she says. "Josie? I was only asking a silly question. Of course I think you're innocent! But I have to *ask*. The evidence against you was so compelling."

"Right, yeah," says Josie. "You don't have to tell me. I spent ten years in prison on the basis of that evidence. Clearly someone found it *compelling*."

"Josie. Let's start again. Please. We can talk this through."

Josie shifts the now empty backpack onto her shoulders.

"It's all there in the file," she says. "Everything. You don't need me, telling the same story all over again."

"But Josie—"

Josie doesn't wait to listen to her. She has already turned to leave.

"Josie, please," Katherine calls after her. "Let's just talk!"

Josie turns back then, pausing with one hand on the door.

"Actually," she says. "There's one thing I did want to ask you."

Katherine nods, too eagerly.

"Yes," she says. "Of course. Why don't you sit back down and we can—"

"Have you managed to track down Hannah Bailey?"

Katherine's face creases.

"Hannah . . . ?"

Her confusion tells Josie everything she needs to know. She pushes hard against the door. As she walks away, she finds that she is trying not to cry.

TWELVE

2004
SIX WEEKS BEFORE THE BIRTHDAY PARTY

"So, what was it like?" Josie asked.

They were at the beach, supervising Nina as she built sandcastles with plastic buckets that Hannah had scavenged from the dive shop's small children's section. It was the hottest time of the day, and Josie would have much preferred to be within the cool stone walls of the pink house, but Evelyn had insisted that she take Nina out, complaining that she was giving her a headache. Already Josie could feel her skin, never quite used to the hot coastal summers, beginning to burn.

"What was what like?"

Josie flicked a handful of sand at her.

"Come on, you can't play dumb with me. What was it like kissing Blake after all this time?"

She turned back toward Nina, momentarily distracted.

"That's it. Tap it on the top with your spade so that the magic gets in. One, two, *three*."

"It was . . . I don't know."

"Was it everything you always imagined?"

"Not exactly what I imagined, no. I was definitely expecting less water."

Josie snorted.

"It's all broken!" declared Nina as she lifted the plastic mould, the sandy mound emerging with its turrets not quite intact.

"It's fine, look." Josie clambered to her knees and patted some extra sand on top. "We can fix it."

And then, to Hannah.

"But what was it *like*? Actually kissing someone? Did he use tongue? Did you, like, French, or was it just a peck?"

"I don't know, sort of in between, I suppose?"

"Josie?" Nina said, wheedling. "Did Hannah kiss Blake?"

"'Course not, Neens," said Josie. "'Cos boys are gross, right? Hey, why don't you try another one?"

She rolled over, wiped the sand off her hands.

"So, what?" she said. "Are you and Blake, like, a thing now?"

She tried to keep her voice light. Tried to keep the edge out of it, but somehow, it remained. She knew Hannah could hear it by the way she tossed her hair back, the way she said, "Are you jealous or something?"

Josie snorted.

"Me?" she said. "Jealous of you snogging Blake Drayton? Give over."

"Anyway, what happened to you? You disappeared on me."

Josie shrugged.

"You must have been off with Blake," she said. "I didn't go anywhere."

"But you did," Hannah persisted. "I looked everywhere for you. How did you even get home?"

"One of Tamara's friends gave me a lift."

"*Tamara's* friends? You don't know any of Tamara's friends."

"Funny how quickly you get to know people when you get ditched at a house party in the middle of nowhere, though, right?"

Hannah fell silent. Josie couldn't quite look at her. She flexed her feet against the sand, her gaze fixed on the sea.

"You're not telling me something," said Hannah at last.

"There's nothing to tell, Jesus," said Josie. "I got bored. I found some people who were heading back the same way as me, and I hitchhiked the last bit. I'm not the one sneaking off with Blake bloody Drayton."

"Josie." Nina looked aghast. "You said a bad word."

Hannah stood.

"I should go," she said. "I told Mum I'd be home for lunch. And I have to work on my Oxford application this afternoon."

"Oxford application? That's not code for meeting up with Blake, is it?"

"And what if I was?"

"I'm only looking out for you, Hannah."

"The deadline is September and I've barely even—"

"Sure. Fine. Whatever. I'll see you later on then, I guess."

"You're really not going to tell me where you went?"

For a moment, Josie was still. She watched as wave after wave crashed down on the beach.

"Fine," Hannah said at last. "I'll see you later on."

Josie did not turn to see her go. She just watched the waves. The never-ending in-out rush of the sea.

@TRUECRIMEFANGIRL_2002
POSTED FIVE WEEKS AGO

Hey, true crime girlies, and welcome back to my series on the Tamara Drayton case. Now, if you're new here—and, like, where the eff have you been if you are?—then this case has it all. Rich kids behaving badly, secrets, lies, love affairs, betrayal, and, of course, murder. Or was it? That's what we're here to figure out. So strap in, because we are getting in. To. *It*.

First of all, I want to give a big, juicy, true crime thank-you to everyone who watched, liked, and shared my first video about the case. It's my most-liked video ever. Wow. Appreciate you guys.

So today I thought I'd do a special little feature on some of the people the police overlooked in the Tamara Drayton case. Because I have seen your comments, and I get it. If it wasn't Josie Jackson who killed Tamara Drayton, then who was it? Well, guys, a few people who used to know the Draytons, or who were in the Côte d'Azur that summer have been in touch. And oh my god, the stories I've been told. That place was just a hotbed of secrets and lies and intrigue. In fact, I might have to do a whole separate series on who was at the birthday party that night and all the crazy shit that's come out about them since, because, wow, there is a LOT.

Now, some of this is pretty well-known stuff, so if you're new here, and I know that lots of you are, there is just tons of information out there about all the various theories, all the background to the case. These are just some of my faves. And trigger warning on this one for drug use.

So first of all—Harrison Andreas. I mean, jeez, what a scumbag that man was. So, for those of you not in the know, Harrison was Evelyn Drayton's third or fourth husband, depending on which way you split it. Now, the rumors are that there was trouble in paradise for these two, and Harrison was actually having an affair and planning to leave Evelyn. In fact, Harrison filed for divorce four weeks after Tamara's death and believe me, that guy got a huge settlement.

But here's the thing. Harrison and Evelyn's prenup had an infidelity clause, meaning that Harrison forfeited his right to any of the Drayton fortune if he was unfaithful. And look, Harrison moved in with a new girlfriend the day after the divorce was finalized, so I think we can all speculate that he was indeed unfaithful. But guess what? Some of Tamara's friends have since come out and said that Tamara actually knew about Harrison's affairs—in fact, she could have been the only person in the family who had proof that Harrison was cheating. Could Harrison have wanted to unalive Tamara so that he still got a huge divorce settlement without Tamara messing things up for him? Lots of people think so.

And what about Evelyn herself? By all accounts, Evelyn Drayton was a pretty reckless mother. She drank, she partied, and she basically didn't give a crap about her kids. And we know that Tamara was into partying, too, and lots of people think the so-called drowning might have been a convenient cover-up for Tamara OD'ing. You can totally see it, right? Tamara gets her hands on Evelyn's stash, gets carried away, and boom. Evelyn's looking at a manslaughter charge. And we already know that Evelyn was pretty close to the pathologist who carried out the autopsy on her daughter. Is it possible that she persuaded him to play down how intoxicated Tamara was that night?

And don't even get me started on Rocco Mae. That's Blake and Tamara's deadbeat dad. It turns out that he was actually in the area when Tamara died, even though he'd told Evelyn and his kids he was in his home in Italy. *He* says that he'd visited a few weeks previously and added some time onto the end as a holiday, with his wife and youngest children coming out to meet him at a rented villa about a thirty-minute drive away from the Drayton home. He claims that there were tensions between him and the twins, and in particular, between the twins and his wife, Flora, which is why he didn't want Tamara and Blake to know he was still around, but this all just sounds super sus to me. And what were these tensions anyway? Were they enough to be a motive for murder?

Or how about Blake? Everyone says that he and Tamara were close. Like, really, weirdly close. I mean, I'm not saying it's a reason to suspect him, but I just have a weird feeling about it, you know?

And that's not to mention all the guests that were there that night. You'll have heard of Damien Wright, big Hollywood producer who was arrested after fatally shooting his daughter Olivia Wright, actually a friend of Tamara Drayton's, back in the twenty-tens. Police said it was an accident, but there's lots of speculation otherwise. Well, guess who was on the guest list at Evelyn's party that night?

The police said that nobody else had any motive to hurt Tamara Drayton, but I, for one, disagree, and as always, there is so much more to this case than meets the eye.

Please give me a follow if you want to know more, and let me know in the comments. Who's your number-one suspect?

Crimeathon67: Gotta be Harrison. That pic of him gives me major chills
CathrynJameson: I heard that one of Evelyn's best friends had had a miscarriage a few days before the party. Could be like a kind of woman gone nuts with grief sitch!?
Justice4JJ: OK, hear me out, Rocco Mae hiring a hitman?
BenJackson__washere: Evelyn Evelyn Evelyn. Always said that woman RADIATES guilt. Also, it's mad how many people who were at the house had shady shit going on!? Like whatttttt.
Posiegirl: This speculation is WILD. Let a dead girl rest in peace, guys.

THIRTEEN

2024

Gabby shows up at the house that night, the exhaust on her battered car announcing her arrival long before she knocks on the door.

"Have dinner with us," Calvin says to Josie as he goes to answer it.

But Josie makes her excuses. She says that she's tired, and that she'll take a plate up to her bedroom instead. It's not exactly a lie. The early start and long, hot day *has* exhausted her. But it also wouldn't have been a lie to say that she can't stand the thought of dinner with her brother and his girlfriend. Gabby's kindness, and the inevitable questions about her meeting. Josie does not have the energy to deal with either.

From downstairs, Josie can hear the sound of Gabby and Calvin talking. Laughing. She's surprised to realize that they're speaking to each other in French. Calvin used to be so bad at it, when they first moved here, but now he's fluent. To Josie, everything is stuck in the past. Everything is the way it was twenty years ago.

※

When Josie wakes the next morning, there are sounds coming from the room next door. A rhythmic tapping of a headboard against the wall. A low, animal moan.

It takes Josie a moment to fully come to consciousness. To understand what she is hearing. When she does, she scrambles to her feet, face burning. She grabs a thin sweater and pulls on a pair of pajama shorts, hurrying down the stairs so quickly that she turns her ankle on the bottom step and has to hop across the kitchen floor, desperately trying not to make a sound, trying not to be there at all.

It's only when she's outside that it occurs to her that she has nowhere to go. She hasn't dressed properly to go down to the village, to kill an hour or two in a coffee shop. She has no friends who she could shelter with until the coast is clear, to laugh off the awkwardness of hearing her brother and his girlfriend having sex. In fact, there's nobody here who would want to see her at all.

She walks slowly to the edge of the driveway, onto the scrap of a road. There's a broad stone post inscribed with the house number that she still remembers her dad hammering into the ground, irritated that nobody could ever seem to find them, waiting for letters from home that rarely came. She perches there, her flip-flops grazing the ground.

She'll tell them she couldn't sleep, she thinks. That she went out for a walk to clear her head.

She wonders, briefly, how long Calvin will put up with her staying. How long before having his sister hanging around starts to grate on him and he begins to long for his own space again. She pushes her toes into the foam soles of her flip-flops. She'll find somewhere new to live, as soon as she can save enough for a deposit. Where exactly she'll go, she isn't sure. Like always, the future seems to gape in front of Josie, vast and undefined. Sometimes, she imagines her life as a fall from a very high cliff, trying to grab on to the first thing that might stop each inevitable plummet. Sometimes, she finds a safer place to land. Sometimes, she manages to clamber up a few feet. Sometimes, the earth seems to crumble away from beneath her, and she is falling, falling all over again.

She lifts her face up toward the early morning sun, closes her eyes, and waits. She doesn't open them, even when she hears the sound of a car rolling slowly up the hill. Even when the engine cuts, a handbrake creaking on.

"Not disturbing you, am I?"

She opens her eyes.

The man in front of her is tall. Tousled dark hair and a lean body. A deep voice with a lilt of French beneath a good English accent. Someone who's been here for a while, who's used to tourists, and who can spot Josie's British genes from a mile off.

"No," she says. "I was just . . ."

She trails off. Gestures one hand, uselessly.

"I thought it was you I saw yesterday," he says brightly.

"Yesterday?"

"At the dive shop?" he says. "I waved at you, through the window. Didn't you see?"

He shakes his head, incredulously.

"Josie Jackson," he says, as if he can't quite believe it himself. "In the flesh."

"I'm not—" she starts.

But he's looking at her like he knows her.

"Do I—?"

"You don't remember me?"

She shakes her head.

"Oh, come on," he says. "I know I was only a kid back then, but I was always running around after you and Hannah. I thought you guys were so cool."

That's when it clicks.

"Nicolas?"

There's a vague memory, like an object just beneath the surface of water. Hannah's little cousin. He lived somewhere else—somewhere inland—but he and his parents would come out here to visit. When Josie was fourteen, he had stayed for the entire summer. His parents were getting a divorce, and he had been offloaded with Hannah's family while they sold the house and squabbled over custody, as Hannah told Josie in whispered asides when Nicolas wasn't listening. They had spent all summer trying to cheer him up, taking him down to the beach and showing him their favorite places to cliff-jump. They had taught him how to dive, just below the surface of the water where small shoals of fish would dart away from them, the world still and quiet.

"Everyone calls me Nic now," he says. "But that's me."

"God," says Josie. "You're still here. Does anyone ever leave?"

He shrugs.

"You did," he said. "And Hannah. Hannah left."

The name hangs between them.

"Where did she go?" Josie asks.

Nic rubs the back of his neck, as though trying to knead out a knot.

"England," he says. "You know she always wanted to go there. She moved the year after . . . everything. Went to university."

"London?"

The possibility that Josie and Hannah might have been in the same city, might have passed each other in the street, their lives tantalizingly close and yet a million miles away, feels impossible. Nic shakes his head.

"Manchester," he says. "She met a guy there. Got married. She's got three kids now. They come back a couple of times a year to see her parents. They're cute. I think I have a picture . . ."

He digs his phone out of his pocket and thumbs the screen.

"Ah, yeah. Here. Look."

He holds the phone out toward Josie. She takes it with both hands, scanning the picture. The sea, the beach that she knows so well. A woman, crouching between two young boys, as if they could hide her from sight.

Her hair is shorter, a bob, and her body has filled out. She's wearing a one-piece instead of a bikini, and there's an exhaustion behind her eyes that wasn't there before, but Josie would recognize her anywhere. Hannah. Hannah, twenty years older than Josie remembers her.

"That was before Isla was born," Nic is saying. "She hasn't been here the last couple of years. Said it was too much, with a baby."

Josie wordlessly passes the phone back to him and he takes it with an affectionate smile at the screen.

"Mason's fourteen now. I can hardly believe it. And Noah—the middle one—he's ten. They're good kids. Really good kids. Her parents retired a few years ago, and they wanted to keep the shop in the family. Hannah was never that interested, and she's got enough going on with the kids now, so they asked if I wanted it. And I was hardly going to say no."

Josie doesn't say anything. She can't imagine having a fourteen-year-old. Most of the time, she can't imagine having children at all. There were so many things taken away from her that early-August day, so many paths that her life could have taken, narrowed down to nothing. Dead ends and roads not taken.

"What are you doing out here anyway?" Nic asks, tucking his phone back into his pocket. "Are you waiting for someone?"

"Not exactly," Josie says. "I . . ."

She pauses. Glances back toward the house.

"My brother's got his girlfriend over," she says, knowing that she's blushing. "I figured they could use some privacy."

"Ah." Nic's eyebrows raise slightly. "Yeah. Gabby's not exactly the quiet and retiring type."

"You know Gabby?"

"She's actually my ex. Hence why I'm familiar with your . . . desire to be out of the house."

Josie feels her nose wrinkle. She's always been bad at disguising her thoughts, her face often giving her away. It used to get her into trouble, back when she was a teenager. It still does now, sometimes.

"Gross."

Nic shrugs.

"Hey, Gabby's cool," he says. "We're still friends. We can joke about it."

Josie shifts, folding her arms across her chest.

"What are you doing here, anyway? You weren't . . . you weren't looking for me, were you?"

Nic's face breaks into a grin that shows all his teeth. He has a good smile, easy and open.

"I was actually here to see your brother. He wanted me to drop some stuff before he started work. But it sounds like he's otherwise engaged."

"God, everyone around here really does know everyone."

"Yeah," he says, like it's the most obvious thing in the world. "That's what I like about it." He swings the door of his car back open. "Calvin can wait for his gear. I'm coming back this way later, anyway. You need a lift? You look like you could do with getting out of here."

Josie spreads her hands wide, indicating her pajama shorts.

"I'm not exactly dressed to go anywhere."

He opens the passenger door and starts to sling things into the backseat. A pair of scuba goggles, an armful of wetsuits.

"We've got a ton of stuff down at the dive shop," he says. "Lost property. It's amazing how many people come to a lesson and manage to leave the clothes that they showed up in behind. I'll give you a ride down, if you like. You can help yourself. And then you're a free woman."

"I—"

He straightens and gestures to the emptied front seat, beaming.

"Come on," he says. "This car doesn't get cleaned up for just anybody."

Josie hesitates. But then she thinks about going back to the house. The awkwardness of drinking coffee at the kitchen table with Gabby and Calvin, still glowing with sex.

She stands, grit sticking to the backs of her thighs.

"Fine," she says. "Let's get out of here."

※

At the dive shop, Josie finds a pair of women's jeans scrunched up in the bottom of the lost-property basket. It's always hard to find clothes that fit her right, jeans always coming up too long for her, too tight on her thighs, but when she pulls them on, she finds that they are perfect.

"Thanks," she says when she emerges from the back room.

Nic looks up from the front desk, where he's counting a basket of regulators.

"Hey," he says. "They suit you."

"Oh," she says. "Thanks. They'd probably look better on someone taller. But. You know."

"You're not very good at accepting compliments, are you?"

Josie doesn't have a response to this, so she bends down, pretends to be smoothing the jeans down against her thighs.

"Well," she says. "Thanks again for the lift. And the jeans."

"It was my pleasure," Nic says. "It was cool to see you again, Josie Jackson. After all this time."

She finds herself smiling at this, ducking her head to hide it. It's an unexpected pleasure for her, too, to come across someone from her past. Someone who knows who she is and doesn't flinch away from her. Who doesn't look at her as if she did the worst thing imaginable.

"Hey," says Nic. "I have to open up here in twenty minutes. But do you fancy maybe going for a drink later?"

Josie pauses, one hand already raised toward the door.

"A drink."

"Yeah. Or a coffee. Whatever you fancy."

She doesn't say anything.

"Oh, come on," he says. "Don't tell me you have something better to do."

"Like . . . a date?"

He tilts his head to one side. Smiles.

"Sure," he says. "Like a date."

He must see the expression on her face, because he holds his palms out flat toward her, mock-defensive.

"Wow, OK," he says. "Not the reaction I usually get. Too forward?"

"It's not that, it's just . . ." She hesitates. "Don't you think you should be dating someone your own age?"

"I'm thirty-two!"

"You are not." In her head, Hannah's cousin had seemed so young. Childlike in comparison to their pretense of adulthood.

He laughs. "Alright," he says. "How old are you?"

"Thirty-five."

"I've dated older."

"Showing off now, are you?"

"I'm just saying, it's not a big age gap."

"Alright then. Don't you think you should be dating someone who isn't a convicted criminal?"

There's a glitter behind his eyes. "I always liked a bad girl," he says, deadpan.

Josie laughs, in spite of herself.

"Come on," he says, cajoling now. "Give me your number, and I'll plan something fun for us. I reckon you could do with a night out. That is . . ." He pauses, a smile spreading out from the corners of his mouth. "That is, assuming you have a mobile phone, of course. You never know, with thirty-five-year-olds, if they've caught up with the latest tech."

"Very funny."

"Is that a yes?"

She holds out her hand. She's smiling now. "Give me your number," she says. "I'll contact you."

FOURTEEN

2004

SIX WEEKS BEFORE THE BIRTHDAY PARTY

Hannah did not have to work on her Oxford application that afternoon.
 She was not used to lying to Josie like this.
She always told Josie the truth, even about the stuff she'd be embarrassed to say to anyone else—the fact that she'd once had a crush on their maths teacher, or that she'd once cheated on a history exam and still felt bad about it. And yet, when she had received a text message from Blake that morning, she had known that she would not tell Josie. She had known, somehow, that this was something she wanted to keep for herself.

What are you up to today? the message had read.

Not much, she typed in response. Might go to the beach. Might help out my parents with some diving lessons later.

The reply was almost instant.

You know, I've never dived before. Crazy right?

It took Hannah a few minutes to respond to this. A pause as she agonized over the right thing to say. Was Blake hinting that he wanted to go diving with her? Was she reading too much into it? What if she suggested it, and he responded with complete repulsion at the idea they might spend more time together? What if this entire thing was in her head?

I could take you out, if you like? she had eventually replied. Casual. Like it didn't matter to her either way.

She held the phone tightly in her hand, the screen inches from her face. Holding her breath as she waited for it to light up again.

I thought you'd never ask x

※

Her parents were late coming back from the dive lesson that afternoon. They were irritable, short with each other as they navigated their nightly ritual of counting the day's takings. Hannah could tell they'd been fighting again. When she asked if she could take the smaller boat out—the speedboat that they used for private lessons—they were too caught up in their silent grievances to ask why.

By the time she got to the beach Blake was waiting for her. She was out of breath from hauling diving equipment all the way from the shop, her feet catching in the sand in her hurry not to be late. He was dressed in swimming trunks, his chest bare. The suggestion of a tan.

"I thought you'd stood me up," he called, getting to his feet as she approached. "Here, let me help you with those."

He jogged over and prized an oxygen tank out of her hands, staggered with the unexpected weight.

"Shit," he said, laughing. "They're heavier than I thought they'd be. You must have muscles."

Hannah wasn't sure whether having muscles was supposed to be a good thing. The girls she usually saw Blake with were petite, their bodies neat and toned from horse riding and hockey.

"It's pretty physical," she said. "Come on, we're going this way."

"Aren't we going in the sea?"

Hannah tried to hide the way her mouth lifted into a smile.

"Don't get ahead of yourself," she said. "You have to practice first."

※

There was a natural salt pool close to the beach, only a few feet deep. It was designed for children to paddle in, the water always warm and still, a contrast to the cold, unpredictable heave of the sea.

They practiced in the lagoon-like basin, Hannah showing Blake how to breathe and demonstrating the tricks they taught in classes—removing and replacing his regulator while submerged, clearing his mask. It was dusk by the time they took the boat out, the sun low, the sea bronzed with its reflection. Blake had been eager to move their lesson into the deeper waters, and on the boat he made a big performance of checking his equipment the way Hannah had showed him.

He's trying to impress me, she thought, but then batted the idea away.

"Are you ready?" he asked, as they trod water next to the boat.

And Hannah ignored all the things she knew about diving, all the times her parents had told her not to leave the boat without someone on board, all the times they had told her not to take somebody out alone.

"I'm ready," she said. "Let's go."

And together, the two of them plunged beneath the surface.

Hannah loved diving when it was almost night. Perhaps it was because evening was often the only time when she could actually dive for fun. Not assisting a group dive, shepherding beginners on shallow descents, spending more time adjusting equipment than beneath the surface.

Or perhaps it was the fact that the sea seemed to come alive at this time, creatures emerging into the half-light. Octopuses and luminescent jellyfish. The water a deeper, darker shade of blue. The glow of her flashlight stretching far out ahead of them, reminding her of the vastness of space around them. Making her feel like they were the only people alive.

They descended slowly, using the rope as a guide. Hannah knew that a first dive could be disorienting. That without the gravity of the world above, you could lose your bearings, forget which way was up. She signaled to Blake.

Are you OK?

He nodded. Shot her the *I'm OK* sign that she had taught him back at the salt pool.

The water darkened. Hannah flipped on her head torch, and the world around them illuminated. A shoal of fish darting past, their fins an electric blue. A field of bright green sea grass. A plume of red coral, its arms extending out like the branches of an aged, underwater tree.

The beauty of it never failed to shake something within her. Being beneath the water, for Hannah, was always like coming back to life.

She started to swim from the rope, kicking slowly. She only got a meter away before a hand closed around her arm. When she turned, Blake's eyes were wide behind his mask. Panicked. He tapped at the plastic, a foggy sheen misting the surface. Gestured wildly.

It's OK, she signed to him. Pointed at the surface. *Let's go back up.* Her hand against his to reassure him. *Slowly.*

They weren't particularly deep, and it took them just seconds to ascend. Still, when they did, Blake tore off his mask, gasped for air.

"You did it!" Hannah said. "Your first dive."

He shook his head, tossing his wet hair out of his face, his bravado gone.

"Are you kidding?" he says. "I completely messed up. I panicked."

"No way. Most people don't manage to get into the sea on their first lesson at all."

She was lying, but it felt like a kindness. His face was flushed, salt-burned.

"You want to try again?" she said.

He looked out to sea, toward the orb of the sun, now so close to the horizon that it looked huge and blazing.

"Nah," he said. "I think that once was enough, for now."

"OK, let's go back to the beach."

He shook his head.

"Let's stay out here, for a bit? It's nice. Peaceful."

He turned to look at her, and his face was lit up by the sun.

"I like being here with you."

Hannah pulled up the anchor and taxied the boat out farther. The water softened, waves passing beneath them in slow swells. They lay on their backs so that their heads were close together, their faces turned up toward the fading pinks and oranges of the sky.

"I can see why you enjoy this," Blake said.

"The boat?"

"Diving."

"I wouldn't exactly call that diving," Hannah said, testing how it felt to tease him.

He laughed, and the sound felt like liquid gold in her stomach.

"Do you come out every day?"

"Not every day," she said. "Sometimes it feels too much like work. It's something I have to do, to help my parents out."

She didn't tell him how, as much as she loved diving, it often felt like a reminder of all the things she didn't have, the precarious line they were always walking. The days when her parents canceled trips because not enough people signed up, when the bell over the shop door never rang.

"I get that," Blake said. "Sometimes I feel like so much of my life is about who my parents are. Like who I was going to be was already decided, before I was born. Like I never had a choice."

Hannah trailed her fingers against the surface of the water, considering this. She wouldn't mind not having a choice, if it meant she were a Drayton. If she could live in the pink house, and have staff, and never have to worry about money.

"What would you want to do?" she said. "If you had the choice?"

"Honestly?" Blake said. "If I had the choice, I wouldn't have been born a Drayton in the first place."

He shifted so that he was propped up on one elbow.

"People think it's great," he said. "This life. They think they would want the money and the attention. But they have no idea what it's like having the legendary Evelyn Drayton as a mother."

There was a twist behind his words, something sharp and bitter.

"Right," said Hannah carefully. "She's a bit . . . well. She's not your typical mum."

Blake snorted at this.

"That's an understatement," he said. "And it's not fun, you know? Having all the guys at school know who your mum's slept with. Knowing that their parents gossip about us. Laugh at us. Think we're trash, because we're still *new* money, even though my granddad made his fortune back in the fifties. But we don't have houses and a family name that goes back generations. So—as far as they're concerned—my mum is some dumb heiress whose only notable achievement is pissing away our grandfather's cash."

Hannah had never heard him talk like this. It was as though that moment beneath the water—that flash of vulnerability she saw in his eyes—had carved something out of him. Created an open hollow that he now spoke to fill.

Blake flashed a sideways look at Hannah, and seemed to catch her surprise.

"You didn't know that she's running out of money?" he said. "She's always been running out of money, as long as I can remember, and yet she can't stop spending it. Somehow, every time we're in crisis, she conjures up a miracle."

He leaned back again now, so that he was no longer looking at Hannah. So that his face was tilted toward the sky.

"So I guess, in answer to your question, I would choose to be someone different entirely," he said. "Someone from a good family. Whose surname isn't a joke to people. Someone who has stability. Actual *money*, not just pots of dwindling assets. People think they want to be part of our world. That's what you want, right? But you have to understand that we're not in that world either. Not really. I'm on the outside as much as you are. We don't belong any more than you do."

Hannah almost flinched at that. She had been so careful to play it cool. Never to let Blake know how badly, how desperately, she wanted to be like him.

And yet . . .

Blake thought that they were alike. He was wrong, of course; she knew that. Whatever subtle class differences existed between Blake and the people he went to boarding school and on skiing trips with were infinitesimally small compared with the vast gap between his life and hers. The fact that Blake could even notice the intricate hierarchies within his social sphere only proved how deeply embedded in it he was.

But what Hannah really heard was that he thought they had

something profound and important in common. Something that really, truly seemed to matter to him.

"I didn't want to come out here this summer," Blake said. "I wanted to go stay with my dad, in Italy. He just bought a vineyard over there. Me and him were going to get Vespas and drive down the Amalfi Coast. It would have been so cool."

"Why didn't you?" Hannah asked.

She felt the shift of Blake's head tilting beside her, a half shrug.

"Mum said she wanted us to be all together. She and Harrison are at each other's throats all the time, and she thinks that if we can play happy families for the summer, he might stick around."

Hannah thought of what Josie said at the pool yesterday. She wondered if Blake already knew.

"She's so deluded," he continued, and his words had a hard edge to them. "Harrison doesn't want me here. He doesn't give a shit about me and Tamara and Nina. He *especially* hates Tamara. And no amount of pretending is going to sort out whatever dysfunctional shit he and my mum have going on."

He broke off, and the only sound was the gentle slap of waves against the boat.

"Maybe you can do the Amalfi Coast another time," Hannah said.

"Yeah," Blake said, brightening slightly. "We're probably going to do it at the end of summer instead. After Mum's gone back to London."

They both fell quiet. If she was still, Hannah could hear the soft in, out sound of his breathing. She could hear the beating of her own heart.

"Hey," said Blake. "Do you have any plans tonight?"

"Tonight?"

For just a moment, Hannah had been outside of time. She had forgotten that there was a tonight that would come after this. That there would be dinner waiting for her in the microwave at home, evening television, chasing sleep with the memory of this evening keeping her awake. She had forgotten that there was anything outside of her and Blake, this boat, the slow drift of the sea.

Blake sat up.

"We're going out," he said. "Me. Tamara. Barnaby. You wanna come?"

And even though Hannah wanted nothing less than to be with Tamara and Barnaby, even though she wanted to stay here until the sky turned black, wanted to stretch this moment until it split at the seams, Hannah nodded.

"Sure," she said. "Let's go out."

Barnaby's car pulled up outside the dive shop late, after Hannah's parents had already gone to bed. She had dried her hair, slicked on mascara. She was secretly pleased when she opened the car door to realize that Blake would be sitting in the back with her, Tamara in the passenger seat. Tamara didn't turn round to look at Hannah as she climbed inside. Across the darkness of the back seat, Blake's hand slid toward hers. Their fingers intertwined.

They drove into the nearest city, abandoning Barnaby's car in a no-parking zone.

"It's not like we can't afford the fine," Barnaby said.

He looped his arm around Blake's shoulder and ruffled his hair. Blake grimaced and pushed him off, but they were laughing.

"Come on," said Barnaby. "Let's get fucked up."

There were drinks. Vodka shots. A casino, where Barnaby put down a thousand euros and just rolled his eyes and laughed when he lost it. More shots. Barnaby, sliding his arm around Tamara's waist. Tamara pulling a face and slapping his hand away. Cocktails in a rooftop bar where the city seemed to shine, a haze of color and light. A nightclub where the music ignited something in Hannah, sent a thrum of ecstasy down her spine. A round of drinks that Blake paid for with a handful of cash. A bottle of champagne that fizzed through her, that felt like drinking stars.

They moved on to another club that backed onto the beach. Darker, busier, the music unfamiliar. Strobe lights and a heavy bassline. Tamara and Barnaby downing tequilas with salt and lemon. Blake, leaning his head down close to Hannah's ear, the soft brush of his hair against the side of her face. Saying that it was so hot in here. So loud. Asking if she wanted to go outside.

Blake needed to use the bathroom, so Hannah offered to queue for his jacket at the cloakroom while he went. She stood in line, her arms folded across her chest, a comfortable, easy haze to her vision. The group of girls in front of her shifted forward, and as Hannah followed she felt a breathtaking strike of clarity, as if seeing herself from above. She was here. She was going outside with Blake Drayton, alone. This was it. This was the moment that everything would change.

"You're still here? Jesus."

Blake was next to her, slipping his arm around her waist as if it was the most natural thing in the world.

"Thanks for saving my spot," he said, quietly, so that he had to lean in close to her ear.

"Anytime," said Hannah, and she really, truly meant it.

Outside the air was cool. Sweat chilled against Hannah's skin, and she wrapped her arms around herself, realized that she was shivering.

"You're cold," Blake said, a statement, not a question. There was a certainty about him that sucked something out of Hannah, made her want him.

No. Not want him, exactly. Want to *be like* him, to be part of this world, where you always have answers, rather than questions. Where things were clear and assured.

"Here."

He took off the jacket that she had queued for and slipped it over her shoulders. The inner lining was still warm from his body. The smell of him encased her.

"Come on," he said, taking her hand.

They walked down to the beach, Hannah's ankles turning inward in her only pair of heels. She took them off, the sand cool against the soles of her feet. They both smelled of fresh sweat, the chemical hum of alcohol. There was a magic to the city in the early hours, shutters closed on the houses and shops that lined the seawater, the feeling that this was an impossible, nonexistent time. A witching hour where anything could happen.

"I'm so hammered," said Blake, running his fingers through his hair, almost disbelieving.

"I had so much fun tonight," said Hannah.

She meant it. She had always known that this world was out here. This feeling that nothing mattered. That she could go anywhere, do whatever she wanted. She had just needed someone like Blake to hold the door open for her.

The touch of his fingers was so light against her thigh that it sent a strange, deep convulsion through Hannah. She wanted him to press his hands hard against her skin. She wanted to be able to feel him. To be able to sense the contours of his bones against hers.

"I really like you, H," Blake said. His words were quiet. Slurred. "I've liked you for years. Ever since we were kids."

His hand skimmed from her body to her face. Touched her chin lightly, a tremor in his hand. An anticipation. Turned her face toward his.

"I like you, too," she said.

When he kissed her, his mouth was hard and hungry and somehow familiar. He tasted like salt. Like heat. Like summer.

Hannah knew what would happen, even before Blake rolled on top of her. Even before his hands moved from her face to her waist, his breath coming faster, urgency radiating out of him. She knew, it seemed, exactly what to do, even though the whole thing had always seemed baffling and alien to her. Even though she and Josie had spent hours snorting with laughter as they discussed logistics—what went where, and who did what. It was as if this was how it was always supposed to be, Hannah and Blake, here on this beach, the sky blank and dark above them, the nighttime air cool and sharp against their skin.

He reached down and slid her underwear off. She was glad that she'd dressed in one of those flippy little tennis skirts, just like the girls that Blake usually hung out with. She didn't even have to take it off.

"You're already wet," he said, and there was a soft surprise in his voice that made Hannah feel good about herself, like she was doing something right.

Later, Hannah would remember how rough the sand had felt beneath her. How there had been a dull pain between her legs for the next few days that sent an unexpected thrum of pleasure through her, a reminder of what had happened between them.

But, in that moment, all Hannah felt was the beating of his heart against hers. The certain knowledge that something good was finally happening to her.

It was over quickly. Afterward, Hannah pulled her underwear back up and felt the scratch of grit against her inner thighs, a wetness on the fabric.

"Fuck."

Blake was rebuckling his belt, a dazed, disbelieving look on his face.

"That was . . . unexpected," he said.

To Hannah, it was anything but. It was what she had wanted from the very first time she saw Blake, before she really even understood her own desire. Before she knew what that muscular twinge inside her even meant. There was a clean inevitability to it, the sense that everything had been leading to this moment.

From behind them came a loud, sharp wolf whistle. A whoop. Barnaby sauntering down the sand toward them, Tamara a few steps behind.

"There you are," said Barnaby. "Wondered where you pair had disappeared to."

He dropped down onto the sand beside them.

"Hope you two have been behaving yourself."

"Doesn't look like it," said Tamara.

The words were cold and flat. Hannah ducked her head. Blake was already volleying back, making some joke about Barnaby hardly being one to talk.

"Come on," said Barnaby. "Club's closing. We should be getting back."

As Hannah stood, she could swear that she could feel the heat of Tamara's stare.

✳

In the back of the car, Hannah leaned her head against Blake's shoulder and closed her eyes. She knew that Tamara would probably shoot them a dirty look, if she saw. She knew that this thing between her and Blake was undefined, that resting against him was the kind of thing a girlfriend would do, and she was not his girlfriend. She knew that, if she hadn't drunk so much, she would worry about all these things, overthink whether she was being too forward, if she was annoying Blake's twin. But right now, she didn't care.

Barnaby drove fast, his foot pressed hard against the accelerator, the car drifting into the center of the road. Once, he had to sway to avoid a lorry barreling toward them, the blast of the horn cutting through a sleepy, half-drunk daydream that Hannah had been having. She and Blake in Oxford together. Pints of beer in tumble-down pubs, sex in a single bed in her halls. She had gripped the back of her seat when Barnaby swerved, but then the lorry passed and they had all been laughing, saying what an idiot the truck driver was. As if he were the reckless one.

Later, Hannah would look back on that moment and cringe. She would be horrified by how untouchable they had all felt, as if they were asking the world to break them. The frightening hubris of seventeen-year-olds. She did not yet know that somehow, somewhere, someone was always going to get hurt.

But just then, Hannah sat in the back of the car and thought only of the warmth of Blake's arm against hers. The twinge between her legs. An exquisite pain.

The sun was rising as they followed the coast home, the sky a shade of gold. The promise of another day. Another future, now within Hannah's reach.

23 August 2004, 11:48

Extract from interview with **Evelyn Drayton**.
This extract is taken from Evelyn Drayton's fourth interview with the police.
Present is legal representative for the Drayton family, **Florent Portier**, and translator **Felicity Carmichael**.
Leading the interview is lead investigator **Martine Allard**.

M Allard: OK, Ms. Drayton, we're going to go through this again, but this time we're really going to take our time with it. I understand that you're upset, and I understand that you and your family have been through a lot—

E Drayton: That's an understatement.

M Allard: You've been through a lot, and this process is extremely distressing for you. But we're just going to go over, one more time, what your daughter told you yesterday.

E Drayton: I don't know how many more times I can say this. Nina crawled into my bed, where I'd been napping, and she told me that she saw Josie Jackson fighting Tamara in the pool, and she saw Josie push Tamara underneath the water.

M Allard: And you said you were napping. Did Nina wake you up to tell you this?

E Drayton: I—I think so. I was dozing. Half-awake, I think. I've been sleeping a lot. It's been hard to get out of bed lately.

M Allard: So there was no conversation leading up to this? You weren't discussing Tamara's death with Nina?

E Drayton: No. No, I don't think so. I was sort of half-awake, and

Nina said, "Mummy, I know a secret." Yes, that's what she said. "I know a secret." I know I'm not supposed to smoke in here, but . . .

M Allard: It's fine. Go ahead. And how did you respond to that?

E Drayton: Well, I don't really remember. I don't think I said anything, at first. As I said, I wasn't quite awake. And then she said, "Mummy, I saw Tamara and Josie fighting." Well, I was awake then, let me tell you.

M Allard: What did you say then?

E Drayton: I don't know, I suppose I asked her what she meant. And that's when she said it. That she saw them fighting in the pool. That Josie . . . that Josie *killed* Tamara.

M Allard: Did she use those words? Did she say that Josie killed Tamara?

E Drayton: Well, I can't remember, exactly. Maybe. Or she might have just said that she pushed her. I don't know. And then I shouted for Blake, so that he could hear it. And I got Nina to repeat what she'd told me, and she said the exact same thing. "I saw Josie and Tamara fighting, and Josie pushed Tamara under the water." Clear as a bell.

M Allard: And what happened next?

E Drayton: Well, we called the police, obviously.

M Allard: You didn't ask Nina any more questions?

E Drayton: I can't really remember. I don't think so.

M Allard: And would you describe Nina as a truthful child?

E Drayton: Of course. She's a *child*. Have you ever seen a child try to lie?

M Allard: What do you mean by that?

E Drayton: I have three children, Inspector Allard, and let me tell you, Nina's the worst liar of all of them. She has this look on her face when she lies, like she's waiting to get caught. You can spot it a mile off. Tamara, on the other hand, now, Tamara was different. She was always so smart, right from when she was tiny. She could tell little white lies, little fibs. Her dad always used to say she was manipulative, and I used to tell him he was mad. Kids can't be manipulative. But he swore she was. Not like other kids—you know, kids lie and say they haven't had any treats today so that they get a second bag of sweets, or say that they've already brushed their teeth so that they don't have to. Tamara wasn't like that. Tamara's lies were bigger. She—I'm sorry. It's hard. Talking about her. But she was so clever, even when she was very young. Her dad didn't like it, but I did. I'd look at her, and I'd find it so impressive. She's going to be brilliant, I used to think. She's going to have people wrapped round her finger.

M Allard: I know this is hard, Ms. Drayton.

E Drayton: You asked me about Nina, and I'm telling you. Nina doesn't lie. Nina *can't* lie.

M Allard: And what were your impressions of Josie Jackson? I understand you knew her quite well.

E Drayton: Not well, no. Her mother worked for us. It's not as if we knew her socially. But yes, she was strange. Quiet. Moody. Most teenagers are, of course, but Josie was worse than most. She was rude, too, one of those kids who talks back, thinks they're smarter than they are. I only really gave her work because her mother's been with us for such a long time. And Nina loved her, of course.

M Allard: She was at your house often?

E Drayton: A few days a week, in summer. Although she used to hang around a lot, even when she wasn't working. That's what I found so odd about her. I found her sneaking around the place a couple of times, did I tell you that? Just hanging around the house, when she had no business being there. Oh, she always had an excuse. Had always left something somewhere, or said she thought her mum was here when clearly she wasn't. I used to find it strange, but I suppose I didn't think much of it. God, I wish I had done now. I wish I'd challenged her.

M Allard: And were you aware of any relationship or rivalry between Josie and Tamara?

E Drayton: God, no. In fact, I always warned Tamara and Blake to stay away from her. The local kids around here—well. They're feral. I didn't want my children thinking people like Josie Jackson were *friends*, just because they were often around. Blake used to mix with people like Josie sometimes, but not Tamara. In fact, Tamara actively avoided Josie, more or less. So, actually, yes, maybe there was—not

a *rivalry* because Tamara was worlds above Josie, of course. You couldn't compare them. But a . . . I don't know. A dislike? Maybe.
M Allard: Can you tell me more about that?
E Drayton: Look, really, the last person I want to be talking about right now is her. And to be honest you shouldn't be talking to me again. You should be talking to Josie bloody Jackson. Because that bitch killed my daughter. And she needs to pay for what she did.

FIFTEEN

2024

Nic is already seated at an outdoor table when Josie arrives at the restaurant. There are white tablecloths, railings wound with ivy, waiters in buttoned-up shirts. Beyond the terrace, the sea is a hazy shade of gold. It's a notoriously expensive place, the kind Josie's mum would once talk longingly about visiting but could never afford. Not that Josie can afford it either. She had balked when Nic had suggested it. I'm kind of broke at the minute, she had texted him back. His reply had been swift: My treat x

"Hi," she says when a waiter shows her to the table.

Nic stands, his chair scraping back against the ground. He looks different, in a pale blue shirt and chinos. Older. He leans in to kiss Josie on the cheek.

"You look great," he says.

"Thanks." Josie plucks at the lengths of the lilac tie-dyed dress that falls to her feet. "It's actually Gabby's. She lent it to me."

She had only had a few going-out outfits from Paris. Figure-hugging black dresses, skin-tight jeans. City clothes. Nothing that had felt right out here.

Nic laughs. "Only round here," he says, "could you go on a date with someone and she turns up in your ex-girlfriend's dress."

The waiter pulls out Josie's chair and she lowers herself down. "She was pleased," she says. "That we were going out tonight, I mean."

It had pained her, how delighted Gabby and Calvin had been when she had told them. Gabby clapped her hands together, and Calvin's shoulders seemed to soften, as if he had been holding a weight on them this whole time.

"Nic's a good guy," he said over and over, as if he couldn't quite believe it. As if he was floored by the relief of someone good wanting his sister.

Nic nods.

"He worries about you, I think."

"He's got nothing to worry about. I'm good. Better than ever."

The waiter arrives to hand Nic a wine list.

"I'll be honest with you," says Nic as soon as he's out of earshot. "I know absolutely nothing about wine."

He holds the leather-bound list out toward her and she shakes her head.

"Me neither," she says. "Do you think that they'll look down on us if we just order the cheapest one?"

"Or two of their cheapest, finest lagers," Nic says.

"Whoa." Josie holds her hands up in mock horror. "You're meant to be ordering a drink, not getting us kicked out of this place."

She likes making him laugh. She likes the way his whole face floods with warmth when he does. She has to remind herself, as she often does in these scenarios, that this cannot lead anywhere. She cannot let herself like Nic, even in spite of his laugh, their shared history. Like so many other things, the luxury of attachment is not something that Josie gets to have.

"Can I get you started with any drinks?"

The waiter's return is so smooth that it makes Josie jump.

"Erm . . . maybe this one?"

Nic stabs a finger at the wine list. "The . . . Montepulci . . . d'Abrusso?"

"The Montepulciano d'Abruzzo?" the waiter says, with a perfect Italian flair, one eyebrow raised.

"Erm. Yeah. That one."

"A few more minutes with the food menu?"

"That would be great."

"Just let me know if there's anything that you don't . . ." The waiter's eyes flit up and down, taking them both in. "Understand."

As he hurries away with the wine list, Nic's face flushes.

"Is it just me or was he . . ."

"A complete snob?" Josie says. "Yeah."

She picks up her menu, her eyes automatically skipping to the row of numbers that line the right-hand side of the page.

"Jesus. This place. These prices are crazy."

Nic is scanning the menu, too, his eyes flitting back and forth.

"Mmmhmm," he says.

"Are you . . ." Josie lowers her voice. "Are you sure you can afford this? Seriously. I'd be just as happy with somewhere a bit cheaper."

"No," Nic says, sounding uncertain. "It's fine."

"I don't mind. Really."

"It's fine," Nic says.

He runs his fingers along his shirt collar, sticking too close to his neck.

"I just wanted to take you somewhere nice," he says, in a smaller voice.

"It is nice. It's just. Well . . . I don't actually know what half these ingredients are."

He glances up from the menu, meets her eye across the table.

"I mean, what's samphire when it's at home?"

There's a flicker on his face then, a smile almost catching his mouth.

"Oh, I was actually thinking of going for the sea buckthorn," he shoots back.

They grin at each other, a secret alliance formed.

"You know," she says. "They haven't taken our order yet. We could absolutely still cut and run."

Nic hesitates. Places down his menu.

"I actually know a really fun spot not that far away from here," he says.

"Do they do sea buckthorn? Because I really had my heart set on the sea buckthorn."

They pause, the possibility hanging briefly between them. It sends a hum of excitement through Josie. Like schoolchildren, daring each other not to get caught.

"There's a path down to the beach right over there."

"On the count of three?"

"One, two, *three*."

※

They go to a tiny shack on the beach, away from the main strip. Wooden benches are set out on the sand, fairy lights strung up between poles. There's music, a bonfire in a metal barrel, a makeshift dance floor of wooden pallets.

They order bottles of beer and thick, buttery baguettes stuffed with crab meat. Nic tells Josie about the shop, and his year backpacking in Southeast Asia in his late teens, the two seasons diving in Thailand. Josie tells him how she always wanted to go traveling without feeling awkward about the very obvious reason why she never has, and they compare bucket lists. Goa. Cuba. The Philippines.

They're two drinks in by the time their food arrives, and an ease has fallen between them.

"You know," says Nic. "I always had the biggest crush on you when I was a kid."

Josie swallows a mouthful of baguette.

"You did not. Nobody had a crush on me."

"For real! When I was about twelve or thirteen. I basically thought you were the perfect woman."

"I dread to think what thirteen-year-olds look for in a woman."

"I just thought you were super cool. That day that you and Hannah first took me diving?" He let out a mock wolf whistle. "I didn't realize that girls did stuff like that, before then. Man, I was smitten."

"You were creepy *and* sexist when you were thirteen?" Josie says. "No wonder it took us this long to go on a date."

"I mean, I hadn't actually talked to many girls at that age, so my understanding of them was fairly skewed," says Nic. "Obviously, you and Hannah proved me wrong. You were always much braver than I was. Still are, probably."

Josie wipes her fingers on a paper napkin.

"Sorry to burst your dream-woman bubble," she says. "But I haven't been diving in years. I only ever really did because it came with the territory, if you were friends with Hannah."

Hannah had known the water. The best swimming spots and the best diving spots. She knew where the water was clear and safe and where there were jagged rocks right beneath the surface that could catch you and tear your skin to shreds.

"I'm not even sure I could do it now," she admits.

"'Course you could. It's like riding a bike. Hey, we could go tomorrow, if you like? Take the boat out, go for a swim around the bay? Diving optional."

Josie almost says no.

A date on her third day here was a crazy, out-of-character decision, but two dates in two days?

But then, she imagines the rise and fall of the waves. The cool, clean water.

"I can probably move a few things around in my diary," she says, with a slight upturn of her mouth that shows him what he surely already knows. That Josie doesn't have things to move around in her diary. That she doesn't even *have* a diary.

Nic raises his beer.

"It's a date," he says.

Josie raises hers back.

"It's *maybe* a date," she says, but he's already clinking his bottle against hers.

They order another round of drinks, and Josie can feel the world growing soft and dappled around them. Nic undoes his top shirt button, ruffles his hair. He looks good. She thinks how easy it would be to go home with him tonight, how uncomplicated. Someone who knows her past without her having to tell them. Without having to worry what they will think of her.

"So we don't have to talk about it, if you don't want to," says Nic. "But you coming back—is it anything to do with a certain documentary?"

Josie swallows the last bite of crab.

"You know about that?"

"Everyone knows about that. It's created a bit of a buzz round here, actually. Lots of people not happy about it. Not exactly good for business, your town being infamous as the site of a murder."

Josie wipes her fingers on a napkin.

"Maybe you're right," Josie says. "Maybe we don't have to talk about it."

"But that's why you're back?"

"Sort of," Josie says.

And then she surprises herself by telling him everything.

She tells him about getting an email from the producers a few months back, before the newspaper article that had changed everything. Their excitement about the social media storm that had revived the case. Their promises that *people were starting to see things differently now*. The way they had suggested, so casually, that Josie might be able to get hold of her case file.

You're the only person who can access key documentation about the investigation, the email had read. And believe me, we've tried! We think that this, combined with the renewed interest in the case, could shift the public's perception of what happened to Tamara Drayton.

She told him how she had initially ignored the email. The people from the production company were not the first who had contacted her. She had, when she had first been released from prison, agreed to a few interviews, hoping to be able to scrape together enough money for a new start. She had felt idiotic and humiliated when she'd seen the results. The worst had been a magazine spread by a journalist who had seemed so kind when they'd met up but had written the article as if they were entirely convinced of Josie's guilt. *When I meet Josie Jackson she has the look of someone who has seen and done the darkest imaginable things*, read the opening line. After that, Josie had decided that she would talk to nobody. So far, she'd stuck to her decision.

And yet, in spite of her insistence to Calvin that she wouldn't be participating, Josie had found herself filling out an application form to access her case file. She had told herself that it was nothing to do with the documentary. That it was a part of her legal history. No different, really, from how other people kept copies of their birth certificates or marriage licenses. That she would probably be denied access anyway. When she got a phone call to say that the file was awaiting collection, she had been as shocked as if she had never applied for it in the first place.

"And then when I got it, it just sat there, staring at me," Josie says. "Or at least, that's how it felt. All this information, and what was I meant to do with it? All this stuff that people have talked about, and posted about in stupid online forums, and speculated over for years, and now I had it. It would be mad to just keep it in a desk drawer, wouldn't it?"

"But you don't want to do the documentary?" Nic says.

"I *thought* I wanted to do the documentary," Josie says. "When I came back here, with the file, I'd sort of talked myself into it. Like, what did I have to lose?"

Nic nods.

"Right."

"But when I met up with that producer and she was asking me if I did it . . . it just sort of brought it all back. All the questions, and all the people doubting me. Why would I put myself through that again?"

"But you gave them the file."

"I didn't want it. In fact, I wanted it as far away from me as possible. And they wanted it, and . . . I don't know. I suppose it made sense, in the moment."

Nic leans in closer.

"But what if this documentary could actually be a good thing? It feels like these people are taking it seriously. What if this could change people's minds about what happened?"

Josie shakes her head.

"You don't understand," she says. "What they're like. How they twist your words. Turn the slightest thing you say against you. And besides, what are they going to do? Are they going to turn back time? Are they going to give me back all the years I spent in prison?"

Nic's mouth slides shut.

"Look, I've had years to come to terms with what happened," Josie says. "I know it must seem like this huge, big deal to everyone else. But to me, it's my life. I can't change it. All the worst things have already happened, and now it's time for me to move on."

"I get it," says Nic. "But what if people believed you this time? What if the police actually *did* reopen the case? What if they found out what really happened that day?"

"But what if they didn't? What happens if I put myself out there again, let everyone know where I am and what I'm doing, only for them to decide that I'm some evil kid killer all over again?" She can hear her voice rising, her words coming fast. "I've done that before. I've been through all of this. I am not going to let them tear me apart again."

"OK, OK." Nic holds his palms out flat toward her. "Look, you're right. We don't have to talk about it."

"I understand," says Josie. "Why this might seem like . . . I don't know. An opportunity. But honestly? I've seen this kind of thing dozens of times before. A new podcast, or some TV special comes out, and all of a sudden people go crazy about the case. But it doesn't change anything. It never does. And pretty soon, people forget. They move on, and I'm still here, still trying to put some semblance of a life together, still standing in the wreckage. That's what nobody understands."

Josie crumples her napkin, wilted with grease.

"At the end of the day, Nina Drayton has never changed her story," she says. "And as far as the record goes, she was the only witness."

She takes a deep breath. She is thinking about Tamara. She thinks of her often, even now. She can see her so clearly. Ripped jeans, even in the summer heat. The smell of cigarette smoke and perfume.

"I've had years to come to terms with this. Over half my life. As long as Nina Drayton says I'm guilty, I'm guilty. I've accepted it. I'm trying to move on. And I just wish everyone else would, too."

Nic looks thoughtful.

"But what if Nina *did* change her story? What if—"

"Hey, lovebirds!"

"Oh god," says Josie. "Don't tell me that's—"

"Fancy seeing you guys here."

Gabby swoops up to the table, dragging Calvin behind her.

"You look so cute together!"

"Sorry," says Calvin, red-faced. "We didn't realize you'd be here."

"You don't mind if we join you, do you?" Gabby is beaming, sliding into the seat next to Josie.

"Gabby." Calvin looks like he wants the ground to swallow him up. "They're on a D-A-T-E."

"I did actually do my exams in prison, you know," Josie says. "I know how to spell."

She glances at Nic, their unfinished conversation still hanging there, unsaid. There's a flicker of a discussion that passes between their eyes. *Is this OK with you?* The intimacy of it surprises her.

"It's cool," says Josie. "As long as you guys get the next round in."

"It's a deal," says Gabby. "Calvin. To the bar!"

※

The night is so different from what Josie is used to.

She is used to dark, discreet bars. Toilets with UV lighting. People who talk more than they listen. People who drink because they are trying to forget, rather than because they want to create a night worth remembering.

With Gabby and Calvin and Nic, it's easy. They play stupid drinking games, the kind that Josie never learned because she missed out on going to university and those late teenage years of bar hopping and trying to break the ice with strangers. They talk about work—easy, inconsequential problems about rude customers and late deliveries of stock. Gabby tells Josie about how she first visited the town as a teenager with her high school boyfriend, how they had fantasized about moving out here and opening up a café. How the dream outlasted Gabby's relationship, and she had come back alone thinking that she would stay for a summer, heal from heartbreak. Instead, she never left, a dream becoming her reality. It reminds Josie all over again how special, how magical this place can be. How it can take hold of your heart and refuse to let go.

When a song that Gabby loves comes on, she squeals and grabs Josie's hand, tugging her to the dance floor. Gabby dances with short, happy bounces, and briefly the two women catch hold of each other and spin round and round. Josie is tipsy enough not to feel self-conscious. The music is inside her, as deep as her bones, and she throws back her head and sings the lyrics at the top of her voice.

"Hey." Gabby pulls Josie close so that she can speak in her ear. Her eyes are shiny. "Calvin and I were talking before we came out. The girl who does the afternoon shift at the café is leaving next month. I was going to advertise, but—well. You need a job, right?"

Josie leans back. They are still swaying to the music, Gabby grinning and glowing, Josie temporarily dazed.

This could be her life, Josie thinks, with a flash of clarity. Spending the day at the café, in a job that she likes, where the work is hard and simple and thoughtless and honest. Coming down to the beach with a group of friends, people who know her. Care about her. Maybe even a boyfriend, someone who loves her in a straightforward, undemanding way. Evenings spent drinking and laughing. The past becoming a distant thing.

The thought has not quite fully formed before Josie trips, Gabby's borrowed dress tangled up around her legs. The two women collapse onto the sand, squealing and clutching at each other, a giggling heap of limbs.

"Alright, you guys." Calvin is there before they can stagger back to their feet, one arm looped beneath Gabby's to pull her up. "Think that you might have had enough to drink."

"But we're having so much *fun*," protests Gabby.

Then Nic is there, too, his hand gripping Josie's, pulling her up. His touch sends a flicker across the surface of her skin, and when she meets his eye, they both hold the gaze for just longer than is necessary.

"Actually," says Josie. "I am kind of tired. Maybe we should head home."

"How about it, Nic?" Calvin says, slapping him on the back. "Nightcap back at ours?"

There's a beat before Nic answers. A promise of what could come passing between him and Josie. The start of something. The startling optimism of their desire. Josie has learned not to expect anything from anyone. She has learned not to dream, but just now, she does. Just now, she lets herself lean into the hope.

"Yeah," Nic says. "I think that maybe I will."

※

They walk slowly, as if they have nowhere in the world to be.

Gabby and Calvin go on ahead, and Nic and Josie lag behind talking, the ambling, easy chatter of two people who've been drinking for the past two hours. Whose mouths are freed up, the intimacy of alcohol between them.

Josie tells Nic about how once, when she was in Paris, she shoplifted a handbag from a designer shop where the assistants were snooty and rude to her, and all of a sudden, the story feels funny rather than shameful, Nic laughing and letting out an impressed whistle and saying that she's basically an anti-capitalism activist. He tells her about a time when he slipped a bag of sweets into his pocket in a supermarket as a kid, and his dad marched him back to apologize later that day, and Josie feels genuinely sorry for the little boy that she imagines, embarrassed and repentant, and has an overwhelming urge to pull Nic in for a hug.

"I'm glad you came back," Nic says, when they're close to the house. "You feel like you belong here, you know?"

To Josie, who has not felt as if she belongs anywhere for a very long time, this feels like the kindest thing he could have possibly said.

Their fingers brush against each other as they turn onto the road leading up to the house, and Josie could swear that she feels an actual crackle of static pass between them. The promise of what comes next is palpable, electric. She is thinking of Nic touching her. Kissing her. She is, with this tiny, almost imperceptible moment of contact, mapping out an entire future for them.

She turns her face up toward his, wondering if this is it. If Nic might kiss her, right here in the street.

But Nic is not looking at her.

Instead his forehead is creased, his gaze fixed somewhere in the distance. His steps slow.

"Wait a second," he says. "Is that . . . ?"

His expression reconfigures, the shock sketched across his face.

"Oh shit," he says. "I think that's Nina Drayton."

SIXTEEN

2024

Nina knew that Ryan would be concerned when she suggested staying.

They were in Nina's childhood bedroom with its fresh white sheets and its cool stone walls, Nina's running gear discarded on the floor. She saw Ryan's eyes twitch toward the crumpled pile of leggings, wary, when she called him in. He would know, of course, that something must be wrong. Nina would never leave anything untidy. Disorder was not in Nina's nature.

"I just don't think there's any point flying back today," she said. "You already said that work doesn't need you in this week. And we're here now. Why not stay the weekend?"

"But the flights are already booked."

"We can change them. And look—" She took a deep breath in, ready to play her trump card. "Mum's birthday party is Saturday night. You know how much it means to her. We can stay for that, and go back early on Sunday."

"Nina," Ryan said slowly. "You said that you never wanted to go to one of your mum's birthday parties again."

"Well, I changed my mind."

She bent to pick up the pile of workout clothes, business-like.

"It might be fun," she said, her voice lighter than she felt. "And it'd be brownie points with Mum. Get her off my back for a bit."

"Nina—"

"You can go back, if work needs you. I don't mind flying on my own, and—"

"*Nina.*"

She looked up at him then, sitting on her bed, his hands laced together, his jaw tight.

"Please tell me," he said, "that you don't want to stay because of this documentary."

Nina folded her leggings in two even though they needed to go in the wash and there was little point making them neat.

"Of course not," she said. "I already told you. I'm not doing the documentary."

"Because your mum and Blake are right," Ryan said. "There's no good that can come of you putting yourself out there. It's done. It's best we leave it that way."

"That's not what you said back in London."

She turned her back on him, started to roll the leggings up into a tight, compact ball.

"What I said in London is that it would be a good idea to talk to your mum and Blake about it. Because I knew that Blake would talk sense. This documentary, Nina—there's only one way it can go, and it's badly. Putting your family under the microscope like that. Putting what *you* said—what you told the world—under the microscope. Nina. You'd be setting yourself up to be torn apart."

"Why?" Nina asked, still not looking at him. "Do you think that if I let them put what I said under a microscope, they'd find out it wasn't true?"

There was a moment of silence. A moment where the only sound was the soft fabric shifting through Nina's hands as she rolled and unrolled the leggings.

"You know I don't think that," Ryan said at last.

"But what if I *was* wrong?" Nina said. "Would I have the

responsibility to find that out? Would I have the responsibility to tell the truth now?"

Another silence. This time, Nina turned to face her boyfriend. He was looking straight at her. He looked, she thought, unbearably sad.

"Anyway," she said brightly. "It doesn't matter. It's not about the documentary. It's a beautiful day, and I don't want to spend it in an airport."

"Nina—"

"Just a few more days, OK? Just a few more days, and we'll go back home."

He hesitated. She could see him thinking. Could see his eyes twitch as he watched her. Trying to figure her out.

"Promise me," he said. "That you're not going to go looking for something."

"Looking for what?"

"I don't know. Something. I don't want you getting obsessed with this. I don't want you to go looking for Josie Jackson."

Nina scoffed.

"Why would I go looking for Josie Jackson?" she asked. "Josie Jackson is the last person I want to see."

And now, Nina stands across from Josie Jackson, and the first thing she thinks is that she has lied to Ryan. Another break in her family, because of this woman. Another reason why she has to make this count.

The second thing she thinks is that she *knows* this woman, an enormous sense of déjà vu that disappears as soon as she arrives.

But then, in a way, Nina *does* know this woman. She has said her name over and over, every time she has explained the death of her sister. She has stood across from her in a courtroom, as she told a story that would change both their lives. She doesn't remember a time before she knew Josie Jackson.

And now, when Nina looks at Josie Jackson, she is five years old again.

She is out by the pool, the sun against her skin, Josie strapping her into her armbands.

She is six years old, standing in that courtroom, the drawing of her sister's death in front of her.

She is seven, and eight, and sixteen, and twenty-one. She is all the ages of her life when she did not have a sister. When she knew that the story she had told had changed this woman's life. When both of their existences were irrevocably rerouted from what they could have been, all because of what did, or did not happen, on that hot August day twenty years ago.

"Josie," Nina says.

But Josie is already stepping back from her. Her eyes are wide. Her mouth, a set line. She looks, Nina thinks, like something preparing to pounce. To fight for its life.

"Josie," says Nina again. "I think we need to talk."

※

Nina expects to be invited inside, but instead Josie leads her to a threadbare patch of ground at the side of the house. There's a rusted metal table and chairs, an ashtray, a light that trembles with a too-white brightness when they walk beneath it. An olive tree, its trunk ancient and knotted.

A man, who must be Josie's brother, hovers for a moment until Josie tells him he can go.

"We'll be right inside," he says, his arms folded across his chest. "If you need us."

Nina thanks him, even though she knows he isn't talking to her. It is clear that the offer only extends to Josie.

They sit opposite each other. It strikes Nina, as she lowers into the uncomfortable seat, how ordinary this woman looks. Josie Jackson has always been the ghost in everything that Nina's family says and does, but now it occurs to Nina that she could probably pass this woman in a supermarket without a second glance. She is so much smaller than Nina had thought of her as. Freckles along the lengths of her arms. A bad blond dye job. A thick, straight line of dark roots against the white of her scalp. A small, heart-shaped necklace resting in the center of her chest.

Nina waits until Josie's brother has disappeared behind the house before she speaks. Josie's eyes are staunch. Wary. She doesn't break Nina's gaze.

"I almost couldn't find this place," Nina says, trying to keep her voice light. Trying to put Josie at ease. "I was convinced I was waiting at the wrong house."

It isn't just small talk. The walk really had taken her longer than she expected, her calves aching with the tilt of the hill. She had imagined Patricia Jackson as she climbed, a woman whose face she knew more from newspaper articles than memory, walking this road every single day. Before the sun came up, and long after it set.

She had imagined Josie, just sixteen, trudging up the path to babysit Nina when she should have been doing all the things that sixteen-year-olds do—going to parties and falling in love with the wrong people; sneaking alcohol and staying out too late. All the things that Nina had missed out on, too; her once permissive mother overprotective, after what had happened with Tamara; the notoriety of her name preceding her in every new friendship, interrupting every teenage crush. Her anxiety and the creeping, terrible fears that so often slipped between her and many of the teenage experiences she should have had. Her mother keeping her home from school when her worries felt particularly sharp, entire terms learned from textbooks. The psychiatrist appointments and chemists and one terrible stay at a private hospital for teenage girls who were, as Evelyn said, "unbalanced." Nina had looked at the other girls with horror, their wasted bodies from starving themselves, their skin scratched with the same compulsions that Nina suffered from, their dazed expressions from the cocktails of medications that were handed out with breakfast. She hated that she saw herself in them. That she, like Josie, was locked away.

But the similarities between Nina and Josie ended there. For Nina, there had been recovery. The relative freedom of her late teens and early twenties. University. A relationship. The promise of a career. Things that Josie likely never got to have. The guilt of it filled Nina up in the same way that it did when she was a small child, immediately after the trial. Josie Jackson had served ten years in prison, a stretch of time that had been unimaginable to six-year-old Nina. Now, she understands all the things that can be lost in ten years. All the things that her words took away from Josie Jackson.

"I'm not here to cause trouble," Nina says.

One of Josie's eyebrows lifts, disbelieving.

"I'm not," says Nina. "I just want to talk. You've probably seen everything that's been happening online. People talking about Tamara again. About the case."

Josie shrugs.

"I don't really bother with all that stuff," she says. "Social media."

"Right," Nina says. "Well, there's been this online video series. And it's attracted a lot of attention. And—"

Josie is holding up one hand to stop her.

"I said I'm not on social media, not that I live in a hole," she says. "I know what's going on. And I can take a pretty good guess why you're here. You've heard about the documentary, and you're scared that something's going to come out, right? You're scared I'm going to participate, and I'm going to say something that will make everyone doubt what really happened."

She pushes back her chair.

"Well, you don't need to worry," she says. "I'm not doing the documentary. And I wouldn't have anything new to say if I did. So if that's why you're here, I don't think we have anything to say to each other. You can rest assured that I'm not going to be the one to call you out."

"No," says Nina. "That's not what I want."

Josie tilts her head to one side, an almost imperceptible motion. This is it, Nina thinks. This is the moment when she says the thing that has always scared her the most. The thing that she has always been afraid to say, even to herself.

"I don't remember what happened that day," she says, the words coming out in a rush. "I don't. I remember patches—little pieces—but I don't remember finding Tamara. I don't remember seeing you . . . you hurting her. And the bits that I do remember. They're so murky. Like looking at something through stained glass. I'm not sure if they're real memories, or memories of memories that have got all mixed up and distorted over time, or if I'm only remembering the stories that I've been told since—"

She breaks off, out of breath. It is the thing she has never said out loud. The thing that she has barely admitted, even to herself. In spite of the essays, and the seminars, and her intricate understanding of memory. This is the thing that none of her research and lecturers have been able to answer.

She cannot, even now, describe how it feels, the muddle of images, the tangled-up thoughts. The childlike sketch that she still sometimes wakes up in the middle of the night visualizing. The obsessions, and the anxiety, and the self-loathing that pile up inside her. A mother who went from neglectful to overbearing, seemingly in the blink of an eye. A brother who still seems to be missing part of himself. A sister that Nina will never know. So many lives, all sent ricocheting in one day, one moment.

And then, a singular, still image of Josie pushing Tamara beneath the water.

"The story is there," Nina says. "I just don't know how to access it. And maybe I *can't* access it. Maybe it's gone, and the more I go over it in my mind, the further away from the truth I get."

There's a moment when neither of them speaks.

"Right," says Josie slowly. "And what do you think that I can do about it, exactly?"

"I want you to tell me everything about that night," Nina says. "Everything you can remember."

Josie lets out a sharp bolt of laughter.

"Why?" she says. "I've already told my side of the story. I told the truth in court. I don't have anything new to say."

"I just thought . . ." Nina hesitates. "You were there that day. And so was I. And maybe if we could just put our stories together, we might be able to find out the truth?"

Josie is already shaking her head.

"This is real life," she says. "It's not some kind of detective drama. It's not a game of Cluedo. We can't just put all the clues together and miraculously find the answer."

"Josie, please," Nina says. "Please. I just need to hear it from you. I just need to know. Where were you when I found Tamara? Why would I say that you did it?"

Josie sighs deeply.

"I've said all this a thousand times before," she says. "I wasn't anywhere near the pool when it happened. I wasn't even near the house. I was down on the beach—the private beach you go down the steps at the back of the house to get to? I was looking for you. You'd wandered off and I—I was worried. I thought you might have slipped away, down to the sea. It's a long way down, you know that. I would have been gone awhile. And by the time I got back up—it was crazy. They'd found Tamara in the water. Everyone was freaking out. I'd missed the whole thing."

Nina waits for more. There must be more. This can't be everything. It can't all come down to this.

"And as for why you would have said it," Josie says. "I don't know. I've thought about it over and over again, but I barely even spoke to Tamara that night. You couldn't possibly have seen us together. I just don't have an answer for you. I wish I did."

"That can't be it," Nina says. "There must be something else. If you didn't do it, there would be something—"

"I told you," Josie says. Her voice is sharp, and Nina feels the brief confidence between them break, Josie defensive again. "It's not a detective show. It's real life."

"But I thought . . ."

Not thought, exactly. Hoped. Hoped for something new, something definitive, something that would hold the truth together.

Josie starts to stand.

"It's late," she says. "You should go."

"I'm going to do it," Nina says in a rush. "The documentary. I've told the producers I'm going to do it."

Josie looks at her like she's crazy to think she would care.

"So?" she says. "Your funeral, not mine."

"Why are you back?" Nina says. "If it's not the documentary, then why are you back?"

Josie lets out a long, exasperated sigh.

"Honestly? I didn't have anywhere else to go. And I thought . . ." she trails off, shaking her head. "I don't know what I thought. But whatever it was, I was wrong. This place isn't good for me. I never should have come back here."

Nina swallows. This place isn't good for any of them. Too many memories, too much pain.

Josie straightens fully.

"I'm sorry about your sister," she says. "I always was. But you can't fix things, Nina. Not for me. It's too late to take back what you said."

@TRUECRIMEFANGIRL_2002
POSTED THREE WEEKS AGO

Hey, true crime babies. Me again! You're back watching my series on the unaliving of Tamara Drayton. And boy, you guys have been loving this series. Loving it! In fact, these videos have been the most popular since my JonBenét Ramsey series, and I know how much you little freaks loved that one.

But you guys seriously need to relax in the comments. Because these videos have attracted some people who are obviously not real true-crimers, saying we need to chill out, and that it's—I don't know—gross to be talking about someone's death like this or something? But you guys need to understand that we do this because we care. Because, at its heart, that's the point of our true crime community, right? We are all about cracking forgotten cases wide open and bringing new information to light, and hopefully getting justice for people. Seriously.

And yeah, we have a bit of fun with it along the way, but that's how we get attention for our cases, OK? So I do not appreciate all the commenters calling me a voyeur, or a tragedy whore, or whatever.

But look, I read my comments. I really do read each and every one of them. And trust me, I have seen the people who have been coming for me, saying that I'm biased, saying that I'm ignoring anything that supports Josie Jackson being Tamara Drayton's killer. So I want to be fair with you guys. I want to switch things up today, and go over all of the evidence that Josie unalived Tamara Drayton.

Because I am nothing if not fair to these victims. And that's what it's all about really, isn't it? Making sure these victims get their stories heard. So let's get into it, and talk about why people think that Josie Jackson is guilty.

So the biggest piece of evidence used at trial was the testimony of little Nina Drayton. Needless to say, that was the smoking gun. Pretty much all the other evidence against Josie was circumstantial. But sure, there's some stuff that's hard to explain away.

So, first of all, there's the relationship between Josie and Tamara. I have a whole separate video about this. I'll link so that you can check it out, but turns out these guys actually knew each other a lot more than either of them had let on to other people, and there was a pretty complicated history there. Enough, some might say, to give Josie a motive for killing Tamara.

Now, second of all, Josie's fingerprints were found in Tamara's room. And this might not sound like a big deal, but Evelyn swore up and down that Josie *never* went into Tamara's room. Tamara was pretty private, and her room was usually locked. The prosecutor suggested that after killing Tamara, Josie might have gone up to her room to dispose of evidence—remember the ten-minute time slot that I talked about before? Tamara's diary was recovered, but numerous pages appeared to have been torn out of it, and Josie's fingerprints were found on the drawer where the diary was kept. Could Josie have ripped out the missing pages? Could there have been incriminating evidence inside that diary?

Another thing that's interesting is that a big part of Josie's defense was that she was completely dry when she was arrested. Her clothes weren't wet, she didn't have a bathing suit with her, she didn't look like someone who had just been in a pool. Now, this is huge, and you'll see it mentioned in absolutely any post or podcast defending Josie Jackson. It's actually the thing that got me on to the case in the first place. But when police were searching Tamara's room several days later, they also found a discarded swimsuit which was covered in Josie's DNA. Like, we're talking so much that she *had* to have been wearing it. But here's what's weird. That swimsuit—it actually belonged to Tamara. Did Josie get into the pool wearing that swimsuit, and then change back into her own clothes before anyone could find Tamara?

So, look, I get that this is a lot to process, a lot of information. But I would love to know what you guys think. Are you team Josie? Or does this stuff change your mind? You know where I stand. Let me know in the comments, and don't forget to like and follow if you want more juicy details on this story.

Crimebusta: TEAM JOSIE!!!

Helena_murderess: Yeah, like, this stuff could so easily be explained away.

Holistichealing89: I mean, honestly, this is making me question everything. Sure, that stuff is circumstantial, but along with the Nina Drayton stuff? It sounds pretty watertight to me . . .

Adrianna3210: This case honestly drives me CRAZY. Tamara Drayton was found fully clothed, but Josie was supposedly wearing this swimming costume? That doesn't fit with what Nina Drayton said. None of it makes any sense! Thanks for giving me another sleepless night trying to figure this out 💀

SEVENTEEN

2004
FIVE WEEKS BEFORE THE BIRTHDAY PARTY

Josie knew, although she would never say it, that Hannah felt sorry for her.

She saw it in the way that Hannah always looked at her with a sympathetic tilt of her head when Hannah did better at school. How Hannah always tried to excuse the fact that she still lived with both her parents by complaining too much about her dad, talking about the fights that often brewed at home with an eagerness that made Josie suspect she was trying to make her feel better about her own parents' divorce. The way that she extended the invites that Blake Drayton occasionally tossed out to her as if she was doing Josie a favor.

Sometimes, Josie wondered if she and Hannah would ever have become friends if Josie hadn't encountered her on her way to the sea in those hazy first few weeks in France. If this meeting, along with the fact that they were both outcasts at the money-soaked school over the hill, had thrown them together far more than any shared interests or commonalities. She suspected that, in another world—back in England, perhaps—the two of them would not have become close at all.

As summer drew to a height, the crowds on the beaches thickening, the sea bloating with swimmers, Josie barely saw Hannah. Hannah said that it was because she was busy at the dive shop, helping her parents out, but Josie knew. She always knew more than Hannah thought she did.

Besides, Josie was busy, too. She was at the pink house most days, babysitting Nina. Evelyn was even more frantic than usual, her quest to hold Harrison's interest giving her a frenzied, manic air as she planned nights out at romantic restaurants, days when she would give Josie a handful of cash to keep Nina busy and entertained.

Josie pocketed most of the money, amused by how demanding Evelyn must imagine her five-year-old daughter to be. Instead, she took Nina down to the beach to paddle in the shallows. She took her to a cheap burger joint and laughed at Nina's evident delight at the mounds of fries and sickly sweet ice cream milkshakes. She took her to the small art deco cinema in the town, a relic of the resort's past, and promised her popcorn if she was good for the entire film.

Once, Tamara, seemingly running out of things to do when her mother demanded a free house, joined them. They went to get pizza at a place usually filled with locals. They sat at the Formica table, Nina swinging her legs between them, a pizza slice the size of her head clutched in both hands.

"What's your brother doing tonight?" Josie had asked.

Tamara took a sip of Pepsi through a plastic straw.

"I think you know the answer to that," she said.

"Do I?"

Josie was feigning ignorance, of course. She wanted to see what Tamara would say. She wanted to know what she thought.

"He's with your friend. Hannah."

Tamara said the word *friend* as if it was too large for her throat. As if she had to force it out.

"Is that a problem?"

Josie's defensiveness was quick, even though she also hated Hannah hanging out with Blake. It was one thing for Josie to think that Blake was no good for Hannah. It was another for Tamara to think that Hannah was no good for her twin.

Tamara peeled a string of cheese from a slice of margherita.

"So what if it is?" she said.

"Because." Josie could feel a spark of anger beneath her words. "He's not better than her, you know. Blake should consider himself lucky to be with someone like Hannah."

Tamara paused, the cheese still pinched between two fingers, inches from her mouth. Josie had noticed that the Draytons had a habit of playing with their food. Her mother was always complaining about the plates that returned, fillings picked out of otherwise untouched sandwiches, pieces of meat cut into minute pieces but uneaten.

"It's not Blake I'm worried about," Tamara said, so quietly that Josie thought she might have misheard her.

"Josie," Nina said. "Can we get chocolate ice cream?"

Tamara stood, her pizza still practically intact.

"I'm going to head back," she said.

"Tamara?" Josie said. "What do you mean?"

But Tamara was already bending down, mussing up her little sister's hair.

"I'll see you back at home, Neens," she said, in a voice that was entirely different. Softer. "You be good for Josie, yeah?"

EIGHTEEN

2024

When Josie wakes up, there is a moment when she is not sure where she is.

The fact does not alarm her. Instead, she feels only mild curiosity. Impermanence is a natural state for Josie. She is used to unfamiliar beds, places she only stays in for a couple of nights or a few weeks before fading into strange and disjointed memories when she tries to recall them. The place where the key always got stuck. The place where the electricity flickered off if you tried to use the microwave and the television at the same time. The place that had a meter for hot water, and Josie would have to search for spare coins when she realized it had run out.

Then, her thoughts recalibrate. Shift into place. She is not in her small shared flat in Paris anymore. She is not in the hostel she moved to when calculating the logistics of coming home, staying in her room, bleaching her hair so that nobody would recognize her from the newspaper article that had blown apart the scraps of a life she had spent years gathering together. She is back in her childhood bedroom. Her brother is probably still asleep next door.

She rolls over, and everything pulls more sharply into focus. The memories from last night arrive, clear and startling.

The drinks. Dancing on the sand. The warmth of Nic's body as she walked beside him.

Nina Drayton, waiting for them outside the house.

She sits upright then, her stomach turning over, a combination of too many beers and the image of little Nina, all grown up, sitting out on their patio.

Josie has imagined so many times what she might say to Nina Drayton, if she ever saw her. She has thought of the girl that she used to know. The things that she said. She has wanted, so many times, to ask Nina if she remembers the long summer days that they spent together, before Tamara drowned. And then, last night, she had barely been able to speak. She let the fury that had been building up within her for years take over.

She found herself unable to look in the face of the woman that Nina had become.

※

Gabby is making breakfast when there's a knock on the door. The three of them still. Calvin's hand hovers midway to the coffee pot. Gabby turns off the hob, a pan already spitting. They don't get visitors.

"Maybe it's Nic?" Gabby says, a trace of hope in her voice.

Josie knows that it isn't. She has been waiting for this. She has known, somehow, ever since she came back, that this would happen.

"I'll go," says Calvin.

"No, *I'll* go," says Gabby, wiping her hands on a tea towel. "I can say you're not here, if it's . . ."

She doesn't finish the sentence. That is how Josie knows that the two of them have been waiting for this, too.

Gabby goes out into the hallway. They hear the click of the latch. The name of the newspaper that the man announces. The pause before Gabby responds.

"Josie Jackson?" she says, as if she doesn't recognize the name.

"I got a tip-off that she might be back?" the reporter says. "I drove down right away. With all the renewed attention on the case, the timing was just perfect."

Gabby's voice comes out clear this time, strong.

"You think Josie Jackson would come back?" she says. "With the way people feel about her round here?"

"The person who called this in was absolutely certain," the reporter says. "Said they used to know her when she was a kid, and they spotted her in town yesterday. I figured she must be staying here. This *is* still her family home, right?"

"That's private information," says Gabby.

"Any idea if she's back in town? You haven't heard anything?"

"I told you, there's no chance Josie Jackson would be back here. She'd be run out of town."

"Well, if you do hear anything . . ."

"I won't."

When she rounds back into the kitchen, Josie and Calvin are silent at the table.

"He's gone," she says. "I just watched him drive off. Don't look so worried."

She bustles back to the hob, presses down on the gas ignition.

"He'll be back," says Josie.

A ring of blue flames blooms beneath the frying pan.

"You don't know that," says Calvin. "It's one rogue reporter. It doesn't mean anything."

"How many eggs do you both want?" Gabby says, picking up a fork from the countertop in a voice that suggests the conversation is over.

And because Josie doesn't want to ruin things—because she doesn't want to spoil Gabby and Calvin's morning off, doesn't want to splinter this small fantasy of normality—she asks for two eggs, please. She doesn't mention the reporter again. She doesn't tell Calvin how naïve he's being. She doesn't tell them that, in the moment she heard the name of the newspaper, she felt the small dream that she had allowed to take root last night fall away. That she knows, even though neither of them will say it, that Gabby won't want her working in the café now that people are looking for her. That she probably won't even be able to *go* to the café anymore, or to the beach. That she'll have to find somewhere new to live, because she knows that it isn't fair on Calvin to stay here. To drag him through this all over again.

She doesn't, as she wants to, tell Calvin that they have the capacity to ruin your life, these people. That once they find you, they won't leave you alone. That word of where you are, and what you are doing, will spread like mold blooming across the surface of food left out in the heat. That once they have you, they won't let you go.

Instead, Josie eats eggs and bread. She drinks coffee. She holds on to this moment, this tiny slice of tranquility—a Saturday morning breakfast, a mug of fresh coffee—because she knows how fragile it is. She knows how quickly it will pass.

She knows, already, that her time here is running out.

※

After breakfast, Josie walks alone to a rocky outcrop that sprawls out beyond the beach, far from the hordes of people who fill the sand.

It was somewhere that she and Hannah used to go often, all those years ago. Josie has lost count of the days that they spent stretched out on the bleached white rock, hoping that their skin would turn the exact right shade of tan instead of taking on the pink hue of sunburn. Paddling in pools among limpets and crabs with their claws braced up, strings of seaweed like dark, glistening pearls. Talking about their plans to get out of here, Josie to faraway and unfamiliar places, Hannah to England.

It was there that Josie had seen Blake Drayton for the first time. He had been standing in a circle of friends, a portable speaker breaking the peace, rupturing the serenity of Josie and Hannah's secret, special place. Josie had noticed how Hannah's body tensed when she saw him, how she rushed to rearrange herself, rolling over and putting a towel over the almost invisible folds of her stomach.

"Who are you trying to impress?" Josie had asked.

Hannah had looked at her like she was mad.

"You must have heard people talk about the Draytons?" she had said.

It was the first time that Josie had heard their name.

It had been the year that Josie moved to France, the single summer tinged with optimism for her family. Her dad had just started to make good money. Her mum was talking about starting up a business out there, perhaps doing nails or hair for the kind of women who would pay well for the service.

Josie's stomach aches when she thinks of the hope they all had. How her mother had practiced French tips on her and Hannah at the kitchen table. How the nail polishes and drying lamp that she had bought then sat abandoned in the hallway cupboard for years after Josie's dad left, her mother having to take any work that she could get.

Everyone said that they should go back home to England after he walked out, but Patricia Jackson was determined to show that they could manage on their own. She said Josie and Calvin would have a better quality of life here. She heard rumors that some employers were so desperate for British staff, so unwilling to mix with the locals, that they would pay the fees at the expensive international school over the hill as part of their employment contract. That was how Patricia Jackson ended up spending her days catering to the whims of the Draytons. It was all supposed to make things better for them, to give Josie and Calvin the best shot possible. Josie didn't fail to see the irony in the way things had turned out.

Josie hadn't known when her mother got sick. She was living in Paris by the time Patricia was diagnosed with ovarian cancer, after months of putting off going to the doctor. Josie called home rarely, and when she did, her mother was always bright. Cheerful. Asking Josie when she would come and visit. Josie never did, even though she often said she would. Back then, the thought of returning had still been unbearable. She was ashamed of how little she had to show for the years she'd been out of prison. She was afraid of seeing the disappointment in her mother's eyes—to see her realize that, despite all the sacrifices she had made, her daughter had made nothing of herself.

Calvin only told Josie right at the end. Patricia had been admitted to a hospital in Nice, he said in a hurried phone call. Things were much worse than they had thought. They didn't have long left.

Josie tried to get to her mother, a frantic, multiple-train, cross-country trip. She arrived an hour too late. Calvin's mouth had been a furious, hard line when he saw her. She went to hug him, and his body had been stiff.

"You don't know what it's been like," he told her.

The funeral was held in England, which felt like a huge insult to Josie. After all those years of working herself to the bone, trying to build a life for them on the Azure Coast, Patricia Jackson had ended up cremated in a squat brick building next to a Kent A-road on a rainy Tuesday afternoon. Gray skies; triangle sandwiches and sausage rolls; a wake held at a working men's club.

Josie hadn't spoken to many people there. She sat in the corner with a paper plate in her lap, finding it easy to not meet anyone's eye. It turned out that nobody really wanted to talk to her either.

It was only afterward, when just she and Calvin were left, that he collapsed into her arms, holding her tightly. It was the first time all day that Josie was glad she came.

They spoke more, after that: Josie started to call her brother, just to chat. Sometimes about nothing in particular. Sometimes about their mother, or people that they both used to know. Sometimes, about that summer.

Talking to Calvin, Josie's recollections of the childhood she spent by the sea began to pull at her in a way they hadn't in years. Good memories began overwriting some of the bad ones. Hours spent on the beach. The rare afternoons when Patricia was off work, and they would take a picnic down to the sand. The slow, sleepy way those days seemed to unfold, the sun tracking their progress across the sky. Josie grew sick of the city, and the fact that she never seemed to see the sun. She missed her mother in a way that she had never imagined she could.

Josie wanted to go home, and for the first time in years, she felt like she knew where that was.

※

Josie almost cancels on Nic that night.

Their preplanned date feels pointless now. She feels foolish for even letting herself imagine that she might have been able to go on a second date with someone. That she might be able to mimic the rhythms of an ordinary life, when her life is so far from ordinary.

She knows now that she will have to leave soon, and she will forget about Nic, and she cannot stand the thought of pretending otherwise. Pretending that this is the start of something, rather than the end.

But then, she thinks of how, years ago, she, Hannah, and Nic would borrow Hannah's parents' boat off-season. How they would take sandwiches and cans of sugary drinks and spend the entire day diving, coming up with salt in their hair and sun on the back of their necks. She remembers the peace of the water, the feeling that she would sometimes get when she was breathing beneath the sea. Impossibility and wonder all at once.

By the time Josie arrives, the beach is quiet, the crowds cleared out. Only a few stragglers remain, cracking open bottles of beer, pulling T-shirts over their swimming costumes as the heat bleeds out of the day.

"You look good," Nic says, even though Josie has opted for a baseball cap and one of Calvin's oversized T-shirts pulled over a borrowed wetsuit, the closest thing she could muster to a disguise.

He leans down to kiss her on the cheek, and Josie feels a heat in her face. The fact that they didn't sleep together last night—didn't even kiss—hangs in the air between them. She briefly imagines how things might have gone, if they hadn't bumped into Nina Drayton. The dance between the kitchen and the bedroom, the anticipation, the flirtation, the moment when their bodies finally touched.

She imagines how this morning might have been. The awkwardness of waking up next to a stranger. She knows it so well: the sense that somebody badly wants you to leave. The next-day understanding that you have nothing more to say to each other, the hazy magic of the night before turned to dust.

Or, she dares to imagine, there might have been the rare, tentative delight of waking up next to someone and feeling the start of something, rather than the end. They would, perhaps, have sat outside drinking coffee together, a little embarrassed, a little excited. Touching each other whenever they could. Letting their fingers linger when

Josie handed Nic a mug. A brush of his hand against her waist. Her foot making idle contact with his leg.

Instead, Nic's lips bump against her skin, the kiss misjudged, and Josie feels a flush of awkwardness. As if she imagined the crackle of something between them last night, the way the air felt tight and steeped with promise and ease.

"You don't look very ready for diving," she says, pulling back, self-conscious.

He's wearing a loose-fitting shirt, a pair of board shorts. He grins, looking slightly bashful.

"Actually," he says. "That's part of the surprise."

"I hate surprises."

"Well, I think you might like this one."

He reaches out and takes her hand, the unexpected contact making her flinch.

"Come on," he says. "I'll show you at the boat."

As they cross the beach to the small dock, Josie thinks how strange they must look together: she dressed for a dive, he as if going out for drinks. She is agonizingly aware of the glances that they must be attracting.

"There's a lot of people around," she says warily.

"Don't worry," Nic says. "We're going somewhere completely private."

He squeezes her hand.

"We're almost there. In fact, if you just look that way . . ."

She recognizes the boat at once. The same one that Hannah's parents used to take tourists out on, all those years ago, her father's pride and joy, looking a little more run-down now, but unmistakably the same. Hannah hadn't been allowed to drive it, and the three of them had taken the smaller, scrappier speedboat out when they were kids. But now, Nic proudly extends one hand to guide her aboard.

"Ladies first," he says.

"Do we really need the big boat, for just the two of us?" Josie asks, embarrassed by the extravagance.

He laughs.

"It's my boat now," he says. "Came with the territory, when I took the business over. Besides. I wanted tonight to be special."

"Oh?"

He grins at her.

"Come on," he says. "I'll show you."

He leads her to the front of the boat where the bow stretches out toward the sea. An unbroken view of the amber-colored sky, the water reflecting back the yellow-red glow.

"Surprise," he says, his voice soft, close to her ear.

There, spread out in front of them, is a picnic blanket. A hamper. A bottle of champagne, two glasses waiting next to an ice bucket. A bowl of strawberries. A beautiful, perfect setup for a date. The most romantic thing that anyone has ever done for Josie.

The sight of it makes her heart sink.

"Do you like it?" he says.

He sounds so pleased with himself, so excited.

"It's—"

"I know it's a bit clichéd, strawberries and champagne and all that stuff. But I thought after the disaster that our first date turned into, I wanted to push the boat out. No pun intended."

"Nic, it's—"

"And we can always go diving another time. But I just thought, for tonight—"

"Nic."

She says it too loudly, too sharply. He stops talking, his mouth still open, a hopeful smile still hovering on his lips.

"It's too much," she says.

He pauses, looking down at the picnic and then back up at her.

"Is it the champagne?" he says with a small wince. "Honestly, it's only one of the cheap ones. I didn't spend a fortune on it."

"It's not the champagne, it's . . ."

Her skin feels too hot, and she wonders if she caught the sun earlier. She gestures toward the picture-perfect setup.

"It's all of it," she says. "The whole thing. It's . . ."

She's struggling to find the words. Struggling to put it in a way that won't hurt him.

"Well. This is something that you do for someone that you really like."

"But I do—"

"No." She holds her palms flat out toward him. "Don't say it."

"I . . ." He looks again between the picnic blanket and Josie, as if searching for a response. As if there's something fundamental that he's missed, some answer that might be hiding behind the bowl of strawberries. "I don't understand," he says at last. "I thought we had a good time last night. I thought we had a lot of fun. I thought that if Nina hadn't turned up . . . well. It felt like it was maybe going somewhere."

"You're right," Josie says. There's something heavy and solid in her throat. "You don't understand."

The sea is calm, but still she feels her legs brace as if prepared for a great wave.

"I can't do this."

"The picnic? Or this?" He gestures one hand between them both.

"Any of it," she says. "I don't know what you want from me, but it's too much."

"I don't want anything from you," he says. "I just thought that we clicked. I thought this seemed like something that could go somewhere. That maybe we could just see where it goes—"

"But that's exactly the problem. I don't have the luxury of being able to just *see where things go*."

Josie closes her eyes, briefly, and takes a deep breath in. When she opens them, he's still there, still looking at her, forehead furrowed.

"You don't understand what my life is like, Nic. It's not like yours, or Gabby's, or Calvin's, or anyone else's. I can never just see where things go, because they always, always go wrong, in the end."

"What do you mean?"

"I mean you want more from me than I can give, Nic. I can't do relationships. I can't do falling in love, or thinking about the future, because in the end, I always have to leave. You'll end up hating me, and I'll end up having my heart broken. It's just how it is. It's how it always has been, for me."

He doesn't say anything. His mouth, poised open as if ready to leap in with a defense, shuts.

"I think I should be getting back," Josie says quietly.

She sees him swallow, the bob of his throat.

"If that's what you want to do," he says. "I'm not going to stop you."

"Fine."

"Great."

"It's not you, Nic, really. It's me."

It's always me, she thinks. Always ruining things. Always hurting anyone who comes close.

He's already turned away from her. He starts to gather up the picnic blanket, packing the champagne back into the hamper.

"I'm sorry," she says.

She isn't sure that he hears her.

She turns and walks away.

She is almost certain that she will never see Nic again.

NINETEEN

2024

For the second day in a row, Nina has not slept.

All night, she lay awake. She relived the conversation with Josie, over and over. Tried to quantify what it meant to her, how it had felt, to see the woman who had killed her sister. Or at least, who Nina had long believed had killed her sister.

Sometime around 2 A.M., Ryan clambered out of the bed, sleepy and stiff, complaining that Nina's restlessness was keeping him awake. He shuffled out, carrying his pillows to one of the spare bedrooms. Nina hadn't cared, hadn't even apologized. Instead, she pulled open the curtains so that the room was lit by the soft, silver light of the moon. Not for the first time, she longed for the cacophony of pills that she used to take. Something to slow her heartbeat, and ease her into the release of sleep.

Instead, she was left with her own thoughts which, it felt, were slowly driving her mad.

She kept going over and over the meeting with Josie Jackson. When she thought about it, the thing that struck her the most was how Josie had stood: her body braced, her legs shoulder width apart, her hands firmly by her side.

It was the kind of position that Nina counseled clients to adopt in confrontational situations, to show inner strength. The kind of pose that someone who was certain of themselves might naturally fall into.

Meanwhile, Nina's own hands had been knotted in front of her. Her spine had been hunched and apologetic. It was not the stance of someone facing the woman who had killed her sister.

The body remembers what the mind does not. Nina really believes that. It's what she always told her clients, when she was in her final year of training. And when she stood in front of Josie, her body was not afraid. It was not defiant. Her body did not tell Nina that she was standing in front of a murderer.

For the first time, Nina felt sure that she did not see Josie kill Tamara.

And now she can't stop thinking about what she might have seen instead.

With the sun beginning to set on the evening of Evelyn's birthday party—an entire day survived without sleep—Nina should feel exhausted. Instead, she feels invigorated. Full of fury and drive.

The house is already full of guests, and for once Nina doesn't care about making a good impression. The thought of making small talk and eating a tiny, measured portion of cake and then worrying about how many steps she'll have to take to burn it off later feels ridiculous.

Instead, she sits alone on the terrace, a bottle of wine on the ground beside her. The air has a heaviness that comes before rain, the sky clouded and yellow, the sea dark. Her mother's party guests have crowded inside the house, afraid that they'll get caught up in the storm. Abandoning the champagne station that her mother had set out in the garden, the crudités arranged on a long table on the front balcony.

Nina knows that Evelyn will be annoyed by the weather. That tomorrow she will be in a foul mood that will seep through the house. But for now, the pink house glows and teems with people. Through the window, Nina can just spot her mother, resplendent in a fuchsia dress as the room hums around her, a queen bee at the heart of a swarm. Nina drains her glass and pours another. There is a frisson of exhaustion that pulsates beneath her skin. Her body is in survival mode now, running on borrowed reserves of energy. Her mind is foggy from the wine, and the lack of sleep, and the same thoughts that skitter through her head like electrical currents. *Josie Jackson. Tamara. The pool. The steps. The heat.*

There's an ashtray abandoned on the balustrade, an empty bottle of beer glinting amber. A fly teeters on its neck, dizzy from the lingering fumes, fat from the spoils of plates left out in the heat for too long, the sugary hit of buttercream and stagnating crumbs of cheese sweating from the humidity. Nina watches it climb inside the bottle, knowing that it will die in there, trapped in the dregs of someone's forgotten drink. Its bloated body makes her feel slightly sick, the green flicker of wings against the glass sharpening her desire to be moving. To *do* something. To release some of the anxiety that simmers in her stomach, and in her limbs, and her chest.

She goes to stand, but the sudden movement sends a hot rush of pressure to her temples. She hasn't eaten today. It gave her a terrible, beautiful high to skip breakfast. To slip the sandwich that Sandra had made her into the bin when nobody was looking. It made her feel powerful and untouchable, but now the wine has gone straight to her head. A livid flush of color that blooms from the back of her skull. A crash as the wine bottle topples to the floor.

She takes a second to stabilize, standing perfectly still as her vision darkens and then clears. When it does, she is looking at the exact spot where her sister drowned. She is almost surprised not to see the azure blue of the pool. To not smell chlorine on the air.

It's only then that she notices her foot. A shard of glass. A jagged tear, the flesh white and parted. When it comes, the pain is swift and sharp. Nina swears under her breath and starts to hobble toward the house, leaving a trail of bloody footprints behind her, dark marks on the blank stretch of ground where her sister died.

Nobody seems to notice as she limps into the garden room, where an enormous white cake has been set up on a teeteringly tall stand. Three tiers, more like a cake for a wedding than a birthday. As if her mother hasn't had enough of those, Nina thinks. The cruelty of her own thought surprises her.

Groups are bunched between the yellowing palms and snakes of ivy that wind across the walls, champagne flutes in their hands. A waiter breezes toward Nina, smiling, holding out a glass toward her. She takes it and drinks it down almost in one.

Nina has been to so many of these parties. She has seen her mother bloom and glow as guests tell her how beautiful she looks, how she's barely aged since last year, or the year before that. People that Evelyn hasn't seen since her last birthday, kissing her on both cheeks like they're best friends. One eye always turned toward the door, wondering who else has been invited this year, which recently divorced celebrity or socialite fresh from a scandal will grace them.

Nina does not usually enjoy herself at her mother's parties. Usually, she's careful not to drink too much, or eat too much. Usually, she's busy ensuring that Evelyn has a nice time, too fearful of the black mood that will encircle the house at the smallest slight or guest-list snub.

But tonight, Nina takes a second glass of champagne from the waiter. Tonight, Nina—who usually cares so deeply about everything and everyone—is far beyond caring.

She moves from the garden room to the kitchen, tracking smears of blood across the terra-cotta tiles.

"Your foot—" someone says.

Nina walks right past them.

She spots Ryan close to the kitchen island talking to a young woman, probably the daughter—or even granddaughter—of one of Evelyn's friends. She has that exact beauty, the strong features that come from generations of pedigree breeding, the natural highlights that suggest winters spent in the sun. Nina knows her type. She knows her type because she *is* her type. She is Nina, without the headlines and the history. Without the skin-picking, and the light-switching, and the counting. The kind of person who, Nina imagines, is able to eat bread without thinking about grams of carbohydrates—or worse, who doesn't even *like* bread, long for it, as Nina does. Who doesn't dream, sometimes, about her dead sister.

She is Nina's type, and she is Ryan's type, too. She is the kind of person who Nina has always been afraid that Ryan secretly wants. The kind of person whose entire being isn't so tangled up in one terrible thing that happened to them that it bleeds into every part of her. Ryan is Nina's safe, stable place. Her biggest fear is that he might want someone safe and stable, too.

Right now, he is laughing at something the woman has said, swigging from his beer. Nina grips the stem of her champagne flute tighter, takes another slug. She hobbles around the edge of the room, slipping between discussions about which boarding school grandchildren are being sent to, the impossibility of finding good chalet girls in Val d'Isere. Nina wants to scream. She wants to shake them all, tell them how little it all matters.

Can't you see? she wants to say. *My entire life is falling apart. Everything I knew about my life is disappearing, right in front of me.*

She makes it through the kitchen without being stopped, across the hallway to the stairs. Her foot is beginning to throb. She needs to get to the bathroom, to find antiseptic and bandages. She grips the banister for balance. Starts to climb the sweeping steps. She can see her mother's pink dress, bright in the corner of her vision.

Halfway up she pauses, bending to assess the damage. Blood is beginning to clot against her skin, an ugly line of black, as though the inside of her is rotten and spoiled. The thought makes her woozy, and when she stands she has to lean both hands on the railings facing out over the room to steady herself. A tide is rising up inside her. She opens her eyes and feels, briefly, as if everyone is looking at her, their eyes twitching upward even as their mouths move, their conversations continuing. Above the hum of voices, she can almost imagine what they are saying. The same things that she's read online, over and over again, except for this time they are being spoken out loud. Coming from the mouths of people who know her. People who were there.

I always said they should never have taken the word of a little girl.
I mean, children do make things up, don't they?
She's never really moved on from it, sadly.
But do you think she was telling the truth?
Do you think she was telling the truth?

The empty champagne flute slips from between Nina's fingers and shatters against the stairs. The sound seems disproportionally loud for such a delicate thing, a crash of glass against stone. The hum of the room softens to quiet. A sea of faces turns up toward her, surprised. Wary.

All except for Evelyn. Evelyn, who is smiling. Expectant. As if she thinks that Nina might launch into a speech, her disaster a spectacle designed for her mother's benefit.

And Nina does not like to disappoint.

"Whoops!" she says, her voice clear in the sudden quiet. "There goes my champagne toast."

She laughs, but it sounds forced. Others join in, an uncertain chuckle rippling through the crowd. They're watching Nina now. Properly watching her. Not the version of herself being talked about online, picked over in internet forums. The real Nina. She's here, and she feels electrified and solid. Not someone who can be swept away in a tide of headlines and social media posts.

"Well, I suppose that as the daughter of the birthday girl, I should be thanking you all for coming to celebrate my mother," she says, louder now. She sees Ryan coming into the hallway, the girl with perfect highlights on his left side. "Sixty-two years old! Who would have thought it?"

Someone starts to applaud, and then stops, realizing they're clapping alone. Above her extravagant pink collar, Evelyn's jaw has tightened, her eyes dark.

"Not that my mother likes anyone mentioning her age," Nina continues. "To most people, she's remained in her forties for the last couple of decades. And, as many of you know, today isn't actually her birthday. Because for the last twenty years, we've been celebrating her birthday a month early. Because it's terrible, really, isn't it? When your own birthday also happens to be the anniversary of your daughter's death."

The room is completely silent now, as if everyone is holding their breath.

"Some of you probably remember it," Nina says. "Lots of you were here. Isn't it mad? How we all still come back? The same party, every year. It's pretty messed up, when you think about it. All we had to do was change the date, and everyone was happy to come and celebrate."

"Nina."

Evelyn is pale. There's a warning in her voice.

"But why should I be surprised?" says Nina. "You were all there that night, weren't you? And you all let a child testify, just because you wanted to feel better about yourselves. Because you didn't want to think that there was anything you might have done to save my sister."

She's openly crying now, tears damp against her cheeks. Through the haze, she can make out Ryan's face. The look of undisguised horror.

"If I had a glass right now, I'd raise it," she says. "To all of you. To everyone who partied while my sister died. And everyone who's done their best to forget it, in all the years since. Because some of us have never been able to. Some people have never been allowed to be anyone other than the kid who saw her big sister murdered."

A few voices are rising up to meet hers now, a murmur of protest, a hum of horror.

"In fact," says Nina. "Maybe someone should bring me a drink up here right now, because I'd really like . . ."

"Nina."

There's a hand on her elbow. Blake, his voice in her ear. The weight of him holding her still.

"It's OK," he says. "Come on. Let's get you to bed."

"I'm not finished," she hisses.

"On the contrary," he says. "I think that you are."

A gentle steer, pulling her back from the edge. His body between her and the spectators below, shielding her from view.

"Show's over, guys," he says. "Everyone fill up your drinks. I think we all need another one after that!"

Then he's leading her upstairs, and his grip is so assured, so gentle, that Nina almost believes that he will fix things for her. She almost thinks that he might be able to take everything away.

"Blake," she says. Her voice is small. Childlike. "Blake, I think I'm going to be sick."

Interview with **David B. Walker**, internationally renowned expert in child witness testimony.

Interview conducted by **Celine Blanco**, investigating magistrate.
19 May 2005

Blanco: Mr. Walker, we are here today to discuss the testimony of Nina Drayton. Before we begin, can you confirm that you've analyzed the interview recordings and transcripts of Nina Drayton relating to the Tamara Drayton case?
Walker: I have.
Blanco: Thank you, Mr. Walker. A key question of this case is Nina Drayton's very young age. Nina was five at the time she was first questioned. In your opinion, can the evidence of a five-year-old child be considered reliable evidence?
Walker: The point of the matter is not the age of the child, but how the testimony is gathered. Nina Drayton is very young, but there have been several cases of children of a similar age being used as witnesses in America, the UK, and other countries, often resulting in extremely important testimony. We don't look at if the child should have been a witness. We look at the witness testimony that they gave. If the police officer conducted the interview in an appropriate way. If the child's answers seemed natural and believable.
Blanco: And do you believe Nina Drayton's answers to be natural and believable?
Walker: I do. Examining Nina Drayton's speech patterns, I believe that she answered in a way that a child speaking honestly would have done. There are certain indicators that a child is not telling the truth—the timing between the question and the answer, changing the topic, talking quickly. In the recordings and transcripts of Nina

Drayton's interviews, I didn't see any of these signs.

Blanco: And the interviewing officer? Do you believe that they conducted the interview appropriately? Do you think that the way the information was gathered was fair?

Walker: Look, to be frank, there's no such thing as perfect evidence. When it comes to children, the waters are always muddied. Children don't communicate the way that you and I do. They don't think the way that you or I do. And with the Nina Drayton evidence, there's plenty of muddying. The information came to the police's attention via Evelyn Drayton in the first instance, which is challenging because we'll never know exactly what Nina first told her mother, what conversations were had then. There were child protection experts and guardians and translators in the room, which can confuse a child. There are lots of things that are imperfect about Nina Drayton's evidence. But do I believe that the evidence was gathered as well as possible, for a case involving a child witness? Yes, I do.

Blanco: So you believe Nina Drayton's testimony to be credible, in spite of her young age?

Walker: I do. Although young, Nina Drayton was clearly able to distinguish the difference between a lie and the truth when asked. She didn't display any signs of lying. And the story she told in the interview was credible. To me, Nina Drayton is as good a five-year-old witness as you can possibly get. In my expert view, Nina Drayton saw exactly what she said she did.

Blanco: So, Mr. Walker, in your opinion, should Nina Drayton's testimony be admissible in court?

Walker: I wholeheartedly believe that Nina Drayton's testimony should be taken seriously, and should be admissible in court.

TWENTY

2004
TWO WEEKS BEFORE THE BIRTHDAY PARTY

Hannah spent a lot of time at the pink house after she and Blake first slept together.

She went over when Evelyn and Harrison were out, or sneaked in late at night, when the rest of the family were sleeping. She and Blake took midnight swims in the pool, kissed pressed up against the kitchen counter, had sex in his king-sized bed. Each time made her feel closer to the life she had imagined, as if his touch pulled her deeper into his world.

She'd been seeing him for two weeks when he announced that his dad was visiting that weekend. They were in that in-between phase—too soon for Hannah to ask him what they were, too far in to mistake this for anything fleeting and insignificant. Blake liked her. She could tell from the way he looked at her. The way he said her name.

"It's a last-minute thing," he said, excitement seeping out around the edges of his words. "He was in Paris for some shoot his wife was doing and said he'd come down before he goes back to Italy."

Rocco Mae's arrival was treated like some kind of state visit, the air stretched thin with anticipation. Fresh flowers started to appear in vases, an enormous grocery order that Patricia accepted from a refrigerated van. Champagne, huge joints of meat even though Evelyn and Harrison rarely ate dinner at home.

"She's pathetic," said Blake. "She says that she hates him, but then she's desperate to impress him."

It was all Blake seemed able to talk about in the days beforehand. He spoke about his father with a tinge of pride. *My dad had a platinum-selling album when he was just a couple of years older than us. My dad once hiked the entire Camino de Santiago without stopping for longer than a night. A top chef said my dad's vineyard made the best rioja they'd ever tasted.*

But in spite of all their preparations, Rocco surprised them all, arriving in the afternoon rather than late in the evening, as planned. He must have let himself in with his own key, announcing his presence by bellowing up the stairs.

"Blake? Tamara?"

Hannah and Blake had been lying in bed, in that sleepy, post-sex haze. She had planned to slip out through the back entrance while Blake distracted Evelyn and Harrison. But now, Blake sat bolt upright, his hair still messy, his eyes alert.

"That's my dad," he said. "Shit. How are we going to get you out?"

"I can wait up here," Hannah said. "You could take him outside and—"

Blake was already shaking his head.

"Mum always puts on a show when Dad gets here," he said. "There's no way."

He bit his lip. He momentarily looked very small and very young, a child caught out in a moment of bad behavior.

"I think you'll have to come down and meet him," he said. "My dad'll be cool about it. And my mum won't say anything in front of him. Is that OK?"

A flicker of something in Hannah's chest. Hope. Acceptance. A thrum of nerves at the idea of meeting Blake's parents, properly this time, not as someone that they occasionally hired to help out at parties—to serve their drinks and clean up their mess.

"Yeah, of course," she said, trying to keep her voice as level as possible. "That's cool."

They dressed quickly. Hannah felt self-conscious, pulling on the clothes that she had arrived in. She could smell sex on her skin, noticed a streak of dirt on her jeans from where Blake had lifted her up onto a low wall when he had kissed her earlier on in the day.

"Come on," said Blake.

He was twitchy, urgent. There was already the rumble of his father's voice downstairs, the drawl of Evelyn's response.

They were all in the hall by the time Hannah and Blake reached the stairs. Hannah could see Evelyn as they descended, heavy circles of kohl around her eyes, a deep-red slash of lipstick. Her hair was half-styled, a tumble of curls down her back, the rest of it clipped up on top of her head. Heels. Behind her, almost hidden by the folds of her skirt, was Nina. She was quiet, peering shyly from behind her mother's legs. Harrison stood territorially in the arched doorway to the kitchen, as if blocking access to the rest of the house. Tamara hung back, her arms folded across her chest. Her face collapsed with relief when she saw her brother, that crackle of twin-speak seeming to pass between them. Then she spotted Hannah and her mouth knitted back together, eyebrows furrowing. A glance back to Blake, and this time Hannah understood exactly what it said. *What the hell is she doing here?*

"Blake, my boy," his dad bellowed.

Blake was smiling. He went straight to his father, gave him the kind of back-clapping hug that Hannah secretly thought men only did to prove something. Then, he turned toward her.

"Dad," he said. "This is Hannah."

Blake's dad looked up, a flicker of interest on his face. But then, of course, he wasn't just Blake's dad. When Hannah looked at him, she saw the 1980s newspaper photographs of Rocco Mae, music superstar, wound around a young Evelyn Drayton, their faces white-hot with the camera flash as they fell out of nightclubs. The famous snapshots of their shotgun Vegas wedding. The infamous pictures of Evelyn's face screwed up with fury the night that Rocco Mae was charged with assaulting a photographer who'd ambushed them as they left a Mayfair bar.

"Hannah," Rocco Mae said. "Nice to meet you."

And then he was just Blake's dad again. A salt-and-pepper-haired man in a clean white shirt. Good-looking still, if now carrying a slight paunch. And Evelyn, not the fiery twenty-two-year-old who'd married a man that she'd only known for three weeks, but a woman in her forties who hovered too close, her face pinched, her eyes darting.

"I didn't know you two were friends," she said, as Hannah descended the last steps.

"I thought you'd given those up?" Rocco interrupted, nodding at Evelyn's cigarette.

Evelyn sniffed.

"We can't all afford a team of hypnotherapists to rid us of our addictions, Rocco."

"Never start smoking, Hannah," Rocco said, almost conspiratorially. "It's a tough habit to break."

He had a way of looking right at her, of making Hannah feel like they already shared some kind of confidence. She could see why he had been such a heartthrob back in the day. Still was, she supposed. She'd seen the magazine coverage when Rocco and his supermodel wife renewed their vows on their Italian vineyard estate last summer. They had twins about Nina's age, who always looked spookily perfect whenever they were photographed, glossy double-paged spreads of the whole family smiling in front of their sprawling countryside farmhouse. They looked nothing like Blake.

"You know full well everyone smoked when I started," Evelyn said. "It was the seventies, for god's sake."

Rocco ignored her.

"Is your friend coming with us to dinner?" he asked Blake. "Hannah? Would you like to join us?"

"You're taking him out for dinner?" Evelyn said. "I thought we were all eating here. I got Patricia to set up the dining room . . ."

"But I'm here early, and I've got reservations," said Rocco, cutting across her smoothly. "Down at La Maison de la Mer. They'll be able to add another seat for Hannah, I'm sure."

"I'm vegetarian now. I don't eat seafood," Tamara said triumphantly, and then, under her breath, "which you would *know* if we ever saw you."

Rocco seemed to ignore his daughter, whipping around to place his hand on Blake's shoulder.

"Actually, I was thinking I'd just take Blake out tonight. A boys' night. Well, the boys and Blake's new friend, I suppose. I'll take Tamara out tomorrow."

Hannah saw Blake falter. A quick, worried glance at Tamara. Tamara's face was impassive, her mouth set into a hard line.

Evelyn let out a small, disbelieving laugh.

"Well," she said. "That's how to parent like Rocco Mae, I suppose. One child at a time."

"I thought it'd be better to have quality time with them," Rocco said. "Me and Flora have been talking about how to be really present with the kids, you know? Give them our undivided attention."

Tamara let out a small, sharp snort. There was a brief, terrible moment of silence. Evelyn, swaying foot to foot, her cigarette burning down in one hand. Rocco, looking straight back, his face still, his jaw set square.

"And what am I supposed to tell Patricia?" Evelyn said at last, her voice smaller now. "Harrison and I can hardly eat a whole leg of lamb between us."

"Patricia's handled worse dramas from you, I'm sure," Rocco said, and Hannah saw the way that Evelyn flinched before she gathered herself again, straightened, frowned.

"Blake, Hannah, how about it? Maison de la Mer?"

"I was actually just leaving—" Hannah started, but Rocco wasn't looking at her.

"Blake?" he repeated.

She watched as Blake hesitated, the eyes of both parents boring into him. He glanced between them. Then, he looked at his sister.

"Yeah," Blake said, at last. "Yeah, let's go to Maison de la Mer."

"Great." Rocco clapped his hands together. "The car's waiting outside."

"Right, perfect." Evelyn stubbed her cigarette out hard. "I'll just tell Patricia that nobody wants the dinner that she ordered in especially, I suppose."

Nobody seemed to be listening. Hannah would have almost felt sorry for Evelyn, if it wasn't for the way that Blake took her hand. Claiming her, in front of everyone.

"Come on," he said, his face brightening. "You'll love this place."

※

For Hannah, going out for dinner was a rare occurrence.

The stretch of coast that they called home wasn't designed for people on their budget, with their tastes. Her mum said she hated the restaurants that patterned the small seaside towns. Her dad said going out was a waste of money anyway.

One of the best things about where they lived, Hannah's mum always said, was how easy it was to get fresh ingredients. Crab caught straight out of the sea, salty mussels that she would douse in butter and garlic and box up for a picnic on top of the cliffs, their fingers greasy as they cracked open the shells. They didn't need expensive restaurants, her parents always told her. They had the best view for free, the best food that they could make at home. They had the best company, as long as they were with each other.

Maison de la Mer was the kind of restaurant Hannah's parents would roll their eyes at. They'd driven past it before, with its sleek white facade, a windowless cube right on the coast.

"Flora and I found this place last time we were here," Rocco said as they clambered out of the car. "Great food. You'll enjoy it."

"And where is her eminence tonight?"

Blake's voice was light, but there was a bite behind it. Something Hannah didn't quite recognize. Rocco simply laughed, patting his son on the shoulder.

"Now, then," he said. "That's a big word for a son of mine. Flora's stayed home. It's a long trip for Atticus and Aurora."

"Me and Tamara used to do it when we were their age," Blake said, but Rocco was already noisily greeting the maître d', shaking his hand like they were old friends.

The interior was dark, candlelit, even though it was still light outside, each table a dimly illuminated orb. As she led them to their table, the waitress explained that the chef had deliberately decided to block off the sea view—the idea was to taste the ocean, rather than see it. Taste, she said, was a more powerful sensation than sight. Rocco nodded along, making small noises of appreciation.

"Brilliant," he said. "Just genius."

He ordered a bottle of red wine with three glasses, and nobody asked Hannah or Blake's age. Rocco Mae spoke like a man who expected to get exactly what he asked for. Hannah wasn't used to wine, and when she took a sip, she found the taste strange and metallic, an undertone of iron that made her think of a time that Josie had sliced her index finger on a rock and, without thinking, Hannah had put her mouth to the wound to stop the bleeding.

Rocco asked for oysters and then steak. Blake echoed his order, and Hannah wondered what the point of sitting in a windowless box was if you weren't going to order seafood for your main course anyway. She told them that she wasn't hungry enough for a starter, choosing a tuna salad for main, the cheapest thing on the menu. The wine left a thick, dry sediment in her mouth, and she found herself drinking quickly in an attempt to wash it away. Blake ordered a beer and switched between the two drinks, a mouthful of wine, a swig from his bottle. He and Rocco talked about school while they waited for their starters, how Blake flunked his mock exams, his university applications. Blake sounded almost proud when he talked about how his teacher had promised to surreptitiously bump him up a few marks on his coursework.

"She reckons that'll get me into Leeds at least. Bristol, if I'm lucky," he said.

"You're a smart kid," Rocco said, a pride in his voice. "Academic. Not like me and your mum."

"And school said that I can go back late, in September," Blake announced, as platters of oysters were placed on the table between them, gray and glistening. "They said it's cool for me to miss a few weeks."

Rocco picked up a dappled shell.

"Oh yeah?" he said. "Why's that?"

Blake stilled, an oyster paused halfway to his mouth. Around them, the restaurant hummed, the clatter of cutlery, the sound of plates being set down on the polished wooden tables.

"The Vespas?" Blake said. "You know. We're meant to be going down the Amalfi Coast together. You and me."

Rocco slurped down an oyster, smacking his lips appreciatively.

"Did we say September?" he said. "I thought that we said maybe next year."

"Yeah. We talked about it last time we spoke on the phone, remember?"

"Well. September might not be the best time for me, to be honest with you, kid."

Blake set down the oyster without bringing it to his mouth.

"You said we would," he said. "You said, if I spent summer with Mum, we'd do our road trip in September."

Hannah felt his body tense beside her. Tight, like a coiled spring.

"I'm not sure that I said that, did I?"

"Yeah," said Blake. "You promised. I've been doing research. You said that I could plan the route."

And then, in a smaller voice:

"I already bought a helmet."

"Well." Rocco lifted a fork to scoop another oyster out of its shell. "September's a crazy time for me. Atticus and Aurora are starting a new school, and Flora's got this amazing job opportunity in Milan, so I'll be doing the hands-on dad thing for a couple of weeks—"

"You *promised*," Blake said again.

There was a tremor in his voice now. Something that threatened to break.

"Well, stuff came up." Rocco sounded close to irritable. He eased another oyster into his mouth. Swallowed. "You know how it is, kid. Don't make me feel bad."

Blake pushed his plate away from him.

"We've been planning this for months."

"Planning? Aw, come on, kid. We were spitballing. You know I'd love to take a trip with you. But I have to put the family first, you know?"

Blake opened his mouth as if to respond, and then closed it. He folded his arms across his chest. Hannah could see, in his eyes, the glint of tears. If Rocco noticed, he ignored it.

"So, Hannah," he said mildly. "Where do you go to school?"

She opened her mouth to answer, but the sound of Blake's chair scraping back against the floor drowned out her words.

"I'm not hungry," he said.

Rocco's expression didn't flicker. He shoveled another oyster into his mouth.

"So cancel your main," he said.

"This restaurant is shit," said Blake. "Who the fuck builds a restaurant without windows right next to the sea?"

He reached out his hand toward Hannah's.

"Come on," he said.

Rocco leaned back in his chair.

"You're not seriously upset about the road trip?" he said. "Come on. You're supposed to be a man now, Blake. You need to start acting like it. Atticus and Aurora—"

"Fuck Atticus and Aurora."

"Hey. I won't have you talk about your siblings like that."

"They're not my siblings, though, are they? They're yours and Flora's kids. I could probably count on two hands the number of times I've met them. Just because we happen to have the same dad doesn't mean anything."

"Well, if you'd come to the vow renewal . . ."

"Flora didn't *want* us at the vow renewal."

"Well, now I think you're projecting."

Blake's jaw was set so tight that Hannah could see a muscle twitch.

"Come on," he said to her again.

She stood, slowly.

"Thanks for the wine, Mr. Mae," she said.

Rocco didn't look away from his plate.

"I'll send you the bill for your steak, shall I?"

"Fuck you."

Blake's hand closed around Hannah's.

"Let's get out of here."

They hadn't called a car, so they left the restaurant on foot. The road was narrow and scrappy, teetering into dirt, forcing them to walk tight to the cliff edge. Blake's strides were longer than Hannah's in spite of her height, her sandals catching on rocks and scrubby patches of grass as she tried to catch up. She forced herself to slow when she turned her ankle on an uneven shelf of tarmac, then stopped when headlights soared into view. Her arms were folded against the night chill, her body briefly silhouetted by the roar of light, but Blake kept walking as the car passed by, his hands dug into his pockets. Hannah had to quicken her pace into a half jog. Her stomach was starting to ache with hunger and her ankle throbbed.

"Blake!"

She called his name, but her words were whipped away toward the sea.

"*Blake.*"

He stopped then, his back still to her. A second car screeched past so quickly that it had to swerve to avoid them, the acrid smell of hot tires against asphalt. Hannah cried out, stepping reflexively back from the road's edge, a horn blaring into the night. She could imagine the driver, hands gripped on the wheel. *Stupid kids, walking along an unlit road.*

"What the fuck are you doing?"

Blake was striding back toward her, catching hold of her wrist. He pulled her away from the sheer drop of the cliff. Toward a squat, brick building on the other side of the road, some kind of abandoned outpost or long-closed substation, the kind of thing that Hannah would pass by often without thinking about.

"I wasn't—"

"You practically stepped out in front of that car."

"I—"

He brought his face so close to her that she could feel the dampness of his breath, flecks of saliva on her face when he spoke.

"Don't you think I have enough of my own shit going on, without having to worry about you?"

"Blake." Her voice was a thread through the back of her throat, thin and taut. "You're hurting me."

He dropped her wrist then. On her arm she could just make out the shadow of his hand, the ache where he had gripped her too hard.

"*Fuck.*"

The word tore out of him, almost a scream. He raised his arm and Hannah flinched, held her hand up reflexively as his fist barreled into the wall. The sound of bones against brick was ugly and deadened, and he let out a bellow of pain, bent double over himself, clutching his fist into his chest.

"Fuck."

She had never seen him like this before. Animal, almost unrecognizable, anger rising out of him like heat. She should walk away. She should leave him here, with his fury. And yet, she felt that thread in the back of her throat again, and this time it seemed to pull her toward him, unspooling into the syllables of his name.

"Blake." It sounded like a plea. Like a prayer.

His head was in his hands, the one that he had used to punch the wall limp, arched beneath the other as if for protection. His shoulders were shuddering. She realized, with a jolt of surprise, that he was crying.

"Here," she said. "Let me look at your hand."

She tried to peel one fist away from the other, but he resisted.

"It might be broken," she said. "Let me see."

And then he was grabbing her wrist again, straightening, pulling her in toward him. His mouth was on hers, and he was kissing her with a fierce urgency as if it was the only way that he could stop her from seeing his tears. Pressing her up against the brick wall. His uninjured hand tugging at her jeans, pushing into her underwear.

"Blake," she said. "Stop it."

She turned her head away, but his mouth was on her jaw, her throat. The wetness of his tears against her skin. She tried to move his hand away. Tried to turn the mewl of fear in her mouth into a laugh, because it would be so much easier if she could laugh this off. So much better.

"Someone will see," she said.

"What?" he said. "Are you frigid now or something?"

The word hit her like a second punch. He pressed his hips into hers, and she could feel that he was hard through his jeans. She imagined the girls that Blake had slept with before, how they radiated sex, how they would probably find this entire situation fun and daring. Hot. She wanted to be like them so badly it hurt. She didn't want Blake to look at her the way that they did, with pity and condescension.

So, she let Blake turn her around, press her against the crumbling wall, pull her jeans down, push himself up between her legs. She closed her eyes and moaned like she was supposed to, pretended to enjoy it, like her teeth weren't gritted so hard that her entire skull ached. She arched her back the way the magazines her mum sometimes read told her to. She said the same word over and over, *yes, yes*, because it was better than saying no.

When it was over, she realized that Blake's hand had been bleeding, and that everywhere he had touched her was now streaked with red. Somehow, Hannah couldn't stop thinking of the wine that she had drunk earlier, that ironlike taste, how impossibly different the evening could have been.

Hannah Bailey never drank red wine again.

PART THREE

TWENTY-ONE

2004
ONE WEEK BEFORE THE BIRTHDAY PARTY

One week before her mother's birthday party, Tamara Drayton borrows Harrison's car and drives down the coast to Montpellier.

Borrow, of course, is a generous word. Tamara, who has not officially passed her test, does not ask Harrison whether she can use his car. She knows that he would only say no. But she also knows that if she simply *takes* his car when he is out fucking the girl who works down at the bistro in town (because another thing Tamara knows is that her stepfather *is* fucking the girl who works at the bistro down in town) then he won't have the balls to bring this up to her mother. And so, Tamara takes the keys out of the top drawer of Harrison's desk and reverses his 1970s Chevrolet Corvette right out of the driveway.

Most of Tamara's life has operated on this kind of bargaining. Having a mother like Evelyn Drayton taught her, from a very young age, that secrets were a currency, and that collecting them conferred a very specific kind of power. If you accessed them at the right time, they could be used to get exactly what you wanted.

It was how she knew about her stepfather's affairs, and her mother's insecurities. It was how she knew that her dad was not, as he claimed, "Italian sober" (fine wines only), but had three separate cocaine dealers in Montpellier, Naples, and London. It was how she knew that Blake was sleeping with Hannah Bailey, even though he had told her that he wasn't—a lie that shook Tamara, who had once believed that her brother would always tell her the truth.

But mostly, Tamara knows the power of secrets because she knows what it is like to have one.

The roof is down on Harrison's car, and as Tamara drives she is buffeted by the summer air. The afternoon is sloping toward evening, slippery with heat. She lights a cigarette, one hand on the steering wheel, thinking that the smoke will ward off the flies and mosquitoes that swarm at this time of day. She drives toward the city as if she is driving away from her life. She drives as if there is nothing in the world that can stop her.

When she was very young, Tamara's nanny told her that she was the bad twin.

The nanny, who lasted just six months, had walked into the nursery just as Tamara was scrawling an enormous *T* on the wall in bright blue crayon while Blake sat quietly, finishing his apple slices and peanut butter.

The nanny had not stuck, but her words did. *The bad twin.*

As she had gotten older, Tamara became fascinated by the idea. She read about changelings and doubles. Germanic folklore and Norse mythology. The idea of twin malevolent entities.

She is thinking about this as she steps into a bar on the wrong side of the city, the kind of place where it's always dark, even in daytime. Thick drapes and carpeted stairs, a room with plenty of corners and places to hide. Tamara briefly considers whether the car will be safe on the graffiti-lined street outside, and then decides that she doesn't care much if it is or not. That, perhaps, Harrison will think twice before his next afternoon rendezvous if his Corvette comes back with a window or two smashed in.

Bad twin.

These are the spiteful, vengeful things that cross her mind. Enough badness for two people.

She orders shots. Two of them. She drinks them straight down, chases them with a beer. A man on a barstool close to her wolf-whistles between yellowing front teeth.

"You can really put them away, can't you, sweetheart?"

Tamara sticks two fingers up at him.

Bad twin.

Later, she finds herself sitting with a man who tells her that he was recently dumped by the love of his life. He buys them more shots. Tells her, tearily, about how he thinks that he'll never meet anyone like her again.

"At least you're not me," Tamara says. She's slurring. She can hear the slant of her words, the way they run into each other. "At least you're not in love with someone who you can never, ever tell."

"Ah, you're young," the man says. "You'll get over it."

He knocks back another shot. Tamara hasn't been counting how many they've done, but something in the churn of her stomach tells her that it's too many.

"Anyway," he says. "Why can't you tell them?"

She takes another shot anyway. It burns all the way to her stomach.

Bad twin.

"Because," she says. "There's something wrong with me."

The man tilts his head to one side, focused now.

Tamara leans in closer.

"Can you keep a secret?"

TWENTY-TWO

2024

The car's air conditioning starts to give up somewhere close to Avignon, the vents beginning to splutter in and out, blasting them all with intermittent puffs of cool air. By the time they see signs for Marseille, it has given out entirely, and they sit, marinated in their own sweat, the windows fully rolled down.

"This is the last time we're doing the tunnel over," says Hannah's husband, Eric, hitting his hand against the air vent for the eleventh time. "Next time, we'll fly."

Hannah doesn't answer, because it would be the fiftieth time they've had this debate since becoming parents, Eric lamenting the horror of the eighteen-hour trip, Hannah pointing out the impossibility of wrestling all three children and the countless clothes and toys and pushchairs that they need for four weeks in France onto a flight.

"My dad will take a look at it when we arrive," she says. "I'm sure it's something he'll be able to sort."

Her words are supposed to be soothing, but Eric sighs and taps against the vent slightly more aggressively.

"That's the other thing," he says. "Your dad already thinks I'm such a shirt. He'll love the fact I know nothing about cars. I won't hear the end of it."

"Oh, stop it," says Hannah. "My dad loves you. You know he does."

"*Mum.*"

A small foot digs into the back of Hannah's seat.

"Tell Mason it's my turn with the iPad."

"It's not your turn with the iPad. You had it for ages."

"*You've* had it for ages. You're not even using it."

"You only use it to play stupid baby games."

"You're the stupid baby."

"You're a stupid shithead."

"*Mason.*" Hannah's voice makes everyone jump. "Apologize to your brother right now."

Just then Isla, strapped into her booster seat, decides it's the perfect time to start wailing.

"Apologize for what?"

"For calling your brother a shithead."

"Mum!"

"Mum, you just said shithead."

"No, I didn't." Hannah is twisting round to ply Isla with yet another strawberry lollipop. The sugar high is going to be unbearable to deal with, but she can't stand the screaming. Not now, not at these temperatures. "I said an s-head. I didn't actually say the word—"

"Look, boys, I can see the sea!" Eric roars, cutting Hannah off before she can finish.

Hannah turns back, grateful as Noah starts to chatter about how Uncle Nic is going to teach him how to dive and Isla slobbers happily over her lollipop. They're a good team, she and Eric, even in thirty-degree heat. Even after spending seventeen hours in a small metal box together.

She's glad that he's here, glad that she has him to come back with. Without him, she would never have come back at all.

※

For years after she left this place, Hannah did not return. She couldn't stand it. Her home had been so marred by tragedy, so overshadowed by the arrest of her best friend.

She had moved to England. Thrown herself into her studies, living in an unfamiliar city—not Oxford, in the end, but Manchester—drinking cheap pints in student bars and staying in the library until late at night. She got a waitressing job in an upmarket pizzeria, and the Christmas shifts gave her a good enough excuse to avoid going home at the end of autumn term.

She met Eric at a silent disco at the student union midway through her first year and slept with him the same night, with an impulsiveness and clarity that took her by surprise. They were an item right away, finding each other on nights out to go home together, and meeting each other's flatmates, and missing seminars to sleep in late, and going on dates to chain restaurants that did midweek deals. It was so unlike her relationship with Blake that sometimes she couldn't quite believe it. She would sometimes lie awake listening to Eric breathing, unable to believe how easy it had been. She let herself, for the first time in over a year, feel happy. Hopeful. But when Eric would ask when he'd meet her parents, Hannah always had an excuse.

It wasn't until Mark and Marie decided to retire that Hannah could stand to come back. Against all odds and everyone's expectations, the dive shop had begun to flourish after Tamara Drayton's death. The media storm had brought attention to their strip of sea: a developer bought land just down the coast and built a mega-hotel; locals who owned smaller, cheaper houses on the other side of the hill seized the opportunity to rent out holiday lets to people who had seen the impossible blue of the sea on news reports. Suddenly, after years of struggle, the dive shop was busy—just as Mark and Marie were ready to wind down.

Eventually, they had decided to pass the family business on to Nic. A trusted friend would manage the day-to-day running until Nic was ready to take over, and Mark and Marie would receive a split of the future profits. It would be enough for them to retire and live more comfortably than they had for years.

Hannah was twenty-three then, and had just found out she was pregnant. It was an accident; she was only partway through her accountancy exams, and she and Eric were living in a small flat up three flights of stairs, completely unsuitable for a baby.

Still, there had been no question that they'd keep it. They had gone to France that summer for the first time, and Hannah's mother had been delighted, pressing her hand against Hannah's rounded stomach as her dad made jokes that weren't really jokes about how he'd have liked to have met his daughter's boyfriend at least once before he knocked her up.

Since then, they'd returned almost every year. Each time, the memory of that terrible summer had faded just a little bit. Motherhood was so consuming, so exhausting, and with Eric working long hours as a teacher at an inner-city comprehensive, holidays in the Côte d'Azur became something that they looked forward to. Time as a family. Time to forget the stresses of home—the fact that they never quite seemed to have enough money, or that Hannah had lost touch with all her university friends when she'd been changing nappies and they had still been out partying, or the nagging sense that she should really go back and finish her accountancy qualifications, or at least get another job, but then childcare was so expensive, and could they really afford it, and what was the point of spending all day in an office away from her kids if they would only just about break even?

But when they arrived at the sea, all that faded away. This tiny town, which had always felt so claustrophobic, so stifling when Hannah was a child, started to feel like an escape. She began to feel the muscles in her shoulders release every time she drew within sight of the famously blue sea.

Her mother is waiting outside the house when they pull in.

"You made it!" she says as they clamber, sticky and sweat-soaked, out of the car.

She reaches out her arms for Noah, still young enough not to be embarrassed by open displays of affection. Mason hangs back, shy all of a sudden, sullen, and Hannah feels a brief twinge of sadness at how quickly it all passes, that lack of self-consciousness and easy affection of childhood. In just a few years, Noah will be a teenager, too, and Hannah will no longer be able to reach either of her sons in the way that she used to.

"Where's my little girl?" says her mother. "Oh. There she is. Come to *Grand-mère*."

She scoops Isla out of the car seat, showering her with kisses.

"Look at you. You all look exhausted. Come inside, quickly. Granddad's in the house."

They let Noah fly past them, Mason trailing behind. Eric gives his mother-in-law a brief squeeze before hauling two suitcases out of the boot and following his sons.

The second they're alone, Marie kisses her daughter on both cheeks.

"You look tired," she says.

"You would, too, after that car journey."

"I didn't mean it like that," says Marie, but she doesn't elaborate any more.

"Let me just get some of the cases out," Hannah says. "I'll be in in a sec."

Her mother doesn't move.

"I wanted to tell you," she begins, "before anyone else does."

She sways Isla back and forth on her hip, a movement that seems instinctive. She would have rocked Hannah like that once, unthinkingly, as if she could soothe anything away.

"Josie Jackson is back," she says. "Your father saw her yesterday, down near the beach."

Hannah bends over a wheelie case, pretends to be struggling to release the handle. It gives her a second, just long enough, for the bolt of unease to pass.

"I know," she says. "Nic texted me."

"Word gets round fast here," Marie says. "People won't be happy. When they realize she's back."

Hannah straightens.

"It's her decision," she says. "If she wants to make a rod for her own back, so be it."

"Do you think you'll go and see her?" Marie asks. "Do you think that you might want to . . . I don't know. Talk to her? You girls used to be such good friends."

Hannah swings a backpack onto her shoulder and turns to look her mother straight in the eye.

"Why would I do that?" she says. "Being friends with Josie Jackson almost ruined my life."

```
NEW VIDEO
@TRUECRIMEFANGIRL_2002
POSTED TODAY AT 11:22
```

Hey, true crime girlies, and welcome back to a week in my mad life. And *what* a week it's been. I mean, this has honestly probably been one of the craziest few days I've ever had. You might have spotted little ol' me on actual national television yesterday, because yes, the mainstream media are getting on this bandwagon now, and my true crime baby is going big.

But first of all—have you guys noticed anything different? Anything at all? Well, take a look around, because I'm not in my usual spot. In fact, I'm not even in my usual country. That's right, kiddos, I'm in Europe! Getting all continental up in here. And before you all come for me in the comments, yes, I know Europe isn't a country, so let me be specific. I'm in the South of France, baby! In fact, I'm standing about a hundred meters away from where Tamara Drayton's body was discovered. Because, yes, all the rumors are true, and I am out here to film a very exciting project. So watch this space!

But you guys know me, I'm not really about all that glitz and glamor, you know? I'm here for the true crime community, and bringing you guys the details that the media are scared to talk about is what I actually love doing. And I know a lot of you guys frickin' loved my autopsy series that I did about a year ago—and yes, if you remember "Lacerations and Dead Girl Frustrations" then I know that you're an OG follower. So I thought I'd throw it back and talk about Tamara Drayton's autopsy today.

So Tamara Drayton didn't actually die at the scene. Officially, her time of death was recorded as 06:38, and she passed away in the hospital. Now, my real true crime junkies will know that things are a little more complicated if there's been any hospital intervention between the victim being found and their actual death. It gets a little trickier to determine certain things. It can mess with the forensic evidence, and it can mean that some of the bruising and injuries on Tamara's body could have been from the pretty invasive treatment she would have received as doctors tried to save her—I mean, have you ever seen anyone do CPR before? Because that shit is brutal. Not to mention that it means we have no idea when Tamara's injuries were inflicted, or how long she was in the water for, because she didn't die until hours later.

But what we do know is that the police were immediately suspicious. And guess who the first person that they wanted to question was? Yep, you got it. No other than Harrison Andreas, who everyone was pretty quick to point out hated his stepdaughter. We actually know that Harrison was interviewed multiple times by the police, but honestly, there were a lot of suspects' names that got thrown into the mix at this stage. Pretty much everyone who was at that party had to answer for something.

That, of course, was before the police talked to Nina Drayton.

But here's where things get really interesting. Tamara Drayton also had a number of injuries to her body. In fact, this was allegedly what made the police immediately want to investigate this as a homicide. In particular, she had what is described in the autopsy as a "catastrophic head injury." And this lines up with the crime scene—forensics noticed that there was blood in the water and on the side of the pool. They use this to paint a picture of a fight that got out of hand—maybe Josie pushed Tamara into the water, or maybe they were already in the pool, and Josie grabbed her and smashed her head against the side of the pool? Tamara would then be incapacitated, at least momentarily. Potentially long enough for Josie to hold her under the water, and for Tamara to lose consciousness. It's a pretty grim way to go, for sure, but it lines up with Nina Drayton's story.

But that's not all. Something that really grabbed my attention in the autopsy was that Tamara Drayton also had bruises on the left side of her body, and in particular, signs of recent soft tissue damage on her left ankle. Like a sprain, or a similar injury. Now, investigators are pretty quick to say that this fits with their theory. By the time the autopsy report comes back, Josie Jackson has already been arrested, and they say that these injuries could have been sustained from Tamara's fight with Josie. But it just doesn't seem to fit, you know? Like, would you really get bruises underwater? Wouldn't the water actually slow the impact of something hitting you? And whoever heard of someone spraining their ankle in a pool?

Is it possible that the fight could have happened outside of the water—and if so, shouldn't that totally change the police's theory on how the crime happened? How do they even know that they're looking for forensics in the right place?

And if the fight was really that intense then why do we not have any injuries recorded on Josie Jackson? She's a pretty small girl. Could she really do that much damage in a fight?

Anyway, there's so much in this autopsy that's interesting, and I am going to link it. Have a read and let me know what you think. Did Josie Jackson actually beat the shit out of Tamara Drayton? Or is there something more going on here? Let me know in the comments!

Avalonsaccount: No way JJ could have beaten up TD like that. Deffo behind the accidental drowning theory. Maybe T couldn't swim with a sprained ankle? Or wasn't she a big druggie? Could have been on something?
JocelynV:): You guys are seeing what you want to see. Broken ankle and head injury 100% aligns with the Josie Jackson = guilty theory
Crimeaddict82: Hellooo—this definitely points to murder to me, but there's absolutely nothing to link the injuries to Josie Jackson!?

Leah_Drayton: I would say accident. Like, maybe she slipped, and hit her head on the side and couldn't get out of the water? Except for that doesn't explain the OTHER injuries. All of them together just makes me think someone MUST have done this to her. And honestly, Josie Jackson still seems like the best bet to me.

TWENTY-THREE

2024

The morning after the party, Nina goes out onto the terrace just as the sun is beginning to rise.

She has perhaps seen more sunrises this week than she has in the rest of her life put together. She has waited for each day to slide in with a sense of dread and anticipation. But today, she barely notices the mottled pink sky. She barely sees the light begin to warm the silver plains of the sea.

Today, Nina is thinking about her sister.

Tamara would be thirty-seven by now. Nina cannot imagine what she might have been like, cannot assign an adult personality to the few scraps of the teenage girl that she barely remembers. There are a thousand possible versions of the person her sister might have become. An overachiever like Nina, with a string of high grades and degrees. Someone who improvised their way through life, like Blake—always seeming to land on their feet, falling into highly paid jobs and relationships with a succession of beautiful people. Or, perhaps, she would have rebelled, dropping out of university to go backpacking in Bolivia, or to work a job that her mother disapproved of, or to run off with an unsuitable boyfriend they would all worry endlessly about.

No matter what, they would have been close, Nina thinks. She has friends with sisters. Women from school or university whose siblings would come and visit, who would reminisce about squabbling over stolen clothes and staying up late comparing crushes. When Nina heard those stories, she always felt a sense of loss, as if she was glimpsing a world that was unknowable to her. A relationship she couldn't quite fathom, but longed for nevertheless.

Nina did not exactly miss Tamara—*couldn't* miss someone she had barely known—but she did miss what the two of them might have been. She felt the absence of her sister in a profound but not exactly painful way, like a nonessential organ. An appendix, or a singular kidney. A thing that she could manage without, but that she would always know wasn't there.

As she picks over the remnants of last night—the shattered wine bottle and streak of blood—Nina thinks about how they might all be different, had Tamara lived. If Nina would have picked some other career. If she might have friends other than Claire, hobbies other than sharpening every piece of herself until only edges and corners remained.

Blake might have met someone who he would stay with for longer than a year. Instead, it was as if nobody could fill the space that his twin had left behind. Evelyn might have found a way to be happy, to be more of a mother to Nina. Instead, she looked at Nina as if her youngest daughter reminded her of everything that she had lost.

Nina gathers up the pieces of glass, glinting green in the early morning light. It brings the entire night back to her. Blake holding back her hair as she vomited bile streaked red with wine. Ryan, furious. Nina, telling him that she wanted to stay. Telling him that she had spoken to the documentary makers and scheduled in a meeting with them on Monday. Typing out an email to her new employers that she's too embarrassed to look at now, certain it will be littered with typos and drunken mistakes, telling them that there'd been a family emergency. Asking them if she could put her start date back by *just a few days.*

Ryan had woken up early that morning for his flight home. The room was still dark, illuminated by the light of his phone as he gathered his things.

"You're really not coming?" he said.

"I'll be back in a couple of days," she replied, her voice sounding small. Uncertain.

"This isn't like you," he said. "Come on, Nina. You're more sensible than this. You can't just not show up to work because of some ridiculous whim."

"It's not ridiculous to me," she said, but she knew it was useless. He hadn't been listening to her.

He hadn't kissed her goodbye.

Then there was the video, posted a few hours ago by a gossipy but prominent news outlet. A clip that must have been filmed by a party guest, Nina standing on the stairs, her words slurred. Beneath the clip, comments flooded in so quickly that Nina couldn't scroll fast enough to keep up.

Fucking nutter.

Nina WHO? Report on some REAL NEWS not these z-list NOBODIES

This girl needs professional help

Nina watched the video three times. The commenters had a point. In her own professional capacity, she could see that she was looking at someone who appeared on the edge of something dark and dangerous.

She was looking at someone who was losing control.

She hoped that Ryan wouldn't see the video, or worse, her new employers. She had spent years avoiding the public eye, and now here she was, in the center of the storm. There was a surreal quality to it, like she was watching someone else break down. Like the Nina Drayton in the video clip was someone she didn't know, had never met.

Now, with the sea hazy in the early-morning light, Nina wonders briefly if it's too late to fix things. She could, after all, still make an afternoon flight. Arrive home by dinner, in time to iron her outfit for tomorrow, and check that she has her highlighters and her notepad and the color-coded Post-its in her bag, these talismans for her new, grown-up life. She remembers how she felt buying them, that tug of anticipation, the promise that everything was falling into place.

It feels so long ago. Now, the thought of moving forward feels impossible. The pull of her past is too consuming, too bottomless. There are things she cannot leave alone; there are things she has to settle first.

When Ryan said she was sensible, Nina had the strangest feeling that he was describing someone else entirely. She feels unpredictable, brimming with an unexpected energy that's honest and raw. For the first time in her life, she's unconcerned with the expectations of others, the need to be good, and tidy, and well-behaved.

She hears the pad of feet on the terrace behind her, and twists around to see Evelyn crossing the tiles with a mug in each hand.

"I made you a coffee," she says as she approaches, her voice milder than Nina expected. "It's absolutely vile, but Sandra isn't here yet so I had to improvise."

She sits down next to Nina, bare feet hanging off the edge of the terrace, and hands her a cup.

"Jesus," she says, taking a sip from her own mug and wincing. "That really is terrible. Maybe I shouldn't have given Sandra the morning off after all."

"He's gone," Nina says. "Ryan."

She expects her mother to ask her what she means. Where he's gone to, and for how long. Instead, Evelyn just nods.

"They always go, darling," she says, like it's the simplest thing in the world. "*C'est la vie*, as they say round here."

Nina is fairly certain that her mother, in spite of spending most of her life *round here*, doesn't actually speak any more French than this, but she doesn't comment on it. For a moment, they just sit in silence, their eyes on the horizon. Nina is waiting for her mother to start berating her, to say how disappointed she is. When nothing comes, Nina speaks instead.

"Does it make you sad?" she says. "Being out here?"

Evelyn doesn't look at her.

"Nina," she says. "There are kinds of sadness that you can't even imagine, until they happen to you. And then they happen, and you forget there's any other way to feel. Do you mind if I smoke?"

Nina is so taken aback by the request that she only blinks at her mother. Her mother, who doesn't ask permission for anything. Who is barely seen without a cigarette in her hand, a wreath of smoke around her head.

"I'll take that as a no," Evelyn says.

She produces a packet of cigarettes, lights up, and takes a long, thoughtful drag.

"So no," she says as she exhales. "I don't feel any sadder here than I do anywhere else. Because it's everywhere, that sadness. And you keep on moving because you have to. You survive, because you're lucky to have been given the chance to do so. Because it's all that you *can* do."

In the distance the sea glitters. A bird dips and rises in the air overhead, a lazy, swooping dance.

"Did you think that I was telling the truth?" Nina asks. "About what happened?"

Evelyn looks right at her then. She's bare-faced, besides the thin, faded tattoo of her eyebrows. For a moment, Nina can see the beauty that she once was. The eighties it-girl, the woman that the world fell in love with. The woman that Evelyn has never quite been able to let go of since.

"I think that in a situation like that," Evelyn says, "you believe what you have to, to stay alive."

Nina's heart sinks.

"So you don't really believe it?"

Her mother exhales a purple stream of smoke.

"Belief is a choice, Nina," she says. "I choose to believe in my children. You have to. It would destroy you, otherwise."

"But wouldn't it be better to know? Wouldn't you go looking for the truth, if you were me?"

Evelyn stubs her cigarette out, right on the border where the stones turn a lighter shade. Right where their lives changed forever.

"I think," says Evelyn. "That the past comes back to you, no matter what."

Something flickers across her face then. Her features rearrange, and all of a sudden, she looks distracted. Changed.

"Look," she says. There's something strained in her voice again. A forced brightness that wasn't there before. "I didn't come out here to talk to you about all that. There's actually something I wanted to tell you."

She sits up straighter. Rolls her shoulders back.

"I'm selling the house."

Nina just blinks at her.

"What?"

"It's been a struggle for years, darling. You know it has. It's falling apart, the upkeep is madness. And my dad's work will be out of copyright soon, and we'll stop getting royalties, and . . . well. There's not much left in the pot, otherwise." She lets out a strange, strangled laugh. "You know I've never been good with money. There seemed like so much of it when I was younger and now . . . it just goes so quickly, doesn't it? I should have been better with it really, invested or something, but . . . well, you just don't think about it at the time, do you?"

There's a tightness behind her words, as if she's holding something back. As if, if the brightness falters from her voice, the fear will creep through.

"But you love this house," says Nina.

For the last few years, Nina has watched as her mother downgraded her London townhouse to a two-bed flat. As she started to sell her vintage designer pieces. Let go of staff, until only Sandra remained. Nina has known for a long time that the money was running out, but she never imagined that her mother would sell the pink house. It is the focal point of their family. Their legacy. An entire mythology between stone walls and sea views that Nina assumed would last forever.

"Of course I do. Do you know what it's going to do to me to sell this house? The decision alone has nearly killed me. But it's impossible, Nina. And I know, I've been foolish. All those bloody divorce settlements, and all the houses, and the parties. I just didn't realize the money would run out. I've always had it, you know? I've never known any different. I assumed it would be there forever, even when everything else . . . even when every*one* else left me."

She takes a deep breath.

"And after last night," she continues. "Well, you said it yourself. Time to move on. To stop living in the past."

She smiles a wavering, hopeful smile.

"It's time, Nina," she says. "I'm moving on. And you should, too. This is going to be our last summer at the pink house. So let's not let all of these silly rumors ruin it."

Their last summer at the pink house.

There will be no more nights beneath the bougainvillea. No more birthday parties.

No more avoiding the place where Tamara was pulled out of the water.

But all Nina hears, all she understands, is that there will be no more opportunities to put things right.

That this is, perhaps, her last chance to find out the truth.

TWENTY-FOUR

2024

Josie has left an entire afternoon free to pack. She opens up the suitcase that she arrived here with, not even put away yet, and begins to fold T-shirts and ball up socks. Quickly the stretch of time starts to feel ridiculous. An entire afternoon to pack up the few scraps of her life she brought with her. She has only been here for a week. She has almost nothing to show for it.

Gabby knocks on her door just as Josie is searching for a bracelet that she kept, back from that brief period of living in Devon. Her boyfriend back then, the first man she had loved, had given it to her for her birthday just six days before he had found out the truth. It surprises Josie now, how little she remembers about that period, one of the few lengths of time that she recalls being truly happy. Only a few small, snatched memories. Cups of tea on the sofa on rainy days. The small, unexpected joy of eating dinner together in front of the television every night.

"Need any help?" Gabby asks.

Josie shakes her head.

"There's not much left for me to do."

Gabby hovers in the doorframe.

"Need some company?"

Josie's hand catches against the bracelet, its thin gold threads entangled around a pair of tights. How long until this week becomes a vague and faded memory? How quickly will it melt into the patchwork of Josie's life, a tangle of places and people that she can't quite remember? Cheap costume jewelry that she can't bring herself to get rid of, even when the gold fades to a gray tarnish. Phone numbers that she never has any need to call anymore. The specific smell of someone whose face she can no longer remember.

"Yeah," she says. "I could use some company."

Gabby shuts the door behind her and slides over to the suitcase. She ignores Josie's refusal of her help and picks up a T-shirt, beginning to fold it into a neat, compact square.

"Where are you going to go?" she asks.

Josie frees the bracelet and drops it on top of the pile of clothes.

"Kent, at first," she says. "I can stay with my mum's sister for a couple of weeks. Just while I'm figuring things out."

"And then where?" asks Gabby.

"I don't know."

The words fall heavily between them, a rock sinking toward an ocean floor. Josie can't bear to think about what she'll do after her aunt's hospitality runs out. She only knows that she can't stay here. Not with reporters showing up at Calvin's door. Not with the worry that they'll be at Nic's flat next, or at Gabby's café.

"You could just stay, you know," Gabby says. "Calvin's devastated that you're leaving. We both are."

Josie is already shaking her head.

"Everyone knows where I am now," she says. "Nobody wants me here."

"*We* want you here," Gabby says.

Josie zips up her toiletries bag with one hard, decisive motion.

"Look, I get that you're trying to be nice, but you don't know what it's like," she says. "It almost killed us last time. I can't do that again. I can't do that to you, or to Calvin, or to—" Her voice catches. "To . . . to anyone else," she says.

"People talk in places like this. So what? You've got the job at the café, if you want it. You've got us. Let them talk."

There's something solid in Josie's throat. Something that she has to swallow down so that Gabby can't see how badly she wishes that were true.

"I can't," she says. "I'm not strong enough to go through all that again. Sorry."

The suitcase is almost full. Gabby presses down on the small pile of clothes inside as if to make space for something more. Josie isn't sure what.

"Nic messaged me earlier," Gabby says. "He said he's been trying to get hold of you?"

"Oh, yeah?" Josie says, as if it's news to her. As if she hasn't seen the messages lighting up her screen.

Hey. Is everything OK?

Are you ignoring me?

I'm sorry if I upset you. If you want to be left alone that's cool. I just want to make sure you're alright.

"Look, I know that me and Nic used to date, so maybe this is weird for me to say, but he likes you. I can tell," Gabby says. "And he's a good guy. It wouldn't hurt, would it? Just to let him know you're OK?"

Josie slides past her to pull the suitcase shut.

"He wouldn't like me," she says. "If he knew what being associated with me would do to him. If he knew half the things other people think of me."

She sets the case upright on the floor, ready to leave.

"In fact," she says. "I don't think that he'd want anything to do with me at all."

```
NEW VIDEO
@TRUECRIMEFANGIRL_2002
POSTED TODAY AT 13:12
```

Hey, true crime fans, and thanks for coming back to check out my series on the Tamara Drayton case.

Now this is a video that I have had a lot of requests for. And besties, as you all know, these videos are all about you. I always, always want to give you true crime addicts all the juice, and that's why today we're talking about some of the weirder bits of evidence for this case—our true crime Easter eggs, shall we say. Now, if you're new here, these are fun little clues and crazy coincidences that might have absolutely nothing to do with the case. But if you know me, you know I love a rabbit hole, and is anything ever really a coincidence anyway? So buckle up, my little true crime bunnies, and let's get digging.

So first of all, let's talk about Harrison Andreas's car. Now, people freak out over this, and it is kinda crazy. So, on the night of Evelyn Drayton's birthday party—the same night that Tamara Drayton gets unalived—Harrison Andreas's car gets stolen from the garage of the Draytons' property. I know! Wild!

The car is found abandoned not far from the house, and basically police kind of sniff around this for a little bit. It actually ends up being part of the reason why they take Harrison in for questioning, and why he's the focus of their investigation for the first few days.

But ultimately, and honestly, kind of unbelievably, they decide that the two events—the car being stolen and crashed, and Tamara

Drayton's death—are unrelated. They fingerprint and forensically test the car, and frankly, it's a hotbed of DNA. I mean, let's be honest, we all know that Harrison Andreas was a total creep, so he'd probably screwed half the town in that car. But what we know for sure is that the family's DNA is found inside, plus at least two unidentified samples and a number of partial fingerprints. The police also report that Tamara's fingerprints specifically are found on the steering wheel. Which isn't *that* suspect. Like, Harrison said that Tamara was always sneaking his car keys and driving his car, like, classic teenage rebellion stuff, and she was probably giving people rides all the time, like you do when you're seventeen.

But yeah, there's literally hundreds of theories out there on this, and I'm not surprised at all. I mean—how often does your car get stolen, and more to the point, how often does your stepdaughter get found half-dead in your swimming pool? Both kinda freak incidents, but for them both to happen on the same night? Kinda wild, right?

So a lot of people agree this makes Harrison pretty suspect. Like, what if he was trying to escape a crime scene and ran his car off the road? Or what if Tamara took off with his car—which she was known to do—but this time Harrison got pissed? Like, *really* pissed? Pissed enough to kill her?

But the police get DNA samples and fingerprints for pretty much everyone at the party, and those unidentified samples don't match anyone. Again, the police decide that the stolen car is unrelated. But what if it isn't? That would have to mean that the car was either moved by someone in the family, or someone who wasn't at the party at all. And if you believe that the stolen car is related to Tamara's death . . . well. It definitely gives you a lot to think about.

Now, on to my second Easter egg about this case—and this one is big. Were Tamara and Josie actually closer than everyone says?

So, I could make an entire series on just the relationship between these two girls, because there is so much going on here. But the accepted wisdom is that these girls were not friends. In fact, Tamara kind of disliked Josie. Josie was a bit of an outcast, and despite Josie spending a lot of time at the Drayton family home, the two of them rarely interacted because they were just so different. Like, Josie's family literally worked for the Draytons, and the Draytons weren't exactly mixing with the help, you know?

But then, when Josie's house gets searched, the police actually find some stuff that Josie claims tells a very different story. Gifts that she says were given to her by Tamara Drayton. In fact, Josie says that she and Tamara were actually friends. Had been for years. And the jury is out on what is going on here—is Josie trying to suggest some kind of preexisting relationship as a reason why she couldn't possibly have killed Tamara? Or is she telling the truth, and the two women were actually a lot closer than people suspected? And if they were, then why the secrecy? Why did nobody else believe that the two of them were friends? Does this protect Josie, or does it give her some kind of motive for murder?

OK, guys, I could talk about these forever—and believe me, there is so much more to this than meets the eye. Because you real true crime addicts will know that this isn't the only interesting thing about Josie and Tamara's relationship. But guys, I'm going to have to make a separate video about this, because I'm running out of time. Like and comment if you'd like a part two on these deep dives into the night of Tamara Drayton's death, because there's so much other stuff I have to tell you guys!

EllieBelly: Can't believe that I've never heard about the stolen car before?! That shit crayyyy.
Murderhouse790: How did Harrison Andreas never get charged!?
Victim_987: You can't just leave us hanging like that. Like, were these two friends or not!?
ClaraKensleysMom: This is the case that never stops giving.

TWENTY-FIVE

2004

ONE WEEK BEFORE THE BIRTHDAY PARTY

Tamara met Josie Jackson when she was twelve.

It was the second summer that Josie had lived on the Côte d'Azur, and the first summer that Tamara had been without Blake. He had gone to the Amalfi Coast to stay with their dad, a trip that Tamara had been uninvited from after fighting viciously with her stepmother during their obligatory Christmas visit to Italy.

With Blake gone, Tamara found that all the clichés about twins were true. She felt like half a person. Like her left arm or right leg was missing. That her thoughts went unfinished, trailing off where her brother was supposed to pick them up.

Tamara spent that summer at the pink house, roaming its vast rooms, sitting alone on the edge of the pool, wishing that she had controlled herself around Flora. That she had been better, somehow; more like Blake. Instead, she had been the bad twin again.

She started to sneak out. Late at night at first and then earlier and earlier in the day. She was surprised to find that Evelyn didn't seem to notice—or perhaps simply didn't care. Tamara would go down to the beach alone, or to one of the cafés that sold fresh fruit juice and ice cream. She watched the local children playing in the sea, unafraid of the waves and the tides.

Tamara never went into the sea herself. She had always been a little bit afraid of water, the legacy of a mother who was baffled by the idea of ferrying her children to swimming classes or spending afternoons supervising them at the pool. Despite spending every summer of her life at the pink house, Tamara was not a strong swimmer.

That was how she first met Josie Jackson.

Tamara was sitting alone on the beach, her legs drawn up to her chest, watching the other kids play in the sea. Watching one girl in particular: sinewy and small, her dark hair bunched back into a ponytail, her swimming costume slightly too large for her. There was a small floating platform, and Tamara watched as the girl clambered onto it before diving into the water over and over again, her body a tight, soaring arc before it disappeared beneath the waves.

After a while, the girl seemed to notice Tamara watching. Her dives became higher, more performative. Tuck jumps and twists. Tamara looked away, embarrassed that she'd been caught staring. She pretended to be watching a swarm of surfers disappointed by the flatness of the waves instead.

"Aren't you going in the water?"

The girl had crept up without Tamara spotting her, her voice making Tamara jump. She dropped down onto the sand, hair still dripping wet. Tamara's arms tightened around her knees.

"I . . ." She hesitated. "No. I don't really like going in the sea."

"You must be a tourist."

The girl said the word with a kind of smugness. A sense of belonging here, even though Tamara would later learn that she'd only been living in France for a little over a year.

"No, actually." Tamara felt her chin stick up at this. "We own the pink house? Up on the hill?"

There was an authority to it.

"I'm Tamara Drayton."

She was used to people recognizing the name. She was already accustomed to the raise of eyebrows, the impressed way they would say, "Not one of *the* Draytons?"

"Oh yeah," the girl had said, as if it was nothing. "My mum just interviewed for a job there. I'm Josie, by the way."

She reached her hand down, idly tracing shapes in the sand.

"So how come you don't like the sea?" she said.

Tamara swallowed. There was something about this girl. An ease. An openness that seemed to spool out and wind its way into Tamara.

"I'm not the best swimmer," she said.

Josie's hand slowed in the sand.

"Serious?" she said. "I thought the pink house had a swimming pool."

"Yeah, well." Tamara shrugged, helplessly. "I don't mind the pool so much. But the sea . . ."

She stretched out one hand toward it, as if by explanation. The vastness. The emptiness.

"Well." Josie sat up straighter, propping herself up on one arm. "Do you want me to help you?"

"Help me?"

"Yeah. It's easy, once you get used to it."

In spite of herself, Tamara had found a smile creeping onto her face.

"OK," she had said. "Alright. You can help me, if you want."

※

When Tamara gets back from her night in Montpellier, Blake is waiting up for her, sitting on her bed in the light of a single lamp, his arms crossed over his chest.

"What do you think you're playing at?" he asks.

"What do you think *you're* playing at?" she echoes him. Grins. The room is swaying slightly, a slow, back-and-forth tilt, as if they are in the bow of a ship.

He stands.

"Harrison knows you took the car, by the way. He's been fuming all afternoon."

"So? What's he going to do? Call the police on me?"

He pulls a face.

"You stink of booze. You shouldn't be driving."

"Sorry, Mum."

"Yeah, right. Like Mum would care. Seriously though, Tam. I don't know what's got into you this summer."

"Like you've never let Barnaby drive you anywhere drunk."

"Tamara, stop." He places his hands on both of her shoulders, maneuvers her to sit on the bed. "It's like you're in self-destruct at the minute. I can't talk to you when you're like this."

"So don't. Don't talk to me."

"Tamara—"

"You've been too busy fucking Hannah Bailey all summer to bother with me anyway."

She regrets it as soon as she says it, the petulant, childish way that it sounds. But mostly, she regrets how it invites her twin brother, the person she loves most in the world, to lie to her again.

"I'm not—"

She covers her ears with her hands.

"Don't," she says.

"Don't *what*?"

He prizes her hands away from the sides of her head. His grip is firm. Strong. It reminds Tamara, briefly, of when they used to play-fight as kids. How, for two glorious summers, Tamara had been taller than her twin, stronger. How she used to be able to wrestle him to the ground, triumphant.

Now, her brother has filled out, gained muscles that Tamara doesn't have. Now, she looks Blake straight in the eye, and her voice is a hiss.

"Don't lie to me, Blake," she says. "I know you. I can tell."

For a moment he is still. His body is all hard lines and angles. His hands are still around Tamara's wrists. Then, something inside him collapses. He lets go of her. His shoulders slump.

"Fine," he says. "Yes. I had sex with Hannah Bailey."

Tamara should feel triumphant, but instead something inside her drops. As if she had still, somehow, held on to the hope that this might not be true.

"You're an idiot," she says. "Do you think no one's going to find out?"

He collapses down onto the bed. Lowers his head to his hands.

"I don't know," he says, muffled. "I wasn't thinking."

"Do you like her?"

He pauses. Then:

"I don't know."

"You do, then."

He doesn't say anything.

"She likes you."

Still, nothing.

"Oh, Blake." Tamara can't help herself. She sits on the bed beside her brother. Wraps her arm around him. "You are in so much trouble."

He nods.

"You won't tell anyone?" he says thickly. "She's different from us, you know? In a good way. I couldn't help it."

"Who would I tell?"

"I don't know."

"You have to end it though. You know that, right?"

Slowly, Blake nods.

"And Blake?"

"Yeah?"

"Whatever you do," Tamara says, "do not let Hannah find out about Cordelia."

TWENTY-SIX

2024

There is a smudge of orange foundation on the collar of Nina's shirt.

She notices it in the bathroom, after a makeup artist has spent the best part of an hour plastering her face with products that she assured Nina were necessary to prevent her looking *washed out* by the cameras. She looks washed out anyway, the result of barely sleeping or eating for the last few days. But she will sleep after this interview, she is sure of it. She will finally, finally be absolved. Everything will be better, brighter, once she tells the world the secret she has carried inside herself for so long. She will be able to breathe at last.

A runner manages to find some stage chalk to conceal the blot of orange on Nina's collar, winks as she rubs the mess away.

"Tricks of the trade," she says.

And then, Nina is arranged on a sofa, bright white lights pointed at her, in front of a set that she knows will have been hastily assembled to look like the living room of a society heiress. It's much nicer than any of the Draytons' properties are in reality. All fresh, white linen curtains and shiningly new furniture. Nothing at all like the crumbling interiors of the pink house.

"Nina! Hi! So good to meet you!"

A woman breezes up to Nina, bending to plant kisses on both her cheeks.

"Katherine. I'll be conducting the interview today. You've been briefed? Yes? Wonderful. Now, the most important thing to remember is to talk to *me* and not the camera. We're just two friends, having a coffee and a chat, alright? Oh, and we won't be including any of my voice or questions, so if you could start your answers by repeating back the question. And don't worry too much if you mess up. This is only a first interview. And we'll only be pulling out the tiniest bits, don't worry. Most of it will end up on the cutting-room floor, so just talk as much as you like, take us wherever your mind takes you, and I'm sure that you'll be just wonderful."

"It isn't Imogen interviewing me?" Nina asks, dazed.

"Oh, *Imogen*? You mean 'truecrimefangirl' two thousand and whatever?"

The implication of inverted commas around Imogen Faye's screenname is obvious, and Nina suspects that Katherine is not pleased to be superseded by a twenty-two-year-old TikTokker.

"God, no. Imogen's a bit . . . well, you know," Katherine trails off with a raise of one eyebrow. "She'll really just be doing the to-camera stuff, you know? A few little segues and voiceover segments. You really have to work with these social media kids now, you know. Gets their audiences on board. And an audience like Imogen Faye's is well worth having. Anyway. Are we ready?"

Before the camera starts, before Katherine begins, Nina thinks of what she should have been doing today. Her new job. The curt email response that she received this morning from the HR manager informing her that they understood, but that *as she is in her probation period, they unfortunately can't authorize any absence that exceeds three days*. Her messages to Ryan that have gone unanswered over the last twenty-four hours, the longest they've gone without speaking in their entire relationship.

"OK, Nina," Katherine is saying. "Three, two, one. Let's go."

※

The interview is not what Nina expected.

She is eager to get to the point. To the day of her sister's death. But instead, Katherine fires off a flurry of questions that make Nina feel disoriented. That make her mind feel thick, as if she's reaching for something within the intangible mess of her memories that she can't quite access. What was Tamara like? Josie? How were the days leading up to Tamara's death? How did Tamara seem? When was the last time that Nina remembers interacting with Josie before the day of the party?

Nina tries her best. She says things she knows about her sister, although she isn't sure if they are thoughts that she has formulated herself or things she's only heard before—from her mother, or from Blake, or from articles that she's read, episodes she's pretended not to watch.

When she talks about what that summer was like, she isn't sure if she is talking about that summer specifically, or an amalgamation of all her childhood summers, a montage of memories that come together into one hot, suncream-scented soup. She finds herself saying generic, pointless things, hating how vague they sound. A time for the family to be together. A break from their lives in London. Happy memories.

She tries to talk about Josie but finds herself swaying between two different versions of the teenage girl she barely remembers—the impression of someone warm and kind, and the impression of someone dark, and dangerous, and cruel. Are both versions of Josie real to her, or is one a construct of all the things that have been said about Josie since Tamara's death? Does Nina know anything about Josie at all?

"And now." Katherine is leaning in. "If we could shift to the actual day of Tamara Drayton's death. Can you tell us everything that you remember?"

This is it. The question that Nina has been waiting for. She sits up slightly straighter.

"Well, this is the problem," she says. "I don't actually remember what happened the day that my sister died."

She expects the room to change. The atmosphere to shift. She almost imagined a collective gasp rippling around the ring of producers and cameramen surrounding the set. But instead, Katherine goes on with just a small raise of her eyebrow.

"Understandable," she says. "You were very young, of course. But absolutely nothing?"

"Nothing," Nina repeats. "I really don't remember whether Josie went anywhere near my sister."

"Well, no use flogging a dead horse if there's nothing you can say about it," Katherine says breezily. "Let's move on to your role in the trial."

And just like that, the moment is gone, the opportunity snatched away from Nina. She keeps answering questions, keeps telling Katherine what she remembers about the police interviews and the trial. It is only as they move further and further away from talk of the day of Tamara's death that Nina realizes.

Katherine doesn't seem to care whether or not Nina remembers at all.

※

Nina corners Katherine later, when a senior producer announces a break and they are guided into a room where baskets of fruit and plates of pastries are set out on a long trestle table.

"Katherine!" Nina says. "Katherine, hi. Can I just . . . do you mind if I just grab you for a second?"

"Grab away," Katherine says, still rooting through a basket of brightly packaged snacks.

"Well . . . it's just . . . the question about whether I remembered what happened to Tamara? I thought we'd talk about that a bit more? I thought that that might be—you know. Quite a big thing. That it'd be a sort of turning point. After all, I'm basically saying there's a good chance Josie Jackson didn't do it. Isn't that something we should focus on a bit more?"

Katherine is inspecting the ingredients on the back of a protein bar wrapper.

"Well," she says. "Do you know what *did* happen to Tamara?"

"Well, no," Nina says. "Like I said. I don't remember."

"Mmhmm," Katherine says. "You see our problem?"

"I . . ." Nina trails off.

"The thing is, Nina." Katherine begins to unwrap the protein bar. "That this isn't exactly new evidence, you understand? Sure, you don't remember *now*. And don't get me wrong, that's incredibly interesting. It gives our viewers something to think about. But if I was watching at home? Well, I'd be asking myself what's more reliable. Do I believe the testimony of someone—albeit a little kid—who says that they saw exactly what happened—and their memory is fresh, right? They saw it happen literally a couple of days before they speak out."

She breaks off a piece of the protein bar.

"Or do I believe that same kid, twenty years later, who says that they don't remember anymore? Not that they remember that they made the whole thing up, or that they know what really happened. But that they simply don't remember *anything* anymore."

She places the small, compact square of ultra-processed nuts and chocolate into her mouth.

"Honestly, I'd believe the little kid," she says between chews. "I don't remember my first day at school, or the day my dad left, but that doesn't mean it didn't *happen*. It doesn't mean I didn't know about it, and understand it, and remember it at the time. You see?"

She swallows noisily.

"And anyway," she continues. "We have a *fantastic* neurologist, all lined up. He's going to give us some great material about false memories, and how trauma can lead to us blocking things out. All that good stuff. What you said was *brilliant*. I can just see it now. You saying you don't remember, and then cutting straight to Dr. Edmonson to explain why you don't remember something now that you remembered so vividly at the time. It'll all flow together brilliantly. All very thought-provoking, for our viewers."

"So it doesn't matter?" says Nina. Her voice comes out faint. She feels, suddenly, very far away from this woman. Almost like she isn't in the room at all. "It doesn't matter that I've . . . that I've *confessed*?"

Katherine laughs then.

"Oh, sweetheart," she says. "You have nothing to confess to! You're just telling us your side of the story, as you remember it. Nobody expects someone to remember exactly what happened, all that time ago. We have the case file for that."

She stuffs the remainder of the protein bar into her handbag, pats it conspiratorially.

"I'll need my energy later!" she says. "And between you and me?"

She winks at Nina, an exaggerated flutter of her eyelash extensions.

"I think that Josie Jackson is guilty as hell."

NEW VIDEO
@TRUECRIMEFANGIRL_2002
POSTED TODAY AT 15:22

Hey, true crime babies, and welcome back to my series on the Tamara Drayton case. I am still here, still on the beautiful Azure Coast, as they call it, and we are starting filming really, really soon. But in the meantime I've been doing some serious snooping. In fact, yesterday, I actually went and took a look at the pink house, and you bet your girl went and knocked right on that door. There was no answer, sadly, but hey, you gotta try, right?

But on top of that, I'm going to be dropping some huge, really juicy information soon. Now this is a super big deal, and I'm not allowed to talk about it yet, but let's just say that I got access to Josie Jackson's case file yesterday and oh my god—I can't wait to share some of the new information that's inside. Like, this shit isn't even public yet. It's gonna be big. Give me a follow to make sure that when I post about it, you don't miss out.

I have to wrap this up, but keep investigating, keep asking questions, and keep talking about this case, guys, because we are getting justice in real time. You love to see it.

Drewpow: Noooo you cannot leave us hanging like this!!
Claireflowers: R.I.P. Tamara Drayton. You would have loved Truecrimetok.

TWENTY-SEVEN

2004
ONE WEEK BEFORE THE BIRTHDAY PARTY

The month that Josie taught Tamara to swim had stretched out like a long, late summer sunset. Achingly slow at first and then over quickly, like the sun dropping beneath the sea, day turning into night.

They hadn't used the pool at the pink house. Josie's mother had recently started her job as housekeeper, and had already warned Josie not to mix with the Drayton kids. She was nervous, Josie told Tamara, that Josie would say something to annoy or upset her mother's new charges, something that would get back to Evelyn.

Tamara had her own reasons for wanting to stay away from the pink house. Her mum had recently split from her latest husband and was on the warpath. Tamara preferred to be out of the way as much as possible.

Instead, they met at the salt pool early most mornings, before it got busy. Tamara didn't need to worry about anyone seeing her there—everyone she knew had their own pools, their own private places to swim. Here, Tamara could strap on the armbands Josie brought from the dive shop without feeling self-conscious. Josie could bellow out instructions, telling Tamara to kick harder, to tilt her head forward. The two of them could float, Josie's hand supporting Tamara, her touch gentle against her waist as she showed her how to keep her body flat and firm, the feel of her hand sending a strange electricity beneath the surface of Tamara's skin.

On the day before Tamara returned to England, Josie brought her to a part of the beach she had never been to before. A rocky platform, the sea lapping up against it, the dark kind of blue that suggested immediate depth. A flight of rusting steps screwed into the rock, as if the entire ocean was Josie's private swimming pool.

"Do you feel ready?" said Josie.

"Not really," said Tamara.

Josie smiled and reached down to squeeze Tamara's hand.

"Good," she said. "That means that it's the perfect time."

Josie had gone in first. She swam a few meters out and trod water. Tamara could just make out her legs beneath the surface, the white of her skin as she kicked.

"Are you good?" she shouted.

Tamara was shivering, even though the morning was warm, only the faintest breath of autumn in the air. She nodded. Gave Josie a thumbs-up. Took a deep breath. Lowered her foot onto the ladder.

The water was so different from the calm, lukewarm salt pool. Immediately the chill of the sea took the air out of Tamara's lungs. The swell of a wave lifted her, the spray against her face. Driving her back toward the rocks, salt in her mouth and eyes. A spark of panic in her gut, her legs scrabbling for the ground and finding only water beneath her.

She swallowed a mouthful of water and choked on it.

It was exactly what she'd been afraid of. She was going to drown out here, just like she'd always been scared that she would.

And then, just above the rise and fall of a wave, she saw a flash of white. Josie, bobbing in the distance. Waving, beckoning Tamara toward her. Tamara took in a gasp of air. Leaned her body forward, the way Josie had showed her to. Started to kick her legs.

It seemed to take a very long time to reach Josie. Tamara counted each kick, each hard, scissoring motion of her legs, each drag of her arms against the resistance of water. At first, she didn't seem to be getting anywhere. Josie remained, a flash of skin, the bob of her ponytail, far away. Tamara lost sight of her behind a wave, and then when she emerged Josie was closer. Larger. Tamara kicked harder. Each stroke carried her toward Josie now. The waves seemed to level and slow. She could hear Josie's voice, carrying on the wind. Cheering. Chanting her name.

She swam the final few strokes with salt in her eyes, her vision blurred. When she reached Josie, their limbs collided, and all Tamara could hear was Josie whooping. Tamara caught hold of her and wrapped her arms around her shoulders, both kicking their legs frantically to stay afloat. Dragging each other down at the same time as they held each other up.

"You did it!" Josie said.

Tamara was laughing. There was seawater in her eyes, on her skin, in her mouth. She felt alive. Invincible.

This was how she would always remember them.

※

Tamara is leaning out of her bedroom window smoking when she hears Josie downstairs. The click of the front door, the murmur of voices.

"Yeah," Josie is saying. "Yeah, I can come back tomorrow."

She sounds tired. Tamara knows that she's been taking care of Nina all day, ferrying her down to the beach, reading her picture books. Keeping her out of Evelyn and Harrison's way.

For the last two summers, since their dad stopped inviting Blake to stay with him in Italy, Tamara and Josie have spent time together less frequently. The days down by the sea have thinned.

Their friendship has always been a secret, ever since those days at the salt pool. It had remained a guilty delight, knowing that their mothers wouldn't approve—that Patricia would be on edge about it, and Evelyn would inevitably make some snide comment about *the Jackson girl*, about how she was a bad influence. But recently, Tamara has found herself inventing other excuses. Early-morning swims and late-night meetings have faded to occasional encounters when Josie is working at the house. Tamara has found herself wondering if their mothers are really the reason for her own desire for secrecy, or if there is something more that she is afraid to admit to. She does not like what this might say about her.

Tamara stubs out her cigarette and scrambles to her feet. She darts downstairs, out to the side of the house, where she knows that the garden exit will intersect Josie's path up the hill. She emerges when Josie is still a few steps away, her spine hunched, eyes fixed down toward the ground.

"Hey," Tamara says.

Josie's head jerks up.

"Hey."

Her voice is weighty with suspicion. The ease and warmth that used to hum between them like a current has flickered down to a faint pulse. Tamara finds herself wanting another cigarette, even though her throat still burns with smoke from the last one.

"Are you doing anything right now?" says Tamara.

Josie shrugs, wary.

"Not much."

"Do you wanna go down to the beach? We could sneak some vodka out of Evelyn's alcohol cupboard."

Josie sighs. Rubs the heel of her hand into her eye.

"I'm kind of tired," she says. "It's been a long day."

"Oh, come on," says Tamara. "We haven't hung out in ages. Just for an hour?"

Josie hesitates. Between them, Tamara sees the truth that neither of them will speak. They haven't hung out for ages because of Tamara. Because of the distance she has laid between them.

Because they're not children anymore, and the differences in their lives feel too vast, too awkward, to bridge.

"Fine," says Josie. "An hour. But then I'm going to bed."

Tamara feels a smile spreading up but fights to keep her mouth still. Tilts her head to the side, casual.

"I promise," she says. "An hour."

When they get down to the water, Tamara hovers at its edge.

"Do you want to go in?" she asks.

She so badly wants Josie to say yes. She wants to be in the water with her. She believes, in some impossible way, that it will take them back to who they once were. Two girls, without all the complicated things that have arisen between them over time.

Josie screws up her nose.

"I don't have a swimming costume with me," she says.

"We could paddle?"

"I'm OK. Thanks."

"Vodka, then?"

Josie accepts the bottle and they sit on a broad, smooth rock. There is a chill in the air, and Josie pulls her knees up to her chest as she passes the vodka back to Tamara.

"What have you been doing this summer?" Tamara says.

"Working, mostly."

"Right. Obviously."

Tamara takes a swig from the bottle and then offers it back to Josie. Josie shakes her head.

"I'm good," she says. "Mum will freak out if I come back hammered."

Tamara removes her hand, stung. Already, the night is not unfurling how she had imagined. She had hoped that they'd get tipsy. That they'd swim. That she'd see Josie ease back into herself, her guard gradually falling away.

"My mum, too," she lies, knowing that Evelyn will not care—perhaps will not even notice.

Josie shifts slightly.

"She'd freak out if she knew you were with me," she says.

Tamara doesn't answer.

"I guess she doesn't know about Hannah and Blake yet?" Josie says.

"Hannah and Blake?"

Josie rolls her eyes.

"Don't act like you don't know," says Josie. "Hannah's a good person. I don't want her getting hurt."

The words sting. *I'm a good person,* Tamara wants to protest. Or at least, she wants Josie to think she's a good person. Josie had always treated her as if the fact that she was a Drayton didn't matter. As if she didn't see all the darkness inside Tamara.

Tamara knows how close Josie and Hannah are. She's jealous that Hannah gets Josie all year round. Tamara doesn't mind that their friendship has always been a secret from their parents and siblings. It stops people asking questions; makes it feel more special somehow, sacred. But sometimes she wonders why Josie doesn't at least tell Hannah about her. Wonders what Josie feels like she has to hide.

"It won't last," Tamara says.

"What makes you so sure about that?"

There's a defensive spring in Josie's words. The same spike that Tamara heard in the pizza restaurant. *He's not better than her.* Tamara had kicked herself afterward for letting Josie think that was what she meant, realizing that she had inadvertently laid another inch of distance between them.

All of a sudden, she is tired of protecting her brother.

"He has a girlfriend," she says.

She feels Josie stiffen beside her, alert.

"A girlfriend?"

Tamara lifts the bottle of vodka and takes a swig. Too late to go back now. "He's been with her for a while," she says. "Her name's Cordelia."

"*Cordelia?*"

Josie says the name like it's a bad punchline.

Tamara shrugs.

"She's old money," she says. "Like, *proper* old money. Her dad's an earl. Mum's descended from some European royalty or something—Spanish, or maybe Portuguese. I can't remember. Anyway. Blake's obsessed with . . . well. Not with *her* exactly. But, I guess, what she means. What she represents. He's always had a chip on his shoulder, about us being *new money.* Always been embarrassed about it. I know, I know . . ." She breaks off, preempting the snort of laughter that emits from Josie's mouth. "But, look. It's big, being associated with a family like that. It legitimizes you. Gives you access to all these parts of society that no one else can touch. Sure, Mum knows a load of has-been actors and supermodels from the seventies. But you have no idea the power that families like Cordelia's have. The connections. The doors they can open."

She hates herself for saying it, for knowing these things. For understanding these fine distinctions, the knowledge of the intricacies of class and wealth that have been baked into her since birth.

"He's not going to break up with Cordelia," she says. "Not for Hannah. He *needs* Cordelia. Or, at least, he needs her family. Her dad's got him an internship at a big investment bank next summer in Switzerland. He's talked about renting out this beautiful house for him and Cordelia in Zurich. Then, they'll go and stay with her family at their place in Lake Garda. It's everything he wants, Josie. He's not going to throw it away for—"

Josie stands then. Brushes sand off her thighs.

"I should go," she said.

"But we just got here."

"I'm not in the mood, Tam."

Josie hasn't called her that in a long time. Their eyes meet. Josie looks so sad.

"Everything's different now," she says. "It's not how it used to be, when we were kids."

Then she turns and walks away. Leaves Tamara alone, with only the sound of the waves. The endless stretch of the sea.

TWENTY-EIGHT

2024

There is something uniquely depressing about a budget airport hotel.

Josie's room is on the ground floor. The space is anonymous and plain. A sheen of misted plastic tacked to the lower portion of the window in a faint nod to privacy. A beige carpet. A bathroom with a plastic shower stall. A desk placed against the window, as if anyone would want to gaze onto the blurred concrete concourse beyond.

Josie washes beneath a slow stream of water, using up all the tiny bottles supplied to clean off the scent of her journey. Calvin's car to the station. A crammed train carriage that left a stale, sweating smell on her skin.

Calvin had held her tight on the platform, as if he didn't want to let her go.

"You sure about this?" he asked.

"As I'll ever be," Josie said, and in the reflection of his sunglasses she could see how unsure she looked. How different, and yet the same, as the version of herself who had arrived here a little over a week ago. The optimism of her new beginning already broken.

After her shower, she switches on the television. She sits on the bed, and flicks through channels she would never normally watch.

She imagines the people who have occupied this space before her, none of them staying longer than a night, nobody sleeping easily. Couples sneaking in bottles of prosecco to toast their first holiday. Harassed businessmen hanging up their suits above the chipped mirror. The slightly dazed people who stay here after a flight away from a place, a person, a world that they can never go back to. Who stretch out on this bed and know that tomorrow everything will feel new, and strange, and different.

Josie has been in so many cheap hotels, caught so many early-morning flights. She has sat watching television on beds exactly like this. She barely feels it anymore, the sense that she is leaving one life behind and moving on to another. It is easier to long for the next stage than to mourn the part that has just ended.

Her fingers stray to her phone. She slides her thumb against the screen and pulls up a picture she took on what would be her first and last date with Nic. They had been waiting for their food to arrive, already with that gloss of tipsiness, a starriness on their faces, white-toothed grins. She flicks her thumb again, and there she is with Gabby, a selfie on the dance floor. A picture of Gabby perched in Calvin's lap. A group shot of the four of them that Calvin had cajoled a stranger into taking.

She exits her gallery and scrolls into her conversation with her aunt instead. Her mother's sister, Beverly, a woman that Josie has only met a handful of times since she first left the UK as a child. It's clear that Beverly regrets telling Josie that she could ask for help *anytime* in a stream of uncharacteristic emotion at Patricia's funeral. Her messages are filled with tense questions about how long Josie plans to stay for, warnings about how Beverly's partner won't put up with any press at their front door. Josie promises not to be any trouble, says Beverly will hardly know she's there. Like always, Josie feels that she is apologizing for something that she cannot control, for being someone she is not.

Josie hopes she'll only need to rely on her aunt for a few weeks. She wouldn't have thought of her at all, if she wasn't so desperate. But she needs to leave France if she has any shot of throwing the media off her scent.

She finds herself tapping back into the gallery. Zooming in on the picture of her and Nic. Something in his eyes sends an ache through her chest. She barely knows him, of course. But god, she can imagine it. She wants so badly to let herself reach out toward him. To lean into something that feels like it could be good for the first time in years.

Her phone buzzes in her hand. A message from Calvin.

We miss you already x

She won't let herself cry. She can't. It would be too much of a cliché, to spend the night sobbing in a shitty airport motel. It would be too depressing to bear.

Just out of curiosity, she tells herself, she opens up a browser, checks to see if there are any trains still running. There are two, if she goes quickly. Two choices. Two chances to change everything Josie thinks that she knows about herself.

Her thumb hovers over the screen.

If there is one thing that Josie thinks she is good at, it's goodbyes. Or, to be more precise, *not* saying goodbye. Leaving people behind without a backward glance. Letting each person, each place leave only the tiniest mark on her, an almost imperceptible dent in the fabric of her being rather than a great gouge.

But a slow chipping away of herself is still a hollowing, a lack of history. A numbness that Josie has let grow inside her for years.

Perhaps it's time to start filling that hole.

She taps on the button to buy a ticket.

Perhaps, Josie thinks, perhaps she isn't quite so good at goodbyes after all.

※

Josie takes a taxi from the train station, the road skimming the coast, the sea falling in and out of view, long shadows as the moon rises in the sky.

She does not have a plan, exactly. She understands, still, that she will have to leave eventually, back to England, or Paris, or some as-yet-undecided place. But she also has an impossible-to-resist feeling of something unresolved, an itch that she must scratch.

Josie is so used to leaving things broken behind her. For once, she wants to put them back together. She wants to see Nic, even if only one last time. She wants to say goodbye. She wants to say sorry. She wants to say that she wishes things could have been different, but knows that they can't. She wants to tell him that she'll be back, but doesn't know if she'd be telling the truth.

She wants to do the right thing.

The dive shop is closed by the time Josie arrives, the shutters pulled down, the lights turned out. Upstairs, one solitary window glows. Josie pulls out her phone. Types out a message.

Look outside x

When he comes to the window he's smiling.

"I had a feeling you might come back," he says.

"You want to go for a walk?"

"Yeah. Let's go for a walk."

※

They don't talk until they reach the beach.

They take their shoes off once they get there and sit close to the water, their toes dug in the sand. The reflection of the moon is a shifting slice of silver, shimmering with the dark rise and fall of the waves, as though the sea is a living, breathing thing.

"You're not leaving, then?" says Nic.

"Not yet."

"At some point, though?"

"At some point, yeah. I just felt like there was unfinished business for me to figure out here first."

"Is that what I am? Unfinished business?"

He says it lightly, like he's joking, but Josie doesn't miss the cut of his words, the hurt that hides behind them. She looks right at him then.

"Of course not," she says. "That's not what I mean. I . . ."

She pauses. She has already made her decision. And yet saying it out loud will solidify it. Make it real.

"I'm going to talk to the documentary makers again," she says. "You were right, what you said before. I've already given them the case file. They're going to be telling my story anyway. People are going to be talking about me, whether I like it or not. At least this way, I get a chance to control the narrative. I get a chance to tell my side of the story. I doubt people will believe me, but . . ."

She breaks off. Takes a moment to gather herself again.

"When we talked about this before, I said that things would never change, unless Nina Drayton changed her story. And when I spoke to her—I think that she actually might be ready to do that. If I'm here, if I take part, I can make sure that she goes through with it. I need to talk to her again. I need to speak to Nina Drayton, properly this time."

"And then you're leaving?" Nic says.

"I like you, Nic," she says. "If things were different . . ."

She shrugs. She can't finish the sentence. If the case hadn't gone viral again. If Josie hadn't spent her late teens and a good chunk of her twenties in prison. If, all those years ago, Nina Drayton hadn't pointed her finger at Josie and changed the entire trajectory of her life.

"The documentary is going to attract a lot of attention," she says. "And even if Nina Drayton changes her story, there will still be a lot of people who don't believe her. A lot of people who hate me."

"But how can things be different, unless you change what you're doing?" Nic asks.

"What do you mean?"

He picks up a stone and rolls it between his fingers.

"It just seems to me like this is what you always do. Didn't you say that you've spent the last ten years feeling like you were running away?"

He pulls back his arm and throws the stone. It lands heavily against the water.

"How can you expect things to be different, if everything that you do is the same?"

"I didn't mean . . ." she starts, and then trails off.

Because maybe this is exactly what she meant.

"What should I do differently then?"

He picks up another stone.

"Stay," he says, simply. "Not just for a bit, while you're sorting out *unfinished business*. Stay for good."

"It's not that easy."

"Why not? Gabby and Calvin want you here."

"Just Gabby and Calvin?"

"You're really going to make me say it?"

She tilts her head to one side. He groans, mock-defeated.

"Look, I don't want to put pressure on you," he says. "I wouldn't ask you to stay just for me."

He tosses the stone. This time it's a perfect skim, the flat rock bouncing against the surface.

"But since you said it first," he says. "I like you, too. I like you a lot."

There's a beat of stillness. Within it, Josie sees the last ten years of her life. All the different places and people. All the times she has left. All the times she's gone looking for safety, and found only the ground giving way beneath her again.

Nic is right. Even change becomes monotonous, after a while. The same process of leaving, of starting over. The same worries, and regrets. The same hopes that get dashed again and again. Maybe it really is time for Josie to do things differently.

Her fingers graze Nic's leg. She doesn't think too much. She doesn't wonder if this is the start of something, or the end.

He turns his head toward her, and she leans into him. Her mouth meets his.

It's one of those rare moments where Josie Jackson feels as if she is exactly where she is supposed to be.

※

When Josie wakes the next morning, she is alone.

She must have fallen asleep without meaning to, Nic's T-shirt twisted around her body, the smell of him on her skin. The scent takes her back to last night. How they had come back to his flat and drank coffee on his sofa. Talked for a long time. How, eventually, they had kissed again, slowly this time, his hand on the side of her face. How Josie had wanted him in a way that felt large and complicated, and clean and focused all at once. The scale and simplicity of her desire.

They had taken their time undressing each other, uncovering each new contour of skin, hands tracing new curves and corners like explorers sketching out a map of new territories. Nic had kissed her collarbone, her hip, the sharp indent between her throat and shoulder. When he was inside her, he had intertwined one hand with hers and pressed it down hard against the mattress. To Josie, it felt like they were drowning, submerged, clinging to each other as they reached for the surface.

In some ways, Josie feels as if she has been underwater since the day Tamara died. Now, she takes a deep breath, and is struck by the distinct sensation that she is back above air again.

She pulls on her jeans and opens the door to the living room. Nic is already at the stove, brewing coffee in a battered moka pot.

"Morning," he says. "Sleep well?"

"Yeah." She feels slightly dazed at how natural this feels.

"It's a beautiful morning," Nic says. "If you go and sit out on the balcony I'll bring this out?"

"Actually," Josie says. "There's something I wanted to ask you first."

"Ask away."

It feels so easy, and yet Josie knows that now she must make things hard. She must make things hard, so that she can make them better again.

"You said last night that Hannah's back," she says.

She sees him stiffen. She has to go on.

"Can you talk to her for me?" she says. "Can you ask if she'll see me?"

"I don't know—"

"Please," she says. "It's important. To me, and probably to her as well."

On the stove, the moka pot starts to gurgle. Nic doesn't move to take it off the heat. Instead, he straightens, then nods.

"OK. I'll see if she'll talk."

TWENTY-NINE

2024

They always eat as a family here.

It isn't something that Hannah is used to. When she was a child, she would rarely sit down for dinner with both her mum and dad. There was always something that needed doing at the shop, some excursion that one of her parents would be running, some equipment that needed setting up for the next day. It wasn't unusual for meals to be eaten standing up in the kitchen, or behind the shop counter. Makeshift picnics carried down to the beach.

It was a habit that Hannah had continued into early adulthood. She and Eric hadn't been able to afford a dining table in their first tiny flat, and by the time they could, sitting down for a family meal fell so far down Hannah's list of priorities that it scarcely warranted a look-in. After school and nursery pickups, she'd wrestle trays of chicken nuggets into the oven, throw on a load of laundry while frozen peas boiled on the stovetop, help Mason with his homework while she did the dishes.

Eric would be home for bedtime, and by the time both kids were settled, the two of them rarely had the energy to sit up straight at the table. They'd order takeout, or microwave a frozen meal, slump in front of a box set to eat, always talk about how one day, when the kids were old enough, they'd do things properly. Hannah would cook something from scratch. Eric would get out of work early enough to help. They'd all sit at the dining table together, some happy, wholesome version of parenthood that always seemed to be just around the corner, but that they never quite caught up with.

Hannah had only once thought they were about to make the change from hassled, time-poor parents to the kind of people she saw on Instagram. The kind of mums who wore floaty linen dresses without unidentifiable orange stains, who baked their own cake pops for party bags, and read the back of washing powder packets to make sure that their kids weren't somehow absorbing lethal chemicals through their fabric softener.

Noah had been due to move up to juniors, and Mason was nine, starting to be independent, wanting to hang out with his friends instead of his mum and dad. Hannah was beginning to feel like she'd almost got the hang of parenting. She'd joined an online group for local parents and had made a few mum friends. She'd set up a sleepover a few weeks before, and she and Eric had actually had a date night for the first time in their entire marriage. She'd started to research the local adult education college, wondering if she could finally finish the accountancy qualifications she'd dropped out of all those years ago.

The pregnancy was a complete accident, even more unlucky than the first. While that had been the result of a casual approach to using condoms, she'd been religious about taking the pill since Noah was born. But then they'd had a dodgy curry one night and Hannah had spent the entire weekend throwing up. She thought it was just a myth that you could get pregnant if you missed a few pills, but then there was the inarguable blue line telling her otherwise.

"We said we were stopping at two," she said, tearful, when she had told Eric. When she hoped that he would tell her that it was early, and maybe they should think about getting rid of it, that nobody would need know, because then she wouldn't have to be the one to say it.

"We were," said Eric. "But I guess now we're stopping at three."

Eric would never have thought to suggest an abortion. He wasn't the one giving up the hope for a career, the possibility of a separate identity other than mum and wife. He still had a job, and mates that he went to the pub with on a Thursday night, and people who spoke to him like an actual human being every single day.

But Hannah knew he'd never make her go through with a pregnancy for a child she didn't want.

"You never know," Eric continued. "We always used to say that we wanted a boy and a girl, ideally. Maybe we'll get *two* boys and a girl."

Hannah had thrown away the leaflets about returning to education as a mother the next day.

Now, as her mother sets the table, Isla solemnly following her holding a stack of woven place mats as if the success of the entire meal depends on it, Hannah can hardly believe that she'd considered getting rid of the cluster of cells that would eventually become her daughter. She still feels a stab of guilt when she thinks about the abortion that never was, knows that she'll never tell anyone, not even Eric, that she ever considered it.

She also knows that in some parallel universe she made a different choice. She's still a mother of two. She has a job, and friends, and hobbies, and interesting things to say at dinner parties. Maybe she learned another language, like she's always threatening to do when she's had a couple of glasses of wine and feels a bit useless.

In that parallel universe, she would be completely certain she'd made the right decision. But just now, with her own mother thanking Isla profusely in French each time she offers up a place mat, the thought is too terrible to bear.

With her parents' retirement, dinners have taken on a different tone. The house that they rent out of town is more spacious than the two-bedroom flat Hannah grew up in, big enough to fit a dining table that Mark made out of sanded-down driftwood, with patio doors that open out onto a garden where Hannah's mother grows her own herbs.

They're happier now, more relaxed than they used to be. Sometimes, Hannah wonders if they regret all the time they spent trying desperately to make the dive shop work. All the years of stress, of scrimping to get by. If they could have found other jobs, if they could have been living like this all along, would they have done so?

There are so many pathways in life, so many unknown versions of ourselves that we might be, that she wonders how we don't all go insane with the possibilities. How can anyone know if they've made the right choices? If another, better life isn't only one or two undone mistakes away?

"There's a bottle of Piquepoul open in the kitchen," Marie says, spotting Hannah hovering. "Go and get a glass, if you want one."

"I'm good, thanks," Hannah says.

She's never been a big drinker. A few wild nights when she was a teenager. Student socials at university. But then, she was pregnant with Mason so young that she missed out on actually learning to like wine in her twenties. She has the odd glass every now and again, but it doesn't take much to make her tipsy. She doesn't like the feeling it gives her, the lack of control.

"Nic's coming by for dinner tonight, by the way," Marie says, frowning at a smudge on a bright blue tumbler. "He should be here soon."

She lifts her head and spots Hannah's face.

"What?" she says. "You love Nic."

"He's been seeing Josie Jackson," Hannah says. "Did you hear?"

Marie sets the wineglass down.

"Well," she says. "I'm sure he's not planning on bringing her, if that's what you're worried about."

"'Nother one, Mémé?" pipes up Isla.

"Don't you think it seems weird?" Hannah says, as her mother accepts the place mat offering.

"I trust Nic's judgment," Marie says, as if that ends the matter.

"You've changed your tune."

"He's my only nephew, Hannah. I'm not going to stop inviting him over because of some fling. Besides, you know what Nic's like. He'll be on to the next one before you know it."

"'Nother one?"

"Maybe I will have that glass of wine."

"Top mine up while you're in there, would you?"

It is one of those perfect summer evenings. Warm. A slight breeze. Everyone together. The kind of night that always makes Hannah wonder aloud to Eric if they should consider moving out here, an idea that melts away as soon as the wine buzz wears off.

But tonight, with the news of Josie Jackson being back, the heat and the alcohol only remind Hannah of that summer. Blake. Tamara, a blaze of fury and bad ideas, tearing through what none of them knew would be the last few weeks of her life.

And Josie. Always Josie, always intertwined with Hannah's memories. It seemed, sometimes, like their teenage years merged together in places, until Hannah couldn't make out which memories were hers and which were Josie's. Who got a detention for running a black-market bubblegum-selling operation on the playground, who had their first kiss at a year-eight disco with a boy with cystic acne, who won the year-seven sports day, and who cracked their head open falling over in the egg and spoon race. It was always Josie and Hannah, bearing witness to each other's lives, telling each other's stories until they tangled into one.

That is, until Evelyn Drayton's birthday party. The day that their paths were spliced into two, sent spiraling into wildly different directions.

Hannah goes outside, to the small patch of garden that Mark and Marie dreamed of their entire working lives. There are borders crammed with tomato plants, pots of basil, an explosion of strawberries. A wind chime Marie made at a ceramics class that she's taken up on a Tuesday afternoon. A stone wall that Noah kicks a football up against over and over again. Mosquito candles, the smell of citronella almost overpowering the garden's natural herbal scent, because Marie has become obsessed with the possibility of her grandchildren getting bitten, even though Hannah spent most of her childhood wandering about with tender scarlet swellings patterning her arms and legs.

Mark and Eric sit at the table, a second bottle of wine between them. Stretched out on a wooden deckchair, Mason's thumbs fly against the buttons of his Nintendo Switch. He's fourteen now, a teenager. The thought sends a cold feeling all the way through Hannah. She knows all mothers dread the thought of their children growing up, but this feels different. She understands what teenage boys are like. She remembers.

Hannah had postnatal depression when Mason was first born. Baby blues, they used to call it, something that sounded so impossibly twee to describe the vast, awful feeling that threatened to consume her, that kept her awake at night and made her feel like the worst person in the world when she looked at her child and the feeling of overwhelming love that people had promised her failed to materialize.

It was understandable, everyone said, especially when she'd had him so young. It was hard not to feel like she was missing out, when all of her friends moved on with their lives, leaving her behind.

Hannah couldn't find the words to describe how it was something far worse than that, something much more terrible, more frightening.

Eric was the only person she had told, on a long, dark night, when Hannah had gone to bed with her hair still smelling of milky vomit, unable to remember the last time that she'd slept properly or showered.

"Think of the worst person you've ever known," she said. "The person who's done the most terrible thing to you."

"That barber who gave me that shit haircut before the wedding," Eric said.

"You're not taking this seriously."

"OK, OK, fine," he said. "I'm thinking of someone."

"OK," said Hannah. "So what if Mason turns out like that? What if he turns out *worse* than that? What if we've created something that's evil at its core, and there's absolutely nothing we can do about it?"

Eric didn't speak for a moment. When he did, his voice was so certain that Hannah couldn't imagine how different their experience of becoming a parent must be.

"I don't think anyone's evil at their core," he said. "I think evil is created. A result of circumstance, and your upbringing, and all sorts of things. And I reckon we're pretty good people, right? So I think Mason's going to turn out alright."

She hadn't answered at first.

"*You're* alright, aren't you?" he said into the darkness. "Like, you're not thinking about . . . I don't know. *Doing* anything to Mason? Because you can tell me if you are, you know. We can work it all out."

Hannah had rolled away from him then, faced the bedroom wall.

"Don't be stupid," she said. "What kind of person wants to hurt a child?"

She went on medication not long after that, and the bad thoughts mostly went away. But now that Mason was almost at the age when Hannah had done some of the worst and best things of her life, she would look at him and wonder.

"You alright, babe?" Eric says, breaking through her thoughts. "You look off in your own world over there."

Hannah gives her head a small shake, quickly, before anyone can see, as if she could dash the thought away.

"Fine," she says.

From inside the house, the doorbell rings. It sounds very far away.

"Hannah?" her mum calls. "Can you get that?"

"If it's Nic, he's got a key," Mark says lazily. "He'll let himself in, in a minute. Don't know why he even bothers ringing the doorbell."

"It's fine," Hannah says. "I don't mind going."

She wants to be inside again. She wants the cool shade of the house. A moment to shake off her thoughts, the cold feeling that always sets in whenever she thinks about that dark, terrible time before she got the right pills, before she could look at her own son without feeling a wave of despair. A rare few seconds to gather herself without one of her children asking her for something.

She takes a few deep breaths in the hallway. She feels lighter by the time she reaches the front door. She can see the shadowy shape of her cousin through the misted glass. She doesn't see, at first, that there is someone standing beside him. It doesn't register, until she's already swung the door open, smiling, ready to pull Nic into a hug.

She is looking at Josie Jackson for the first time in twenty years.

She looks so different. So much older than Hannah remembers her, the reconfiguration of her features reminding Hannah that she has also aged in the last two decades.

She is surprised that the gut-shock of horror lasts only for a millisecond before it's replaced by the thrill of familiarity and longing. She is overcome with the urge to tell Josie everything. That she went to England, like she always said she would. That she graduated from university, fell in love. She wants to squeeze her friend by both hands and squeal, *I'm MARRIED*, because now that she's looking at Josie, the thought of being married feels laughably, hilariously grown-up. They used to talk about this stuff all the time. What their ideal husbands would be like, how Hannah would have Josie as her bridesmaid, but Josie wouldn't have bridesmaids because she would elope and get married on a beach somewhere.

All the monumental things that they have missed hit Hannah squarely in her chest, and she stares at Josie, open-mouthed, before finding her voice.

"You're *blond*," she says.

And just like that, all those lost years disappear.

THIRTY

2024

Hannah and Josie go outside, to the small walled garden, and sit opposite each other at a wooden table, still littered with wineglasses, empty beer bottles, a half-eaten bowl of crisps. The detritus of the warm summer evening that Josie has interrupted.

Hannah's mum had looked at her with the horrified recognition that Josie was used to seeing in people's eyes. She had ushered the children inside, said *Mark, come* on, when Hannah's dad hovered, pink-faced, muttering something about it being good to see Josie again, after all this time.

"I'll leave you two, for a minute," Nic says. "I feel like you have some stuff to catch up on."

He slopes inside after his uncle while Hannah reaches for an open bottle of wine. She starts to pour herself a glass, and Josie sees that her hands are shaking. A tremor running through her, like wind across the surface of water.

"I heard you were back," Hannah says, in a rush. "If you were wondering. You know. Why I'm not surprised to see you."

"I'm sorry to ambush you like this," Josie says. "It was my idea. Nic didn't think you'd agree to talk to me. So I suggested that I just . . ." She spreads her hands wide, apologetic. "Turn up."

Hannah smiles. It's faint, but it's there. It makes Josie long to make her smile again.

"Nic's probably right," Hannah says. "I wouldn't have wanted to see you."

She lifts her glass and takes a large swig of wine.

"You and Nic?" she says. "Are you . . . you know?"

"Are we fucking?" says Josie.

She laughs, in spite of herself, as Hannah's hands fly up to her ears.

"Oh my god," Hannah says. "Stop. That's my little cousin you're talking about."

But she's laughing, too, and Josie can't believe how easy it is. How fast they've slipped back into their old roles.

"We're friends," Josie says truthfully.

"Do you like him?"

It's like they're teenagers again, talking about boys they have crushes on. The muscle memory of their friendship coming so easily back to life.

"Yeah," Josie says. "I do."

Hannah pushes the bottle of wine toward Josie.

"God," she says. "I can't believe this. I didn't think I'd ever see you again. I didn't think I *wanted* to see you."

"Nic says you live in England now?"

"Yeah. I went over there for uni and never came back. What about you? I heard on the grapevine that you were there, too, for a while?"

Josie nods.

"London," she says. "And then Devon, for a bit. Didn't really agree with me though, in the end."

Hannah nods again.

"I couldn't come back here at first," she says. "I didn't, for a long time. I couldn't stand it. Not just everything that happened, but *them*. This whole world. The money, and the privilege. The entitlement, and the way they acted as if they had a right to do whatever they wanted with us, just because they could pay us to be there. The way they just took people's whole lives and crushed them, and didn't think twice about it. Like they did with your mum, after she gave her life to the Draytons. Like they did to you."

She has to stop, as if she's run out of breath. Josie catches the glimmer of something bright in her eyes. She thinks it might be tears.

"I never thought I'd hear you speak like that about the Draytons," Josie says.

She only remembers how obsessed Hannah used to be, how she idolized them. She spoke of Evelyn in reverent tones, even though, as far as Josie could see, none of the Draytons had done much to deserve their lot in life. It was one of the reasons why she never told Hannah about her friendship with Tamara. She imagined how Hannah would react. How she would beg Josie to let her hang out with them, and then be fawning and deferent if Josie had said yes. Josie had been embarrassed by the thought of it, and then ashamed for thinking that way about her best friend.

"Yeah, well," says Hannah. "I guess I saw the light."

She straightens, seems to compose herself.

"I thought of writing to you," Hannah says. "You know. When you were . . . *incarcerated.*"

She says the word carefully, like someone who has spent too many nights at home watching American prison dramas on Netflix.

"Why didn't you?"

Hannah blinks as if she wasn't expecting to be asked.

"Because I couldn't," she says. "I couldn't bring myself to do it. I was scared. And I wasn't sure what to do. They don't exactly cover that in *Mizz* magazine, do they? What to do when your best friend gets convicted for murder."

"They don't cover what happens when you actually *do* get convicted, either," says Josie.

It comes out more sharply than Josie intends it to, and she sees Hannah flinch. She has to swallow back the spikiness that always comes when she thinks about those lost years. When she speaks again her voice is level.

"I wrote to you," she says. "My lawyers told me not to, but I did. You never replied."

Hannah nods, slowly. Apologetically.

"I told my mum and dad not to forward them to me, when I left," she says. "I didn't want to see them. I wanted . . . I wanted to leave it all behind me. That summer. You."

A moment of quiet passes between them and, for a second, Josie could almost believe that they are teenagers again. How many summer nights, exactly like this one, have they spent together? How many secrets have they told each other beneath these stars, the words unfurling in the darkness, never to be spoken again?

"Hannah," Josie says. Her voice is quiet now. Serious. "After I was arrested, I waited for you to come forward and back me up. To tell them that you were at the party, too. Why didn't you? Why didn't you say anything?"

Hannah shakes her head. Her face is strained, like she is holding something back. As though, if she speaks, she might burst into tears.

"I know you were there," Josie says. "I saw you there. Why did you lie?"

Hannah lets out a sound like a sob; a fast, desperate exhale.

"Hannah?" she says. "Did you see something? Did they threaten you? Did—"

Her voice catches then.

"Did you hurt Tamara?"

Hannah is shaking her head rapidly now, face tilted down toward her hands.

"Say something," Josie says. "Please."

Hannah stills. Swallows. Tries to compose herself.

"I didn't say anything," she says. "Because I didn't know *what* to say."

She lifts her head then. Finally looks Josie in the eye.

"The problem is," she says. "I don't remember what happened. So when the police asked, the only thing I could do was lie."

THIRTY-ONE

2004

SIX DAYS BEFORE THE BIRTHDAY PARTY

On the fifteenth of August, Josie turns sixteen.

Tamara always remembers the date, even though she never went to any of the birthday celebrations that Josie's mum threw every year. Even though she felt a hum of jealousy when Josie showed her photographs of her and Hannah, their arms around each other's shoulders, grinning over a piped lilac birthday cake.

They celebrated both their birthdays on the fifteenth of August. It was a tradition that had started when they were younger, and Tamara bought a set of friendship bracelets for Josie's thirteenth birthday, a thank-you for the sunrise swims.

"This is cool," Josie had said, jangling her wrist. "Because we both get one, so it's kind of like a present for both of us."

Tamara had flushed, not wanting Josie to think that she was making Josie's birthday about herself. She had spent ages picking out the bracelets, woven blue threads looping around a delicate silver heart with the word *friends* engraved in its center.

"When's your birthday?" Josie had asked.

"December."

"This is perfect then." Josie shook her wrist so that the heart swung to and fro. "You're never here on my birthday, so it makes sense that we both get a present today. We should always do this. It can be both our birthdays today."

For the next three years, they had stuck to their tradition. They exchanged gifts and made up silly rituals. A midnight swim, to mark the fourteenth turning into the fifteenth. Tamara convincing Patricia to bake a cake for increasingly farfetched celebrations during her shift at the pink house—Tamara getting her first period, international left-handers day. They would take the cake with them to their midnight swim and eat the entire thing with forks, giggling at how carefully Patricia had piped a relevant message for whatever occasion they had invented. They would sit out until the sun began to brighten at its edges, their own secret, special celebration before Josie's real birthday began.

Last year, Tamara had missed the celebration. Barnaby's parents had rented a place in Miami for the summer, and Blake and Tamara had been invited out for a week. Tamara had felt a twinge when she had seen that the dates fell over the fifteenth of August, but she hadn't been able to think up a good enough excuse to say no.

When she got back, she went down to the beach early, and waited to see if Josie would show up. She never did, and Tamara had felt the crack that had been forming between them splinter and break. Things had not been the same since then.

Today, on the fourteenth of August, Tamara is on edge. She slopes into the kitchen where Patricia is washing dishes, and asks if Josie has any plans for her birthday. Patricia looks surprised that Tamara remembers, and says something vague about a special dinner at home.

"Sounds nice," says Tamara.

"Yeah," says Patricia, wary. "Yeah, it'll be very low-key but lovely. Sixteen is a big birthday."

Tamara nods. Hesitates.

"Hey, Patricia?" she says.

"Yes, love?"

"Did I tell you that it's my friend's cat's birthday, too? I think it'd be really cool if we did her a cake."

※

That night, Tamara waits at the beach until long after midnight. She sits, staring out to sea, the Tupperware of Patricia's hastily assembled cake beside her.

Josie doesn't come.

When the display on her watch face shows 1 A.M. Tamara stands slowly, careful to keep the cake flat. She stretches out her legs, cramped from sitting for so long. She starts to walk up the hill.

※

Tamara has only been to Josie's house a few times, but she knows which window belongs to her. She picks up a handful of rocks and tosses them at the glass, praying that it's double-glazed. They bounce off with a soft smatter of sound. She waits for a minute. Nothing. She picks up another handful and tries again.

This time, a face appears at the window in seconds. Josie, sleepy, frowning down at Tamara. When she sees her standing there, her eyes widen. She pushes against the window to lift it open.

"What are you doing?"

Tamara retrieves the Tupperware from the ground and holds it out to her, an offering.

"Happy joint birthday," she says in a loud whisper.

"Were you throwing rocks at the window?"

"Might have been."

"I thought people only did that in films."

"It worked, didn't it?"

"I was sleeping, Tamara. I'm up early tomorrow."

"Don't you want to see the cake?"

Josie hesitates. Tamara can see her resolve weakening.

"What did you go for this time?"

Tamara peels off the Tupperware lid to reveal a buttercream cat with ginger fur, *HAPPY BIRTHDAY, MITTENS* hastily iced above it.

Josie clasps her hands over her mouth to stifle a loud, wheezing laugh.

"Tamara," she hisses, once she's recovered. "You did not get my mum to make that."

"I helped," says Tamara. "And I brought two forks. Don't make me eat Mittens on my own."

She can see that Josie is trying hard not to smile.

"Fine," she says. "Give me two minutes."

THIRTY-TWO

2024

When Nina crawls out of bed late on Wednesday morning, she finds the house empty.

She has slept for the first time in days, and she feels like she is crawling out of a months-long hibernation. Her body feels heavy, her brain fogged. She still feels exhausted, in a way that is bone-deep. She wants to close her eyes again. She wants to sleep until everything fades away.

She checks her phone to see a message from Claire.

Hey, everything OK with you? Ryan called me. He says he's worried about you. And have you seriously missed the first week of your new job?!

Nina responds lying flat on her back, phone held above her face.

I have so much to fill you in on. But I'm OK. Just need to stay here a bit longer to figure some stuff out x

She doesn't tell her that her new boss has asked her to come to a meeting on Monday morning to *discuss the terms of her contract*, or that she and Ryan have barely spoken over the last few days. She doesn't tell her that she suspects that—at last—Ryan has seen her for what she is, someone who is flawed, and imperfect. Not the disciplined person that she has tried so hard to be—someone who has her life together, her career planned, her sister's death pushed to the back of her mind. That she is broken. Unfixable. She doesn't tell her that, since the interview, she has spent hours on social media and in backwater internet blogs, reading everything that people have thought and said about Tamara's death. Getting pulled into a world that is entirely different from the one she remembers. The one that she has imagined, for all these years.

She has been unable to stop thinking about what Katherine said to her back in the documentary breakroom. She has asked herself the same question that Katherine posed to her over and over again. After all, who—or what—does Nina trust? The gut instinct that tells her that she was wrong? Or the little girl who said she was telling the truth? Two versions of Nina, both buried somewhere inside her, both impossible to fully access. A summer's day. A story told by a five-year-old child. A story that, for two decades, has defined all their lives.

Evelyn has gone into Montpellier to visit friends, so Nina fires off a text to Blake, asking him where he is. She finds Ryan's contact, and taps the green call button. His phone goes straight to voicemail. He'll be at work, of course, but the silence still bothers her. It makes her consider, briefly, how Ryan will react, when he sees the video footage she filmed two days ago. How he's often said how stupid he finds people who put their life up for public consumption, how they deserve all the ridicule they get.

She presses down the thought before it can fully form. Like her job, her life in London feels far away now, another world entirely. She has something much more important to do here.

She dresses in leggings and a creased T-shirt and walks to the back of the house, through the garden with its sweeping sea view. She paces across grass scorched brown by sun, deadened by years of Evelyn being unable to afford to pay a gardener. She finds herself drifting all the way to the spine of steps that Josie said she had walked down all those years ago, looking for her during the exact window of time in which Tamara drowned.

Nina descends the stone staircase slowly. The path is overgrown, vines splintering the steps. She hasn't been down here in years. Perhaps none of her family has. Not for the first time, the ridiculous excess of everything they own hits Nina with a scald of shame. An entire private beach they never use. A house that could fit the Jackson family home into one of its rooms.

When Nina reaches the beach, she finds a large, flat rock and sits, watching as the waves pull in and then out again, crashing close and pulling away.

It's peaceful down here. Quiet. She closes her eyes and imagines that this is the last moment of her life, before everything changes.

As she heads back up to the house, Nina sets a timer on her phone. She walks quickly, imagining that she is searching for someone. That she has left a child alone, one she is meant to be looking after. It takes her eight and a half minutes. Long enough to be missed. Long enough for something terrible to happen to someone.

It feels like proof, somehow, but not proof enough. No one has ever said that Josie couldn't have made it down to the beach and back in the missing window of time, only that she might not have done. As an alibi, it was weak: there were no witnesses to back it up. The only person who could corroborate that Josie Jackson might have been looking for a small child who had wandered off was the same person who said that Josie Jackson was a murderer.

Nina is out of breath by the time she gets to the terrace. She jumps when she hears a clatter coming from above, a crash against a tiled floor. She makes her way quickly through the house, across the kitchen and the hall, up the stairs and down the corridor to her mother's room.

The door is ajar. Through it, Nina sees a handful of clothes fly through the air and bounce down on the bed, followed by the unmistakable sound of her brother swearing loudly. She pushes against the door.

"Blake?"

Her brother is arm-deep in her mother's chest of drawers, red faced, the skin above the open neck of his polo shirt shiny with sweat. He doesn't look up at her.

"Where have you been?" Nina says. "I messaged you."

"Yeah, yeah. Sorry, sis," he says, still not meeting her eye. "I went into town to talk to a solicitor. You've heard Mum wants to sell the house? It's completely absurd. This is meant to be our house one day. She can't just sell our legacy like that—"

He pauses, mid-rant, to hold up a leather-bound folder that he's unearthed, a pair of tights still hanging from it like an elaborate talisman.

"Aha!" he says.

He flips it open and lets out a small huff of dismay.

"*Wedding* photos?" he says. "And for Harry, too. Surprised she had time to get the film developed before she ditched him."

"What are you looking for?"

"Granddad's will, Nina. Of course, Mum hasn't kept it in the bloody study, where you'd expect, and the solicitor says that we need a copy of it if—"

He breaks off, looking up at his sister, still standing in the doorway, for the first time.

"I heard that Ryan skedaddled?" he says.

"He didn't *skeddadle*," Nina says. "We were planning to go back on Sunday. He has work."

"We'll see," Blake says. He straightens, returning the wedding album to the drawer. "Sorts the men out from the boys, our family. Some people can't hack it."

"Can't hack what?"

"Being a Drayton," he says, as if it's obvious. "People are interested in us, until they get on the inside. Then most people realize they aren't cut out for it. The attention. The gossip. Looks to me like Ryan got out at the first sign of trouble."

Nina doesn't answer him. Blake pulls open another drawer.

"Maybe it's back in London," he says, distracted again. "Although I'm sure he had his will done here. The solicitors closed down years ago, unfortunately—"

"Blake," Nina says, interrupting him. "I went to see Josie Jackson the other day."

He stops still. His face furrows, as if reaching for a thought.

"Nina," he says, and there's a note of warning in his voice.

"She's back," Nina says in a rush. "And she didn't want to talk to me, at first. But now, she's decided that she wants to, and I'm going to meet up with her today, and I thought maybe you might want to . . ."

"Jesus, Nina." Blake shuts the drawer, hard. "What did I tell you about leaving this stuff alone? Haven't you got into enough trouble already?"

Nina's mouth slides shut.

"Next thing you'll be telling me is you want to do this bloody documentary," Blake continues.

"Actually—"

He looks up at her, his face aghast.

"I went and did a preliminary interview," she says. "On Monday, when I told you that I was going shopping in Montpellier."

"For god's sake."

He sits down heavily on the bed, lowers his head to his hands.

"What did I tell you," he says, thickly, his words muffled, "about talking to those people?"

"You said it was my decision!"

"Your *decision* affects all of us, Nina."

He straightens. His face is flushed and livid in a way that Nina doesn't recognize.

"She was my twin sister, Nina," he says. "She was my best friend. I knew her better than anyone. Don't I have a right to say who gets to talk about her? Don't I get a say in that?"

For a moment, he doesn't look like Nina's bold, brash brother who always drinks a bit too much wine, always makes people laugh, always has everyone wrapped around his finger, always seems at ease. He seems crumpled. Broken.

Nina thinks then of all the other things that she doesn't remember. Not just the night that her sister died, but the aftermath. The devastation that swept through this house. The long, slow process of putting lives back together.

But then, she thinks of her own life, spooling out in front of her. All the years that she has carried the guilt of sending someone to prison. How she knows, from experience, that over time this guilt will only get larger and larger until it consumes her.

"I'm sorry," she says. "But I have to do this, Blake. It's my life, too."

There's a silence. It stretches out for slightly too long. Makes Nina itch.

"Nina," Blake says, at last. "I know that this documentary has resurfaced a lot of . . . a lot of *trauma* for you. For all of us. But you're getting obsessed."

"I'm not—"

He holds up one hand.

"Please. Let me finish."

Nina closes her mouth.

"You're not yourself," he says. "You seem . . . well, frankly, Nina, you seem a bit unhinged."

She almost laughs. She's the one who's a psychologist. She's the one who knows about these things.

And yet, she recognizes the look of genuine concern on his face. Her brother, who knows her better than almost anyone. Who cares about her, more than almost anyone. Who has always been there, always loved her unconditionally, as if all the love that he used to have for Tamara needed somewhere to go and settled on Nina.

She thinks, then, of the video posted of her at her mother's birthday party. How even she saw how unstable she had looked. How Ryan had looked at her before she left, as if she was becoming somebody else right in front of him.

"Maybe we should think about getting you to see someone," Blake is saying.

He tilts his head to one side, sympathy leeching out of him.

"A doctor, or something? Just someone you can talk to about things, before you make any big decisions? Have you been taking your medication?"

She shakes her head, mutely.

"I came off medication last year, you know that—"

"Well, then!" he says, as if that decides it. "I really don't think you should be making these kinds of big decisions in your current state of mind."

"I don't *have* a current state of mind," Nina is saying. "Not like that, anyway. I'm fine."

But she sounds less certain this time. The creep of something in the back of her throat.

Blake takes her hand. Guides her to sit next to him.

"Neens, when everyone you know and love is worried about you, it's probably time to listen," he says evenly. "Just don't go and see Josie Jackson today, OK? You can rearrange for another time. Maybe a bit further down the line. When you've had a chance to speak to someone about everything that's going on with you. You're making a huge decision here. You don't need to rush into it."

"I—"

"And I'll call your doctor. The one you used to see when you were a kid? I'll speak to the documentary makers, too. Tell them you weren't in your right frame of mind when you spoke to them. I'll tell them about the medication. They won't be able to use anything you said, if there's any doubt about your mental health. And I can speak to your work, too, tell them what's going on. They, of all people, will understand . . ."

"You're talking to me like you think I'm crazy," says Nina.

Her voice wavers on that last word.

Blake knows. He knows that this has always been her worst fear, ever since she was small. Ever since their mother first took her to a psychiatrist. Since the diagnoses began. The anxiety, and the obsessive behavior, and the need for control. Ever since she was first put on medication.

But she can't deny it—she has been different lately. She knows this. And she is not sure if she is in control anymore.

"Of course you're not crazy," Blake says. "You just need support, Nina. You always have. That's why you have to listen to the people who care about you. The last thing you need to be doing right now is talking to Josie Jackson."

He squeezes her hand. His eyes look so loving, so concerned. For a moment, Nina sees the picture of Tamara that she's seen so many times before. Their eyes, she realizes, are still identical. It is like looking into the eyes of a dead girl.

When Nina finds herself nodding, there's a relief to it. All the stress and the anxiety of the last week taken out of her hands. Allowing someone else to make the decision for her.

"OK," she says, and she sees his shoulders release. "I won't see her today. But Blake? I still want to see her. I can't just leave this."

"Sure," he says, soothing. "We'll figure it all out, Nina. You don't have to worry about a thing."

THIRTY-THREE

2024

They agree to meet at the beach bar, the same place that Josie and Nic went on their impromptu first date.

Without the glaze of several beers, the hot anticipation that had hung between her and Nic, Josie can't help but think that it looks slightly run-down. The wooden picnic benches and piles of polystyrene trays left out by careless tourists look less charming by day. Josie orders a bottle of water at the bar and finds a table as close to the sea as possible, where the clamor of lunchtime punters is more spread out and the groan of the waves will stop anyone from overhearing their conversation.

She sees Hannah arrive, weighed down by beach bags. She dumps them on the sand and gestures to Josie that she's going to get a drink. From the table that she's chosen, Josie can see Hannah's family setting up camp around the abandoned bags. The husband glancing warily toward Josie. The oldest boy, looking like there's nowhere he'd less rather be. Isla, the little girl, perched on a beach towel plied with snacks—packets of crisps and bottles of brightly colored fruit juice. Noah, already knee-deep in the sea.

"Lemonade or Coke?" Hannah places two cans on the table between them. "I wasn't sure if you wanted food, so I ordered some chips, too? Only, don't let the kids see. Noah won't stop moaning if he knows I got chips for myself."

Josie holds up her bottle of water, apologetic.

"Oh!" Hannah says. "I didn't realize you'd gotten yourself something already. And I bet Nina Drayton isn't the kind of person who drinks all this sugary crap."

She lowers herself into the chair opposite, running her fingers through her hair, fluffing her fringe, looking as though she can't find a comfortable position. Josie notices that her nails are bitten down, crescent moons.

"That's OK," Josie says. "I've actually invited someone else along, too."

Hannah's eyes dart up.

"Oh?"

Josie nods. Exhales.

"Yeah," she says. "I thought we might want another person who's on my side."

※

The idea to contact truecrimefangirl_2002—the person who, in some ways, had sparked all of this—came to Josie after she had left the Baileys' house.

She had walked back down to the town with Nic.

"You seem distracted," he said, weaving one hand through hers.

"Can you blame me?" she replied.

Talking to Hannah had ignited something inside her. She found herself thinking about that night all over again, as if seeing it for the first time. About the case file that had briefly been in her possession. About what Nina Drayton had said. Each account, each witness statement, each piece of evidence sliding up against each other, a puzzle tantalizingly close to resolve.

It was one thing to have a theory about what happened. It was another thing entirely to have a platform to tell people about it. Someone that people listened to; someone who had seemed to believe Josie all along.

Now, she sees Imogen Faye crossing the sand toward them. Josie raises one arm to wave her over.

Hannah's eyes bulge.

"Are you serious?" She presses her palms down into the bench as if making to stand. "Josie," she hisses. "You said that this would be confidential."

"Hannah, just—"

Josie's hand reaches out and finds Hannah's arm. The contact seems to shock Hannah to stillness.

"Just trust me, OK?" she says. "I'm trying to help."

Hannah's hands lift away from the wooden seat. She folds them in front of her on the table, glancing back toward her family.

"If she films us . . ." she hisses with warning.

But Imogen is already within earshot, and Hannah doesn't finish her threat.

"Josie," she is saying brightly. "Hi."

She sticks out one hand toward Josie for her to shake.

"And you must be Hannah," she says, aside. "So nice to meet you both."

Josie doesn't move her hand. She takes in the woman standing in front of her. A face that she recognizes from the dozens of videos she pretends not to watch, not to care about. She expected the plum-purple lipstick that she knows so well, the slick of eyeliner, the vocal fry, and the social-media-specific drawl. Instead, Imogen Faye has dark hair neatly pulled back into a ponytail, the red stripe barely visible. Pared back, clean makeup. A black cotton dress with thin straps. A clean, well-spoken American accent.

"You . . ."

"Yeah," says Imogen, looking slightly bashful. "I'm not like in my videos? I know."

She shrugs, spreads her arms wide.

"Truecrimefangirl is kind of an internet persona. I mean, who actually talks about murders like that in real life?" She laughs an embarrassed what-can-you-do laugh. "It started as a bit of a joke. But what can I say? People love truecrimefangirl_2002! I should probably introduce myself properly."

She thrusts her hand toward Josie again.

"I'm Imogen. I'm a master's student in criminology. I'm writing my dissertation on women who are scapegoated in extremely public murder trials, mostly due to factors like class and sexism, and all the other ways that society likes to decide that women are bad, or wrong, or don't fit in with what they expect. And, I'm also truecrimefangirl_2002. An internet personality who talks about those public trials online, in a way that makes people sit up and listen."

For a second, both women just look at her, stupefied. Hannah speaks first.

"So you're a fraud?"

Her voice is sharp, surprising Josie.

Imogen smiles apologetically. Shrugs.

"Are any of us really who we say we are online?" she says. "I'm here to help. As Imogen Faye *and* as truecrimefangirl."

"Don't you think that's a bit . . . *morally questionable*?" says Hannah. "Building a career and income around talking about dead girls on the internet isn't exactly Feminism 101."

Imogen doesn't look at her this time. Instead, her eyes lock with Josie's, as if Hannah hasn't said anything at all.

Josie reaches out slowly, grips Imogen's hand.

"Thank you for coming," she says. "And thank you for believing me."

Imogen smiles then, properly this time, a broad, open beam that takes Josie aback with its warmth.

"You don't have to thank me," she says. "Now. Let's talk about what the eff happened to Tamara Drayton."

THIRTY-FOUR

2004

ONE WEEK BEFORE THE BIRTHDAY PARTY

Tamara and Josie eat the cake at the end of the driveway, hands sticky with icing, buttercream smears in the corners of their mouths.

"Sorry I didn't get you a present," Tamara says. "The cake was kind of a last-minute thing."

"My mum actually came home moaning about the ridiculous stuff your family asked her to do at short notice."

"She did not."

"She didn't mention any names, but—"

"It's a masterpiece. Mittens would have loved it."

Josie shovels a mouthful of cake into her mouth. Swallows.

"I actually did get you something," she says.

"Seriously?"

She nods.

"Technically it's what I got you last year. But I never got a chance to give it to you."

She digs in her pocket and pulls out a small jewelry box.

"It's nothing special or expensive or anything," she says. "You probably have much nicer stuff at home. But I saw a place doing them, down by the beach, and I thought they were cool, and . . ."

She trails off as Tamara prizes open the jewelry box. Inside is a small, delicate pendant. A heart on a silver chain. *J T* inscribed against its surface. A tiny, delicate rendering of a tulip, their shared favorite flower.

"I thought it was kind of like a grown-up version of the friendship bracelet?" Josie says. "I got one for myself, too. I know yours broke years ago and—"

"I love it," Tamara says.

She doesn't tell Josie that she kept the heart from the broken friendship bracelet. That she strung it onto a gold chain. Still wears it, sometimes, beneath her clothes.

She snaps the jewelry box shut.

"Hey, Josie?" she says. "Do you want to go for that swim now?"

※

Up at the pink house, they pull the cover off the swimming pool, one at each side, rolling the weight of it back to expose the sheet of blue beneath.

"You know," says Josie. "Me and Hannah broke in here before the season started to use the pool. Mum went nuts."

Tamara lowers her hand into the water to check the temperature.

"You should break in more," she says. "It's crazy that this house sits here all year with no one using it."

In the light of the pool, Josie looks beautiful. She is wearing a white one-piece borrowed from Tamara that glows iridescent in the light.

"How's your diving these days?" Josie asks with a grin.

In response, Tamara crouches and executes a sloppy, half belly flop of a dive into the water. From the side, Josie mimes holding up a scorecard.

"Ten!" she says.

Tamara is laughing. Josie takes a running leap from the side, contorts her body in the air so that she performs the perfect swan dive into the water. When she surfaces, she's beaming.

Tamara had almost forgotten that they could be like this.

Josie paddles toward her, and they lean back against the side of the pool, their shoulders submerged.

"I've missed this, you know," Tamara says.

She only meant to think it, but then there it is. Out in the world between them. I miss you. Something close to *I love you*. Something close to *I've thought about you every day, and I can't tell you.*

Close, but not quite.

Josie nods.

"I've missed this, too," she says. "When did it all get so complicated?"

"I don't know," says Tamara.

But maybe she does know. Maybe, if she thinks about it, she can piece together how a thousand moments, a thousand things, made her and Josie drift apart. How all the ease and simplicity of girlhood slipped into popularity contests, and who your parents were, and who you loved. How the fact that Tamara went back to London every autumn started to feel awkward, a demonstration of the things Tamara had that Josie did not. How, so slowly that neither of them had quite seen it coming, their early morning swims had begun to feel like an impossibility.

But mostly, it was Tamara's feelings for Josie that had shifted, and Tamara who had pushed her best friend away. She had closed herself off to Josie, because it was the only way she knew how to deal with this new, unknown thing that had reared its head inside her.

"Hey, there's a party on the beach in a couple of days," Tamara says. "A bonfire thing. It's going to be fun. You should come."

Josie turns to look at her.

"You want me there?"

"Yeah," Tamara says. "I want you there. I want more of this."

A half breath passes between them, long enough for Tamara's heart to skitter.

"Me too."

Me too. Another thing that feels almost, but not quite, like everything Tamara wants to tell Josie.

A promise that perhaps Josie feels the same way, too.

In that moment, Tamara thinks about the morning swims, the secret birthdays. The years of loving Josie in a way that feels bigger than the way she has ever loved anyone else.

She sees how Josie is looking right at her now, her gaze holding steady, the silence and the stillness. Her mouth, still wet from her perfect dive. There is only a half inch of water between them.

Before Tamara can let herself think about what she is doing she is leaning in, closing the impossibly small gap between them. Josie doesn't move. Tamara sees the friendship bracelets. That small, silver heart. The way that Josie is the only person who doesn't see the bad twin who lurks inside Tamara, the only one who believes that there is some essential goodness within her. Something that Tamara can almost believe herself, when the two of them are together. When Josie says her name.

There's a strange, shocking moment when their lips meet. Their bodies, slippery with water, their stomachs pressed together. Tamara, easing Josie's mouth open. The unexpected flicker of her tongue.

Then, Josie's hands, pressing against Tamara's arms. The gentle firmness as she pulls away.

"Tamara," she is saying.

She's still so close that Tamara can feel the heat of her breath.

"Tamara," Josie says. "I'm not . . . sorry."

And just like that, Tamara's world falls down around her.

She draws back. Josie looks almost pained, blinking water out of her eyes.

"I'm so sorry," she is saying.

Tamara feels too hot all of a sudden, in spite of her soaked-through skin.

"You're not what?"

Josie sounds almost apologetic.

"Well. You know. I'm straight."

"Yeah, me too." Tamara can hear the defensiveness in her voice.

Josie frowns.

"Then why did you . . ."

"Because," Tamara cuts across her. "I thought it'd be funny. I wanted to see how you'd react."

There's a pause. A silence as Tamara feels her lie fill up the space between them.

"Tamara," Josie says. "It's OK if you're . . ."

"I'm not."

Tamara won't let her say it. She won't. She can't stand hearing her secret spoken out loud. She doesn't want the impossibility of Josie feeling the same way confirmed.

"I'm not," she says again, more clearly. "Alright? God. Why are you getting so weird and uptight about it? Girls kiss girls all the time, it doesn't mean that they're . . ."

She can't say it either. The part of her that she's been afraid of for almost as long as she remembers. The part of her that flinches every time one of her friends makes a joke, or one of the boys in their group talks about lesbian porn, as if the whole idea of women desiring other women only existed for their pleasure. Every time someone says *that's so gay*, like it's the worst thing that something can be. Every time Harrison comments on a news story about campaigns for civil partnerships or adoptions for same-sex couples, sneering, *It's not that I'm against them, it's just that they don't need to be so in everyone's face about it*. Every time her mother agrees with him.

"I'm not being weird about it," Josie says. "I'm just saying that it's OK if you are."

That's when something in Tamara snaps. When her arms fly up, push hard against Josie's shoulders so that the other girl staggers backward, almost loses her footing against the slippery tiles.

"I'm not though," Tamara says, her voice tight, her jaw clenched. "So can you just fucking *leave it*?"

Josie blinks at her, taken aback.

"What is *wrong* with you?"

The words hit Tamara like a physical blow. There it is, the truth. There *is* something wrong with her. She *is* the bad twin, with all the darkness inside of her, no matter how hard she tries to push it down.

"What's wrong with *you*?" Tamara says.

Before she knows it, she's grasped hold of Josie, pushing harder this time. Josie flails and falls back, her head beneath the surface. In that moment, Tamara wants to hurt her. But more than that, she wants to hurt herself. She wants to claw out the part of herself that is in love with Josie Jackson. She wants to hold it under the water until there is no oxygen left to feed it.

Josie surfaces, gasping, blinking water out of her eyes.

"What are you *doing*?" she says, furious. "What is your problem?"

There's a blaze in her eyes now, an anger. A disgust. *Yes*, Tamara thinks. This is what she deserves. If Josie is not going to love her, then maybe she should hate her. There's an exquisite kind of pain in how she looks at Tamara.

"Tammy."

A tiny, scared voice from the side of the pool that makes them both stop.

"Tammy, why are you fighting with Josie?"

Nina is standing in a pair of pink pajamas, her hair in pigtails, wide-eyed. Her mouth is open in a small *o*, threatening tears. She kneads the hem of her top worriedly.

Tamara sees the scene for what it is then. She and Josie, squared up against each other in the water. The tender moment gone, replaced by tension and rage.

"Oh, baby," Tamara says. "We're not fighting."

She paddles to the side of the pool and hauls herself out. Picks up her little sister and pulls her into a hug. She and Blake had been horrified when their mother had told them she was pregnant six years ago, but Tamara has never managed to hate Nina the way she thought she would. Nina, who, ever since the day that she was born, has always seemed like something good and pure and right amidst the Draytons' chaos.

"Were you scared?" she says.

Nina nods.

"We were just playing," Tamara says, her voice singsong. "We were just playing."

She is dripping on the side of the pool. Soaking Nina's dress. She doesn't care.

"Come on, baby girl," she says. "Let's go inside."

And with her heart beating too fast in her chest, Tamara walks away from the swimming pool. She leaves Josie Jackson there, staring at them. Watching them go.

THIRTY-FIVE

2004

THREE DAYS BEFORE THE BIRTHDAY PARTY

Blake mentioned the bonfire one afternoon when Evelyn and Harrison were out of the house. He had thrown a window open, but the smell of their bodies still filled the air. Body spray and sweat, the plastic of the condom. A new fragrance that Hannah was already beginning to associate with sex. With him.

"It's the party of the whole summer," he said. "For real. It's always crazy."

His eyes were bright, still full of that post-orgasm high. One hand trailed across the contours of Hannah's body as if he couldn't get enough of her. She shivered as he brushed the inward curve of her waist.

"What about your mum's birthday?" Hannah said. "I thought that was supposed to be the party of the summer?"

Blake's hand lifted away and dropped onto the covers. He rolled over, reached for his boxer shorts, the light falling out of his eyes.

"My mum's birthday party is bullshit," he said. "Always is. People she barely knows, coming to tell her how great she is, how she doesn't look a day over thirty. It's boring."

Hannah sat up, pulling the sheets over her bare chest. It still felt like a kind of sacrilege, being naked on a bed that belonged to Evelyn Drayton. Linens that probably cost more than Hannah earned all summer.

"Really?" she said. "I always thought it looked kind of fun."

She didn't tell Blake that for years she had dreamed of being invited to one of Evelyn Drayton's parties. She thought of the previous summer, when she had been asked to step in when one of the hired waitresses had fallen ill. She had worn a white shirt and too-short skirt, and stood in the hallway holding a gilt tray of champagne and small, damp canapés that had been left out slightly too long, smiling apologetically when people complained about the heat. She had felt so out of place, her palms clammy, the room heaving with bodies, people who seemed to wear satin without worrying about sweat stains, who talked over one another in increasingly loud and high-pitched tones until their voices drowned out the strains of the string quartet. She had moved around the room with her eyes lowered, exactly as she had been told to do. Giving the impression that she was hardly there at all.

At one point, Blake had taken a drink from her tray and she had tried to catch his eye, waited for him to recognize her. He had, after all, known her almost their entire lives. His gaze had skittered from the glass back to the person he was talking to. He hadn't even looked at her properly. She had been invisible.

Ever since their first kiss, she had imagined how different things might be this year. She had dared to dream that the two of them might attend Evelyn's party as a couple. Hannah in a dress that she would have to convince her mum to drive her into the city to buy. Something long and fitted; something that would turn her body—too tall, too rectangular—into something curved and beautiful. Blake would have his arm around her, his hand against the base of her spine. A waitress, maybe some girl that Hannah went to school with, would offer them a tray of champagne, and there'd be a flash of envy in her eyes when Hannah accepted a glass.

Hannah imagined herself on the inside at last. Part of a world she had skirted the edges of for years, serving its drinks, tutoring its children, clearing up their mess at the end of each high season, the littered beaches, the empty houses. She would belong there, finally, because Blake chose her.

"Don't tell me that you want to go to my mum's stupid party?" Blake said.

There was a taunt in his voice that hadn't been there before.

"God, no," Hannah said quickly. "You're right. It's probably lame."

He was distracted, searching for his T-shirt.

"The bonfire sounds cool though," she said.

He shrugged. His brightness from a few minutes ago dulled, reconfigured into casualness. In some ways, he reminded Hannah of Nina. His moods were so changeable. It was so easy to make him happy; so easy to send him spinning away from her.

She thought again of the night she met Blake's dad. A week ago, but also another lifetime. A week ago, but also this second. For the last few days, Hannah had found the memory hovering around the edges of her body. The sensation of Blake pushing up inside her, the way she had felt inanimate. Not quite human.

She has tried repeatedly to transform the image in her mind into something more palatable. Told herself that they were *both* caught up in the emotion of the night, all the nerves and the rage and the hurt turning into that moment on the clifftop. That maybe she had enjoyed it, too. That maybe she had wanted him just as badly as he seemed to want her.

Still, just the thought of it sent a drum of adrenaline through her, a tightening in the center of her chest that felt almost like panic.

"Oh, you know," he said. "It's pretty cool."

"Maybe I could stop by?" Hannah ventured.

She didn't dare ask if she could attend as his girlfriend. She was afraid to address what this thing—delicate and undefined between them—really was.

Blake pulled his T-shirt on over his head.

"You probably wouldn't like it," he said. "It'd just be loads of people you wouldn't know."

"I wouldn't mind."

"I would."

He rolled over to her, lifted a strand of her hair between two of his fingers.

"I like it better when it's just us," he said. "I don't want to share you with anyone. Not yet."

He tugged at the hair, making her neck jerk toward him.

"Your hair is way too long," he said. "It gets in the way."

She had noticed him saying these things lately. Small, throwaway comments about her appearance. That she looked better in skirts, rather than the jeans or shorts that she usually wore. That she should think about getting her ears pierced, because she'd look more feminine that way.

She knew that changing herself for Blake was the kind of thing that would make Josie roll her eyes at her. That, even a few months back, Hannah would have insisted that she would never do.

Still, she couldn't deny how good it felt when his eyes skimmed over a new skirt that she'd bought a few days back. How she hummed with pleasure when he said that he'd seen a pair of earrings that would suit her, knowing it meant he had been thinking of her when she wasn't there. How, with each suggestion, he gave her the secrets to fitting into his world.

She lifted her hand, easing the hair out of his grip.

"I should probably get it cut," she said. "I haven't had it done for a while."

Blake stretched his arms up above his head, his body lengthening, a schism of skin between his boxers and his T-shirt.

"Hey, Evelyn and Harrison will be back soon," he said, with the air of a conversation that was over. "You should probably think about leaving."

※

The day of the bonfire was also the first day of the heatwave.

The streets were quiet, even as the sun started to set, anyone with any sense staying inside where it was shady and cool. As soon as Hannah applied her makeup she could feel it slide against her skin, a gossamer-thin slick of sweat already melting it away.

No one realized, just then, that this exceptionally hot day was only the start. That they would spend the next week fanning themselves hopelessly, stripping down to their underwear, throwing open the windows, gray rings of perspiration soaked through all their clothes.

Hannah did not know that by the time the heatwave ended, Tamara Drayton would be dead.

Her mum knocked on her bedroom door just as Hannah was applying a second layer of foundation.

"Josie's downstairs," Marie said. She wrinkled her nose. "Is that my perfume?"

"No," Hannah lied.

She snapped the powder compact shut. She had taken the bus to the market down the coast that sometimes sold knock-off beauty products, and asked the woman manning the stall to help her match the bottles of foundation to her skin tone. Still, she didn't look quite right. She couldn't blend out the faintly orange line that skimmed her jaw no matter how hard she scrubbed at it.

"What's all that on your face?"

Hannah zipped her brand-new cosmetics bag closed.

"Just a bit of makeup."

"I didn't think you liked wearing makeup."

"I just wanted to try something." Hannah stuffed the bag back into her bedside drawer. "Can't I try anything new without you commenting on it?"

Her mother held up her hands in mock defeat.

"Fine," she said. "I won't comment on anything I notice around here."

"You should have told Josie I'm not here," said Hannah. "I don't want to see her."

Her mother folded her arms across her chest.

"What's going on with you two?" she said. "I usually can't keep you apart."

"Nothing."

"Doesn't seem like nothing to me. Have the two of you had a fall-out?"

Hannah winced without meaning to. A fallout sounded so childish. This was bigger than that. A distance that Hannah could feel expanding between them, an embarrassment when she would think of how Blake would see Josie. She was so unlike the Draytons, so unlike all the people that Blake was friends with. Hannah was ashamed for thinking it, but it was there now, impossible to suppress.

"She just . . . you know." Hannah shrugged. "Seems a bit childish lately."

Her mum laughed.

"Oh, sweetheart," she said. "You're in too much of a rush to grow up sometimes. One day you'll look back and wish you'd hung on to being a child a little bit longer."

"Mum. I'm seventeen."

"The in-between years," her mum said knowingly. "I remember those."

She picked up a discarded T-shirt from Hannah's bed.

"You and Josie are inseparable," she said. "Don't let growing up come between you."

Hannah stood, her limbs stiff as if they had absorbed some of her reluctance.

"I'm already grown up, Mum."

"Well," her mother said. "Maybe that's the problem."

※

Josie was sitting on the wall outside of their apartment, scuffing her Converse in the dirt. Last summer the two of them had taken a Sharpie and decorated them with stars and hearts and tiny rainbows. Hannah could still see the faded scrawl of her initials close to the heel.

Josie sat up slightly straighter when she saw Hannah emerge, her face brightening.

"Hey," she said.

Her eyes caught Hannah's face and she grinned.

"Oh my god," she said. "What's that stuff on your face? You look like you're doing fancy dress."

Her laugh caught somewhere in her throat when she saw that Hannah wasn't smiling, the sound hooked back by uncertainty.

"I think it looks good," Hannah said.

What did Josie know anyway? Josie, in the same frayed denim shorts that she'd been wearing for two summers now, her eyelashes too pale for her face. Her hair so perpetually pulled back into a ponytail that it crimped when she let it loose.

"What are you all done up for, then?"

Hannah shrugged.

"Just trying something out."

Josie's eyes narrowed.

"It's not for him, is it? You're not getting all dolled up for Blake?"

"No," Hannah lied. "'Course not."

And then, with more conviction than she felt.

"Blake likes how I look, anyway."

She caught a slight roll of Josie's eyes.

"Sure," Josie said.

She straightened, standing.

"Wanna go down to the beach? It's so hot today. We could go for a swim, cool off?"

"I have to tutor tonight," Hannah said.

The lies were coming so easily.

"On a Friday?"

"Yeah. You know what these parents are like."

"Well." Josie bit down on her lower lip and then released it. "Maybe we could hang out tomorrow?"

"Yeah, maybe. I might have some work to do. It's getting kind of crazy for me at the minute."

Josie nodded.

"The Oxford thing," she said.

She sounded almost relieved, as if this explained everything.

"OK, well. Hope that they don't go too hard on you tonight. They better be paying you good to work on a Friday night."

"It all adds up," said Hannah. "I'll maybe see you in a few days."

"Sure. In a few days."

Josie stepped back, turning to leave.

"Hey, Josie?"

Josie turned around, hopeful.

"Yeah?"

"You should probably call, you know. Before you come over here."

Something slipped in Josie's face then. A tremor. A threat of collapse.

"Call?"

"Yeah. You can't just show up at my house and hope I'm free, you know? It makes me feel like . . . I don't know. Like you're not giving me any choice. We're not kids playing out in the road anymore. I've got other stuff going on now."

Whatever was threatening to collapse dropped then, Josie's mouth falling, her body seeming to droop.

"Oh," she said. "I just thought—"

She swallowed. Seemed to gather herself.

"OK," she said. "Yeah. You're probably right. I'll call you in a few days then?"

"Sure," said Hannah, as if it didn't matter to her either way.

Just then, she wasn't sure that it did.

※

Hannah knew the caves where the bonfire was set to take place. They were a draw for tourists, the start of an ancient network formed by millennia of water finding its way through the soft clay veins of the cliffside, burrowing into the earth. An underground network of warrens and grottos, huge chambers and dark corridors.

Hannah's parents used to run excursions down there, but had stopped when a lack of demand made them too expensive to operate. Still, the caves remained a hangout for local teenagers, older kids gathering to sneak stolen bottles of vodka, younger kids daring one another to go deeper into the darkness. The perpetually cool air would often be tinged with the smell of cigarettes, the occasional abandoned beer can floating on the surface of the underground pools.

Hannah had come up with the idea the day that Blake first

mentioned the bonfire. His comments about her not enjoying herself around his friends bothered her. She worried that his line about wanting to keep her for himself hid a deeper truth: that Blake did not think she would fit in with the people he usually surrounded himself with.

The solution, she decided, was to simply go to the caves anyway. She would surprise him by showing up, looking like her very best self. He would be amazed by how well she fit in with his friends. How easy it all was for her to slide into his world.

Hannah saw the sunburn glow of the bonfire at the mouth of the caves long before she reached it. She recognized, among the mill of people, the kids that she had seen grow up around here, returning every summer taller and more polished. Somehow, even more beautiful.

For the first time in her life, Hannah felt like she could be one of them.

She took a bottle of beer from what must have once been an ice bucket but was now a pool of tepid water, fishing around in it in a way that reminded her of apple bobbing on Halloween at her grandmother's house in Lincolnshire. Granny Iris was a fiercely working-class woman who considered a trip to London something to plan months in advance. Once, she took Hannah to see a show in the West End as a special treat. Afterward, they had gone to Harrods, where Hannah had gawped at the rows of velveteen bears and wooden rocking horses in the children's department. Her grandmother had tutted, and promised that she would buy her something from Argos when they got home instead.

Hannah remembered thinking there and then that she would move to London when she grew up. That one day, she would be the kind of person who shopped at Harrods. It was the first time that she remembers wanting something more for herself. More than this life.

"Hey, it's Hannah, right?"

A girl who had long, dark hair and a crop top that showed the silver glint of a belly-button piercing was waving. Hannah knew her, although it took a moment to reach for her name.

"You took my brother for a diving lesson last year?" the girl said. "I came out on the boat. It was just, like, not my thing?"

She had an upward lilt to the end of each sentence, turning statements into questions. Olivia. Her name was Olivia.

"My dad took him," Hannah said. "I was just helping."

"Right."

Olivia grabbed a bottle from the bucket.

"Hey, do you have, like, a bottle opener or something? The boys are always showing off, opening these with their teeth and I'm always like, are you guys insane? I am not wrecking my teeth just so I can drink some shitty lager."

She flicked her head so that her hair fell over her shoulder. It was impossibly glossy, cut into long layers. Hannah had wanted long layers, too, but when she had finally got them last year she had found that the saltwater made the top layer puff up like a mushroom cloud, and she had to spend the entire summer with her hair tied up in a ponytail waiting for it to grow out.

"Who invited you here, anyway?" Olivia asked in a way that seemed genuinely curious, not exactly unkind. Her eyes flicked up and down, as if taking Hannah in for the first time. Hannah felt herself shift, an automatic recalibration of her body, an awareness of her limbs.

"Blake," she lied. "You know, Blake Drayton?"

There was a flash of something across Olivia's face. A smile.

"Well, obviously I know Blake," she said with a tiny roll of her eyes. "Doesn't everyone?"

She flicked her hair again.

"Hey, do you want something else to drink? I think I saw some wine. Or maybe something stronger?"

She dropped the bottle of beer back into the bucket. Hannah hesitated, just for a second. Just long enough for the thrill of acceptance to register. As if Blake's name was all that it took for this girl to want to be her friend.

Olivia's eyebrows were raised. Expectant. Challenging Hannah to say no.

Hannah dropped her bottle, and it sank with a dull clink of glass against the metal basin.

"Yes," she said. "Let's get something stronger."

They walked close to the bonfire where the air was hot and dry, a rasp of smoke in Hannah's throat.

"Some of the girls are just over here," Olivia said.

She led Hannah to the opening of the caves, a place where the rocks sloped upward, forming the arch of a high-ceilinged tunnel.

Three girls sat, half-lit by the flames. Hannah stopped dead when she saw Tamara perched at the top of a rock, as if on a throne.

"This is Phoebe," Olivia said, pointing at one of the girls. "Chrissie. And Tamara."

Hannah's eyes locked with Tamara's.

"We know each other," Tamara said, coolly.

"Oh yeah," said Chrissie, white-blond and wearing a row of gold bangles up an arm. "Aren't you the girl who hangs around with that weird kid whose mum works at the pink house? Jodie something?"

"Josie," Tamara says flatly.

"Yeah, Josie," Chrissie said. "She always looks like she's been dragged through a bush."

Phoebe, a girl whose auburn hair had been disguised with highlights, whose pale freckles were just visible through a thick layer of foundation, giggled.

"Oh yeah, she's always, like, lurking when we're at your house, Tamara."

"She was always such a freak," added Olivia. "Do you remember, Tamara? She was always staring at you when we were in the pool in our bikinis. So gross."

Tamara picked up a bottle of vodka and took a swig.

"Josie?" Hannah said, confused.

Tamara swiped her mouth with the back of her hand.

"Erm, yeah, didn't you know your friend was a lesbian?" Chrissie said the word with a gleeful delight. "She tried to snog Tamara—right, Tamara?"

Tamara didn't meet Hannah's eye.

"Josie tried to kiss you?" said Hannah.

It didn't make sense. Hannah and Josie were always talking about their celebrity crushes, sharing elaborate fantasies about boys at school. Josie would tell her if she was into girls. Hannah was sure of it.

"Yeah," said Tamara loudly. "She just lunged at me. It was so weird. She's basically been obsessed with me for ages."

She passed the vodka to Olivia.

"Hey," said Olivia. "Guess who invited Hannah here."

There was a singsong lilt to her words. She made them sound like a playground chant.

"Who?"

Olivia paused. She looked between the girls, gleeful. Settled on Tamara.

"Blake," she said.

Hannah knew she wasn't imagining the way that Blake's name tightened something in the air. How Chrissie and Phoebe exchanged a glance. They were impressed. Maybe even a bit jealous.

Tamara was lighting a cigarette, unmoved as the others shot eager glances toward her, hunting for her reaction.

"So?" she said. "Blake's probably invited half the town."

"Are you, like, hooking up with him or something?" said Chrissie.

Hannah shrugged. Trying to play it cool.

"Oh, you know," she said. "We're just seeing where it goes."

Olivia passed her the bottle of vodka and she took a large swig. It burned all the way down to her stomach, a petroleum tang.

"You like him?" asked Olivia.

"Everyone likes Blake," said Tamara. "He's the fucking golden boy. Can we talk about something other than who fancies my brother, please?"

"Let's play a drinking game," said Olivia. She turned to Hannah, voice saccharine. "Unless you want to go and find Blake?"

Hannah hesitated. The only reason she had come here was to see Blake.

But then she imagined him catching sight of her from across the beach. Laughing, having fun, already absorbed into his world.

"Blake can wait. I think I'd like to play."

The game was truth or dare. Tamara set the rules. Three truths and three dares, going round the circle, each taking turns. Backing out on a dare or refusing to answer a truth was punished with a swig of neat vodka.

It seemed to Hannah that the game was a way for the girls to spill all the outrageous things that they'd done, all the things they wanted to brag about. Almost everyone picked truth for the first couple of rounds. Tamara described how she'd blown a guy in the school library. Olivia coyly dropped the name of a celebrity's son whose virginity she had taken on a skiing holiday. Phoebe told a long, elaborate story about the worst sex she'd ever had, the other girls shrieking with laughter.

When it was Hannah's turn, they asked her to name her crush, and the question felt so easy compared to the ones that they had already asked one another that she'd glanced between them, almost expecting a punchline.

"Well," she said. "I guess . . . I guess Blake."

Tamara pulled a face, and Olivia demanded that Chrissie take a shot for asking such a boring question.

"Hey," said Phoebe. "Isn't that your friend over there?"

She was looking across the bonfire to the other side of the rocks. They all followed her gaze, but the brightness of the fire snatched at Hannah's vision. She could only see dim silhouettes, half shapes.

"Watch out, Tamara," said Chrissie. "She might try and touch you up again."

Hannah felt her stomach tighten.

"Oh shit," said Olivia. "She's coming over."

From the mess of bodies, the dimly lit crowd, Hannah's vision calibrated and Josie came into focus, her short, compact figure, her trademark ponytail. Her face was open and smiling as she lifted one hand to wave.

"Hannah!" she said, her voice bright and clear, even over the crowds. "You got out of the tutoring job?"

Beside her, Hannah heard Olivia snort. "Tutoring job?" she muttered. "On a Friday night? Jesus. You must be more desperate for money than I thought."

"Hi, Tamara," Josie said. She was looking straight at her, her gaze unwavering, even when Chrissie wolf-whistled and Phoebe snorted with laughter. Tamara stubbed her cigarette out, ignoring her.

"You must be getting mixed up," Hannah said loudly. "I'm not tutoring tonight. Clearly."

Josie's face creased into a frown.

"But you said earlier—"

"What are you doing here, anyway?" Hannah said before Josie could finish speaking. Before she could reveal something that would confirm for these girls how unlike them she really was. "You can't have been invited."

Josie shifted her weight onto her right foot, her hip protruding to one side. Her bare legs were marked with small, pitted scars. Mosquito bites. Grazes that Hannah recognized from when they spent their summers scrambling over rocks and diving into the sea.

"It's a public beach, isn't it?" Josie said, bristling slightly. And then, with less affront, "And Tamara told me about it."

"Tamara?" Chrissie turned around, disbelieving.

Tamara's mouth was a thin line.

"Yeah, I mentioned it," she said. "I didn't say that you should come."

"Oh my god," said Chrissie. "She's, like, stalking you or something, Tam."

Josie was frowning now, confused. She looked at Hannah, appealing directly to her best friend.

"I was just sitting over there, by the fire," she said. "Some of the guys are setting up beer pong. You wanna come and play?"

"*You wanna come and play?*" Chrissie mimicked Josie's hopeful tone, elevating the pitch of her voice until it twisted into a toddleresque mewl.

The others collapsed with laughter. Only Tamara and Hannah stayed silent.

"Thanks, but no thanks," said Olivia. "We don't want you trying to get with us, like you tried to get with Tamara."

Hannah saw Josie flinch. For a moment, she looked very young. Even younger than usual. Then, her face hardened, her hands folding across her chest.

"You told them that?" she said.

She was looking directly at Tamara.

"Yeah," said Tamara. "Well. I didn't want you twisting it. Telling everyone that we were . . . that I was up for it, or something."

Josie didn't move. Her legs remained firmly planted on the sand. Her chin lifted.

"Hannah?" she said. "Are you coming?"

When Josie first started at Hannah's school, she had been picked on by the other kids. They had spotted her secondhand uniform, taken stock of her stature, and crowded around her on the playground on her first lunchbreak. They had tugged at her battered backpack, imitated her accent.

It was Hannah who had broken them up. Hannah who had pushed through them all and clasped Josie's hand. She'd taken her to the back room behind the assembly hall, a place where she would hide when she wanted to be away from the others, reading books and eating her prepacked sandwich. After that, the two of them spent most of their lunch breaks there together, and people had mostly left Josie alone.

"Yeah, Hannah," Olivia said, her tone somehow sweet and acidic at the same time. "Are you going to play beer pong with the boys?"

"Actually," Hannah said. It was as if someone else was speaking. "I think I'm going to stay here."

"Hannah doesn't need to chase after boys, right?" said Chrissie. "She's already with Blake."

Josie opened her mouth. Closed it again. There was a glint in her eyes, the reflection of the fire. She looked furious. She looked fierce.

"I'll come and find you later," Hannah said, quietly.

"Yeah," Josie said. "Right."

She turned to walk away but her foot caught on a piece of driftwood and she stumbled. The girls erupted into laughter.

"Oh my god," said Olivia gleefully. "She's, like, so weird?"

Hannah wasn't laughing. The vodka and the heat were making her head hurt. Her skin was hot, the fire too close.

"Hey, Hannah, look who it is," said Phoebe.

"It's your *boyfriend*," sang Olivia.

"Oh my god," said Chrissie. "I know. I know what your next dare is."

"It's not her turn."

"No, it's perfect, listen."

Chrissie grinned. Her teeth looked sharp in the light of the fire.

"I think it's time for you and Blake to make it official, right, Hannah? I dare you to go and kiss Blake, right in front of everyone."

"No," said Tamara. "Come on, guys. You're taking the piss now. Blake would hate that."

"It's a dare? It's *supposed* to be something a little risky."

"That's not fair, though. You know it's not."

"Oh, come on, it'll be great."

Chrissie turned back toward Hannah.

"Sometimes guys just need that little push, you know? Just to get things over the line."

"He'll probably like it," says Chrissie. "A hot girl just walking up to him and snogging him in front of everyone?"

"It's a *dare*, Hannah. It's meant to be hard."

"Blake'll be hard when she's done with him."

"Oh my god, Olivia, grim."

"Come on, Hannah. It'll be *funny*."

Hannah had begun to rise to her feet, slowly. There was a small rush of blood to her head, like a tiny explosion of stars behind her eyes.

"Hannah." Tamara caught hold of her arm. "Seriously. Don't."

Of course Tamara didn't want Hannah kissing her brother in front of everyone. Tamara didn't think she was good enough for Blake. Across the fire, he was smiling as he talked to someone. Swigging a beer. She had that *there he is* feeling when she saw him. She was starting to think it might be love.

Phoebe had started to slow clap.

"Do it," she said. "*Do it, do it, do it.*"

Hannah walked toward him, one foot in front of the other. She felt like she was floating.

In those last few steps, as the space closed between them, Hannah saw the entirety of their summer together. Lying together at the bottom of her parents' boat, the sky golden above them. Him kissing her on the beach late at night. The taste of his skin. The way that his touch made something within her spark and shiver.

She saw the next year of her life, and the next. She saw Oxford. She and Blake, together in England, Hannah finally becoming more than a summer fling. As if the changing of the seasons with Blake by her side would make her real at last.

He didn't see her until the very last second. When he turned, he was still smiling. Then there was a judder of recognition in his eyes, followed by confusion. Surprise.

"Hi," she said, and she could hear how sexy she sounded. All casual and confident like this was the most natural thing in the world. As if she did this every day. Leaning toward her boyfriend, putting one hand up to rest on his shoulder, kissing him hello.

"What the fuck?"

Blake stepped back from her, frowning. His palms out flat, as if bracing to push her away.

Hannah stumbled, her body misbalanced by the air where she had expected her skin to meet his, the feeling that she was flailing in space. From behind her there was a snort of laughter.

"Whoopsie-daisy!"

Olivia with that singsong voice again. A peal of cackles. Hannah didn't turn to look at them. She could only see him. The look on his face. Something close to revulsion.

"Blake—" she started.

He was shaking his head.

"Wow," he said. "You're pissed."

Then, an arm was slipping around his waist, and Hannah's vision expanded. A girl, a bottle of beer in one hand, the other hooking into a loop of Blake's trousers, an easy sense of ownership. She was beautiful. Long, straight hair. Blue, oval eyes, a petite frame. Skin with the exact right kind of honey-gold tan, the kind that suggested expensive holidays rather than days spent out working on the boat and parents with a laissez-faire attitude to suncream.

This girl and Blake looked good together. They looked right. She looked like the kind of girl who belonged with him. And suddenly, it all made a terrible kind of sense.

The girl's head tilted to one side. Not threatened, but inquisitive. Because, of course, why would a girl like her be threatened by a girl like Hannah?

"Are you alright?" she said brightly. Loudly, as if speaking to a child. "Do you need something? I could get you some water, if you like?"

She turned her face toward Blake.

"Do you know her?" she said, quietly, as if Hannah might be too drunk to understand.

Hannah felt a scorch of embarrassment, heat rising from her cheeks. Blake was looking straight at her.

"Yeah, I know Hannah," he said flatly. "She helps out at the house sometimes."

"Oh!" the girl said. "Yeah, I know you. Don't you work at that little shop in town? The one that sells all the beach stuff?"

Hannah stepped back. She could see it so clearly. His lies. Her stupidity. Her idiotic belief that Blake would ever actually be with someone like her.

"I'm fine," she muttered.

She turned, too quickly, a rush of blood to her head, a flush of light. When it cleared, she could see Olivia and Phoebe and Chrissie, their arms looped around one another, bent double with laughter. Tamara, standing apart from them, her face still.

Hannah walked straight past them, trying to ignore the sound of Chrissie cawing, the rise of Olivia's voice as she protested that it was a joke. She knew, in that moment, that *she* was the joke, to them. She understood, for the first time, that they found the thought of someone like her being with someone like Blake funny. She knew then that she would never, ever be like them.

"Hannah!"

A familiar voice was calling after her. Hannah didn't stop. Didn't slow down. She was almost running now, almost back on the beach, where the rock would turn to sand. The grit between her toes.

"*Hannah.*"

A hand caught hold of hers, jerking her to a stop. Hannah shook it away, not wanting Josie to see that she was crying.

"Stop following me," Hannah said.

"Are you OK?" Josie said. "I saw what happened, and—"

"I'm fine," said Hannah, even though her eyes were stinging, her vision blurred.

"I was worried that something like this would happen, ever since Tamara mentioned Cordelia. I wanted to sit down with you and tell you properly, but—"

Hannah's head snapped up, looking past Josie.

"What do you mean?" she said. "Ever since Tamara mentioned Cordelia?"

Josie looked pained.

"Cordelia," she said. "Blake's girlfriend. She flew out yesterday."

The world slowed.

"Blake has a girlfriend?"

"He's been a total dick," Josie said. "I told Tamara it wasn't fair, messing you about like that. But—well."

Hannah feels as if her skin is burning, as if there's a pressure in her skull that she can't shake off.

"You knew?" she said. "You knew he had a girlfriend?"

Josie flushed.

"Not until a few days ago," she said. "I'm sorry, Han."

"Why didn't you tell me?" Hannah said. "What, were you too busy trying to get with Tamara?"

The words are sharp, coming out before she can think them through. But she wants to lash out. She wants to hurt someone, anyone, so that she is not the only one who feels this gut ache, heart wring of pain.

"Hannah, no." Josie's face tightens. "You know I didn't try and kiss Tamara. She tried to kiss *me*. In the pool, at the pink house. And I said I wasn't interested and she got angry with me. She pushed me. And now she's telling everyone before I can."

"I don't want to hear this."

Hannah started to walk away. Away from the bonfire, and the beach, and her best friend.

Josie called after her again, except this time, she didn't follow.

This time, she let Hannah leave.

THIRTY-SIX

2024

The beach is busy, but around the table the air feels thick and quiet. Imogen hasn't moved the whole time Hannah has been speaking. Hannah could swear that she is holding her breath.

"Nina wasn't making it up," Hannah says. "She *did* see Tamara and Josie together in the pool. She saw them in the pool three days before Evelyn's birthday party, when Tamara tried to kiss Josie."

Imogen shakes her head, as if in wonder or disbelief. Hannah isn't sure which.

"I always thought *you* tried to kiss Tamara," she says to Josie. "That was always the story. The motive that the investigators used for why you would want to hurt her."

"That was what Tamara told everyone," Josie says. "That was the rumor she started. The story Hannah was told at the bonfire. I was pissed off at the time. But now—" Her voice tremors slightly. "She was young," she says, once she's swallowed, steadied herself. "We were all so young. And she was probably scared. She probably wanted to protect herself."

Imogen frowns. Her eyes flicker between Hannah and Josie.

"But why did this never come up?" Imogen says. "I mean, no offense, but if I'm approaching this with the cold, hard gaze of an investigator, it still doesn't add up. It's convenient that this event that only *you* witnessed, Josie, that took place a couple of days before Tamara's death, just so happens to explain everything away. And you're only bringing it up now?"

"I *did* bring it up at the time," Josie says. "But not to explain what Nina said. That didn't click for me at the time either, with everything else that was going on. It was only when I talked to Hannah yesterday—"

"It took me a long time to put two and two together," Hannah intercedes. "I knew about the kiss, but nobody had ever mentioned that Nina had witnessed it. In fact, I only really understood it when I had my own kids, when I saw how their minds work. They remember so many things, but they piece them together in the wrong order sometimes. And it probably became bigger than it was in Nina's mind—Tamara pushing Josie became a full-blown fight. Nina was only five; she'd just witnessed the most traumatic thing any child could have seen. She was probably confused. So she told people the last memorable thing that she'd seen at the pool. The last time she saw Tamara alive in the water."

"They tried to say that I killed Tamara because she'd rejected me, so of course I tried to tell them it was the other way round," Josie says. "But nobody believed me. So many people already knew the story, the way Tamara had told it. So many people already believed that I was in love with Tamara. The motive seemed to fit. Why would anyone listen to my version of events? Especially when, as you say, my version seemed a bit too convenient. It didn't even get included in the evidence at trial."

"That makes sense," Imogen says, nodding.

Hannah feels, in spite of her skepticism at Imogen's presence, a flurry of hope. Perhaps Josie is right. Perhaps, if Imogen believes them, she can spread the word. She allows herself to imagine Josie's name cleared, after all this time.

And yet, something lingers, a heaviness in the air. Imogen and Josie's eyes meet for a half second before they both look away. Hannah catches something between them, some secret she isn't privy to.

"What?" she says. "What is it?"

"Well," says Imogen. "The problem is, this might explain why Nina pointed the finger at Josie, sure. But it doesn't explain what actually happened to Tamara."

"But does it matter?" Hannah says. "Isn't the important thing that we can now argue Josie's innocence? That we can show that Nina didn't see Tamara and Josie in the pool together the night that Tamara died?"

She glances between Josie and Imogen.

"Right?" she says. Her voice is small. Hopeful. "We can clear your name, Josie. That should be enough, right?"

Josie takes a deep breath.

"Actually . . ." she says.

She exchanges another glance with Imogen, longer this time. Long enough for Hannah to understand that there is something they are not telling her.

"Actually," says Josie. "Imogen has a theory about what happened to Tamara, too."

THIRTY-SEVEN

2004
THE DAY BEFORE THE BIRTHDAY PARTY

After the bonfire, Hannah didn't leave her room for three days.

She said she was ill. Her mother pressed the back of her palm to her forehead and agreed that maybe she was feeling a bit hot. She promised to call up the families that Hannah had agreed to tutor, and left soup in a Tupperware container in the fridge.

Hannah did not eat the soup. The nausea was not entirely a lie. Her stomach was clenching, turning in on itself. The thought of food was impossible to bear. She pulled the covers up over her head. She inhaled the sour smell of herself, the faint traces of smoke that still lingered on her skin and in her hair. Her heart seemed to be beating much faster than usual, and she couldn't slow it down.

Every time she dozed off, she awoke to the sear of shame. Remembering everything all over again. How those girls had laughed at her. How easily Hannah had let herself believe that they wanted to be her friend. How Blake had looked at her as if she disgusted him.

What Hannah was experiencing was not just the loss of Blake, but the loss of a dream that had simmered beneath the surface of her entire life. A belief that one day, she could be like the people who came here every summer.

She eventually crawled out of her bed on the fourth day, after her mother started to talk about doctors' appointments and blood tests. She went through the motions of the day—breakfast, helping out at the shop, going home to make sandwiches for lunch—feeling as though she was drifting a foot or two outside of her own body.

Her parents were supposed to be going away that evening, taking the train up to Lyon to visit Hannah's aunt for her birthday. They would be away for a couple of nights. Hannah heard them talking in quiet, worried tones, debating whether they should be leaving her. It was impossible to keep secrets in their small apartment.

"I'm fine," she interrupted them, leaning her head around the door. "I have some work to do on my uni applications. And I'm feeling better. I'll be OK on my own."

She didn't tell them exactly why she longed for privacy. How badly she wanted to crawl back beneath her sheets and grieve without the anxious eyes of her mother watching over her.

That night, after her parents had left with promises to call as soon as they arrived in Lyon, Hannah went down to the sea.

She took off her shoes as soon as she reached the sand and started to run, shedding her clothes behind her. She was in her underwear by the time she reached the shoreline. The coldness of the water took the air out of her lungs. She dove beneath the surface and kicked, the salt stinging her skin, the roar of the tide in her ears. She opened her mouth, and as the water flooded inside she let out a scream, a howl that came from so deep within it felt as if a part of her was tearing away from herself. It erupted into the ocean as air, a dead cry that nobody would hear.

When Hannah surfaced, the hill was silhouetted against the sky. Close to the top, she could see the glow of the pink house. Lanterns bobbing as they were set out on the terrace. Strings of fairy lights, everything ready for Evelyn Drayton's birthday the next night. Once again, the longing seized hold of her, so physical that for a split second, she thought she had a cramp. She had imagined herself on Blake's arm so clearly that the image felt scored onto her vision. Now, she saw Cordelia on his arm instead. Her perfect, shiny hair. Her small, toned body. A dress that fit her just right.

Cordelia struck Hannah as the kind of girl who already had everything. It felt stupendously, cataclysmically unfair that she got to have Blake as well.

Hannah dove back beneath the water. She held her breath for as long as she could, and then, when her lungs were aching, kicked back toward the surface. Her eyes were stinging. She squeezed them shut.

When she opened them again, she saw a figure standing on the shoreline. He was silhouetted in the half-light of dusk, but still she knew who it was. Who *he* was, his hands buried in his pockets, his hair tousled, his head tilted to one side as he watched her.

After all, she would know Blake Drayton anywhere.

※

They went back to her apartment. The air inside smelled of garlic and stewed meat, the meals that Hannah's mother had cooked and refrigerated that afternoon for Hannah to eat over the next few days.

"Do you have anything to drink?" Blake asked.

She didn't have the kind of drinks he would want. The expensive bottles of vodka he and his friends drank, the multipacks of beer. Instead, she found an open box of red wine left over from one of the rare nights her parents drank with dinner and poured him a glass. She passed it to him, painfully aware of how out of place he looked in her kitchen. The room felt much smaller than usual, as if the walls had inched in while she'd been away. She was suddenly conscious of the dated yellow tiles, the washing hung up on a buckled clotheshorse because they had no space for a dryer.

"You're not having one?" he asked.

She shook her head. She wanted to be clearheaded for this conversation. Braced for whatever Blake had to say to her. Besides, the thought of red wine still made something in her convulse.

"I'm not thirsty," she said.

"Right," he said. "Right."

He seemed temporarily stalled, glancing around the room. Hannah found herself bristling. Was he really so shocked by where she lived?

"Shall we..." His eyes hovered on the sofa, covered with diving equipment that her parents had brought back from the shop for cleaning. "Is there somewhere we can sit down and talk?"

"We can talk here."

It was a strange thrill, to see him hesitate. To know that he was thrown by this—that he had expected Hannah to scurry to clear space on the sofa, or offer up her room. It felt like something close to power.

"Fine," Blake said. He straightened, gathering himself. "Hannah, about the other night—"

"You mean about the fact you have a girlfriend?"

Her voice came out steely. Stronger than she expected it to. He winced at the word.

"She's not my... Jesus. She's not my girlfriend, Hannah. Cordelia is... she's an ex. I broke up with her a few months back. But she's... she's crazy, Hannah. She's still obsessed with me. And her parents have a house out here, so she's impossible to avoid..."

"It didn't look like she was your ex."

"I know, I know."

He combed one hand through his hair, agitated.

"She's... it's hard to explain. She's not well, Hannah. She's... she's *unstable*. She went berserk when I tried to break up with her. She was threatening to kill herself. When she turned up at the beach I freaked out. She was acting like we were still together. I didn't know what to do."

"So that's why you pushed me off you?" Hannah didn't try to hide the skepticism in her voice.

"Hannah, you don't know what she's capable of. When I saw you at the beach... well, I was worried what she'd do, if she knew about us. I was worried she'd hurt herself. That she'd hurt *you*."

She hesitated then. She could almost see it. Cordelia, with her pristine exterior, her gilded life. Of course she would believe she was entitled to anything she wanted. Even Blake.

"Hannah," Blake said. "You know me. You know how I feel about you. Do you really think it's all been a lie? Do you think, this entire summer, I've been stringing you along?"

She thought of when he kissed her beneath the waves. When they had had sex for the first time, her body thrumming with alcohol and desire. Something flickered within Hannah then. A small, certain part of herself that said *no*. She could not believe that all of that had been a lie.

At least, she did not want to believe it.

"Hannah," he said. "I don't want Cordelia. I want *you*. I've always wanted you."

And there it was. The thing that Hannah had so badly wanted to hear, even now. Even with her eyes still red and raw from crying over him. That flicker turning into a flame.

"I want to be with you," he said.

"It's really over between you two?" she said. Her voice was smaller than it had been a few minutes ago. Quieter. "You promise?"

He stepped toward her. Placed his wineglass down on the kitchen counter.

"I promise," he said.

He was nearing her now. Reaching out toward her. Hannah held out one hand to stop him coming any closer.

"You have to prove it to me," she said. "You have to show me I can trust you."

"Yes, of course," he said. "Of course."

"How?"

He faltered at this, one arm still extended toward her.

"I . . . how?"

"Yeah." She folded her arms across her chest. "How will you prove it?"

"I . . ." His hand dropped down. "I just . . . I will. You have to let me show you."

"By telling people that you're with me?" she said. "No more hiding. No more sneaking around. If you're serious about this—about us—you'll tell people we're together."

"Yes," he said. "Of course. I can do that."

She was speaking in a way that she hadn't known she could. Demanding things she had never thought to ask. She lifted her chin, emboldened.

"And your mum's party," she said.

"What about it?"

"I want to go to it. If you're serious about me, you'd want me there. As your date."

"Hannah." He reached out toward her again. Snatched hold of her hand. "Come on. We don't need to show the people at my mum's party that I'm serious about you. They're not important. *This* is what's important. Us."

She pulled her hand away.

"I mean it, Blake. Either we're doing this, or we're not. If you want me, then show me that. Show everyone else that."

There was a second—only a second—when she thought he would say no. When she thought he would turn. That he would leave. Then his hands were on her waist. Her back. His mouth close to her face.

"Alright," he said. "Come to the party. Come, and I'll show you. I'm serious about this, Hannah. I want this."

Something in her relented then.

"Come on," he was saying, his breath hot, his touch urgent. "Let's go to your room."

And so, they went. And so, she let him kiss her. Undress her. Let him fuck her on her childhood bed, with a force and an urgency that she was not expecting.

But Hannah was not thinking about how he pushed her hard into the mattress, facedown on the bed. The way that he abruptly flipped her over, pressing his hand against her throat as he came.

Instead, Hannah was thinking of silk dresses. Champagne. Evelyn Drayton looking at her as if she was a person for the very first time.

She was thinking of all the ways that tomorrow would be different. The way that her entire life would be different now.

THIRTY-EIGHT

2004
THE DAY OF THE BIRTHDAY PARTY

The day of Evelyn's birthday is predicted to be the hottest of the year.

Tamara hears the weather warnings on the radio. The talk of sea temperatures and keeping children and animals indoors. Outside the Draytons' house, the asphalt curls and buckles, and when Tamara drives into town with Harrison to pick up a wine delivery at her mother's request they find the town empty and silent, the streets sliced through with heat, nobody wanting to venture away from their pools or their air-conditioned houses. Farther down the coast there are wildfires that give the air a strange, burnished tinge, the sky a shade of gold as if the whole world is burning.

After days of Evelyn throwing increasingly explosive tantrums about the weather ruining her birthday, Harrison hires air-conditioning units, enormous metal things that are wheeled in on sack barrows while Evelyn complains loudly about the expense; about how her father would be *turning in his grave* to see his hallway filled up with *those ugly contraptions*. When they are switched on, groaning and clunking into life, the humidity immediately easing, she falls quiet. Within minutes, she is telling everyone how Harrison has *saved her birthday,* resting her head on his shoulder, looking at him as though he is explaining how he achieved world peace when he talks about how he tracked down a company who could deliver the units last minute.

Later, Tamara hears them having sex upstairs, her mother's performative moans, and hates her for it. Hates how easily Evelyn forgives. How desperately she needs love, and how easily she accepts something far less.

She goes outside and sits on the terrace, leaning her elbows up on the balustrade, and texts Barnaby, asking if he can get hold of some coke for tonight. She needs more than alcohol to take the edge off. She needs something, if she is going to smile, and talk to people, and pretend that she is happy.

Last night, just before sunset, she had walked down to the small private beach at the back of the property, taking with her the diary where she had written down all her thoughts and feelings about Josie Jackson. Where she had recorded each time they had met up with a small, purple heart at the top of the entry. She had flicked through the pages, noticing how the sea of violet stamps had grown thinner over time until, this year and last, they were barely there at all. Just an occasional purple mark on an otherwise blank expanse of summer. She thought of how much those infrequent meetings had meant to her, how she had savored taking out her purple pen to ink each occasion into permanence.

Then she had thought of her life stretching out ahead. Without Josie, but perhaps also without the ability to be who she really was. To love the way that she wanted to. She had seen the shocked way that Josie had looked at her. She never wanted to feel like that again.

As the sun set, Tamara tore every page out of her diary with a purple mark, every single mention of Josie Jackson. She shredded them until the loop of her handwriting was barely visible, and then she released them into the air, let them drift and fall into the water. They looked, in the half-light of dusk, like ashes after a fire.

Tamara has a goal for the party, and that goal is to get exceptionally fucked up.

She has a bottle of Grey Goose, stolen from Harrison's stash. She has coke, bought from Barnaby, hidden in the secret compartment of her bedside table. She mixes vodka with Coca-Cola, so strong that the liquid is a pale, insipid brown. She drinks two full glasses while she gets ready. A slick of kohl around each eye. A tight black dress.

Tamara looks at herself in the full-length mirror. She looks thin, as though she has lost weight in the last few days, her cheekbones concave, her eyes too big for her face. She can almost see the effect of the coke starting to take hold of her. The hum of energy. The chemical glow that flickers beneath her skin.

She drains the last of her drink.

"Just a few hours," she says to her reflection. "You can get through this."

※

When it's time for the guests to arrive, Tamara goes to the staircase and sits on the very top step, hidden by the stone banister. She can make out the feet of the first partygoers, the people who Evelyn always complains turn up too early, as they filter into the hallway. Can hear the greetings of the waitstaff, the offers of champagne and canapés on small silver platters.

It reminds her of when she and Blake were very small, before they were allowed to attend their mother's gatherings. When Evelyn was recently divorced from their father and made no secret of the fact that she thought two young children cramped her style, they would hide in this very spot and long to be bigger, and older, and taken more seriously. To be grown-up enough to join the party.

Now, Tamara barely spends time alone with Blake. Now, the two of them keep secrets from each other, when it used to be the two of them together, against the world. Now, Tamara wants to curl into a ball and make herself as small as possible. So small that she begins to shrink.

She wishes she were younger. She wants to be sitting up here with Blake again, enthralled by their mother. Giggly with having evaded their bedtime, awestruck by the beauty of Evelyn's friends. Tamara wants all of her problems that seem specifically grown-up to go away.

Her mind is drifting when she sees a pair of pale blue heels. The hem of a silken dress. A voice saying *thank you very much* at the offer of champagne in a way that makes Tamara sit up.

Her mother's friends do not thank the staff. And besides, Tamara knows that voice.

She is on her feet, barreling down the stairs before she can think about what she is doing.

"Hannah," she says.

She catches hold of her arm, champagne slopping out of the top of the glass that Hannah is holding. She turns to look at Tamara, alarmed. She looks different. Her hair, usually loose and long down her back, is shiny and groomed, tamed into an elaborate updo. Her makeup is carefully applied.

"Tamara—" she starts.

But Tamara doesn't give her a chance to speak.

"Hannah," she is saying. "You're not supposed to be here."

THIRTY-NINE

2004

THE NIGHT OF THE BIRTHDAY PARTY

The terrace was empty, everyone sheltering in the artificially cool air of the house.

Tamara guided Hannah to the steps that led to the lower balcony, where the pool extended a story below the house. As they passed the water, Hannah thought, briefly, of that day all those weeks ago when she and Josie had stretched out in the sun, their skin glistening and wet, the entire summer seeming to unfurl before them. The promise and the heat.

"What are you doing here?"

Tamara spun round to face her. Her pupils were large, black orbs. She looked angry. Hannah lifted her chin.

"Blake invited me," she said.

"Blake . . . ?" Tamara frowned, and then shook her head. "No," she said decisively. "Blake wouldn't have."

"Is it so unbelievable that your brother might want me here?"

Tamara snorted, a half laugh.

"Unfortunately not."

"What is *that* supposed to mean?"

Perhaps it was the heat. Perhaps it was the alcohol that Hannah had already consumed, telling herself that she needed the liquid courage.

Or perhaps it was all her built-up hopes and disappointments. All the times that Hannah had not felt good enough.

Whatever it was, whatever buried part of herself was surfacing, Hannah was angry.

"You just can't stand the thought of Blake liking me," Hannah said. "You think you're better than me. You think you're better than everyone."

Tamara was turning away from Hannah. She looked tired, as if Hannah was something she couldn't be bothered to deal with.

"Hannah," she said. "Go home."

"Why? I've got a right to be here."

"He's with Cordelia, Hannah."

"Cordelia isn't coming. He told her not to come. He told her it's over—"

Tamara laughed. There was a strange, crazed brightness behind her eyes.

"He doesn't *want* you, Hannah," Tamara said. "You need to realize that. Blake doesn't want someone like you."

There it was. No one had ever actually said the words to Hannah before. Not Evelyn, or Harrison. Not the families of the kids Hannah tutored, or the groups that her parents took on private dive expeditions. Not her classmates at the school where Hannah fought tooth and nail for her scholarship, or Barnaby, or Blake. The silent, seething undercurrent to her entire life.

Someone like you. Someone not good enough.

Someone not like us.

That simmer of anger, just beneath the surface, sparked.

Reflexively she reached out, pushing hard against Tamara's shoulders.

Tamara staggered back. There was a look of shock on her face as her ankle twisted beneath her. Her leg bent at an awkward angle, then gave way as she toppled to the ground.

"Shit, Tamara, I'm sorry. I didn't mean—"

Tamara's face was contorted, screwed up with pain. Her hand went straight to her ankle, tugging off her heels.

"What the hell?" she said.

Hannah moved to help her up, but Tamara jerked away from her.

"Don't touch me," she said. "What is wrong with you?"

Hannah was scrabbling for something she could say, something she could do to take it back. Her cheeks flushed hot with shame.

"Hannah?"

Both their heads lifted. Up toward the steps, where Blake stood watching them. Hannah felt something inside her sink.

"What's going on?" he said.

"Blake—" Hannah started.

"Your fucking *girlfriend* pushed me," Tamara cut across.

"I didn't mean—"

"Hannah."

His voice was level. Calm.

"Come on," he said to her. "Let's go inside."

"Blake, what the hell?"

"Come on," he said again. He wasn't looking at his sister. He was only looking at Hannah.

Mutely, she held out her hand toward his.

They left Tamara out by the pool. Out in the impossible, suffocating heat.

FORTY

2004

THE NIGHT OF THE BIRTHDAY PARTY

Tamara's dress is torn where it caught against a cracked tile. There is a smudge of dirt on her elbow where she caught her own fall. A deep, fierce pain in her ankle.

She hobbles into the house via one of the passageways leading straight from the pool, designed for staff to ferry trays of cocktails and fresh ice out onto the terrace for her grandfather's legendary parties. It leads straight into the service kitchen, a small, airless space with an industrial freezer and dusty cupboards, hardly used now that the Draytons' staff has dwindled.

Tamara can feel her ankle swelling already, the tight throb of her skin stiffening over the injury. She digs in the freezer to find a bag of ice and uncovers another bottle of vodka. She slides to the ground and unscrews the cap with her teeth. She takes a large swig as she presses the ice against her skin. Already, she can see the pale shadow of a bruise beginning to form, can feel a tenderness that extends from her foot all the way up her calf. It's just a sprain, and yet she feels a wound that runs deeper than the thread of purple beginning to pattern her leg. The fact that Blake did nothing to help her. The fact that he has invited Hannah here, when he told Tamara it was over. That her brother has lied to her, yet again.

Tamara waits until the ice is almost entirely melted before she climbs to her feet.

She tests putting weight on her ankle and feels a sharp twinge of pain. She needs something stronger than ice and vodka; some of the painkillers that her mum keeps upstairs. Tamara occasionally sneaks some for herself, knowing that Evelyn won't notice. She likes the rush of endorphins, the twitch of the chemicals taking hold beneath her skin. The way that it makes something release inside her, the grasp of the world feeling a little looser. She gets why her mother sometimes needs everything to feel slightly less real. Understands the need to soften all the small losses that life deals out.

She hobbles up the back stairs, managing to avoid any of her mother's guests, and makes her way through the arteries of the house to the first-floor landing. She pushes open the door that leads to her mother's dressing room, a small enclave that separates her bedroom from the rest of the house. It's messy, as always. Shoes left where they were slung off after a night out. A pile of dresses, tried on and abandoned. Makeup scattered on a countertop. Tamara digs through a drawer, crammed so full that plastic catches against the runners as she slides it open. She holds the small, metallic packets to the light, until she finds what she is looking for. Oxycodone. Much stronger than she needs, but something that she knows will do the job, and quickly. Enough to make it through the night.

Tamara pops two pills out of the packet. Places one into her mouth and swallows. Without anything to rinse it down, it leaves a lump in her throat. She winces as she forces down the second.

She plans, at first, to stay until the painkillers have taken effect. Long enough that she can shuffle downstairs and rejoin the party. She knows that people will be drunk by now, too far gone to notice the dark gaps of her pupils, the static hum of her movements.

But then she hears a murmur from behind the door. A clunk of something heavy being moved. A voice that unmistakably belongs to her brother.

As Tamara stands, she feels only a mild curiosity. Only a vague interest in what her brother is doing in their mother's bedroom. A flicker of hope that perhaps he has told Hannah to leave. That he invited her tonight to break things off with her, properly this time.

She stands. Pushes against the door.

"Blake?" she says. "What are you—"

At first, Tamara does not exactly understand what she is looking at.

What she sees is a white flash of flesh. A dark tangle of sheets. Black lace, limbs that are bent strangely, a body spread out on her brother's bed.

What she sees is her twin bent over Hannah Bailey's inert form. His breathing heavy. Her head rolled back, her eyes out of focus.

It confirms both her worst fear and secret hope.

Tamara is not the bad twin.

Her brother has been the bad twin all along.

"Blake, what the *fuck*?"

Blake scrambles back, his face flushed, fully exposing the sprawl of Hannah's limbs, the lengths of exposed flesh.

Tamara pushes past him, seized with an urge to cover her up, to protect this girl that she barely knows from her brother. She drags the bedsheets up over Hannah. She can feel the heat of her skin, can see that her hair is wet with sweat.

"I wasn't doing anything to her," Blake is saying, but Tamara isn't listening. She is leaning over Hannah, saying her name. Hannah's eyelids flicker, as though she can hear Tamara from whatever distant place she inhabits.

"What's the matter with her?" Tamara says. "What has she taken? What have you given her?"

"I haven't . . . Jesus, Tam, I haven't given her anything," Blake says. "Look at her, she's just hammered. I was trying to help her. Put her to bed. What the fuck are you implying?"

Tamara looks at her twin, who she loves in a way that she can't explain to anyone else, that transcends all the other types of love she has ever felt. Her brother, who is standing at the edge of the bed, hands on his hips, face flushed. Who reaches up one arm to sweep his hair out of his face, a nervous tic that Tamara instantly recognizes. Her brother, who she wants to believe, who she is desperate to trust.

But Tamara knows. She knows.

"Give me your phone," she says.

"Tamara—"

"Give it to me."

Reluctantly, he reaches into his pocket. He holds the small silver device out toward her. Tamara flips it open and thumbs into the picture library.

"Tam," Blake is saying. "I swear I wasn't doing anything. Not like that. She turned up here hammered. You saw what she was like earlier. She'd obviously been drinking to psych herself up or something. And she must have had more drinks since then, and . . . and I was just going to put her to bed for a bit, I swear. Let her sleep it off. And then I thought . . . I don't know. I just wanted a bit of leverage, you know? Something to make sure she wouldn't talk to Cordelia . . ."

Tamara can't quite look at the pictures. She can only focus on small, specific details, the bare skin, the black lace. The slope of Hannah's breasts. The tilt of her thighs.

"Tam, I love Cordelia," Blake is saying. "I fucked up."

Tamara snaps the phone shut.

"You don't love Cordelia," she says. "You *need* Cordelia. You need her family, and her connections, and all the other bullshit that comes with dating her. And you don't understand the difference."

Tamara means what she says. In that terrible, dizzying moment, she is not sure that her brother is capable of loving anything.

"OK," he says. "OK, so I *need* Cordelia. You understand then; I can't risk Hannah telling her. It would ruin everything."

"So you thought you should blackmail her instead?"

"Tam," Blake says. "I—"

Tamara stands. She can't meet her brother's eye.

"You'll have to help me," she says.

"Help you?"

"I'm going to put her to bed in my room. She can sleep it off there."

"Tamara, I—"

"I'm not leaving her here with you."

There's a beat of silence. Blake blinks, stunned.

"Are you serious?" Blake says. "You seriously think I would do anything to her? You actually think she's not safe here?"

"You already have done something to her, Blake." Her voice is thick, knotted with the threat of tears.

"They're only pictures."

"Jesus, Blake, stop," Tamara says.

She bends down, loops her arm beneath Hannah's shoulders to pull her upright. Hannah lets out a soft groan, her head lolling to one side.

"If you won't help me, I'll do it on my own," she says. "Where are her clothes?"

She lets Hannah's weight rest against her shoulder. She's whispering to her, the way that she does with Nina when her little sister is hurt or upset. *It's OK. You're going to be alright.*

"Here."

Blake is holding up a dress. Pale blue satin, a color the exact shade of the sky on a hot summer's day. Of all things, this makes Tamara's heart ache the most. She imagines Hannah buying the dress especially for tonight. Carefully applying makeup, doing her hair. Looking at herself in the mirror. Wanting to look perfect, for a boy who will break her. Tamara eases the dress over Hannah's head.

"Let me take her," Blake says. "I can carry her."

Hannah moans again as he slides his arms around her, her weight shifting from Tamara to him. As if she knows, Tamara thinks. As if she can tell. As she lets her brother lift Hannah, Tamara reaches out, squeezes Hannah's limp hand.

I promise, she tries to convey to her, *I'm not going to let him hurt you.*

Hannah's eyelids flicker again. As if she understands.

FORTY-ONE

2024

"Imogen," Josie says. "Did you bring the case file?"

"Shouldn't we wait for Nina to get here?" Hannah asks.

Josie glances at her watch. Nina is thirty minutes late.

"Actually," says Imogen gently. "It might be better this way. You might want to see this first, Hannah."

She lifts her bag up on the table and pulls out a sheaf of papers. They aren't in the hard cardboard case that Josie recognizes.

"Copies," Imogen says, almost apologetically. "The documentary crew—they're not letting this shit out of their sight. I managed to take photos on my phone and get them printed out when everyone was on lunch."

She spreads them out on the table. They're grainy, not quite what Josie had hoped for. But they're enough. She feels, strongly now, that the truth is within these pages.

"Hannah," Imogen says. "This might be hard for you to see."

Photographs, blown up and in black-and-white. The quality is bad, an early aughts mobile phone camera, blurred again by Imogen's secondhand photography. The images are difficult to make out, at first. You have to look at them for a moment, allow the pixels to recalibrate into an image.

Then, the jut of a hip bone. The fade of light skin into the dark bruise of a nipple. An eye, half-closed, an expression that Josie had initially interpreted as lust, a head tilted back as if the body it belongs to is in the throes of an orgasm.

An expression that could be desire, or could be distance. That could be someone out of their mind with passion, or simply out of their mind. Someone who is not wholly within themselves.

"It's me," Hannah says, blankly.

She picks one of the pictures up, holds it between her thumb and forefinger, as if it's something contaminated.

"These are all of me."

"After Nina came forward and the investigation became criminal, the police took the cell phones of people close to Tamara," Imogen says quietly. "Cell phone technology was much less advanced then, so there wasn't as much that could be recovered. They were primarily looking for messages between family members and Tamara that Tamara might have removed from her own device, and that they were unable to recover. The police obviously thought these were interesting enough to keep on file."

"These were on Blake's phone?"

The piece of paper that Hannah holds has begun to crease beneath her grip.

"They'd been deleted, but the police were able to access them," Imogen says. "Evidently, Blake didn't know his phone had a recently deleted folder. They were timestamped on the day Tamara died."

"But . . . if the police had these images . . . I mean . . . nobody's ever shown me these before."

"I don't think the police ever looked into who the pictures were of. In fact, I don't think they looked into them much at all, or if Blake was ever asked about them. There's a ton of other stuff in here that isn't really pertinent to the case—messages between Evelyn and her party planner, texts between Blake and Barnaby van Beek."

"When I first saw these, I assumed they were consensual," Josie says. "That you and Blake had taken these together when you were hooking up, or even that you'd taken them *for* him."

Gently, she reaches over and takes the picture from Hannah's hand. Lays it out on the table in front of her again.

"But Hannah," Josie says. "These are from the night that Tamara died. And you don't remember them being taken?"

Hannah shakes her head. She is still looking down at the pictures.

"I was drunk," she says. "I don't remember the night well. But . . . I don't understand."

"There's something else you should see."

Imogen is sliding another piece of paper out of the pack. She pushes it toward Hannah.

"The toxicology report." Hannah sounds dazed. "I've seen this before. Online."

"Yeah," says Imogen. "A lot of people have said a lot of things about it, including me. High blood alcohol levels and a complete cocktail of drugs in Tamara's system. Cocaine, antidepressants, painkillers . . ."

"Right," says Hannah. "Tamara had a pretty relaxed attitude to . . . stimulants."

"Exactly. In fact, basically everyone that the police spoke to said that this was totally normal for Tamara. That she took this kind of stuff all the time. Other than alcohol, there wasn't a concerningly large amount of anything in her system—certainly not enough to make her wander off and fall into a pool and drown."

Hannah nodded. "Wasn't one of the arguments for accidental death that drugs were a potential factor, but the court ruled that out?"

"Yes," says Imogen. "Which made sense. At least, it made sense without those pictures. But look at this."

Imogen runs her fingers down the list of drugs, stopping close to the bottom.

"Benzodiazepines: flunitrazepam," Hannah reads. "Benzos are sleeping pills, right?"

"Exactly," says Imogen. "In fact, these were apparently Evelyn's sleeping pills. Evelyn said that she got them under the counter, for insomnia. Said that she wasn't sleeping because of everything that was going on with her cheating scumbag husband. And when the toxicology report is released, she completely sweeps this under the rug. Tells the police that it's no biggie. That she actually gave Tamara some of her pills pretty regularly, because Tamara didn't sleep well. She said that Tamara wanted to nap before the party so could have taken them then, or maybe even shortly before she died, if she was done with the party and wanted to get some sleep without the noise disturbing her. Evelyn actually got investigated, since the pills weren't prescription, but the police decided that it wasn't in the public interest to prosecute."

"So . . . what are you saying?"

"Hannah." Imogen leans in close. "You said that you were drunk that night. But were you surprised by how drunk you got? Did it seem strange to you?"

"I mean . . ." Hannah looks flustered. "Yeah, I guess. I'd never been like that before. Passing out, and not remembering stuff. But then, I'd hardly ever drank champagne before. I wasn't used to it. And Blake kept giving me drinks . . ."

"Flunitrazepam," Imogen says, "also has another name."

"It does?"

Imogen nods. Josie can see something of truecrimefangirl_2002 in her then. Something of that dramatic flair.

"Flunitrazepam," she says, "is also known as Rohypnol."

"Rohypnol?" Hannah looks between Josie and Imogen. "As in roofies? The date rape drug?"

Imogen nods.

"In small doses, it's a treatment for insomnia. But in larger doses . . . well."

"We think you were roofied that night," Josie says. "And we think that whoever roofied you also roofied Tamara."

"But that's . . ." Hannah is frowning. "Wouldn't the police have figured that out? Or the coroner?"

"One of the reasons why roofies are a drug of choice for people up to no good is because it leaves your system really fast," Imogen says. "*Really* fast for some people, and a little bit slower for others, depending on what it's interacting with, and your size, and how much you've eaten, and a ton of other stuff. And Tamara didn't die until almost eight hours after she was found. There were minimal traces of it detected in her toxicology results. Not enough to draw any conclusions. And certainly not enough to disprove Evelyn's sleeping pill story. It was impossible to tell when Tamara had taken them, and whether she'd taken enough to help her have a quick nap, or to totally incapacitate her."

"And toxicology results take a long time," says Josie. "Months. By the time they were released, nobody was paying much attention. Nina had already come out with her story, and that had completely taken everyone's eyes off the toxicology report. The investigators had basically made their minds up. They had their theory, and Tamara being on drugs didn't prove or disprove anything. Nina's story still held up."

"But . . ." Hannah closes her eyes and presses her palms down against them. She shakes her head. When she speaks, her voice is quiet. "You think that Blake roofied me, *and* that he roofied Tamara, too?"

Neither of them speak. Hannah pulls her hands away from her face. She can see, from their silence, their pained expressions, that this is exactly what they think.

"But why would he have taken those photos?" She hears the pleading note in her voice.

Imogen looks at Josie, who gives her a small nod. "Hannah, I know it's hard to hear this, even now, but . . . Blake was still seeing Cordelia at the time of the party. In fact, he was still seeing her for about a year after the party, until she dumped him when she went to university the next autumn. My guess? Blake wanted to have something on you, some form of blackmail, in case you threatened to expose him for what he was: a cheating asshole who had been unfaithful to his wealthy, connected girlfriend all summer."

"He was . . . he was still with Cordelia?"

Even twenty years later, the betrayal is a knife. Imogen's and Josie's faces swim in front of Hannah's eyes, and she has to duck her head, taking a deep, gasping breath of the sharp, salty air.

"But I wasn't the only one who knew," she says, her voice tight, fighting for something to undo what Imogen is telling her. "Josie, you knew. And Tamara. Tamara knew—"

She breaks off, the logic of Imogen's argument smacking her full in the chest. Tamara knew. And Tamara ended up dead.

Neither Josie nor Imogen speak. They don't need to. The facts are there, laid out before them all for the first time. Hannah closes her eyes.

From what feels like very far away, she can hear her family. The distinctive sound of Eric's laugh. Isla's childish babble. The sound of Mason and Noah calling out to each other as they paddle in the sea. Just like her and Josie, when they were girls.

When she finally regains her composure, she's made a decision.

"Actually," she says. "There's something else you don't know about that night."

And then, Hannah tells them everything.

FORTY-TWO

2024

Nina is not sure whether or not she is awake.

She is lying flat on her back, the sun a hazy yellow through a gap in the curtains. At first, she thinks it must be morning, and then she is not sure how it can be, if she hasn't been asleep. But then, perhaps she *has* been asleep, because she can't remember any conscious thought for a very long time now. But if she *was* asleep, then maybe she still is, because she also cannot remember waking up.

She is briefly concerned, before the worry mellows out. The center of her chest feels warm and heavy. Her limbs feel light.

She realizes that she knows this feeling well. God, she's missed it. She's forgotten how good, how *easy* it feels, to simply eradicate the fears that usually feel so large and consuming. It only takes one of the small white pills that Blake went to fetch for her. Although, she might have taken two. Or three? Blake had given her the pills and a glass of water to wash them down, and she had felt so tired, so relieved that her big brother was making the decision for her, that she hadn't questioned it. She needed sleep so badly that she was willing to do anything.

It had felt so momentous when Nina had come off the pills last year, but now her reasoning feels ridiculous. Why would you ever resist this? The bliss of feeling like there was absolutely nothing to worry about, nowhere to be. She wants to exist in this state forever. She wants to sleep for a thousand years.

Beside her, her phone is humming, but Nina can't summon the will to answer it. She sees the caller ID flash up, *Josie Jackson*. The name that has filled her with dread and guilt for years is now just a name. Just a combination of letters. Just a message that says Nina, please answer, it's important. Nothing that Nina has the energy or the will to worry about.

The light is softening again, simmering. Nina rolls over. She closes her eyes.

FORTY-THREE

2024

That night, Hannah finds herself going through the motions.

Those strange, half-familiar images of Hannah's body as it was twenty years ago had been like seeing an old friend—or an old enemy—across the room. After she told Imogen and Josie her story, she had risen unsteadily to her feet. Made some excuse about Isla needing a nap, rounded up her children, murmured *later* when Eric asked if she was OK. That promise, passed between them, of togetherness and truth. A promise that Hannah has broken over and over again across the course of their marriage.

Josie had said that they would stay and wait for Nina, by then almost an hour late. She had told Hannah that they'd give her time to absorb what she'd seen, had promised that she would message if there were any updates, but Hannah has not checked her phone. Besides, there is something Hannah needs to do first.

She gets through dinner and bath and bedtime. Negotiating another hour before lights out with Noah, and letting her dad and Eric take care of the washing up while her mother reads Isla another story. With an unexpected schism of time to herself, Hannah escapes into the garden and turns her face to the pale night sky.

It has been impossible not to think about that summer ever since she heard Josie Jackson was back. Impossible not to think about the heatwave, and Blake, and the iridescent edges of girlhood. Impossible not to think about Tamara Drayton.

But now, Hannah is tangled up with other memories. The dinner with Blake's dad; the taste of blood in Hannah's mouth. What happened after, Hannah convincing herself that the whole thing was erotic, somehow; sexy. That it was proof of just how badly Blake wanted her, how much he needed her.

Those pictures felt familiar for a reason. Not because Hannah has ever seen them before, or even knew about their existence. She had no idea that those photographs had been taken. But what *was* familiar—what sparked an agonizing, uncanny lack of surprise within her—was that, deep down, Hannah has always known what Blake Drayton was capable of. She has always known, and she has let him get away with it.

Eric emerges from the house, his hands dug in his pockets, his face soft. He lowers himself into the chair next to Hannah and reaches out for her, his hand finding the small of her back. It's a gesture he picked up years ago, when Hannah was pregnant with Mason. When the lower curve of her spine was always aching, her hips perpetually sore. When the pressure of his thumb against her muscles would ease the pain. A small habit of touch that has never left them, even after Mason was born, even after they had convinced themselves that they would never have any more children.

Sometimes their entire relationship feels like a story of such small gestures—in-jokes and touches weighted with almost-forgotten meanings. It means that Hannah can't imagine being with anyone else. There would never be enough time, enough love, to build a palace out of the small bricks of kindness and history in the way that she and Eric have. A love completely unlike the heady infatuation with Blake Drayton that she experienced all those years ago. The excitement and the longing. Falling for somebody because of what you imagined you might be when you were with them, rather than because of who they were themselves.

With Eric, it's safety. Trust. Nineteen years of loving each other. Of making the choice to love each other over and over again, even when things felt exhausting, or boring, or hard. Eric always chose Hannah.

Now, Hannah's going to have to ask him to choose her again.

"Eric," she says.

He looks at her. His eyes are gentle in the dusk light. Kind. She is going to have to break his heart.

"I need to tell you," Hannah says. "About the worst thing I ever did."

FORTY-FOUR

2024

For the last twenty years, Hannah has not sought Blake Drayton out.

She has stayed away from the main strip of the town on her visits back to the Côte d'Azur. Always picked the quietest spots on the beach. Intentionally avoided anywhere she might run into the Draytons.

But the day after meeting with Imogen and Josie, Hannah walks up the road to the pink house for the first time since the day that Tamara Drayton died.

The coral-colored stone, a touch more faded than she remembers it. The large, wooden front doors that she was never able to use, always going in and out of the back entrance, always hidden, always staying quiet.

Hannah has had enough of staying quiet.

She lifts one hand and knocks, hard, on the door.

For a long moment, she thinks that nobody is home. In the distance, a cricket calls. The air stands still.

Then, she hears a scuffle of movement behind the door. Feet on hard tiles. The slide of a bolt.

She is expecting staff. A housekeeper. For a bizarre half second, she almost expects to see Patricia Jackson.

She is still struck by this, still humming with the strangeness of expecting a dead woman to answer a door, when the door swings open.

Standing face-to-face with Hannah is Blake Drayton.

He is completely different, of course. His shoulders have filled out, his chin squared. His hair is shorter, the blond sweep of his fringe that used to drive girls crazy cut back. His eyes have dark circles, the hint of age.

Hannah might even have second-guessed that it was him, if not for the way he moves, the puff of his chest. The things that she recognizes in him are the things that don't change about a person, even when they get older, even when their face and body grow and shift. The self-assurance. The way he takes up space in the world. The confidence that Hannah always longed for.

"Hannah fucking Bailey," he says, a twitch of amusement on his face. As if he has been expecting her to come here all along.

Hannah fucking Bailey lifts up her chin.

"We need to talk," she says.

He hesitates for just a second. In that second, Hannah thinks of Tamara. She thinks of all the ways things might have been different.

She thinks of all the chances she has missed to put things right.

"Well," he says. "I guess you'd better come in."

※

The pink house is not how Hannah remembers it.

Memory is duplicitous like that. The pink house is a place that has lived for years in her mind, as a shrine to a time that no longer exists. A place that Hannah has revisited so often in her memories, each version shifting slightly—reformulating rooms, reshaping the fall of the light, the color of the walls—until the image no longer resembles reality.

The hallway is smaller than she remembers. She can see right through to the kitchen and onto the small back terrace, even though she could have sworn that it was tucked out of sight. The smell is different—mustier and slightly damp—and yet still she catches the scent of Evelyn's perfume. Blake is so different—gone is that golden sheen of youth—and yet she still feels something within her turn toward him. Some ancient attraction, a Pavlovian response to the way he looks at her. When she looks back at him, she is seventeen again.

She feels that tug of longing, and she hates herself for it.

"Can I get you anything?" he says. "A drink? Some water?"

He seems so relaxed. So at ease, when Hannah's heart is a drum roll. She shakes her head.

"I'm fine. Thanks."

"Well, then, shall we go outside?"

He gestures toward the terrace.

"Is Nina here?" Hannah asks.

Blake tilts his head to one side.

"She's upstairs," he says. "Sleeping. She's not been feeling well lately."

He places his hand on Hannah's arm, as if to guide her outside. Hannah catches the smell of him, the sharp cut of his aftershave, the heat of his skin, the hum of sweat. He's nervous.

"We can talk here," she says, pulling away from him.

Blake smiles then, a grin that doesn't quite reach his eyes. It makes his face look sharp and cruel.

"You think," he says, "that I'm going to talk to you where my sister might wake up and hear?"

He grips her shoulder, harder now. A pressure that takes Hannah back to that night. The taste of metal and wine in her mouth.

"I've got dirt on you, Hannah Bailey," he says, his voice low and hard in her ear. "Don't do anything to piss me off."

FORTY-FIVE

2024

When she first hears the footsteps, Nina is dreaming.

She is dreaming about green, open fields. About people who are not quite human. Faces with a strange, uncanny gloss that marks them apart. When Nina tries to speak to them, their eyes widen. Their throats bloat, like words are trapped inside them. Their features begin to rearrange, until they are terrible, unreal creatures. Demons created before her eyes.

At first, the footsteps are within her dream. They are the sound of these monsters nearing her. They are the sound of her own shoes, pounding against the ground as she tries to escape from them.

Then, slowly, the dream slips away. She is confused, at first, about where she is. Why she is sleeping, when it seems to be the middle of the day.

Then she remembers the sleeping pills. Sliding into the blissful, thoughtless, unconscious state that they promised. Last night, perhaps. Or yesterday afternoon. She isn't sure. Time slopes away from her, a river flowing too fast. Her mind is quiet. Her bones are heavy.

Then, as if carried from the mist of her dream, she hears a noise.

She listens, her mouth cotton-wool dry, her mind fogged. There it is again. A distant tap of footsteps. Not from the corridor that runs on the right side of her room, but on the left. Nina lifts up her hand, the stone of the wall cool against her fingertips. Through the haze of her thoughts, the impossibility of anyone walking on the left side of her room is clear. That wall is shared with Tamara's bedroom.

A room that has stayed empty and locked for the last twenty years.

Briefly she is struck with the image of her sister. Tamara, captured in a thousand photographs. Defiant, even in death. The straight, unsmiling way she had of looking at the camera. Spikily beautiful. A girl that Nina barely knew.

But then, between the fog of drugs, she sees an image of Tamara that makes her breath catch in her chest. Not Tamara as Nina knows her from photographs, but a girl laid out on the side of a pool. Her skin almost translucent. Her body bent at unnatural angles. Her head bloodied. Her eyes closed.

Nina imagines, on the other side of the wall, the ghost of her sister opening her eyes. Raising her blood-streaked head, her face distorted by the terrible concave wound at her right temple. The silent gape of her mouth. The plea in her eyes. Asking Nina, after all this time, to save her.

This is when Nina remembers something else, summoned from the depths of her childhood. That, although the door next to hers belongs to Tamara's room, there is a space between the two walls. A hollow carved out by the crazed geometry of her grandfather's architectural imaginings. The secret structure that weaves between the walls of the house. Passageways and corridors designed for staff to navigate the house unseen. They haven't been used for years, not since Nina was a child. Most of them were blocked off long ago. Nobody would even know that they were there.

Only the people who had existed here long ago. Who knew the secrets of the pink house. Who were accustomed to existing unseen alongside the Draytons.

Nina scrabbles to her feet now. She runs her hands along the wall, trying to remember: a time when she was tiny, when Josie Jackson had promised her an adventure, and had taken Nina into the servants' tunnels. Nina had been stunned to learn that there was an entirely hidden world within the walls of the house where she had spent much of her childhood.

Her mind feels sharper now. She opens her bedroom door, out into the corridor. She remembers standing here; Josie Jackson taking her hand, and her own whispered promise not to tell Evelyn.

There is a thud from the end of the landing, like wood striking wood. A woman's voice.

"*Fuck.*"

There was a door; Nina remembers it now. Wooden, discreet. Exactly where a large cabinet has stood for years. She had forgotten what hid behind it.

She hurries down the hallway, toward the cabinet. As she pushes against it with her shoulder, her fingers scrabbling for something to grip on to, she feels a pressure from the other side. Without thinking of any potential danger—without really considering who the woman's voice belongs to—she finds that they are working together.

But then, perhaps she already knows. She already realizes that there are only a handful of people who know this house like she does. Who understand its secrets.

With one hard push, the cabinet finally eases away. The door swings fully open, and standing there, in the empty space it leaves, is Josie Jackson.

She holds one finger up to her mouth. One more secret. One more hidden thing.

FORTY-SIX

2024

Out on the terrace, the world feels too bright. It is too sunny for the weight that sits in Hannah's chest.

Hannah turns to face Blake.

"I know what happened," she says.

He slings himself into one of the chairs set out around a small white painted table. Folds one leg over the other, a pretense of ease that Hannah sees straight through.

"What happened when?" he asks.

"The day Tamara died," Hannah says. "I know about the pictures you took of me. I know you drugged me."

She almost thinks that she sees something pass across his face then. A flicker of something behind his eyes. And then it's gone.

"I don't know what you're talking about," he says.

"Don't give me that." Hannah's heart is beating fast. "I've seen the photographs. I've seen the autopsy. Rohypnol. It's not a coincidence that Tamara had roofies in her system the same night I passed out and didn't remember anything. Did Evelyn pay off the coroner to play it down? Or was she sleeping with him?"

"That's a very serious accusation to make about my mother, Hannah."

Blake's voice lilts, faux serious. He is mocking her, a pretense of confidence.

"You're forgetting," Hannah says. "That I saw what happened."

He stills at this. For just a second, she sees his composure slip. A flicker of fear behind his eyes.

"We *both* saw what happened," he says, quietly. "And I protected you. For years. And now you're accusing me of—what? Spiking my sister? Killing my sister?"

His mouth twitches, as if the thought is ridiculous.

"It was your fault that she died," Blake says. "It's your fault that Tamara is dead."

FORTY-SEVEN

2004
THE DAY OF THE BIRTHDAY PARTY

For a long time, Tamara has tried to ignore her fears about her brother.

They began years ago. First, a night when they had been out drinking in London, at a bar that didn't check IDs, as long as they had their parents' credit cards. Tamara had seen Blake slip his arm around a girl who was so drunk that she could barely sit upright. His hand on her thigh. Offering to take her home in a taxi. She had felt an unexpected, slippery dart of relief when one of the girl's friends had said that she'd go with her instead. Later that night, Tamara lay awake wondering if she would have intervened, had the girl's friend not done so first.

There had been the time that Blake was sleeping with a girl with an older boyfriend, a secret that only Tamara knew. When the boyfriend found out, he turned up at their house when Evelyn and Harrison were away, and beat the crap out of Blake, right there on the doorstep, the girl standing a few feet behind doing nothing to stop him. A few weeks later, pictures of the girl were posted all over the corridors of their boarding school. Pouting at the camera, her body bare, her breasts pushed up. It had been a huge scandal, and the girl had had to switch schools. Nobody knew who posted the pictures.

Nobody except Tamara.

She tried to convince herself that it was a coincidence the girl's nudes were leaked so soon after Blake had been slighted. That he would have done the right thing for the girl he tried to take home from that London bar.

And yet, there had been other things. Other small signs. The way he sneered at their mother, talked about her relationships with men as if they were the things that lessened her, cheapened her. The way he talked about Cordelia to Barnaby, calling her a slut for doing the things he had asked her to do in bed. Showing his friend the nudes that Cordelia had sent him, the dark hollow of hair between her thighs that Blake said grossed him out. Eventually, he made her shave it off because the pictures that Tamara later glimpsed were smooth and pink like raw meat, speckled with a rash from the razor.

So as much as Tamara tried to ignore these things, something dark and irrepressible told her that there was something cruel in her brother. That Tamara was not the bad twin, after all.

It was why she had tried to warn Josie, all those weeks ago. Why she had resisted Hannah's relationship with her brother so strongly. She understood the power that Blake had over Hannah, larger and more frightening than the power he had over the girls in their own social circle. And she loved Josie, after all. She did not want Josie's friend to get hurt.

As the sky darkens, the moon rising, Tamara goes out to the balcony that backs out of their mother's bedroom. She comes here, sometimes, when she wants to think. The one place in the house where she and her brother are expressly forbidden from going. A place where she can be alone, without the connection that hums between them interrupting her thoughts. In her hand, she holds her brother's phone. It looks so small. So unassuming.

It feels like a grenade waiting to blow apart everything Tamara wants to believe about her twin.

She insisted that Blake leave once he had deposited Hannah onto her bed, physically pushing him through the door and locking it behind her. She pulled the sheets up over Hannah's inert body, gently removed the pins from her hair so that they didn't dig into her scalp as she slept.

Outside, her brother had pounded on the door. He had called out to Tamara. Begged for his phone back. Tamara stayed in the room with Hannah, even after he fell quiet. She had been able to feel his presence, like always, through the door. A prickle on the surface of her skin telling her that her twin was close. She had waited until she heard a shift of movement. The sound of footsteps walking away. The thread that stretched between them feeling thinner. His phone, digging into the palm of her hand.

Now, as she taps into the photo album, she finds that she is holding her breath.

She is braced for what she will see. The unnatural arrangement of limbs. The terrible vulnerability of Hannah's body. Even so, the pictures make Tamara's heart still. She flips through them, steadily, the shock of each new photograph refusing to lessen. Each small, awful confirmation of the kind of person her brother is.

She flips into his messages next and finds the thread of his conversation with Cordelia. Not breakup texts, but Blake telling his girlfriend that he's sick. That he'll be staying in bed for the duration of their mother's party. That Cordelia should stay home. The confirmation Tamara needs that her brother planned this. That he brought Hannah here with the intention of getting these pictures.

The hum of coke in Tamara's system has twisted, the pleasant buzz from earlier contorting into something ugly. Her heart is beating too fast. Her lungs are stiff, metal rather than flesh, so that each breath is labored. She is painfully aware of her insides, can imagine the guts and bones of herself, the way that her chest tightens and her stomach twists with each image. She's aware of the blood in her veins, the same that inches through her brother's body. The differences in DNA that separate Tamara from her brother, tiny fractures of genetics that once seemed small now feel like vast chasms. She used to think that they were almost the same person. Now she feels as far from Blake as she ever has.

She scrolls back to the photo album, her thumb hovering over the small digital rendering of a bin that will wipe it clean. It feels like the simplest thing to do. To protect Hannah by destroying anything that Blake could use against her.

But then, she finds herself exiting the album, the photos untouched. Perhaps they do not belong to her. Perhaps this is not Tamara's decision.

She is struck by an urge to speak to Josie; Josie will know what to do. Josie will be able to talk to Hannah. She will tell her about the pictures in a way that will hurt the least. Together, they can offer Hannah the opportunity to decide what to do with them.

With a small lurch, she thinks of the things that Hannah might do with the photos—the things that she has every right to do. To show them to Cordelia; even, perhaps, the police.

The thought makes Tamara hesitate for only a moment. She cannot protect her brother any longer.

She starts to stand, staggering as she does. Her ankle is still throbbing. The pills have eradicated the pain, but not the pulse of her muscles swelling, the twinge of protest as she puts weight on her foot.

"Tam?"

Tamara spins around, almost losing her balance as she does. She hadn't heard him behind her. Hadn't heard the slide of the patio doors from her mother's bedroom. She hadn't, she realizes with a twinge of surprise, sensed her brother close to her. It's as if the thread between them has finally snapped.

"Tam," Blake says again.

He looks smaller than usual. Forlorn. He is holding a drink in each hand. He extends one out toward her.

"Please don't hate me," Blake says. "I couldn't stand it if you hated me."

Something within Tamara crumples then. A softness blooming within her, in spite of everything. A memory of the two of them, hiding at the top of the stairs together when they were young. The two of them against the world. She supposes, really, that the softness is love. That it never really goes away, even when someone does the worst possible things.

"Can we just talk?" Blake says. "Please?"

FORTY-EIGHT

2004
THE DAY OF THE BIRTHDAY PARTY

Blake had heard a thousand times how lucky he was to be a twin. For all his life, people found it fascinating. The idea of being bound to someone, like he was to Tamara. The fact of your entire existence being so inexorably tied to another being that the very concept of you barely made sense without the other. The thought that you had never, from the moment of your conception, truly been alone.

Blake always nodded when people said this. He always smiled politely; always said, truthfully, that he could not imagine a world without his sister.

But the truth of the matter was that Blake had always hated being a twin.

He and Tamara were close when they were younger, of course. How could they not be? They had never known anything different. Back then, Blake didn't quite understand that other people didn't know what it was like to have every sentence finished for you, every thought understood, every formative experience shared. Tamara always said that there was a connection between them, something that fizzed in the air, just short of mind reading. Whenever she said that, Blake would think how ridiculous the entire idea was. How could Tamara know that there was something different between them, when neither of them had ever been anyone else? How could she possibly discern the kind of twin-magic she believed in from plain familiarity?

To Blake, the twin-speak that they created was a symptom of boredom, a language that formed naturally from the patterns of their lives, in-jokes and linguistic tricks that anyone could learn. The psychic connection that Tamara claimed was just simple cognition. It was easy to know what someone was thinking when you had been present for almost every thought that they had ever had, every word they had ever said.

But the older they got, the more Blake felt his own personality, his own desires twisting out of him, the more that the intimate knowledge that his sister held over him felt cursed. He would see the way that she looked at him. The way that she judged him. The way that she would adopt a slightly pained expression when he talked about girls, and about parties, about the things he and Barnaby would do when they were away at school once he and Tamara had separated for single-sex sixth forms.

Not that he was doing anything wrong. They were young, weren't they? They were *supposed* to be doing things that they would one day regret. Things they wouldn't tell their mother about (although, of course, having a mother like Evelyn Drayton shifted the dial of acceptability somewhat). And it wasn't as if Tamara didn't have secrets. It wasn't as if Tamara was perfect herself.

Sometimes, he felt like Tamara saw things in black-and-white. Sometimes he felt that she saw them as not the same, but opposite sides of the same battered coin. That only one of them could be good. That her role in their relationship was to always, always be the one watching over him. Looking out for him. Judging him. That somehow this made her *better* than him. The thought angered him; made something seethe and twist inside, a resentment that had been boiling for what felt like a very long time.

When Tamara glanced up at him from her position on the terrace she looked tired.

He held the drink out toward her.

"Peace offering," he said.

She hesitated before shifting over on the deckchair. She took the drink out of his hand. For a while, neither of them spoke. Blake tried, for a moment, to feel that connection that Tamara always swore was between them. Instead, he found only space. Only air. Only heat.

"I don't understand," Tamara said at last. "What happened to us. We used to be close, didn't we? We used to be more than just siblings. More than twins, even."

She turned to face him then. Her face was raw with sadness.

"What happened?" she said. "What happened to *you*, Blake? I don't feel like I know you anymore."

Because you don't, Blake wanted to say. *Because maybe you never did.*

"The Blake I know would never do this," Tamara said quietly. She lifted the phone.

"Tam, please."

"Please *what*, Blake? I have to say it. Someone has to say it to you, or I'm scared you won't stop."

Her voice trembled in a way that Blake knew preceded tears. This, he supposed, is what Tamara meant by their connection—knowing someone so well that you knew exactly what they would do next.

But this was Tamara's mistake. Because Tamara did not know what Blake would do to her next. She still trusted him. That was why she was still holding her drink; still taking small, desperate gulps to hide the threat of her tears.

"Sometimes I think," she said, once she'd composed herself. "That there's something wrong with you."

He snorted then, in spite of himself.

"Something wrong with me?"

"You hurt people, Blake. And you don't seem to care. It scares me."

"Because I took some pictures? Jesus, Tamara—"

"It's not just the pictures, Blake. It's all of it."

"All of *what*?"

She shook her head.

"Tam? Tam, say something."

She lifted her head.

"I'm sorry. But I can't let you do this."

"What do you mean?"

"The pictures. I'm going to send them to Hannah. And to Cordelia. They have a right to know they exist, to know what you did."

With this, fear darted through Blake. He thought that Tamara might tell Hannah, might even tell Cordelia. But now, he realized that his sister had the ability to destroy him.

"Tamara." He leaned toward her. "Give me the phone."

She stood, holding it at arm's length away from him. Like they were children again, fighting over a toy.

"No."

"Tam, don't be stupid."

They were not acting the way he had hoped they would, the sleeping pills he had dissolved into Tamara's drink. They had taken effect on Hannah so quickly. She had been dopey within five minutes, unconscious in fifteen. Shouldn't Tamara have at least been dizzy by now? He should have been able to slip the phone away from her, to delete the pictures while she was still woozy. But his sister stood, her legs planted firmly on the ground, the phone tight in her grip. Wholly alive, and strong, and certain.

"I'm not being stupid," she said. "I'm doing the right thing, Blake."

She stepped back, the phone held out of his reach.

"I'm not going to fight you on this," she said.

But really, she did not have a choice.

Because this, for Blake, was a fight for his life. For the life that he had always wanted, a life that he was so close to achieving.

He lunged at his sister, grasping hold of her arm. She staggered back, shocked. He was stronger than her, and an inch taller. He had been born first. He had existed for thirteen whole minutes in this world without her. Thirteen minutes that would always be the difference between him and her.

He wrenched the phone from her hand, tearing it away triumphantly.

He did not mean to push her.

He had only meant to press his hand against the center of her chest to keep her away. To stop her from wrestling the phone back from him.

He did not mean for her foot to catch on the low stone border that ringed the terrace. Did not mean for her to stagger backward, dangerously close to the edge.

As one arm reached out, he meant, perhaps, to save her. Her arms flailed, and their eyes met, hers wide, pleading.

He had not meant for this to be the last time he looked at his sister and saw her looking back.

Briefly, stupidly, Blake was reminded of a magic trick he had seen at one of their end-of-term balls at boarding school. Tamara had volunteered and had been folded into a glittering, person-sized box. The lights had gleamed, the box opened, and Tamara was gone. She refused to tell Blake how the trick had worked afterward, had only tapped the side of her nose, whispering that it must have been magic.

And now, as Blake watched, she disappeared again. One moment she was there, balanced, one foot still on the terrace's edge. And then, she was gone. Only empty space where his sister had stood. Only the air. The sky. The sea.

He dived toward the edge after her. His feet skittered against the stone, stopping just short of where Tamara had fallen. Below them, he saw the pool. Tamara. For just a second, he felt a wash of relief. She had landed in the water. She would be alright.

Then, he saw the dark bloom that came from her head. The blood, almost black against the pale blue of the pool, dissipating into the water. He saw the streak of red on the side of the pool, a mess of something that must have come from his sister's skull. The way that she was facedown. Unmoving.

Later, he would think back to that moment. He would go over and over those few unthinking seconds. That half breath when he should have turned and run downstairs. When maybe—just maybe—he could have saved his sister.

But Blake stayed still. He stood, his fists clenched, looking down at the water. The blood. Tamara.

And in that moment, Blake felt an unexpected sweep of peace. His fears of a few minutes ago were gone, and for a fraction of a second, something terrible crossed Blake's mind. Something that, although he would never tell anyone, he would always remember thinking:

This solves everything.

So Blake did not move.

He simply stood and watched as the blue water turned a strange, pale shade of red.

At the start of Blake's life, he had had thirteen minutes without his sister. Thirteen small, precious minutes alone. And then, kicking and screaming, there she had been.

As the life bleeds out of his sister, Blake thinks about the next thirteen minutes, and the next. He thinks about an entire existence made up of thirteen-minute increments. An entire life stretching out ahead of him, without Tamara.

He feels something give then, like a muscle snapping in his chest. An overwhelming feeling that he doesn't recognize flooding through him. A sensation that he has only experienced once before, for exactly thirteen minutes.

The feeling that he is entirely alone.

This is when Blake knows that she is gone. When he knows that his sister is beyond saving. When he finally understands that his sister was right about the magic that existed between them.

This is when Blake knows that he has made the biggest mistake of his life.

FORTY-NINE

2004
THE DAY OF THE BIRTHDAY PARTY

Hannah felt as if she had been asleep for a very long time.
    A wave of nausea washed over her as she tried to sit up. There was a sear of pain in her skull, worse than any hangover she'd ever experienced. The room was dark, and yet she could make out the strains of music. Talking. Laughter. She fought to recall where she was. The memories came back in hazy, half formations, like glints of light falling through the branches of trees sifting in the breeze. There and then gone. There and then gone.

Evelyn's party. Champagne. Blake. Evelyn's bed.

Her stomach turned over. She fumbled for a light switch, her hand hitting a lamp. The room flushed bright. She was in Tamara's bed, tucked beneath the sheets. A wash of panic seized her. Hours must have passed. She had never been so drunk before that she couldn't remember how she got somewhere. She had heard people talk about being blackout drunk like it was a badge of honor. Nothing like the fear and shame that hummed through her now.

She clambered to her feet. Closed her eyes as the world spun. She must have still been drunk, and yet this was like no kind of drunkenness she had ever experienced. Like being drunk and hungover at the same time. She grimaced as she imagined what must have happened:

drinking too much, trying to calm herself after her confrontation with Tamara. She must have passed out, forcing Blake to put her to bed. The thought made embarrassment unfurl inside her.

It felt vitally important to find Blake. She had to apologize. She had to pull herself together, to show him that she could be the girlfriend he wanted. The room swayed as she crossed it. First, she would get some water. She would be fine after some water.

She remembered that they'd been drinking in Evelyn's bedroom. There would still be glasses in there. There was an en suite bathroom where she could fill them up. She could gather herself there, away from any of the other party guests.

She navigated deeper into the labyrinthine house that Hannah knew as well as her family's own small flat. In a way, it felt as much a part of her legacy as it did the Draytons'.

She pushed against the door to Evelyn's room. Into the dressing room, and then to the main bedroom. The room was thick with heat, the patio doors that led out to the terrace left wide open. Evelyn would be annoyed, blaming everyone else for her own oversight, for forgetting, as she got ready for the party, to shut out the stifling air.

Instinctively, just like someone who had been raised serving people like the Draytons, Hannah moved to close the doors, and there he was. Blake. Her Blake. Silhouetted against the white light of the moon and standing alone, on the very edge of the terrace. A wave of emotion passed through Hannah. Something like relief. Something like love.

She began to walk toward him.

"Blake—"

Then, she stopped. Blake was not looking up toward the stars, or out to the sea. His gaze was fixed downward. His head lifted and Hannah knew immediately that something was wrong. She could see the twist of his face, the sheen of shock. The way that his eyes were wide and full of fear.

"Hannah," he said.

Her eyes followed his. Toward the water. The pool. A bloom of red against the unnatural blue of the tiles. A body, floating, arms outstretched. Like someone ready to leap. To fly.

A wave of nausea contorted inside her, and for a moment she thought she would vomit. Her hands flew up to her mouth. Blake was gripping her wrist, pulling her back from the edge.

"Don't scream," he said. "Please don't scream."

"It's Tamara," she said, uselessly. As if he wouldn't know. As if he wouldn't recognize his own twin.

"I know," he said. "I know."

"Have you called an ambulance?" she said. "We have to call an ambulance."

The world swayed again, and she found that she was leaning into him. That he was holding up her weight, his arms wrapped around her body. Making quiet, shushing sounds.

"It's too late," he said. "I saw her fall. The way she hit her head—Hannah, it's too late."

The shush turned into a sob. A choke.

"What do you mean?"

"She's . . . Hannah, she's . . ."

He could not say it. Hannah could not hear it.

"We have to try." Hannah's voice was strangled. Slurred. Everything still felt hazy, not quite real. Perhaps it was not. Perhaps she could fix this still. "We have to get her out of the water."

His arms loosened. His eyes were wet.

"You have to leave," he said.

"I . . . what?"

"I saw her fall," he said. "It was her ankle. She was disoriented. She must have hit her head when you pushed her. She was limping. Confused. Her foot gave way. I tried to grab her, but I couldn't."

He pulled back, his face level with hers. Urgency radiated from him.

"Hannah," he said. "You need to get out of here, before anyone realizes what you've done."

✳

They moved through the twisted stairwells and hidden passages that weaved from the upper landing down to the house's basement level. Hannah felt as if she was in a dream, the world sloped and blurred around her. As if she was drifting in some unstoppable way toward a decision that was already made.

They paused at the door that led out to the pool. Blake squeezed Hannah's hand.

"I could come with you," she said, desperately. "I could help. Maybe we could still help her."

He shook his head.

"You can't be here," he said. "Do you know what would happen if anyone realizes what you did? You'd get arrested. It's manslaughter, at least, if she . . . if she's . . ."

There it was again, the thing that he could not say.

Hannah did not think to ask how anyone would even know about the fight. She did not think to ask, even, why Blake was so certain that his sister was dead. How he could be thinking so clearly, so sharply, when Hannah could barely see beyond this minute, this second. When all she wanted to do was run to Tamara, to help her, no matter the personal cost.

These were the thoughts that would come later. Deep in the night, when Hannah could not sleep. She would still wake up with the image of Tamara's body floating in the water right behind her eyes.

"You have to go," Blake said. "We can still make people think it was an accident. I can protect you, Hannah. But no one can know you were here."

He moved his face so that he was close to her. So close that she could smell his sweat.

"We stay quiet, OK?" he said. "I love you. I'm going to protect you."

He was trembling. Hannah could see that, in spite of his stoicism, his solidity, he was scared. She truly believed that he was scared for her.

Just then, a child's scream cut through all the other distant sounds—the muffled clink of glasses, the hum of conversation. A cry that was unmistakably Nina Drayton. That unmistakably came from the pool.

"Go," said Blake.

One last squeeze of her hand. A gentle push. Then he was gone, running to both his sisters.

FIFTY

2024

Blake is silent now, as Hannah forces herself to hold his gaze. As if he, too, is remembering. As if he, too, is seeing that night, as if hours have passed instead of years.

"You told me that you would stay quiet for me, because you loved me," Hannah says again. "But really, I was staying quiet for you."

"Hannah," Blake says. "You hurt Tamara. She fell. She tripped, because of an injury you inflicted. I stayed quiet to protect *you*."

"But that doesn't make any sense," says Hannah. "It never did. Why would you protect me? If you really thought it was my fault that Tamara was dead, why would you protect me?"

Blake is standing, slowly now.

"For years, I thought you protected me because you loved me," Hannah says quietly. "It's what I wanted to believe—you counted on me wanting to believe it. But you didn't care about me. You only invited me to the party so that you could drug me, and . . . and . . . take those pictures. In fact, I think you planned to do it the night you came to my parents' place, only I didn't want anything to drink. Which is when you realized it would have to happen at your mother's birthday."

She can see that his fists are clenched. His jaw is set, hard. Behind his feigned nonchalance, Blake is afraid.

"You didn't protect me, because there was nothing to protect," Hannah continues. "The only person you were protecting was yourself. Because Tamara didn't trip, did she? She was pushed."

Blake doesn't speak. A muscle twitches in his jaw.

"I never understood why I woke up in *Tamara's* room," Hannah continues. "Why you wouldn't have put me to bed in your room, or even Evelyn's. It only makes sense if Tamara put me to bed. If Tamara knew that my drink had been spiked. If she knew about the photographs. And you couldn't risk anyone knowing what you'd done to me. You couldn't risk your reputation being ruined."

She knows from his silence that she is right. His quiet bolsters her, and her voice grows stronger.

"You wanted to make sure I didn't tell anyone what I saw," Hannah continues. "So you let me believe it was my fault. You tried to scare me into lying about being at the party. You thought that the police might believe it was an accident. There were no witnesses. And Tamara was drunk, and high. You counted on the police thinking she'd fallen into the pool, and that you would get away with it."

"Hannah, I'm warning you . . ."

"But the police started looking at you anyway, didn't they? They knew, right from the start, that it wasn't an accident. They took your phone. They started poking around the house, on the terrace. And you panicked."

She takes a deep breath. She can't believe how, after all these years of feeling off, of feeling wrong, the events of that night have only now begun to make sense.

"And, conveniently, that's when Nina mentions that she saw Josie and Tamara in the pool together. You knew right away that she wasn't talking about the night that Tamara died. But you needed something to distract the police. Another scapegoat, because you couldn't *actually* use me, could you? You couldn't tell the police that I'd been at the party, and that I'd fought with Tamara, because then they'd question me, and I'd tell them about seeing you on the terrace."

He is still now. Completely focused on her. No longer smiling. This is how she knows that finally, finally, twenty years too late, she has hit on the truth.

"Was it you who coached Nina to tell everyone what she'd seen?"

she asks. "At the very least, you must have confused her? Made her change her story just slightly? Or was it your mother, when Harrison got taken into questioning? Were you pissed off that your mother was willing to protect Harrison but not you? Was it her idea to throw Josie under the bus, or yours?"

"I wouldn't sound so smug if I were you," Blake says, his voice sudden and sharp. "You were happy to drop your best friend in it, after all. I didn't hear *you* speak out when Josie got arrested."

"I was scared," Hannah says, though it's the truth she has been evading for years. "I thought that I was responsible for Tamara's death. I thought I'd go to prison for it. And you were making sure I said what you wanted me to. You were completely in control of me by then."

Her voice trembles as she says this.

She is thinking of those days, after Josie was arrested. How she and Blake had met, late at night, when nobody would be watching. How he had told her how much he loved her. That he had already lost his sister, and he couldn't stand the thought of losing Hannah, too. Hannah had taken his twin away from him, but *now you're the only good thing left,* he had said. *Tamara wouldn't want me to lose you, too.*

Then, there were the times when he was less kind to her, less gentle. When they would have sex in a way that left bruises on her skin, a pain between her legs. The memory of his hands on her throat. Afterward, he would remind her that she had better not go to the police, because if she did, he would destroy her.

When she was at home in bed alone, trying to stop the tears from coming, Hannah told herself that she deserved this. Blake's anger was justified: she had caused Tamara's death, and this was her punishment.

After she and Blake had parted in that dark corridor, Hannah had been unable to leave the pink house via the gate that led directly past the stone steps at the side of the property. Already, people had been filtering outside—toward Nina's sobs, and the pool where Tamara was floating, oxygen-starved now, clinging on to the very last scraps of her life.

The only other exit that remained connected to the servants' tunnels was the garage. She was panicking by then, not thinking straight, her hands shaking as she unhooked Harrison's car keys and clambered into the vehicle. She couldn't think far enough ahead to wonder what she would do with the car once outside the house. All that seemed important was getting away. Leaving the pink house behind her as fast as possible.

As soon as she pulled out of the driveway, she knew it was a mistake. She had no plan for what she would do with the car, no idea where she would take it. And besides, she was too drunk to drive. She could feel the way the steering wheel slipped, the car swaying even as she maneuvered it out of sight of the house. She had abandoned the car halfway down the hill, tossed the key in the undergrowth.

When she was called to her first police interview, she was sure that they had found her fingerprints in the car, or that someone had seen her driving. In hindsight, it was a foolishly attention-attracting way to leave the scene of a crime. She had no idea that Josie had already been arrested that morning, and the interview confused her. So much of it had been about Josie—what her role would have been at the party, her relationship with the Draytons. When the police had asked her, right at the end of their questioning, if Hannah herself had been at the party, she just shook her head. She said that she had been at home, working on her Oxford application, and had gone to bed early. As Evelyn Drayton could confirm, there was no reason for her to have been invited to the party.

By the time the second interview came around, it was too late for Hannah to go back on her story. She was a side character by then, someone to support the vague motives that the police had been toying with, to back up all the things people were saying about Josie. Josie had been obsessed with Tamara Drayton, everyone said so. Olivia and Chrissie told the police what Tamara had said to them the night of the bonfire. They described Josie as intense, strange; they claimed that just a few days before Tamara's death, Josie had tried to kiss her. They hadn't known the details, but it hadn't mattered. It was a motive: romantic rejection. And it fit with Nina's story.

The police wanted to know about Hannah's relationship with Josie. Was it true that they were unnaturally close? There was a rumor they had practiced love bites on each other, turning up to class with the skin of their forearms puckered with pale violet bruises. On the side of Josie's Converse, the shoes that she was wearing when she was arrested, there was a small inked heart with the letter *H* in the center of it.

Had Josie once had a crush on Hannah? And, more important, could she have moved on to someone else? Was Josie in love with Tamara Drayton?

And Hannah had found herself shrugging. Saying yes. Maybe. She didn't know.

By omitting the truth, she was embroiled in an unimaginable lie.

Hannah's mum had sent her to stay with Nic and his mother after that. There were swarms of reporters all over the place, people peering through the window of the dive shop and forcing them to close before the end of summer. It was better for Hannah to be away from it all, they said. Somewhere the specter of Tamara Drayton wouldn't hang over everything.

But when the end of summer arrived, the blaze of August fading into the soft heat of September and then a damp, cool October, Hannah had not returned. She had stayed with her aunt, spending most of her days indoors, playing video games with Nic and avoiding the news.

Over time, the text messages from Blake had thinned. Hannah would call him, surreptitiously, buried beneath her bedsheets late at night, only for the phone to ring out to nothingness. She heard that they had left the pink house, gone back to England. She imagined him in London, barely thinking about her at all.

Hannah had missed three months of school by the time she returned home. The Oxford application deadline had come and gone. Her teachers had tried to be understanding, promising she could catch up. There were other universities, after all. Oxford wasn't everything.

Hannah hadn't listened. She didn't care where she went anymore, as long as it was somewhere else. As long as she was far away from home. When she was accepted by Manchester, she had been inordinately, impossibly grateful, even though she had never been to the city before, could barely imagine living there. All that mattered was the promise of a fresh start. A place where people wouldn't know who she was. Where she could try to forget all about Blake and Tamara Drayton.

Her parents had been unsure, still talking in concerned tones about the cost of university. That was until a letter had arrived. A check from Evelyn Drayton. Hannah showed it to her parents, who had been astounded, unable to fathom that Evelyn Drayton would want to do something to help them. Hannah had spun a lie about how she had been giving Tamara some tutoring when she had been at the pink house. That the money was probably a thank-you for all that Hannah had done.

What she did not show her parents was the note that came with the check. Handwritten. *Blake tells me you've always wanted to study. Maybe it would be good for you to be away from here.*

What she did not tell them was how clearly she understood this message. How a desperate feeling of unease had overtaken her when she read it. This, she understood, was hush money. It was a payment for Hannah's silence. And if Evelyn Drayton wanted Hannah to stay silent, there was something more to Tamara's death, something that she had not—at least at first—understood.

Since then, Hannah had tried to press down the ache of worry. She had tried not to think about Blake. Tried not to think about what it would mean if she had lied for him, unwittingly protected him.

But when Imogen showed her those pictures, she could not ignore it anymore.

Now, she stands in front of the man who changed the course of Hannah's life completely.

"I can't do this anymore, Blake," Hannah says. "I can't keep lying."

Blake lets out a sharp, hard laugh.

"You've been happy enough to lie for the last twenty years, haven't you?" he says. "What's changed now?"

"Everything," she says.

She thinks of Josie. The years her best friend lost. The guilt that has festered inside Hannah for decades, growing too big, too consuming to ignore.

When her son was born, Hannah had been scared of what he might become.

But when she watched her daughter, she was scared of something else. The things that she might say yes to, even when she didn't want to. The lies she might believe. The lies she might be forced to tell.

She stands up slightly straighter.

"We let an innocent person go to prison," she says. "*I* let an innocent person go to prison, because I was young, and I was stupid, and I was scared. But I'm not scared anymore. I'm not scared of you."

Blake takes a step closer.

"Don't you get it, Hannah?" he says. "*You'll* go to prison. We both will. And for what? Josie Jackson's already done the time. Why should we put ourselves through that? What for?"

"Because," she says.

Because she's imagined a life where she lives this lie for the next twenty years, and the next. As it gets bigger and bigger, until there's no space left inside her.

"Because it's the right thing to do," she says. "And because Josie never left prison. Not really. She won't be free of it until we tell everyone what really happened."

"It's over for us," Blake says. "For both of us, if you go to the police."

Hannah has considered this. She has considered the consequences. And yet, her decision is made.

"It's already over."

That's when Blake takes another step toward her. That's when Hannah sees the flash of desperation in his eyes.

That's when he pushes her against the wall of the pink house.

That's when Blake grabs hold of her throat.

FIFTY-ONE

2024

The world goes quiet.
    There is a rushing sound in Hannah's ears. The heat of Blake's breath against her face. The weight of him pushing down on her. She thinks of Mason and Noah and Isla. She thinks of Eric.

She sees, as her vision turns red, Tamara Drayton. Not as she has seen her for the past twenty years, gray and limp on the side of the pool. She sees her laughing with Blake, the flicker of energy that always seemed to dance in the air between them. She sees her smoking cigarettes out on the terrace. She sees her looking at Hannah, that steely determination in her eyes. The life within her. The fire.

Her vision is blurring. The light turning into static, a rush of stars. The world is silent and still, other than the pulse of her blood. The roar of sound that fills her skull.

For a second—for just a moment of strange clarity—Hannah wonders if this is what it was like for Tamara. If she, too, was filled with this strange feeling of being outside of herself. Of the world rushing away from her, with nothing she could do to stop it.

"Get *away* from her!"

Through the hum of her body fighting for air, Hannah does not quite register the voice. Only the feeling of a weight lifting from her.

Air rushing back into her lungs. The sensations return to her body, and she is scrabbling for her own throat, clawing at the place where Blake's hands held her tight, choking in her hurry to suck in oxygen.

Through explosions in her vision, she sees Nic, his arms around Blake as he pulls him away. She sees Josie. Imogen, her phone in one hand, held up toward them. Nina, looking straight at her brother, a slightly dazed look in her eyes.

"Take your fucking hands off me!"

Blake struggles against Nic, but her cousin holds him tightly around his torso and drags him backward.

"Nina." Blake's head thrashes back, trying to see his sister.

Nina's face remains impassive, her mouth a straight line, her eyes hard.

"You lied to me," she says softly. "All this time, you've been lying to me."

"You let them in?" Blake is saying. "You let Josie Jackson into our house?"

"I let *myself* in," says Josie.

"But I let the others in," says Nina. "The rest of them. After Josie told me everything."

Nic releases his grip and Blake, still braced against him, flails free, losing his balance and collapsing onto his hands and knees. Above him, Imogen holds up the phone and taps the screen. Hannah sees two figures twitch into life.

It's over for us. For both of us, if you go to the police.

"Nina," says Blake. "It's not what you think. I can explain."

"Did you really think I'd come see you without telling someone?" says Hannah. Her voice is quiet and unwavering. "Did you really think I'd let myself be alone with you?"

He looks at her with horror, and then back at Josie.

"You planned this."

"Nina would never have believed me," Hannah says. "It had to come from you."

"Nina." Blake is looking straight at his sister, not listening to Josie. "Nina. Please."

Imogen holds her phone aloft. Facing them all, her thumb hovering above the screen.

It's then that Hannah sees the video is already loaded into a social media app. That, beneath her hand, there is one large block of text.

Post video.

"You did this to me," Nina says. "All the years of guilt. All the attention, and the lies, and almost destroying myself wondering why I didn't remember. Wondering if I had told the truth."

"Oh, come on, Nina," Blake says. "This isn't about that."

"Then what is it about?" Her voice is shrill. "What is it about, Blake? Is it about the fact that you *drugged* our sister? That you forced people to stay quiet for you? That you let an innocent person go to prison because of it? All to save yourself."

"Nina." Blake's voice is wheedling. Desperate. "Please. It's not like that."

"It's too late," Nina says.

She turns toward Imogen. Her voice is hoarse. Her eyes, when Hannah catches them, are glistening with tears.

"Do it," she says.

Imogen is holding the phone up toward her, her thumb a half inch above the post video icon.

"You have to decide together," she says. "If you want this. Once it's out there, there's no going back."

Blake struggles against Nic again, swearing loudly, but Nic is taller than him, stronger. Hannah's gaze flickers from Nina to Josie. When she meets Josie's eye, they are exactly as she remembers them. They could be teenagers again. Hannah nods slowly.

"Yes," she says. "It's time."

And there, with all of them watching, Imogen's thumb jerks against the screen. A small wheel darts into motion, signaling the upload. In a moment, the video will appear on the feeds of Imogen's millions of followers.

Blake breaks free of Nic then, lunges for her. His arms reach out. His hands clasp at the air in front of him. He is fast, but Hannah is faster. Flying toward him, knocking him forward, both of them tumbling toward the floor. Her legs on either side of him, pinning him to the ground as he flounders, winded.

Imogen lifts her phone up, wordless.

Your upload was successful.

There is a pause. Seconds. Less. And then Imogen's phone comes alive. Vibrating against the palm of her hand, the notifications lighting up her screen. Across the world, the very first people are reacting. Liking. Commenting. Sharing.

A new truth is rising, like divers breaking the surface of the sea. Breathing for the first time.

PART FOUR

```
NEW VIDEO
@TRUECRIMEFANGIRL_2002
POSTED TODAY AT 18:32
```

Hey, true crime fans, and welcome back. Or, I suppose, I should say welcome back to *me*. Because, as you know, I've been pretty quiet on here lately. Things have been looking a little different. And I really appreciate all of your comments, and questions, and everyone who's got in touch asking if I'm OK. The truth is that I'm fine. In fact, I'm better than ever. But there's been a lot of changes around here. And I felt that I owed it to you guys to tell you about them.

Now, lots of you will remember my involvement in the case of Tamara Drayton last year. And if you don't, check out the pinned video on the top of my page. But for anyone who hasn't watched yet—I teamed up with some of the key players in the case to help get footage of Tamara Drayton's twin, Blake Drayton, confessing to having withheld key information about the case.

But in spite of how wild the whole thing was—and again, so many videos on my page, if you want to check this out—this case got me thinking a lot about my work over the last few years. I started this page so that I could share all the juicy, filthy details of some of my favorite murder cases. And honestly, I've loved telling these stories to you all. But when I got mixed up in the Tamara Drayton case, I ended up getting to know a lot of Tamara's loved ones, or people directly involved in the case. And honestly? It made me need to take a step back. It made me wonder what I'm actually *doing* here? Like, who am I helping? And does the fact that we actually ended up helping to get the conviction of an innocent person overturned outweigh all that? What about all of the other cases we've talked about where that hasn't been the outcome? Where people have probably had to listen to me pick over all the details of a loved one's death, not because we're searching for the truth, not really, but because some internet freaks like me find it entertaining? Don't they matter, too?

Guys, I don't know the answer to all this stuff. But what I do know is that it's time to retire truecrimefangirl_2002. It's been fun. Life-changing, in fact. We had a good run. But now? It's time for new things. And you're probably going to be seeing a lot less of this face on your screens. And maybe that's a good thing.

Comments have been disabled on this post.

FIFTY-TWO

2025

TWENTY-ONE YEARS AFTER THE BIRTHDAY PARTY

Twenty-one years after her sister died, Nina opens up the newspaper to see her own face smiling back at her.

The article is a double-page spread. NEW DOCUMENTARY EXPLORES A DECADES-OLD TRUE CRIME CASE THAT HAS KEPT PEOPLE GRIPPED FOR TWENTY-ONE YEARS. A picture of Nina, her face split in two by the page crease so that it looks slightly contorted.

Nina folds the paper without reading it. She doesn't need to. She already knows what it will say. She knows that it will tell the story of her sister's death—only now, the story of Tamara Drayton will be threaded through with another story, one of twenty years of deceit. A story of how Blake and Evelyn lied to everyone, including Nina, about how Tamara died, and why.

Nina has spent the best part of this year coming to terms with the fact that her mother and brother kept her quiet and sedated for the years after Tamara's death, making her believe that there was something not quite right with her. Now she understands that her childhood tendency toward anxiety and worry was something deeper and darker—a reliance on pills that would excuse any inconsistencies in her story, and repress any compulsion that Nina might have to question their version of the truth.

The article will of course mention the reopened investigation, fueled by Hannah Bailey's testimony against Blake and Evelyn, and the overturning of Josie's conviction. A new trial presenting evidence that's now twenty years old, and an expert who, after all this time, ruled Nina's story to be unreliable.

The cracks that this sent through Nina's life splintered all the things that had once held her life together. Ryan had balked at Nina's new position in the spotlight, said that it wasn't good for him and his business to be associated with her, a conversation that had ended their relationship with stunning swiftness and simplicity. Gone was the beautiful, modern apartment where she had imagined their life unfolding; gone, too, was the pretense of perfection, a need for Nina to be someone that she was not. Last to fall: the pink house, which had sold to developers a few months back. Nina heard they were planning to tear the whole thing down, replace it with a sleek, white hotel with three pools. This, she couldn't help but feel, was probably a good thing.

Because the thing was: each splinter, each crack that ran through the center of her life, had opened up space for something new. Nina had been surprised by the kindness that she had been shown. The brilliant light that broke through the darkest days. The job that had been patient with Nina and given her a later start date told her that she should take as much time as she needed. Claire, who had offered a place to stay as soon as she answered the phone to a sobbing Nina on the day that Ryan broke up with her. The dozens of people who messaged her, wrote letters, commented on her newly public social media profile.

You've been so brave.

I can't believe what you've been through.

Your sister would have been so proud of you.

Most of all, it opened up space for Nina to understand herself—or at least, the version of herself she used to be. The person that she had spent a lifetime trying to escape through pills, and exercise, and rituals that she couldn't explain or justify. The person who had spent years buried in study, trying to understand what had happened to her, when all along the truth had been there. Not within essays, and theories, but in the stories of the people who Nina had never thought to ask.

So, instead of reading the story, Nina gets dressed and leaves her flat. It is a beautiful summer's day, the kind where the light is egg-yolk yellow and hopeful, even first thing in the morning. She goes to the small florist a couple of streets away from her and buys an armful of tulips, flowers that she now knows were her sister's favorites. Another part of the last year, for her, has been discovering these small things about her sister, snippets gathered from the people who knew and loved her. Learning about Tamara—the real Tamara. A person whose life was, for so long, overshadowed by the story of her death.

Nina is determined to change that. From now on, she wants to make today, the anniversary of her sister's death, about her life.

There is just one thing she has to do first.

※

Josie takes a taxi to Nina's flat, threading through the streets of South London. She leans her head against the car window and closes her eyes.

She almost said no when Nina had invited her over. She has been in London for four weeks, and the city is beginning to wear against her, the excitement fading, exhaustion seeping through to her bones.

I wanted to mark the day somehow, Nina had written in a text. Please say yes x

Twenty-one years since Tamara's death, and one year since Josie's life changed all over again. One year since they were all able to move on at last.

"Do you mind?" she had asked Nic, showing him the text message from Nina.

"Of course not," he said. "It feels right, in a way. Marking the anniversary. Why not do it with Nina?"

Josie replied: Just tell us where and when. We'll be there x

Now, Josie walks the two flights of steps up to Nina's attic flat. As it always does, the impossibility of the situation strikes her: she and Nina Drayton, friends.

"You made it!"

Claire opens the door to Nina's flat, beaming.

"Calvin and Gabby are on their way," Josie says. "Their flight was late landing."

"No problem at all." Nina is a few feet behind Claire brandishing a serving spoon, pink with the heat from the kitchen. "Help yourself to drinks. Whatever you like. I'll be with you in just a minute."

She dashes back into the small galley kitchen at the back of the flat. She looks at home here, even though she only moved in a few months ago. She told Josie that it was the first place she had chosen for herself. Not a place passed down through family, or already owned by a boyfriend. Hers.

"Of course, it's a whole lot smaller than I'm used to, and in a neighborhood that estate agents like to call *up-and-coming*," she had said over congratulatory gin and tonics at a nearby pub. "But I like it. And I can afford it myself. And that stuff matters, doesn't it?"

And Josie had agreed that it did.

Josie and Nic make their way to an ancient-looking drinks trolley stacked with liqueurs and spirits that haven't been fashionable since the eighties and help themselves to two glasses and the remains of an already-open bottle of wine. In a vase on the side, Josie sees a clutch of tulips and smiles. Unthinkingly, her hand strays to her throat. The necklace that she has worn every day since her release from prison. *J T* engraved on a silver heart. A small, perfect tulip.

She and Nic clink their glasses.

"To you," Nic says.

Josie smiles.

"To both of us," she says. "Thanks for coming over here, when it's peak season."

Nic shrugs.

"There's always another summer," he says.

Josie squeezes his hand. She loves him. She loves the simplicity of that belief: always another summer. It's something she has never quite allowed herself to believe before. She thinks she would like to now.

They said that they were going to take things slowly at first, she and Nic. Their relationship, if that was what they were going to call it, had been so fast at the beginning, and they wanted to give dating a try. A normal relationship, another thing that Josie had never really managed before. But after a few months of spending a couple of nights a week with Nic and living out of a backpack, Calvin had asked Josie how she'd feel about selling their childhood home.

"Me and Gabby want to move in together," he had said over mugs of tea at the kitchen table. "And . . . well. I don't want us to move in together here. It feels like a bad omen, this place. Too many . . ."

He trailed off, and Josie nodded. She understood exactly what he meant. Too many memories. Too many ghosts. Too many heartbreaks, and wrong turns, and losses.

They contacted an estate agent that afternoon.

Calvin used the money from the sale to buy a flat close to the beach.

"Do you think you might buy somewhere?" he asked.

"I don't think so," Josie said. "I actually had something else I was thinking of doing with the money."

It was an idea she had back when the truth about Blake Drayton came out. For Josie, the news elicited an outpouring of sympathy. Letters from people who claimed to have always known she was innocent. Emails from around the world. But it also sparked messages from dozens of people, too many to count, who would tell Josie over and over again that their loved one had also been wrongfully convicted of a crime that they did not commit. Sketchy evidence, the wrong place at the wrong time. Victims of decades of domestic violence who had finally snapped. People who had been judged on their sexuality, or their race, or their past wrongdoings, rather than the facts of the case. Women who were released after a wrongful conviction was overturned only to come back to nothing—long-forgotten by their now grown-up children, abandoned by past partners. Having to start over, after the justice system spat them out.

That was when Josie knew what she wanted to do with her life. She would start a charity providing legal aid for wrongful conviction appeals, and support for people once they were released. She would help the kind of person that she had once been.

She registered the charity the day the money from the house sale landed in her account.

The last year has been grueling. Flights back and forth between France and the UK. Begging consultants and advisers to give her a cut-price rate and then funneling every spare penny back into the organization. Meetings with her lawyer, who was filing a wrongful conviction claim to get Josie the compensation she deserved after losing a decade of her life. Working odd shifts at the café, when she could.

And now, finally, her hard work is beginning to pay off. Josie has checked her accounts, and dares to hope that this month she might be able to start paying herself a small wage. She carries the knowledge of this inside her like a small, secreted jewel. Her first salaried job ever, and from an organization she herself founded. The thought makes her glow.

"Josie! Nic! You found something to drink?"

Craig, a human rights lawyer who Nina met when he was doing pro bono work for Josie, emerges from the kitchen. He sweeps Josie into a hug, delivers a bracing handshake to Nic.

"So good to see you both," he says. "Nina was so pleased when you said you'd come."

He and Nic immediately launch into a detailed conversation about plans they've already sketched out for Craig and Nina to visit next spring. Josie watches them, and feels a swell of love for Nic rise out of the center of her chest. She hasn't told him about how close she is to making an actual full-time salary yet. They're going to Iceland next month to see the northern lights, something that has been on Josie's bucket list since she was a child. Her first proper holiday. She'll tell him then. Give them something else to celebrate.

"I'll get it!" Josie says when the door goes.

It's Imogen, in London to promote the launch of the documentary. Her first (and last, if her newfound determination to stay out of the public eye is to be believed) television appearance. They've agreed to watch it together when it airs tonight. It seems fitting, when the documentary was what brought them all together in the first place. That prompted them to go looking for the truth at last.

"Dinner's ready!" Nina says, emerging from the kitchen clutching an enormous casserole dish at the exact same time that the doorbell rings again.

Craig gets to the door just as Nina carefully sets down the food in the center of the table, her hands ensconced in oven gloves.

"Perfect timing!" he says, throwing it open.

Gabby bundles straight past him to throw her arms around Josie. She smells like airports and hastily applied deodorant, but beyond that Josie still catches the faint whiff of the sea. That place, so much a part of them all that salt still clings to their skin.

"We've missed you!" Gabby says.

Josie hugs her back, hard, while Calvin and Craig shake hands. She's missed them, too. She misses her life back on the Côte d'Azur. Dinners at Gabby and Calvin's place that last until midnight, candles stuck in empty wine bottles, leftover pastries from the café for dessert. Nights sitting out on the sand, crates of beer, the crash of the tide. Early mornings with Nic, mugs of coffee out on the balcony, the soft dawn heat. A life that is so small and simple in some ways, yet so much bigger than she ever dared imagine for herself. Laughter. People who love her. Work that gives her purpose. Peace.

"Sit down, sit down," Nina is saying. "The documentary starts in half an hour, and I want to clear up before then."

They cram around Nina's small dining table, Nic having to balance on a comically small stool, Craig on a folding garden chair. Nina asks Nic about the dive shop as she plates up. Gabby asks Josie how she's feeling about seeing the documentary, after all this time. Imogen talks about a new opportunity she has, lecturing a series at a prestigious American college about media coverage of female murder victims.

"Anyway," says Nina. Tendrils of hair have escaped from her ponytail. She raises a wineglass. "Thanks so much for coming, all of you. It's been quite the summer."

They all lift their glasses with murmurs of agreement.

A buzz at the downstairs door cuts through the background hum of a Spotify playlist. Nina's smile tightens.

"Are we expecting anyone else?" says Craig, half standing, uncertain.

"Actually, yes." Nina is already on her feet. "There's one more person I thought should be here."

She presses the door release.

"Well, come on, Nina," Craig says with an uncertain laugh. "You're not going to tell us who it is?"

Nina doesn't answer. From the speaker, a folk singer croons. Gabby glances at Calvin, a look of confusion on her face. Nic sets down his fork. No one speaks.

A knock on the plywood door, and Nina pulls it open.

And there, standing in the doorway, a bunch of white tulips clutched in the crook of her arm, is Hannah.

※

The day after the video of Blake Drayton's confession went viral, Hannah had gone back to the pink house.

She went out to the terrace, to the place where Tamara Drayton had drowned. Standing on the place where the pool once was, Hannah cried. For Tamara, but also for the person that Hannah herself was, back then. A lost, confused girl, not much older than Mason.

That afternoon, she had gone to the police station, and told them everything. About her relationship with Blake, and what happened after Maison de la Mer. The bonfire. The night of the birthday party. The way that she had lied for Blake, over and over again.

As she spoke, she felt something inside of her uncoil and release. The truth, unraveling its wings and preparing to take flight. The knot had been there so long, she had stopped noticing it.

To Hannah's surprise, she had not been arrested on the spot. She was being treated as a witness, rather than a suspect. Still, she spent the next few months on edge, waiting for a phone call, a knock on the door.

There was an investigation, and a decision was quickly reached. Yes, Hannah had lied to the police, but she was young and vulnerable. The statute of limitations was short for that kind of crime, and if she was willing to testify against Blake, her role in it would disappear.

Two months ago, Blake was found guilty of manslaughter—the

same crime that he had dangled in front of Hannah as a threat all those years ago. Evelyn was charged with assisting an offender, a trial that had floundered and collapsed on the basis of weak evidence, the truth eroded by time. Hannah had heard that she was living in Paris, awaiting Blake's sentencing. Apparently she was newly engaged to what would be her fifth husband, the arrest of her son and estrangement from her daughter not dampening her belief in her right to a happy ending.

And so, Hannah's life went on. Mealtimes, and school runs, and social media posts, and longing, and sleepless nights. Birthdays, and arguments, and bills, and grief, and love, and all the small things that make up life, that make it easy to forget. She was the same, and yet irrevocably changed.

And now, Hannah stands in the doorway and looks straight past Nina. She looks past Gabby, and Calvin and Nic. Hannah stands in the doorway, and the only person that she sees is Josie.

"Hi," she says. "Do you think we could talk?"

※

They go outside, to a small shared terrace with smatterings of flowers in terra-cotta pots, a bench painted bright pink. London stretches out around them, rooftops silhouetted against a pale ochre sky, the sunset just coming into view.

When Josie was still locked away, Hannah would occasionally watch the sky turn crimson—all the beauty, and the light, and the darkness coming together—and be struck by the fact that Josie could not see it. That Tamara would never see a sunset again. This realization never failed to floor her. In some ways, every sunset since Tamara's death has led her here.

Josie is gazing out at the sky. The sweep of color, the lilac clouds spooling like bruises against skin, the pale sphere of the rising moon.

"Do you remember," Hannah begins. "When we would sit on the beach and watch the moon come up over the cliffs? We used to say that moonrises were better than sunrises. Although I'm pretty sure I only thought that because I was never awake in time for sunrise."

Josie turns to face her. Her skin is golden in the strange, honeyed light.

"Why wouldn't you talk to me?" she says. "After . . ."

She trails off, but Hannah understands. After the day that Imogen's video went viral. The day that their lives changed forever for a second time.

In truth, Hannah had not been able to face her former best friend. The shame had been colossal. The guilt that she had hoped would dissipate had clung on. She had seen it in Josie's face on the day that Hannah confessed. The sadness. The exhaustion. The fact that nothing that Hannah said or did would give Josie back the time she had lost.

She had been relieved when Josie had not attended the trial. Glad that she hadn't had to face her.

And yet, over the past year, she has thought of Josie every day. She has wanted to do this every day. Now or never, Hannah thinks. Speak now, or forever hold your peace. And Hannah has spent more than enough time not speaking out.

"Josie," Hannah says. "I am so sorry. I've been carrying this guilt inside me for years. And look—I know it doesn't fix anything. But I wanted to say I'm sorry for not coming forward back then. And, I suppose, for just not being brave enough. Not standing up to Blake Drayton. Not protecting you. I never got the chance to tell you before. And I wanted you to know."

The sun is almost gone. Only a schism of light, just above the rooftops, remains.

Hannah looks at the woman standing beside her, and she sees Josie Jackson. The girl whose name had been notorious and terrible. A byword for evil, and then, a byword for injustice.

But Hannah also sees Josie Jackson as she was nearly thirty years ago. The lost child who wandered up to Hannah's parents' shop and asked the way to the beach. The girl who Hannah grew up with. Who she loved. Who she betrayed.

She sees the two of them, peeling back the cover to the Draytons' swimming pool with all the world stretching out ahead of them. Infinite summers. Thousands of sunsets.

"I don't know if I deserve it," says Hannah. "But I hope you can forgive me."

Josie's eyes are damp. It occurs to Hannah that she has never seen her friend cry. Slowly, Josie nods her head.

"I already did," she says. "You never had to ask."

Something inside Hannah splits in two then. Relief flooding through her like a wave breaking against the shore. Josie is hugging her, and she still smells the same, like saltwater and summer. Like Hannah's childhood, and all the best and the worst years of her life. Like coming home. Like high season.

Josie pulls away then, looking past her, out at the sky. The last embers of the sun.

"So," says Hannah, searching for her gaze. "What do we do now?"

This is when Josie looks at her, and Hannah sees a world inside her best friend's eyes. The hurt, and the healing. The years lost, and all the years ahead. The sadness. The forgiveness. The hope.

"We go on," Josie says.

She takes Hannah's hand, and they could be girls again. They could be two girls, looking out over the sea.

FIFTY-THREE

2004

In the seconds before Tamara loses consciousness, she thinks of Josie.

The first time she saw her. Early mornings, the salt pool at sunrise. The two of them, kicking beneath the water.

She can feel a strange sensation in her head, a numbness that wasn't there a moment ago. A moment ago she was above the water, and now, somehow, she is here. Somehow, the world has turned blue around her, and she can see the refracted glow of fairy lights above.

She thinks then of how, last night, after she had shredded her diary, tossed the pages into the sea, she had gone up to her room and found Josie waiting for her there. How they had sat on her bed together. How Josie had told Tamara that it was alright. That there was nothing wrong with her; she understood why Tamara was sad, and angry. Why she lashed out.

She loved Tamara, too. Just not in that way. Not like that.

But you will find someone who does, she had said. *You will find someone who loves you back.*

In those words, Tamara felt the bad twin inside her wither and die. Maybe there was hope. A chance for Tamara to be good at last.

It was only yesterday, but now it feels so far away. It feels like a thousand years ago, and yet it also feels like it is happening to her right now. As if Josie is here with her, saying these words all over again. *You will find someone who loves you back.*

Tamara knows that she is underwater. She knows that the world is slipping away from her. That she should reach for the surface. But she is tired. So, so tired. There is a warmth, a peace here. Sleep, folding her close. Darkness, drawing in.

In the last moment before she leaves this world, Tamara is swimming. She is kicking hard against the water. She is breaking its surface, and above the waves is Josie. Waving her arms. Calling Tamara's name.

Cheering Tamara on, as she swims across the sea toward her.

ACKNOWLEDGMENTS

The process of writing a second novel was infinitely more challenging than I could have imagined, and a great deal of gratitude is owed to many people, without whom I never would have gotten to the end of the tricky first draft, let alone to a finished book.

I remain endlessly thankful for my agent, Ariella Feiner, whose faith in my work is a constant reassurance and motivation. I'm extremely grateful for Frankie Gray at Transworld and Sarah Cantin at St. Martin's Press for reading so many failed attempts at novels on the road to this one, and for continuously showing their faith in me to eventually write something both true to myself and worth reading; to Thorne Ryan, who came on board for some exceptionally valuable edits with Sarah; and to all of the above for continuing to push me as a writer, and helping to bring my stories to the world. I never stop being thankful for the opportunity to do this.

Thank you to everyone who works so hard behind the scenes at Transworld, St. Martin's Press, and United Agents. At St. Martin's Press, thank you to Drue VanDuker, Jennifer Enderlin, Anne Marie Tallberg, Lisa Senz, Michael Clark, Lizz Blaise, Allison Ziegler, Paul Hochman, Sophia Lauriello, Gabriel Guma, Danielle Fiorella, and Sara Thwaite. At Transworld, thank you to Anna Carvanova, Irene Martinez, Eloise Austin, Milly Reid, Anna Nightingale, and Phil Evans.

Throughout the writing of this book, I learned the importance of being part of a writing community, for both cheerleading and commiserating. Moseley Writer's Group was an invaluable source of support, and I learned a lot about how to be a better writer from their many pub sessions. A particular thank-you to Alison Gibson, Shane Grant, Sofia Kokolaki-Hall, Imogen Mornement, Stephen Mackman, Mike Venables, and Faith Walsh, who read an early draft in its entirety and kindly offered pointers.

I was also hugely grateful to have met, chatted to, and been cheered on by many people from the very generous and supportive debut author community, but a special thank-you goes to Claire Daverley, whose kindness, friendship, and voicenotes kept me sane on many days throughout the writing and publishing process.

I was very lucky to have authors and readers show enormous generosity and kindness since the publication of my debut novel. Thank you to all the authors who read and endorsed my book, and thank you to all of the reviewers, bloggers, and booksellers who supported and shouted about *The Girls of Summer*. A special thank-you to The Heath Bookshop, which is one of my happy places, and its brilliant booksellers, who show every day how books can make a community a better place. Nuneaton Waterstones and Warwickshire libraries do wonderful work shouting about local authors and—as places which fueled my childhood love of reading—will always have a special place in my heart.

Outside of the writing world, I am lucky to be surrounded by people who offer an excellent distraction from any book woes. Thank you to all of my wonderful friends who listened to me complain about the bad days, celebrated the good days, and agreed that spicy margaritas were an appropriate reaction to both. I won't name names, but you know who you are. Thank you to my family for all your love and support, particularly my mum and dad, who turned up to all my events and taught me to love books before I could even read them myself.

And last, but far from least, thank you to Joe. My life has changed in so many ways since I wrote my first book, but you're still my favorite part of it. This one's for you.